RED
LIGHTNING

RED LIGHTNING

John Varley

ACE BOOKS, NEW YORK

THE BERKLEY PUBLISHING GROUP
Published by the Penguin Group
Penguin Group (USA) Inc.
375 Hudson Street, New York, New York 10014, USA
Penguin Group (Canada), 90 Eglinton Avenue East, Suite 700, Toronto, Ontario M4P 2Y3, Canada
(a division of Pearson Penguin Canada Inc.)
Penguin Books Ltd., 80 Strand, London WC2R 0RL, England
Penguin Group Ireland, 25 St. Stephen's Green, Dublin 2, Ireland (a division of Penguin Books Ltd.)
Penguin Group (Australia), 250 Camberwell Road, Camberwell, Victoria 3124, Australia
(a division of Pearson Australia Group Pty. Ltd.)
Penguin Books India Pvt. Ltd., 11 Community Centre, Panchsheel Park, New Delhi—110 017, India
Penguin Group (NZ), Cnr. Airborne and Rosedale Roads, Albany, Auckland 1310, New Zealand
(a division of Pearson New Zealand Ltd.)
Penguin Books (South Africa) (Pty.) Ltd., 24 Sturdee Avenue, Rosebank, Johannesburg 2196,
South Africa

Penguin Books Ltd., Registered Offices: 80 Strand, London WC2R 0RL, England

This book is an original publication of The Berkley Publishing Group.

This is a work of fiction. Names, characters, places, and incidents either are the product of the author's imagination or are used fictitiously, and any resemblance to actual persons, living or dead, business establishments, events, or locales is entirely coincidental. The publisher does not have any control over and does not assume any responsibility for author or third-party websites or their content.

Copyright © 2006 by John Varley.
Text design by Kristin del Rosario.

All rights reserved.
No part of this book may be reproduced, scanned, or distributed in any printed or electronic form without permission. Please do not participate in or encourage piracy of copyrighted materials in violation of the author's rights. Purchase only authorized editions.
ACE is an imprint of The Berkley Publishing Group.
ACE and the "A" design are trademarks belonging to Penguin Group (USA) Inc.

ISBN 0-441-01364-3

PRINTED IN THE UNITED STATES OF AMERICA

This book is dedicated to the memory of
Don and Mary Stilwell,
and to Jim, John, Jane, Joe, Janice, and Jerry.

1

★ ★ ★

MARS SUCKS.

If you're from Mars, you already know what I'm talking about. If you're from Earth and have read all the glossy travel brochures and watched all the fancy promos, you're thinking I must be nuts. What sucks about swanky hotels and souped-up sand buggies? What sucks about the longest ski slopes ever built, and low-gee rock climbing where you race up the Valles Marineris like a lizard on a wall? Mars is like the biggest cruise ship in the system, nothing to do but have fun, fun, fun, and your daddy never takes the T-bird away, like it says in one of Dad's corny old songs. What's wrong with that?

Nothing, for a few weeks.

At least, none of the Earthies seem to mind it, they've been coming over like rats to a big red Gouda cheese ever since I was a kid, more of them every year. First it was just the rich ones. Not that it cost all that much money to get them there but because the cruise lines could charge whatever they wanted to since there weren't enough cruise ships to take everybody who wanted to go.

But Earthies know a good thing when they see it, and soon there were a lot more ships, but there weren't enough places to stay once they got here. Can't just dump a lot of overmuscled Earthies out on the sand in man-shaped Ziploc baggies with a bottle of oxygen. (Well, *I* wouldn't mind it, but you sure would use up a lot of Earthies that way. Not enough, of course; Earthies reproduce like rabbits, and not even their habit of tossing nuclear bombs around seems to make a dent in the population.)

Now we're building more hotels, and you know what that means: more Earthies. And if you want to know the *biggest* reason why Mars sucks, you've got it right there.

Earthies.

On any given day there are more Earthies on Mars than Martians, Reds and Greens together. In the summertime there can be twice as many, and all I can say is, it's a good thing that summer only comes every two years.

MY NAME IS Ramon D. Garcia-Strickland, but don't ever call me Ramon unless you want a fat lip or you're a teacher I can't hit. I'm Ray to my friends, and to all the decent teachers, too. And don't ask what the D. stands for, either. I swear, parents can get the goofiest ideas, and I don't care if it *is* a name that goes back six generations in Mom's side of the family. Trust me, if that name ever got out I'd be having fistfights every day.

I was born five years after the first four people set foot on Mars. You may have heard of it, if they still teach history at your school. (I understand they've pretty much given it up at a lot of schools on Earth, but they still drill it into you at Burroughs High.) Which is okay, I like history, it's one of my best subjects. Even if I didn't like it, nothing short of an A is acceptable to my mother, who makes sure we get our studying done every evening before we're allowed out.

I mention this because one of those first two men on Mars was my father, Manny Garcia, and one of the first two women was my mother, Kelly Strickland, though they weren't much older than me at the time. You want to talk Martian pioneers, you're talking about my family. Even if you don't know any history you might have seen the movie or the TV series on an oldies channel, and you may have thought it was just made up, like most movies, but this one was true.

For just a little over a million dollars they built a spaceship called *Red Thunder* out of old railroad tank cars. They didn't do it alone. They couldn't have done it all without my uncle Jubal, who is a crazy genius.

You should have heard of Jubal, since he's the most important man on Earth, but I once ran into an Earthie about my age who said he was into music and he didn't know who John Lennon was, so you never know.

Okay, first, my uncle Jubal and my uncle Travis aren't really my uncles, we aren't even related, but me and my sister started calling them that when we were very young and that's how we think of them, as family. An odd family, but my own. Travis is Travis Broussard, who was once an astronaut on Earth, back when space travel involved strapping yourself into a very dangerous guided missile rocket machine and keeping your fingers crossed. You wouldn't get me up in one of those Space Shuttles or VentureStars for any amount of money. I'm not crazy. The VStars even *looked* like tombstones.

Travis had a cousin, Jubal, who might have been almost anything he wanted to be until his religious maniac father beat him on the head with a two-by-four studded with nails. After that, he was suited only to be a mad scientist. He made something that was truly revolutionary, something that to this day no one has completely figured out: the Squeezer.

Now I'll bet you know the dude I'm talking about.

It violated just about every law of physics you want to name, but it worked, and what it did was squeeze stuff really, really, *really* hard. Any stuff at all: air, water, rocks, garbage, that big Earthie bastard who beat the crap out of me a couple years ago when I objected to him putting his hands on my girlfriend (don't I wish!). You could take a cubic mile of seawater and squeeze it down to the size of a football, and then you could make a little hole in it, a discontinuity, and what came out was one hell of a lot of energy. You could use that energy to power a rocket like no rocket anyone had ever seen, a rocket that didn't need to carry one hundred times its own weight in fuel just to get out of Earth's atmosphere. That's because the football didn't have the mass of the seawater you squeezed, it didn't weigh anything, not even the Planck mass, it had gone somewhere else for a while. You could float it in the air like a silver soap bubble. In fact, if you didn't keep your eye on it you could easily lose it, it would just blow away. One of Jubal's early bubbles did just that, and my father found it, and that's how they came to go to Mars.

Free energy. The only known free lunch in the universe.

But nothing is really free.

THAT DAY IT all started was pretty much like any other weekend day. I had spent most of it in Phobos and was on my way back down when my phone rang. Not the very best time to get a call, but it was from Jubal and I knew he'd be waiting by his phone for an answer and would worry if I didn't get back soon. He understands time lag as well as anybody, but he's a nervous man, and a lonely one, and I'm one of his favorite people, so I never keep him waiting. I called up a picture window on the inside of my pressure suit helmet and ticked ANSWER.

What I saw was a man with a round, jolly face and a wild shock of white hair and white beard. Jubal's hair had all gone white at an early age, which led a lot of people to think he was older than he really was, which was in his fifties. You can't tell it from a head-and-shoulders phone shot, of course, but he was quite a small man, not much over five feet, though chubby.

"Hi-de-hi, Ray," he said, "an how happy I am for you to see me!"

Jubal's got his own way of talking. A lot of it is a thick Cajun accent and strange syntax. When Dad wrote his book he tried to reproduce it pretty much exactly, but I'm not going to do that. It strikes me as a little condescending. But there was a definite flavor to his speech that is delightful, and I'll try to retain that.

Then there was the usual pause. He denies it, but I'm sure he's waiting for me to answer back. He can't help himself. He comes from so far back in the swamp and such poverty that he didn't make his first phone call until he was eight or nine. He's usually pretty loud, too, unlike his face-to-face mumble, as if he had to shout to be heard all the way to Mars.

"How's da weather up dere?" he said, and chuckled. This is about as sophisticated as Jubal gets in the joke department. He knows very well that the weather on Mars is one of two things: bad, or very bad. It also has to do with my height, a joke tall people quickly get tired of, but with

Jubal I didn't mind. He always says it as if he's just that moment thought of it . . . and maybe he has.

"We got our usual storm blowin' here," he went on. "De penguins don't mind it, so neither do I. Was out rowin' dis morning, me, an I seen me a whale. Coulda been a big blue, or maybe a fin. I taken off after it, but de Captain tole me dat was a no-no. I had to let that big boy go, me, or de Captain he would of put a few rounds into him, just for meanness sake."

Jubal lives on the Falkland Islands. The only other things that live there are millions of penguins, and the military contingent there to protect him and the scientists and staff there to take care of him. The man in charge is actually a former general from Russia whose name Jubal can't pronounce and I can't remember, but Jubal always calls him the Captain.

When Jubal goes rowing, which is his favorite activity when he's upset or thinking, he's accompanied by two heavily armed destroyers and there are at least three fighter planes in the air at all times. The protection around the President of the United States is nothing compared to the security around Jubal.

He chattered on for a while about things that would be important only to me and him, like where I should go to college after I graduated from good old Burroughs High. Then he sighed deeply, as he always does when he's about to sign off.

"Well, I be goin', Ray, my friend," he said. Then he did a double take and smacked himself on the forehead with the flat of his palm, another gesture that was pure Jubal. He hates it that some functions of his brain are not like they used to be. Well, wouldn't you? "Almost forget, me. I sent you another package, few days ago. It ain't nothing much special, no, but don't worry about it. Jus' a little gizmo I made. Don't do much, that thing, but it maybe can open things that nothin' else can open. An maybe one of dese days I be sending you something else. Can't tell right now, me. Anyway, you take care, and don't take no wooden alligators. Bye."

He laughed, as he always did at his ridiculous sign-off. There's no way to really explain the joke; it has to do with something that happened between him and my father a long time ago.

Sending me something? He did that all the time. Sometimes it was ridiculous stuff, toys of one sort or another. Jubal had trouble keeping track of time. Sometimes he seemed to think I was still twelve, or even six. He was almost devoid of social skills. Travis had told me that had been true even before his injuries. He had something called Asperger's Syndrome, which I gathered was a point on a line called the "Autistic Spectrum." Some autistics aren't able to function at all, while others are true geniuses with some social deficits. Some people think Newton, Einstein, Tesla, and a lot of other great people of the past had Asperger's.

Anyway, Jubal was always sending me stuff. He was a pretty good artist, so sometimes it was drawings, usually of the Louisiana bayou country. Or he'd send me or my sister, Elizabeth, flowers. Other times it would be some little gadget he'd made, some clockwork fancy or flamboyantly useless machine. Once he saw this old plastic box at an online auction site. What it did was, you flipped a switch and a little plastic hand came out of the box, grabbed the switch, and turned it off. A machine whose only function was to turn itself off. Loved it. So, *a little gizmo, don't do much, that thing.* Pure Jubal.

I checked the systems on my board and saw I had a few minutes, so I immediately ticked COMPOSE and started talking.

"Hi-de-hi, Uncle Jubal," I said. "All the wooden alligators here are frozen, as usual. I'm looking forward to the new gadget. The stuff you send me is always fun, you are one of the funniest guys I know. Nothing much doing here, just schoolwork and hanging out on the weekends, wasting time. The new band isn't doing so well. In fact, I think you could say we've broken up. No big loss, the guy on lead synth is a real a—a real awful person. And like I told you a while ago, I've finally realized I'm never going to be a big star and have to beat off all the adoring women with a big old stick. But it's fun. I'll send you some downloads next time. Right now I'm about to be pretty busy, since I left Phobos about fifteen minutes ago and the air is starting to get thick. Oh, did you get the pics of my low-gee pad up here? Pretty neat, huh? Stay well my friend, and take care of the penguins. Over and out."

I ticked off, silently cursing myself. I almost said "asshole," and profanity or obscenity upset Jubal horribly. You'd think that after all these years it would be second nature to clean up my mouth when I'm talking to him, and I haven't slipped since I was ten and saw how hurt he was. Close call.

And I was cutting it a little close on the reentry, too. The board started to make a few odd beeps and boops, and if I didn't see to it soon, the computer would take over and report it to Mom and Dad and I'd be grounded for a month, at least.

NO QUESTION ABOUT it, one of the things that *doesn't* suck about Mars is airboards. And it may be the one thing Earthie kids my age envy us. You can't use them on Earth—please!—and to use one on Mars you have to be a Martian. In fact, if a lot of Martian parents had their way, nobody would be able to use them at *all*. Hence the computer beeping at me, and less obvious safety measures.

We call them boards to be cool, to fit in with surfboards, which we obviously can't use on Mars, and skateboards, which we can and *do* use, and are able to do tricks nobody could even think of on Earth.

What they actually look like is a snowmobile or a Jet Ski, sitting on a longer, wider surfboard. You straddle the engine and air tanks, sitting on a motorcycle seat, and there's a clear Nomex aerodynamic shield in front of you, but other than that, you're in open space, nothing but your suit to protect you from vacuum.

I fired the jets for the last time as I felt the very thin atmosphere begin to tug slightly on my board. Below me, Mars was spread out like a giant plate of lasagna. Sorry, but that's really the best analogy I can come up with. Orange tomato sauce and cream-colored pasta, with a few smears of black olive here and there. The only things that didn't fit the picture were the single, monumental peak of Olympus Mons and the perfect row of Ascraeus, Pavonis, and Arsia Mons east of the big boy. All four gigantic extinct volcanoes showed white caps of frozen water and carbon-dioxide ice.

I checked all my helmet displays, and everything was copacetic. Airboarding is fun, but you don't want to forget that you can reach some serious high temperatures on the way in, and that you've got a reentry footprint you don't dare ignore. Too high and you're okay, you'll skip out and have to try it again, a long way from your target, and endure the merciless ridicule of all the people you know when you get down. Too low, and you can toe right into the soup, decelerate at a killing rate, and fry. Falling off your board on Mars is not an option.

You do have to do a little skipping, but the best way to kill your velocity is slaloming. You have handlebars on the front, and of course you're strapped down tight, so you hang on and shift your body left and right, maybe hang five, which means putting one foot out into the airstream for a few moments. Wear your heavy boots for that one.

I swooshed left, toward Olympus, traveled for a while almost parallel to the triple peaks, which might have been put there by the god Ares as a flight path indicator. When you get over Pavonis, it's time to jog right again.

The gee forces were building up, shoving me down into the seat, and a faint ghost of a shock wave was curling over the top of the windshield and buffeting my helmet. That air was cold when it hit the windshield, and pretty hot when it left. The clear material began to glow light pink.

I was getting to the hottest part of the trip, pulling about a gee, which was easy. I dug a little deeper into the air and pulled a bit more. Then I started getting a little blue color in the air. That was a very tiny bit of the ablative coating of the board bottom burning off. About every fifth or sixth trip you had to spray some more on it, sort of like recapping a bald tire on Earth. But you could mix in some chemical compounds that didn't have anything to do with slowing you down, like strontium or lithium salts for red, barium chloride for green, strontium and copper for purple, magnesium or aluminum for intense white. Same stuff you use in fireworks. Not a lot of it, and the resulting firetail is not as spectacular as a Landing Day display, but it'll do.

If you've got bubble-drive power, you can theoretically start off at any time of day for any destination, and the same on your return. But it can take a long time, even accelerating all the way. The most practical thing is to take off for Phobos during a launch window that lasts about an hour, and when you return there's an ideal time to leave to get to Thunder City—which is just about the only place worth going on Mars.

That means that a lot of people were reentering at the same time I was. Off to each side of me I could see multicolored flame trails as other boarders showed their stuff. As usual, there were varying degrees of skill. I watched as much as I could while still keeping my eyes on all the telltales and keeping my feel for the board. To my left I saw a board getting a little too close. I saw on the display that I was about half a mile ahead of him, which by the rules of the air gave me the right of way. He kept coming, and I got a yellow light on the heads-up. Jerk. I punched the console and a yellow flare arched out in his direction. In about a second he saw it and banked away from me. A window popped up on my display and I saw a kid about fifteen years old, his face distorted by the gee forces he was pulling.

"Sorry, space," he said.

"Stay cool," I said, which he could take any way he wanted.

Below, about fifteen thousand feet, I saw Thunder City, and I banked again and went into a long, altitude-killing turn. Looking out to the side, I got a wonderful view of what had been my hometown since I was five.

My, how it had grown.

When my family arrived the first hotel on the planet, the Marineris Hyatt, which my father was to manage, was still under construction. People were still new at this, at constructing buildings in an environment as hostile as Mars. The hotel was finished almost a year behind schedule. But it was full on opening day, and Earthies were clamoring for more rooms. So we built them.

Now you could hardly find the original Hyatt, which had come within a hair of being torn down before my mother and some others led a campaign to save it as our first historical building. It was converted into our first, and so far only, museum. Next to it was the Red Thunder, which Dad now ran, and where I had lived for the last five years. It was still the tallest and most impressive freestanding building in Thunder City, but wouldn't be for long. I could see three new hotels in the works, all of which would be bigger.

The city was built in an irregular line, which had grown to about seven miles. There were a lot of domes, both geodesic and inflatable, the biggest being a Bucky dome almost a mile in diameter. It was all connected by the Grand Concourse, of which an architectural critic had said, "It represents the apotheosis of the turn-of-the-century airport waiting room." Yeah, well. We can't have open-air promenades with old elm trees on Mars. So most of the trees on the concourse are concrete, with plastic leaves. It's all roofed with clear Lexan, and maybe it's tacky, and maybe it is nothing but a giant shopping mall, but it's home to me.

The slightly zigzag line of the concourse pointed toward the Valles Marineris, five miles away. There was one hotel out there, on the edge, and I swung over the Valles as I deployed my composite fabric wings to complete my deceleration. Like the old Space Shuttle, the board wasn't capable of anything but a downward glide with those wings, but if you were good and had a head wind and maybe a thermal, you could stretch that glide pretty far. I went out over the edges of the Valles, which is just a fancy word for canyon. The Grand Canyon of Mars, so big that it would stretch from New York City to Los Angeles. You could lose whole states in some of the side canyons. I felt a little lift from the rising, thin, warm air. When I say warm, I mean a few degrees below zero. That's balmy on Mars. But I didn't linger. I banked again and soon was down to three thousand feet over my hometown.

Other than the usual hotel construction there were three big things going on down there. Dad hated one of them, and Mom was opposed to all three. Dad was a confirmed Green and Mom was a passionate, some might even say rabid, Red.

On Earth, a Red is a communist—and I admit I'm not too clear on just what a communist is since we don't seem to have any on Mars, or at least they don't call themselves that. Something about everybody sharing everything, everybody being equal. What's so bad about that? I don't know what all the fuss was about, but apparently Earthies spent most of the last century hassling over it.

On Mars, a Red is a conservationist, usually a member of the Preservationist Party. "Keep Mars Red!" You'll see the posters everywhere you go.

A Green on Earth is a member of one of the national ecology parties. They are against pollution, in favor of wildlife conservation and stuff like that. None of that matters a lot to a Martian Green *or* Red. There's pollution, but not much, and no wildlife at all. Here on the red planet, a Green is a terraformer.

Got it? Red means leave it the way it is. Green means build more hotels, warm it up, and fill the air with oxygen.

Myself, I'm a member of the Beer, Bang, and Rock n' Roll Party, and so is just about everybody else I know. We don't think about it much.

So what do I think when I *do* think about it?

A little of both, I guess. The Reds seem pretty stupid to me. I mean, who cares? We've been exploring Mars for over twenty years. If there was life anywhere, we would have found it by now. To my way of thinking, no life equals no ecology. Which means Mars is just a big ball of rock and ice and carbon dioxide, and who cares what somebody does to a big pile of rocks?

Don't get Mom started on that subject, though. You've been warned.

On the other hand, who do the Greens think they're kidding? They've got their test site running a few miles outside town and it's shooting thawed permafrost into the air at a rate that will eventually let us go outside wearing nothing but a very thick parka and take off our respirators for as much as ten minutes at a time.

In about a hundred thousand years.

I could see the plant sitting out there by itself, surrounded by a security fence to keep Red protesters out. Of course, they plan to build thousands of the things, much bigger. But even the most optimistic numbers I've seen won't turn Mars into an approximation of an Earth environment until long after I'm dead. And that environment would be like what you'd find at ten thousand feet over the North Pole.

Again: Who cares?

The other part of the Green philosophy is building stuff.

Even Dad has started to worry about that part of the Green point of view. Not the Grand Canal, he likes that part just fine. That's the second big new thing you see from the air. What they're doing is, they're digging a ditch from Thunder City to Olympus Mons. One day in a few years they plan to sell rides to the Olympus ski runs on big sleds, jet-powered iceboats, instead of flying people there. You can put restaurants on big iceboats, and you can't on small passenger rockets. They envision a leisurely two-day trip, extracting your last dime in the casino. It's sort of a pseudoretro thing. Mars never had canals, but wouldn't it have been swell if it had? In about three years we'll have one.

We already had part of it. The first fifteen miles were complete, almost half a mile wide, straight as a stick, full of water and frozen solid. It continued inside to meet the Grand Concourse, where it was actual warm water suitable for swimming, lined with exotic plastic "Martian" plants and architecture from a 1930s science fiction magazine cover. It was already very popular.

Then there were the Martels, and for once Mom and Dad agreed on something. I could see them sprawling out to the north, into the less desirable real estate beyond the city, like a bad case of acne with multicolored pimples. Dad would give anything to pop them.

The big travel companies finally realized there is a great hunger for off-Earth travel among the middle classes who can't afford the Red Thunder, and who find Luna too black, too underground, and too boring. A few years back somebody built the first of what have come to be called Martels, just glorified tents, really. You can have them up and running in a week.

And there goes the neighborhood.

Sure, they look sort of okay now, from the ground, with none of them more than three years old. Your typical Martel room has a queen-sized bed and a dresser and a stereo and a little curtained area where you can shower and brush your teeth and not much else. Sort of like Boy Scout camp, only you don't have to work for merit badges in suit maintenance and knot-tying. All they are is triple-insulated domes of heavy-duty plastic held up by air pressure and crossed fingers, mass-produced in Ghana or Ecuador and shipped out here by the thousands to sprout on the red dirt like psychedelic mushrooms—they come in twenty-four loud color combinations—whose main purpose seems to be to make Mom hiss and spit every time she sees them.

They're all freestanding units, like teepees for Martian Indians, which some Earth motels actually used to be—teepees, I mean—like I've seen in Dad's collection of postcards of old motels. Their one luxury is a big triple-paned Lucite picture window offering a great view of red dirt, in the calm season, or of red dust when it blows, which is frequently. Oh, yeah, and a view of pink sky when it's calm. When it's blowing you lose even the pink sky, since during a good howler visibility is reduced to about a centimeter. And the howlers can last for . . . well, for a lot longer than your honeymoon vacation package deal. *Yeah, Mom and Dad, we spent five days and four nights on the goddam rock ball and didn't even see the goddam pink sky.*

The last thing worth mentioning in the rooms other than the tacky lithograph glued to the curving wall is a staircase leading down to your front door, which takes you to the tunnel corridor that can stretch up to half a mile of no-pile insulated carpet until it gets to the big central dome—the *Vacation Fun Center!* in Martel-speak—which consists of a bored clerk working his way through Marineris U., the *No Lifeguard On Duty!* Olympic-size pool (if there was a ten-meter freestyle event in the Olympics), and a TV/game room where your kids will spend all their time between bouts of whining *Can we go home yet?* Oh, yeah, and in the mornings, the "Complimentary 'Ancient Martian' Breakfast." Until the Martels arrived none of us *new* Martians knew that the ancient Martians liked to start the day with weak coffee and stale muffins. In fact no one had ever discovered the slightest trace of any ancient Martians at *all,* so you can't say the arrival of the Martels hasn't done *some* good. Who knew?

"Yeah, but just wait until those cheap plastic toilets start to overflow," Dad says when the subject comes up. "Wait till the duct tape springs a leak some night when it's 125 below. Wait till one whole wing blows out entirely and fifty or a hundred guests try to breathe the air. In five minutes we could have a big disaster on our hands, a whole lot of frozen bodies to ship back home, and how is that going to look for the whole industry?"

You notice Dad doesn't spend a lot of time grieving over the potentially dead Earthies. He claims to love 'em, they're his livelihood, but he doesn't expect much of them except rudeness, impossible demands, lack of common sense, and about six concussions per week from refusing to wear their helmets indoors.

Dad knows a bit about cheap motels. He is the fourth generation in the hospitality industry in our family. My great-great-grandparents opened a little two-story drive-up just down the road from Cape Canaveral and called it the Seabreeze. About the time John Glenn took his first trip into space, they renamed it the Blast-Off Motel. My grandmother inherited it, and my dad spent all his early life there. In that time it went downhill quite a bit. It was never very fancy, but by the time Dad met Uncle Travis and Uncle Jubal, Grandma was about to go bankrupt. And then the whole *Red Thunder* thing happened, and it changed his life.

Mine, too. Without that trip, I'd surely be growing up as an Earthie. Makes me shiver just to think about it.

Because when all is said and done, the only place that sucks more than Mars does, is the Earth.

2

★ ★ ★

REASON #2 THAT Mars sucks: exercise.

Mom says I shouldn't complain. If I was on Earth, she says, I'd be doing the same thing, only it would be spread out over the whole day, including the nighttime, when I was asleep. Did I say Mom can find the bright side of anything? Well, she can. I mean, she does have a point, but adding in the extra exercise I'd get just by inhaling and exhaling at night as a cherry on the top of the hot fudge sundae of life is exactly what I'd expect of Mom.

Like I said before, since the chances of you being an Earthie are overwhelmingly better than the chance of you being a sensible person, I'll explain what I'm talking about.

The fact is, more than once I've run into Earthies who got here and didn't know Mars has less gravity than the Earth does. The surface gravity of Mars is a little more than one-third of a gee. Thirty-eight percent, to be precise. A gee is the acceleration of gravity on Earth. I mass about 180 pounds. That means I weigh about 68 pounds on Mars.

Mom's point being, if I was on Earth I'd be carrying that full 180 around all day long. Everything would be almost three times as hard to do as it is here. Walking upstairs to the top of the Red Thunder Hotel, twenty stories, would leave most people breathing hard. I thought for a long time that's one of the reasons why so many of the Earthies that come here are real, real fat. It must be tough for them at home, but here they can dance and jump and run . . . though it's not a pretty sight. Mars must be a delightful place to visit for fat people. I pictured travel agencies advertising for real porkers. But Mom said no, it's just that more Earthies are fat than Martians. (Well, she didn't say Earthies, she never does. Some people think it's an insulting term. She says "People from Earth," or "Earthlings." The funny thing, an Earthie once told me they don't like being called Earthlings. She said it was creepy. Go figure.)

So by now you're wondering what's the big problem. I'll admit, it's not immediately obvious. I see vids of people walking around on Earth, and they just look . . . weary. Not their faces; they may be smiling and laughing, having fun. It's their body language. They move like people who are exhausted, plodding along, *tromp tromp thud thud*. Gravity pulls their faces down. By the time they're thirty, they're starting to look old. Gravity kills, no question about it, and you don't have to fall off a building to know that. Just look at a fifty-year-old Earthie.

The fact is, if you never went back to Earth—went "back home" as most of the grown-ups put it—it wouldn't be a problem. Get it now? Some people here have emigrated for their health, they'd be dead already if they'd stayed in a one-gee field. They're never going "home," Mars is home, whether they like it or not. If they like it, they can be perfectly happy here with just the reasonable exercise that their doctors recommend, though a lot of them admit that they're homesick.

For the rest of us, it's a choice we have to make. Some people say it's easy, no big deal, but they're wrong. I've been here since I was five. Mars is home to me. But I have some memories of Earth, I've been back four times, and for many decades to come, Earth is going to be the place. You know what I mean?

The place. The place where it's happenin', dude, as Dad would say.

The place where most of the interesting people are. The place where the new stuff comes from. Sure, we've got our music here, some fairly good groups. The Red Brigade had a few tunes that scored some heavy downloads—you say "Red Brigade" and most English-speaking kids on Earth would know who you're talking about—but most of them aren't much more than pressurized garage bands.

All the other cool stuff comes from the Blue Planet, too. For a while there kids on Earth were wearing stereos that had been designed on Mars, but other than that, the things people are wearing come from where they've always come from: Los Angeles, Tokyo, St. Petersburg, Shanghai, Bombay. The cool places.

If you're interested in history, like I am, most of it's on Earth. We've got exactly one real historic spot on Mars: the *Red Thunder* landing site, where they built a replica of the ship. Everybody goes there to get their picture taken. All the earlier robot landers were gathered up and put in the museum to prevent vandalism.

So what are you going to do? It's a documented fact: Every year you stay on Mars makes it harder and harder to ever return to Earth. Well, harder to return and lead anything like a normal life.

So that awful day I was doing what I have done two hours per day for most of my life. Working out. There's two places to do that. There's a gym at school, and one beneath the hotel where me and my sister, Elizabeth, and other hotel workers and their children do our sweating, in the basement, beneath the big gym with a view where the Earthie guests are encouraged to exercise and usually don't. I seldom go there. It's no fun watching a little Earthie girl press twenty pounds more than you can. I'd finished my hundred with my right arm and was up to fifty or so with my left.

I'm not one to wear my stereo when I work out. No special reason, I just don't like to, and neither does Elizabeth. So I was on the chin bar with my eyes bare naked, as we say, when I saw something I'd only seen a couple of times before. Everybody in the gym stopped what they were doing and stared off into cyberspace.

"Uh-oh," I said. Beside me, Elizabeth paused with her chin just over the bar and glanced at me.

"What?"

I gestured with my head, and we both dropped to the mat and scrambled for our gym bags. I got out my brand-new MBC V-Crafter 2030 stereo with the cool gold-tinted bug-eye lenses and the black-and-gold

Burroughs school colors tiger-stripe pattern on the wings. While I was doing that I heard a few people gasping. Somebody assassinated? A spaceship crash? A blowout? I put them on and ticked the flashing red NEWS icon. A window opened in the middle distance, the stereo effect making it seem to hang motionless over the running track. In the center of the window was a view of Planet Earth, hanging there like a blue agate with swirls of white.

Only there was something wrong with it. Somebody had made a fine white scratch mark on it, straight as a jet contrail, right over the Atlantic Ocean.

Only . . . the scratch extended out to the northeast, right to the edge of the window. A rocket launch?

Then I realized that if I could see the scratch from that distance—and the window superscript said this picture was from a camera on the moon—it had to be a big scratch.

You can't see the pyramids from the moon. You can't see the Great Wall of China, no matter what they might tell you. You can see Manhattan Island and Hawaii with a pair of good binoculars and a steady hand; I know, I've done it.

You could have seen this scratch with your bare eyes.

Big.

I wasn't getting any sound. I looked around and saw several people cupping their ears, like you do when you're listening intently to your stereo. Were they not hearing anything, like I was, or just concentrating, blocking out external sounds? I smacked the side of the left wing of the set and heard static, and that irritated the sore spot on my temple, under the wing, where the little vibrator with the bio-battery (guaranteed for twenty years!) had been implanted at the store when I bought the set. Simple as an ear-piercing, they told me. For some reason I'd had a bad reaction on that side—"I swear, Ray, this is the first time this has ever happened!"—and I'd had to wear a little donut-shaped pad over there until a few days before. One more smack . . .

Hah! Now it was working. No moving parts, and about the highest tech of all high tech until they figure out how to implant the whole stereo-computer display right into your head and eyeballs, and yet a good whack fixes it sure as it fixes a balky washing machine. One of life's mysteries.

"We have calls in to the Lunar Observatory, but the system seems to be overloaded at this time," the female announcer's voice was saying. "The image you are seeing is live, from the Armstrong Observatory in the Sea of Tranquility." As she spoke that relativistic lie, the camera began a zoom in toward the white line, giving me a view that was somewhere between three and twenty minutes old.

We call it live. But I couldn't interact with anyone on Earth concerning whatever it was I was seeing until—I ticked up another small window, this one showing the current Earth-Mars lagtime—almost thirty minutes.

The streak was still there, like a scratch on the imaginary window that floated in my field of vision just above the warning track. Then it was gone.

"This is tape of the event," the announcer was saying. I couldn't tell any difference from what we'd been seeing before. The Earth hadn't rotated, the cloud patterns were identical. Of course, it takes at least an hour to see much change in either of those things. Then, suddenly, there it was again. One moment a clear shot of the Atlantic Ocean, northern spring, with South America just about centered in the southern hemisphere, North America off to the northwest quadrant, the lights of Europe and western Africa speckling the eastern limb of the globe. The day/night terminator slanted down from Hudson Bay to Maine to the bulge of Brazil; it would be getting dark in the West Indies and the Eastern Seaboard of the United States soon. The next moment, the streak appeared fully formed. I centered a cursor over the spot where the streak began, and my stereo informed me it was about twenty-five degrees north latitude, sixty degrees west longitude, just above that little curve of flyspecks called the Leeward and Windward Islands.

It just didn't add up. What could make a thing like that?

Then they shifted back to the live picture, and the camera pulled back. And pulled back some more, and more, until we were getting the widest angle shot we could get from the moon with that lens with the Earth still centered, and I heard people gasp. I might even have been one of them. The streak just kept going, right to the edge of the picture. Maybe five or six Earth diameters, bright and white and perfectly straight. Lenses changed again, and now the Earth was a blue marble . . . and still the streak extended to the edge of the picture. Each Earth diameter was about eight thousand miles. I ticked up a ruler and positioned it over the streak. The part I could see was over almost a quarter of a million miles long. If the Earth was a clock, the streak was a hand pointing between one and two.

"Is it fading a little?" somebody asked.

"No, it's getting bigger," said somebody else.

"Wider," Elizabeth corrected. "It's getting wider, and it's a little fainter."

I thought she was right. There was no wind where this streak was, but if it was a gas cloud of some kind, you'd expect it to expand in space.

"Down there at the bottom, where it hits the Earth," came another voice. "Isn't it getting wider? Sort of a cigar shape?" I thought it was more of an oval, an ellipse, but it was plain enough. I felt my skin prickle in goose bumps.

"Something hit the Earth," I said.

"Yeah, but . . ."

"No, that doesn't make sense."

"Sure it does," I said. "See, it came in from two o'clock, and it hit in the water."

"No, why would it leave a trail like that? An asteroid wouldn't leave a trail—"

"Would a ship leave a trail like that?"

"No ship I ever saw. It's big, and it's still expanding."

"Plus, look how fast it must have been moving before—"

Somebody did that fingers-in-the-lips whistle that I've never been able to master, and we all looked for the source. To no one's surprise, it was Matt Kaminsky, the senior captain of the swimming team.

"Let's pool, people," he said.

No, he wasn't talking about taking a dip in the lap pool behind me. He meant he thought we ought to pool all our cyber resources, link up, so we'd all be on the same page, more or less. I had five windows running at that time, all different news sources. No telling what everybody else was watching. There being no objection, the motion carried. We all switched our stereos into network setting, and Matt pointed to the east wall of the gym. Windows began appearing in a mosaic as we all turned to face it, hanging a few inches out in front of the equipment there. They were stabilized windows, meaning that if I turned my head, they stayed there in front of the wall, didn't move with my field of vision. Now we knew we were all seeing the same stuff at the same time. There were all the usual suspects: CNN-Mars, EuroTV, TeleLuna, CBS. Some showed talking heads and print crawl lines, others were picking up different angle shots of the streak from various manned and unmanned satellites and orbital resorts. A couple were showing tourist-eye views from people who just happened to be looking at that part of the Earth when the streak appeared. There was no point in that, really; the resolution wasn't as good, and being closer to the Earth didn't reveal any new detail.

Matt pulled up a few more windows, including some I had never seen. There was a public feed from the Jet Propulsion Laboratory, and a false-color image from the United States National Weather Service. That one looked interesting, but I didn't know how to interpret it. There was something happening at what I was thinking of as the impact point, something with a lot of reds and yellows, and I thought I could almost see it expanding as I watched. I checked the count clock that had started when the urgent bulletin came in. We'd been watching for eight minutes, and the event had happened no more than five minutes before that. The visible-light image was just white in the impact area, a lozenge of what looked like a puffy white cloud that was growing. Unseen producers were running recordings backward and forward at high speed, and they all showed the same thing. The streak would appear instantaneously, fully formed, and then the white area would expand until it froze in real time. Big as that area was, we couldn't see it growing in the live feeds.

All the windows were showing the same view, but from widely different angles. From a satellite over the North Pole it was possible to see that the streak seemed to graze the Earth's atmosphere, maybe dip into the ocean.

Wait a minute, I thought.

"Wait a minute," I said, before the thought was fully formed in my mind. Several heads turned in my direction.

"Maybe I had it backwards," I said, and wondered why I'd said it. Then I had it.

"It think that streak is moving *away* from the Earth. I think it hit on a tangent, right there above the ocean, and . . . sort of . . . skipped."

"Like chucking stones over water?" Matt asked. I could hear he wasn't buying it. "You know how fast it had to be traveling to—"

"Well, it had to be going fast," I said. "To just *appear* like that."

"I make it the speed of light," somebody said. "Or close enough as not to make much difference."

"How do you figure?"

"The distance covered, that we can see from some of these views, is about a quarter of a million miles, and I can't see which direction it came from. That means some small fraction of a second. It takes light—"

"Look, look!" somebody else shouted. "The JPL screen!"

That window was showing a slowed-down rerun from some distant satellite with a high-shutter-speed camera. Frame by frame, we could see the streak form. It definitely began on the ocean and shot off to the northeast very quickly, even slowed down as it was. Down at the bottom of the window was a clock counting off hundred-thousandths of a second, and a computer-generated computation of speed: .999*c*. C, in case they didn't teach any physics in your school, is the speed of light in a vacuum: 186,000 miles per second.

Nobody had anything to say when that figure came up.

I began to realize this was going to be one of those *Where were you?* moments. *Where were you* when you heard about New Delhi and Islamabad? For my parents, it was *Where were you* on September 11, 2001? For Grandma it was John Kennedy's assassination, and before that it was Pearl Harbor. This was going to be that bad. I didn't quite know how or why yet, but I felt it.

A few seconds later most of the screen cleared for a moment, and then somebody appeared, same shot, in all of them. It was a black woman—short, judging from the shoulders on either side of her—and she looked out of breath, like she'd run all the way to the cameras. The crawl at the bottom of the windows identified her as the Honorable Shirley Tsange, acting director of UNGWS. I ticked the acronym and was told it stood for United Nations Global Warning System. There was a lot of shouting from reporters off-screen, flashes going off, the usual turmoil of the press pack.

She started speaking without preamble, raising her voice almost to a shout until she got some quiet. She was reading from a prepared statement.

"At 1836 Greenwich Mean Time, a high-speed object of unknown origin impacted the North Atlantic Ocean at approximately sixty-seven degrees west longitude and twenty-four degrees north latitude. The global early-warning system had no indication at all of this object prior to impact, but the impact itself triggered numerous automatic systems that have been monitoring and extrapolating possible effects of the impact since that time. Ten minutes ago the data became alarming enough that I, acting for the director of the UNGWS, issued a tsunami alarm, which went out immediately. The following countries are expected to be immediately affected, in order of their proximity to the impact:

"The Bahama Islands, Puerto Rico and the British and American Virgin Islands.

"Anguilla, St. Martin, St. Barts . . . in fact the entire chain of the Leeward and Windward Islands." I winced, recalling that just a few moments ago I was thinking of those places as "flyspecks." That's what they are, on the map, but those flyspecks were inhabited by human beings.

"The Dominican Republic. Haiti. The Turks and Caicos Islands. The eastern provinces of Cuba.

"But first . . ." She paused, and put down the paper she was reading from. "Sorry, I should have skipped right to this part, things have been happening very fast, and the warning is already out, automatically, so . . ." She paused, took a deep breath, and we could all see just how shaken she really was.

"First, the residents of the Bahamas are in the worst danger. The highest waves seem to be propagating in their direction. We offer the following advice:

"First, if you are able, get to high ground. The initial wave is in the eighty-to-one-hundred-foot range, possibly larger. We can't see much because of the atmospheric storm forming over the impact site. You need to get higher than one hundred feet above sea level, the higher the better, as the wave will have considerable inertia. We realize that the Bahamas are low-lying islands, and high ground may not be an option. Failing that, get to the highest floors of a reinforced-concrete building.

Experience in the Indian Ocean has shown that these structures are quite likely to survive.

"Do it *now*! The sirens are sounding. Do not delay. If you are in a vehicle, I understand the roads are already clogged. Abandon your vehicle and look for the sturdiest structure in your vicinity. Estimated time of arrival of the first wave is twenty minutes for San Salvador Island, Cat Island, and Eleuthera, shortly thereafter for the eastern regions of Grand Bahama Island.

"Once in a safe location, *stay there*. There may be more than one wave, as there have been in past tsunamis.

"The first sign of the wave's approach will be a rapid recession of the ocean. Observers describe it as a 'sucking away.' Much of the seafloor may be exposed. Then the wave will arrive, and eventually begin to recede, but *do not return* to flooded areas until you hear the all clear from the local authorities."

One of the taller men standing beside her leaned over to whisper in her ear. She looked harried, nodded, and went on.

"Right . . . ah, as a precautionary measure, we are recommending the immediate evacuation of coastal areas and river estuaries from . . . from the Florida Keys to New York City and Long Island. Please get away from the ocean at once, and seek high ground or the highest shelter you can find."

My heart seemed to stop for a moment. I looked at Elizabeth, and she was looking right at me, and at that moment I could read her mind.

High Ground? In Florida?

"Grandma!" we shouted at the same time, and turned and began to run.

3

THE PLANET EARTH probably has ten video cameras for every inhab-
itant. They cover virtually every area where people live, street by street,
block by block.

Okay, that's an exaggeration. There are still villages and towns and
maybe even a few cities in Asia and Africa where there's no monitoring
cameras. But where this tsunami was expected to hit, coverage was virtually total.

What I was doing as I ran, and I assume Elizabeth was doing the
same thing, was calling up beachcams in the Daytona area. Fixed views,
pan-and-scan, caller-operated, you name it.

It was hard. The traffic must have been enormous, the servers were
being overloaded. Time and again as I tried to tick on the next one down
the beach, hit-or-miss, I'd get "Unable to complete connection. Please
try again later."

I had the code number of one of the beachcams on top of the Blast-
Off Motel somewhere in memory, but I was hurrying too fast to find it
and work the stereo at the same time, so I had just entered DAYTONA
BEACH and started ticking through the available cams. I got a view of the
ocean from, I thought, about a half mile south of the motel. There was

nothing to see but beautiful blue sky and shining sea and glistening white sand. It was late on a February evening, peak tourist season . . . and no one was on the beach. There were plenty of towels and umbrellas and coolers. Then I saw a few tiny figures here and there, and they were all running. One couple was loaded down with beach gear, stumbling along in dry sand. What, were they trying to save a ten-dollar umbrella and a two-dollar cooler when doom was approaching, just over the horizon? A few others seemed to be frantically searching for other people. My breath caught in my throat when I saw a child, five or six, standing alone and crying. *Oh, god, I don't want to see this.* I ticked to another cam.

We were hurrying through the lobby, dodging people standing still as statues as they watched their own personal newscasts in their personal stereospace. I'd seen it a few times before, when some big news was breaking—last time it was the incredibly important flash that Hollywood heartthrobs Brad and Bobby Gonzalez were breaking up. It's called a freeze crowd. If you aren't wearing your own stereo, or if you didn't give goose crap about the affairs of two empty-headed pretty boys, it looked like time had stopped, or that somebody had sprayed everyone with liquid nitrogen. A few others were hurrying, like us. Most likely they had relatives on the American East Coast or Caribbean islands, like us.

See, our grandmother lived in Daytona Beach.

I mean, right *on* the beach.

The Blast-Off was bigger than it had been in my dad's day, but it was still a mouse among elephants. The "Blast-Off Tower Wing" had been added to the old two-story structure the year I was born, though Grandma admitted it was a grandiose word for a building whose neighbors were twenty-five and thirty stories high.

Which would stand up to a tsunami better? I wondered. A ten-story mouse or a thirty-story elephant?

And they'd said to get up high.

How high is high?

WE CAME TEARING around the side of the front desk at a speed that normally would have earned us a chewing out even from Dad. NO RUNNING, JUMPING, OR SKATEBOARDING IN THE LOBBY! The signs were posted everywhere, you couldn't miss them, and right under it NONRESIDENTS MUST WEAR HELMETS AT ALL TIMES! It was for Earthies, who are always hurting themselves or somebody else by something as simple as trying to turn a corner too fast without leaning over far enough. As for jumping . . . there's a reason why all the ceilings in the Red Thunder Hotel are padded.

We didn't wear no stinking helmets, of course. Not since we were eight. We'd have died of shame.

Actually, only one staff member noticed us at all. The rest were staring at the various news channels on the walls behind the desk. Nobody was getting checked in or out, but that was okay; nobody was trying to. The freeze crowd effect was still working for most of them.

As we barreled around the corner Elaine, a beautiful Indonesian clerk who I'd had a crush on since I was old enough to have crushes, and our best friend on the day staff, looked over at us with an expression of concern on her face. She knew where our grandmother lived. And I suddenly remembered that she was a survivor of the '04 tsunami in the Indian Ocean. She had told us about it once, I couldn't remember the circumstances. She had been three, and her whole family was wiped out. She was found in the branches of a tree, barely alive, three days later. No wonder she looked concerned.

We ran down the ramp in the narrow hallway. The Owner's Suite is in the Frank Lloyd Wright prairie style, like the rest of the Red Thunder, and if that doesn't make a lot of sense to you, you're not the only one. The decor is all wood, angular and spare, and the big room is dominated by a floor-to-ceiling wall of what looks like glass panes, angled inward at the top. It shows a nice vista of hotel row, which is a long line of whimsical towers and attached pleasure domes that reminds a lot of people of the Las Vegas Strip.

It's actually just vidpaper. We were standing about ten feet below ground level; there was nothing but concrete beyond the glass. But it fools the eye. Just as good as the view from the very expensive penthouse suites.

When we get tired of it, we switch it to some Earth scene.

Dad doesn't wear stereos. Never. He hates them, and would be a lot happier if they'd never been invented. He'd be a lot happier if no one in his family ever wore them, but he knows that's a battle he can't win. He gets even by making the desk clerks use old-fashioned screens and key-boards. "This is a first-class establishment," he says. "Our clients don't want to see a bunch of people wearing space cadet goggles." That was years ago, when stereos really did look sort of goofy. The ones me and Elizabeth and most other people wear these days are slim, formfitting, you'd hardly know them from regular wraparound bubble sunglasses except for the thicker frames and wings, and the strap that keeps them on your head. Stereos are tough, and not as expensive as they used to be, but you don't want them dropping on a hard floor too often at four hundred euros a lens.

So Dad was standing and staring at the wall opposite the "view" windows, which was also vidpaper but divisible into different electronic windows. He had a dozen of them going, his eyes darting back and forth.

Dad isn't an imposing figure, in his slightly stuffy and definitely out-of-fashion navy blue suit with the Red Thunder emblem on the chest. He's of medium height, getting a little thick around the waist, and his dark hair has receded right to the top of his head and is gray on the sides. Once we were standing side by side at a mirror so he could see how tall I'd grown (I topped out at six-foot-six, which is not tall for a Martian child—the low gravity lets us shoot up like beanstalks—and I wasn't even Mars-born; no telling how big some of those kids are going to grow), and he muttered "I used to look like Jimmy Smits. Now I look like Cheech Marin." I didn't know who either of those guys were, but I googled them and I have to say he wasn't entirely wrong.

Mom, on the other hand . . .

My parents are different in so many ways I have sometimes wondered what it is that keeps them together. Dad's a Green, Mom's a Red. Dad hates stereos. Mom . . . well, whoever first invented the wearable computer, he probably had my mother in mind. Mom has always got fifteen things going at once. She has always had the newest hardware, the newest programs. Dad says she changes computers more often than a lot of people change their underwear, and Mom says he should change his underwear more often. Then they laugh. Usually.

She was on the move, which is the normal state for her. Elizabeth says that when Mom isn't on the move, she's either sleeping, sick, or dead, and she never allows herself to get sick and doesn't even sleep much.

She doesn't show any marks from her hectic lifestyle. Her face has a few more wrinkles than she had in those pictures from the *Red Thunder* days, there are streaks of gray in her hair, and her skin is much paler than it used to be when she lived in the Florida sunshine because she never has time for sitting under a sunlamp. Of course, wearing a stereo, you can get all sorts of work done sitting down, but if it's a tan you're trying to get done, you'll end up looking like a raccoon. But even working on the stereo she's a multitasker and a pacer. Simply working on the stereo when she could be doing something else at the same time is never enough for her, so she's usually in movement around the apartment or her office doing physical chores or getting from point A to point B, even if there was nothing wrong with being in point A in the first place. Dad says that when they were going together on Earth he hated to be in a car when she was driving. She was always doing several things at the same time, like talking on her cell phone, thumbing the controls of her pocket computer, eating a sandwich because she didn't have time to stop for lunch . . . "I never actually saw her painting her toenails while she was driving," Dad told me, "but I wouldn't have been surprised." She banged up a few fenders. Luckily, her father was a car dealer with a body shop.

Their arrangement seems to be that he runs the hotel and she runs everything else. She pretty much does what she wants to do, which probably would have been harder for my Latino dad if he'd grown up with a father in the house. He doesn't seem to mind. When something is really, really important to him he will speak up about it, and Mom will work out a compromise and make a promise, and that seems to satisfy him. He knows Mom usually gets her way, but he also knows she never breaks a promise.

"Elizabeth, Ramon, you have to start packing, right now," Mom said. I've been *Ray*, had started *insisting* on it, since I was ten but every once in a while I was Ramon again to my parents, and most of the time it meant I was in big trouble.

"Why?" Elizabeth asked.

"Because we have a ship to catch, and it leaves in four hours."

"A ship . . ." I stopped myself. I was going to ask where, but the answer was obvious.

"Mother," Elizabeth said, "how can you think of packing at a time like this? We need to see what's—"

"I can think of it because somebody had to take care of the details, Elizabeth, and because it was hard to get these tickets so quickly, I had to call in a lot of favors to bump a few tourists, and . . . shush!" She held out her hand and listened to someone she was talking to on her stereo.

"Sell them," she snapped. A short pause, then, "I don't care if they're at fifty percent of what I paid for them. By the time the sell order gets to New York they'll probably be down another ten percent, and after that . . . well, who knows. I need to have that sale registered *at once*, in case . . ."

For a moment I didn't get it, and then my jaw dropped.

In case . . .

In case New York isn't answering the telephone in another few hours. In case Wall Street is ten stories deep in seawater.

Mom was selling stocks. Too bad everybody on Earth had a twenty-minute jump on her. I wondered for a moment what stocks you'd sell if you knew a tsunami was on the way. Insurance companies, I guess.

But maybe it wouldn't be so bad.

"Mother, we want to see what's going on."

"Elizabeth, that's what stereos are for."

I went and stood beside my father. He put his arm up around my shoulder, absently, never taking his eyes off the screens on the wall.

"Ten thousand remote cameras on the Florida coast," he was muttering. "Maybe twenty thousand . . . why can't I find . . . ?" He looked down at the remote in his hand, and his shoulders slumped. He tossed the remote onto the couch behind him, and sat down. Actually, it was more like a collapse. He sat there with his shoulders slumped and his face in his hands. I was about to sit beside him and offer what comfort I could, when he suddenly leaped to his feet and shouted.

"Dammit, Kelly, how can you do that at a time like this?"

There was dead silence for a moment. Mom stopped moving and took a deep breath.

"I'm sorry, hon, but there's not a damn thing we can do about what's happening there, except what I've already done."

"I know, I know . . ." Dad didn't seem to know how to express what he was feeling at the moment. I didn't either, but I think I could feel it.

"Manny, children . . . I don't want to seem cold, but you know we can't do anything about Betty's situation. But I know this. She's a smart woman. She's a survivor. If this is survivable, she will *survive* it. What we have to do as a family is get there as fast as we can. I've already arranged for that. And while we're waiting, I want to try to salvage what I can from some investments that are likely to be affected by this before they shut down the markets."

"What would those be, Mom?" Elizabeth asked.

"That's the tough part. People are unloading different things. I don't know. What I do know is, something this big impacts economies and affects people who are nowhere near ground zero. Banks and insurance companies fail under the kind of pressure this wave may represent. Governments may fall. I don't know how to protect us from that, but I'm trying to figure it out. Can I go ahead? Please?"

She wasn't being sarcastic. Dad didn't say anything, and Mom took that as a yes, but when she continued she went to a corner of the room and kept her voice down. Elizabeth and I joined Dad on the couch, on either side. We put our arms around him.

We didn't have long to sit. A computer-simulated wave was reaching Mayaguana Island, which they had calculated was the first place the effects of the tsunami would be seen. There was a reporter stationed on top of the highest tower on a resort on the easternmost point of the island, and she was standing in front of the camera with the blue ocean behind her. She looked a bit nervous. I figured she had every right to be. There was still a chance, according to the stories we'd been seeing, that this whole thing would be a giant fizzle, but that opinion was losing support as new satellite data came in.

"The reports I'm hearing from the news center," she was saying, "tell me that satellite imaging is being hampered by a storm that has formed over the site of the impact. An infrared camera is being moved as I speak, and it should be able to make a better calculation as to how much energy was delivered by the object. The impact was not, let me repeat, not, registered by seismographs, which leads the oceanographers to believe that it did not strike the seabed. That's the good news. The bad news is that if it was energetic enough, if there was enough . . . ah, kinetic energy in whatever it was that struck the Earth a short time ago, and if enough of that energy was transferred to the water . . . well, we might be in for quite a wave in the next few minutes.

"I'm told that the ocean is deep to the east of my position on Mayaguana Island, that we are on the edge of the Bahamian Rise, so we may not see much of the wave's approach until it gets here."

A computer graphic appeared on half the screen, showing how a tsunami can travel over deep water and hardly be seen or felt, then how it would pile up as it reached shallow water.

"We don't know precisely when the wave will arrive," the reporter went on, "but I don't mind telling you I'm a little nervous." She didn't have to tell us. She was very pretty, as TV reporters usually are, and was wearing a bathing suit with a light shirt pulled on over it, like she had been relaxing in the sun when her phone rang and hadn't had time to change into more sober clothes, and her face was shiny with sunburn lotion, and given the location and the way she and the other people on the roof were dressed, it was probably quite warm up there. But she was shivering.

"We're on the roof of a six-story building here, and I've been assured it sits on a concrete foundation and is made of steel and concrete, so—"

Behind her, some of the people looking over the railing began to point and shout. The reporter jumped, then her instincts took over and she hurried over to the edge. Somebody cleared a space for her, and the camera operator panned until we could see over her shoulder. There was a thick line of white drawn on the water halfway to the horizon.

"Look! Look down there!" somebody was shouting. The cameraman moved to the rail and pointed his camera down. The water was being sucked away like a giant bathtub draining. It was *fast!* The beach extended out a hundred feet, then three hundred, then more and more until it seemed it would reach the distant white line. The camera zoomed in on the wet sand and rock, and I could see fish flopping around, including a big shark of some sort. There was some more shouting, then everything got very quiet as people were overcome by the sight of an ocean that had vanished. I heard some people crying, a woman shouting something unintelligible. Maybe a prayer.

"This is . . . uh . . . what we were told to expect," the reporter said. "This suction effect is the first thing we were told to expect . . . I'm repeating myself . . . Jerry, are we getting this? Jerry . . ."

The line of white in the distance began to swell, and was no longer completely straight. It was hitting shallower water, starting to pile up, and it was doing it unevenly, responding to differences in the ocean bottom that we couldn't see.

"We can see it now. Are we getting this, Jerry? It's not what I expected, I thought we'd see a green wall, rearing up like in a surfing video . . ."

As she spoke, the line of water did begin to rear up. It was hard to tell how tall it was, there were no boats out there to give us a scale. But I could hear people shouting. My guess was it was forty feet high, maybe. I think they got waves like that in Hawaii sometimes. Maybe it wouldn't be so bad.

Then I estimated it might be more like eighty feet. It began to curl over at the top, and now it reared up even more. We could hear it roaring.

"My god," the reporter said. "They told me it might sound like a freight train, but this is a thousand freight trains, all of them coming right at us. It's so fast! It's almost to the beach now . . . eighty, maybe ninety feet high . . ."

The curling part broke, but the sea was noticeably higher behind it. No way to tell how high. By the time it crashed on the beach it was partly concealed by a crown of foam and spray. A hundred feet high? Maybe more.

"My god, is it . . . it looks like it might be higher than the building! No, no, it's . . . I can't tell, I can't see . . . here it comes . . . Mother, I love you, I love you . . ."

At that point the camera operator was running, and he dropped his equipment. It landed sideways, and then the lens was spotted with water and the sound was incredible and I saw some running bare feet.

The screen went black.

I DON'T KNOW when Mom joined us on the couch. She was just there, squeezing my hand so tight it hurt, but I was squeezing back. The four of us sat there, stunned, not saying anything.

The next few minutes seemed like a kaleidoscope. I'm a member of the stereo generation, as they call it, and I'm pretty good at opening five or six or a dozen virtual windows and parking them somewhere in my peripheral vision and just leaving them on, semitransparent, but if something interesting happens in any of them I'll quickly tick it over into the center, and all the time I'm watching or reading that window I'll be aware of the other ones. People who are alarmed by this call it permanent sensory overload. People who can handle it call it multitasking. Both sides of the argument think my generation's minds are wired differently.

Whatever. I'd never had a problem with it, but until that day I'd never been confronted with maybe fifty or sixty different windows, all clamoring for my attention. The problem was, everything was happening at once. The house computer's discriminator was being overloaded by the number of news images, each with a top-priority rating. They were coming in from all the islands of the Bahamas, from stationary spycams and personal stereocams, from helicopters and airplanes and hi-rez satellites. They were filling the telewall of our apartment with a rolling crazy quilt of disaster.

We watched in silence, or sometimes turned away with a moan, as the waves arrived at Samana Cay, Acklins Island, and Crooked Island. No sooner had those cameras gone abruptly to black screen than the wave was assaulting Long Island, Rum Cay, and San Salvador. And the Turks and Caicos Islands.

Cat Island, Great Exuma, Eleuthera.

The Dominican Republic, Haiti, Puerto Rico.

Anguilla, St. Martin, St. Barts, Sin Maarten, St. Kitts and Nevis.

Cuba.

Places I'd never heard of, places I'd barely been aware of, and places I'd heard of but knew little about. All of them full of people living in tropical splendor, or taking a vacation from colder climates, people just like us, sitting in front of their telewalls or old flatscreens or even old box TVs, or watching out from their windows, or fleeing for their lives, or trying desperately to find their loved ones before the hammer of God descended on them. People who had had hopes and dreams and plans, people who might have worried about hurricanes or fires or car wrecks or falling off a boat and drowning but had never expected the horror that was bearing down on them. It was the first time in my life that I realized just how quickly everything could change, how one minute you could be strolling down some sunny street in the Bahamas and the next you could be staring death in the face.

It was somewhere between the impacts on Andros and Abaco and the arrival of the wave front at Grand Bahama Island that I noticed something in the one window I had kept functioning on my stereo. It was down in the left-hand corner of my field of vision, where I always parked it. It was the log of my incoming calls. There were forty or fifty names of friends who wanted me to log on to a group chat.

I guess it was the Earth icon that caught my eye. I've got a fair number of chathogs on Earth, but by the nature of the time lag they were more like old-fashioned pen pals—it was seldom important to get back to them right away. But this one was marked FLORIDA, USA, and any of the people I knew in Florida might be writing their last words to me at that moment.

I ticked on the icon, and when the number came up I shouted and got to my feet without even realizing I was doing it.

"It's Grandma!" I said, and quickly ticked the incoming window over to the house computer with an ultra-urgent priority. A window opened up right on the center of the wall. The picture formed, and was chaotic for a moment, then settled down. At first I didn't know what I was looking at, then saw it was an old laptop computer sitting on a chair. Grandma's face was on the screen. She looked a little harried, but calm.

"—how much time we have left, but I had to take a moment to do this," she was saying. I found Mom and Dad and Elizabeth were standing beside me. I felt Dad grab my hand.

"There's never enough time to tell everyone you love how much you love them, is there? I know, I've told you all. But trouble is coming, and they're saying it may be big trouble, maybe the biggest of all, and I have a lot of things to do, but I have to take a moment to do the most important thing of all in case . . . well, in case this is the last chance I have to tell you."

Dad squeezed my hand so hard it hurt, but I didn't complain. Elizabeth took my other hand.

"Kelly, I am proud to have you for a daughter-in-law. I haven't told you before, but I never thought it would last, you being . . . well, from a different sort of people." She laughed. "People with money. There, I said it. I thought you were slumming, and you proved me wrong. I've never been so happy to be wrong in my life."

I heard Mom sob, and she sat down hard on the couch, like her legs had been cut out from under her. Dad sat beside her and hugged her, and Elizabeth and I were left standing. I didn't look back at my parents. I don't like to see my parents cry. In fact, I don't think I'd ever seen it before. Surely not when Mom's father died. The only thing I ever heard her say about that was "Well, now they've got a Mercedes dealership in Hell. But they better keep their hands on their wallets."

Mom and her late father hadn't gotten along.

"Ramon and . . . sorry, Ray, my big boy, and Elizabeth, I'm so proud of you guys I could just bust when I think about you. I wish y'all could have come to visit me more often, and I wish I'd had the guts to take a trip to see y'all on Mars, but watching y'all grow up in the videos you sent me was the next best thing, and I guess it may have to do. I love you so much."

Grandma never even liked to go out on a boat on the ocean, and she hated to fly, so she'd never set foot on a spaceship, even though her son had helped build the first really good one. My throat was hurting something awful, and my nose was stopped up. Yeah, I was crying pretty good, I guess.

"And Manny . . . oh, Manny. You've done your mother proud, young man. I can't tell you—"

I thought I was about to burst, and suddenly the camera moved. I gasped, thinking *My god, the building is falling over!* It jerked around for a while, then showed Grandma's face. She was holding the little camera at arm's length, looking into it. She looked very tired.

"Okay, you'll get that as a message attachment if you get it at all. Let's get practical here." She set the camera on something steady and backed up a little bit. We could see her from the knees up, and I realized she was standing on the roof of the Blast-Off Tower. There were other people in the picture, none of them familiar. Grandma was wearing an automatic pistol in a holster on her hip and had a serious-looking rifle over her shoulder.

"It's been chaotic, but I expect it'll get worse." She smiled grimly and patted the handgun. "For now, we've just opened our doors to anybody who's in the area. I'd say we're at about twice capacity right now. Most of the people seem to have gone to the bigger hotels. They might be surprised later. I figure anybody who's in here when the wave comes is my guest. I've shut off the water in the tank up here on the roof, and turned off the gas, and the tank of diesel is full, and the generator is tested. You know I keep my emergency hurricane supplies up here where they won't get flooded, so I've got enough food to keep this bunch going for at least a week, and I've had volunteers bringing up stuff from the restaurant.

"So the only question is . . . how big is it? If the building holds up, I figure we'll be okay. I've been thinking back to '04. Manny, you're too young to remember it well, I guess, but it was a pretty big deal. I wondered what it would be like if it hit here. I figure that help will arrive a lot quicker, but it will still be pretty hairy for the first week or so. So I just wanted to let you know I'm prepared . . ."

She looked off to one side and smiled.

"See, Manny," Mom said. "I told you she was a survivor."

"She's a tough old broad, all right."

Grandma was beckoning to someone off camera.

"Come on, Maria, you have to say hello, at least. Come on!"

My aunt Maria came reluctantly into the picture, moving slowly with a cane, camera-shy as always. She wrote to me frequently, but never sent videos, scoffing at all that newfangled nonsense. I was shocked at how old and fragile she looked. She had always been . . . well, Mom says she's an "ample" woman, which means at least chubby. Not a lot over five feet tall, dark-skinned, her hair all white now. She wasn't exactly thin, but her skin seemed to hang off her.

"My god, she's lost thirty pounds," Elizabeth whispered to me. Her tone wasn't happy, it was clear to both of us this wasn't a healthy weight loss. Was something happening to her that no one had told me about?

Aunt Maria was no sooner in the picture than Grandma looked off to her left. I could hear people shouting.

"I think it's coming," she said. She faced the camera again. "I'm going to move the camera again, so y'all can see this. We may not be talking for a while, so let me say again I love you all, I love you so—"

The screen went blank.

4

★ ★ ★

LARGE INTERPLANETARY PASSENGER liners don't have to be streamlined because they never land anywhere. The ship does have to withstand acceleration of one gravity for extended periods, so it can't be spidery and insubstantial like so many Earth- and Mars-orbiting satellites, but as long as you distribute the mass evenly along the axis of acceleration you've got pretty much a free hand in design. So you'd think that interplanetary ships would be inner-oriented: that is, the outside would reflect what's on the inside and nothing else. Sort of like the old Lunar Excursion Module, the first human vehicle that never had to operate in air.

You'd be wrong. They mostly look like Buck Rogers or Walt Disney.

The ship that would take us to Earth, the *Sovereign of the Planets*, was run by Royal Caribbean, which seemed ironic to me considering what we'd witnessed a few hours before in our home.

We got our first glimpse of it in free fall after a three-gee boost up from Marsport. Dad was looking a little green in the face despite the antinausea drugs, which are a lot better now than when he was young. Not that they took any with them on the voyage of *Red Thunder*. The one thing that never occurred to him and my uncle Dak was that they'd get spacesickness. So naturally they both spent most of their free-falling time heaving up their guts, while Mom and Uncle Travis and Alicia got along just fine. He laughs about it now, but it's best not to tease him. I think he's deeply ashamed that he never became a good space traveler. A hard blow for a boy who grew up crazy about space and eager to be an astronaut.

The thing about luxury interplanetary travel is, if people have a choice between a nondescript, tossed-together collection of nuts and bolts that you can hardly tell from a bulk cargo carrier and a fantasyland traveling glitter dome that looks part Arabian nights and part Buck Rogers, they'll go for the fantasy every time. People like sleekness, even if it isn't there for any aerodynamic purpose. They like luxurious colors, they like sexy curves.

Bottom line, when they get on a spaceship they want it to look like something that can really go *vrooooooooom!*

There's really no point in getting into a long description of the *Sov*. You can get pictures at the Royal Caribbean cybersite. The main body of the ship is graceful and tapered at both ends, like a real rocket ship. Things stick out for no real reason: big swept-back fins and art deco ornamentation and toward the front a stylized statue of Mercury, the corporate logo of RC Deep Space Lines, that's only about half the size of the Statue of Liberty. The colors are silver with crimson racing stripes. Heck, if it would sell more tickets, they'd gladly fit the ship out with big headlights like a '56 Pontiac and big mag wheels with racing tires. As it was, the thing glittered with lights that raced around the hull in a continual light show, sometimes pausing to spell out the names of the acts who would be performing that night in the theaters and clubs and pictures of the delights to be had at the Mercury Buffet.

PAI-GOW POKER!

FOUR-STAR DINING IN THE ROTUNDA,
RESERVATIONS RECOMMENDED!

CELINE DION TWICE NIGHTLY IN THE INTIMATE STARZ
CABARET!

"MEMORIES OF HIP-HOP" IN THE MAIN THEATER!

24-HOUR ROOM SERVICE!

They didn't advertise anything for my generation while I watched the message boards, my generation mostly didn't have the money for a stateroom on the *Sov*, so it was heavily tilted toward the old farts, older even than Mom and Dad. That's okay. Get six or seven of my generation together in a room with our stereos on, and we can make our own entertainment.

The *Sov* was large, but she wasn't the biggest ship in space. She was built for the Earth–Mars run, four to eight days out, four to eight days back at one gee, depending on the positions of the two planets. I'd call her *pretty* big, as opposed to *huge*, like the liners that go to the outer planets, or *gigantic*, like starships.

The docking was about as exciting as the Staten Island Ferry pulling into its berth—less exciting; I'd have enjoyed riding a water ferry, something I've rarely done. The flight attendants strung the safety line down the center aisle of the shuttle and then bounced around snapping everybody's tethers to it, all the time chanting the mantra for space-stupid Earthies: "Please remain seated and do not remove your seat harnesses until you are requested to. Departure will be in strict order, from the front to the back of the spacecraft. Blah blah blah blah . . ."

I resented the hell out of being treated like a clueless Earthie, but what can you do? Instead, I sat there beside Elizabeth, and when our turn came we meekly unbuckled and allowed ourselves to be handled like baggage, passed slowly and carefully down the line at a very low rate of speed, one hand on the safety line as we were instructed. One plus: no carry-on luggage in a free-fall transfer. Nothing but the clothes on your back and whatever you could carry in your pockets and your stereo, buckled to your face. You don't even want to imagine what it might be like with 150 Earthies swinging backpacks and briefcases and small suitcases around just as though gravity would rescue their careless asses like it always did back home. Talk about your deadly missiles!

Into the ship, and I'll admit it was a little disorienting, going into a strange place in free fall can do that to you. Not really that much to see, anyway, between the shuttle and the assembly room, which would be reconfigured when we boosted and become the main theater, right near the stern of the ship, but which right now was set up to hold the entire complement of passengers. Just ordinary corridors, most of them curving slightly with the hull of the ship, with stewards stationed at every turn to slow passengers who'd gotten too enthusiastic and get them headed in the right way without any broken bones.

They had it down to a science. In the assembly hall they were packing them in like sardines, in three layers, two of them temporary fold-up bleachers with bucket seats and seat belts. I was settled into mine, between Elizabeth and Mom, and in a few more minutes the hall was full. Very much like a ride at Disney World.

Within five minutes we were treated to a big-screen picture of the *Sovereign of the Planets*, from one of the shuttles we'd just left. They didn't waste any time. The longer they spent in free fall, the more vomit bags there were going to be to dispose of, drugs or no drugs.

"Ladies and gentlemen," came the announcement. "We are beginning our acceleration. We will take three minutes to achieve four-tenths of a gravity, just slightly higher than you have been used to on Mars. Please remain seated while this is done, with your seat belts firmly fastened. Some of you may experience some nausea as gravity returns. Please notice that there are plenty of spacesickness bags in the pouch behind the seat in front of you. You may also want to take the in-flight magazine and look at the ship's map you will find inside, to familiarize yourself with the layout of the ship. The captain will be joining you shortly after full acceleration is achieved. Thank you." This was repeated in Spanish, French, Chinese, Arabic, and Japanese.

I felt the weight gradually pushing me down into my seat, until I felt normal. The few extra pounds weren't noticeable . . . yet. All the way to Earth, the boost would be gradually increased—except for the ten minutes of weightlessness when they turned the ship around to decelerate—until we were being blasted by the full, deadening weight that Earthies carried around all the time. It would be like carrying a slightly overweight twin on your shoulders, and I wasn't looking forward to it.

I heard a few sighs of relief, and one prominent cry of "Oh, god, not again!" followed by retching. Then the lights dimmed slightly, and a man came out onto the stage. He was dark brown and dressed in a really snappy white uniform with lots of gold braid and patches, the winged Mercury and the old Royal Caribbean logos prominent among them. There were gold stripes on his sleeve.

"Ladies and gentlemen, welcome aboard the *Sovereign of the Planets,* registered in Oslo, Norway," he said, in a reassuring baritone. "I am Captain Swenson. I have a whole routine I usually deliver at this point in the cruise, a little opening ceremony, but considering what has happened, none of it seems appropriate. I know some of you have lost loved ones in the disaster, and many more of you are worried about the fates of other loved ones. This ship will, of course, be at your service with all our communications facilities to help you find out what can be discovered, but I am not optimistic about learning a great deal before our arrival. Let me fill you in on what I know.

"The loss of life is very large. Speculations are running very high indeed, but I don't want to indulge in those here. What is confirmed is that infrastructure damage has been catastrophic. The systems we refer to collectively as the cybersphere have been crippled by power outages and the inundation of many large central computer installations. It's going to take time to repair that sort of damage. Large areas of the Caribbean and the North Atlantic are going to be back in the pre-electricity era for quite some time. Maybe as long as a year in America, probably longer in places like Haiti and other of the poorer islands. News reporters and government agencies and the United Nations are having to go physically to the affected sites to assess the damage and plan the rescue and recovery operations. Needless to say, things are chaotic at this point. So don't expect to know much for quite some time."

I swallowed hard. The last time I'd looked at the news somebody was talking about fifty thousand dead. Somebody else said five hundred thousand. Anyone want to try for a million? The fact was, nobody knew crap at this point, but the talking heads have to say something.

Captain Swenson shrugged helplessly, and motioned to the side of the stage. Other uniformed crew members came out of the wings and solemnly joined him in a line, all snowy white and gleaming brass and spit and polish.

"I really don't know how to carry on from here," he said. "My engineer knows his job, the cooks and the stewards will continue to do what they would have done on any other voyage. The bars will be open in ten minutes. So will the casino. But you signed up for a pleasure cruise, and I don't know what to do about that. It's going to be hard to organize the sort of fun things you have been expecting. So much of it now seems inappropriate. I know I wouldn't want to be one of our stand-up comics right now. But should I cancel the entertainment? Should I cancel the dances? The fact is, a long space voyage is pretty boring without some sort of diversion.

"Here is what I've decided. All normal entertainment will be canceled for the first twenty-four hours of the voyage. Memorial and religious services will be held here in the theater and in the other meeting places as you desire them. The cruise director will be happy to help you organize them in any way she can. Just ask. After that . . . we'll play it by ear, okay?" He sighed again. "Lifeboat drill will be held in one hour. All passengers are required to attend. Please consult your ticket for the location of your proper station. That is all." He turned on his heel and walked off, followed by his crew.

THE ELEVATORS OUTSIDE the theater had long lines of people waiting to get on, so we headed for the stairs, like a few others. On the way up, Mom suggested that we take the stairs all during the trip, and I groaned a little, but I knew she was right. Every hour we were going to weigh a little bit more, so we might as well start adding in that little extra bit of conditioning.

Didn't mean I had to like it.

The theater was on the lowest passenger deck, the first deck.

Our stateroom was on the fortieth deck.

Could be worse, I realized, as we exited through the pressure door onto our deck. I walked to the circular railing that overlooked the atrium and looked down forty floors to a bubbling fountain in a parklike setting. Each deck was a concentric ring, tapering slightly toward the bottom. I looked up, another forty decks or so, to the multicolored glass artwork hanging up there, beyond which were all the dining rooms and shops and most of the other facilities. Ouch! I'd be paying for my meals in sweat.

It was quite a vista, and we all paused to take it in.

"Makes you feel sort of old, doesn't it, Kelly?" Dad said, with his arm around my mother's waist.

"A little," she admitted. "But only if I worry about it."

I realized they were taking about the old *Red Thunder*, which hadn't been exactly cramped, but didn't have anything aboard that wasn't really needed, bare insulation on the walls, and indoor-outdoor carpeting on the floors. For amusement, when they weren't standing watches, they'd had a box of dominoes, playing cards, and a Monopoly board. Or so they said.

The designers of the *Sovereign of the Planets* had spared no expense to make you forget that you were in a spaceship at all. It might even be an ocean cruise ship, like Royal Caribbean's *Sovereign of the Seas II*. I checked out their website, and the interiors look a lot alike.

It's all gleaming brass and wood paneling and tasteful color schemes, easy-on-the-eyes lighting fixtures. The potted plants stuck here and there are the same species that thrive indoors. The art hanging on the walls in one ship are fanciful tropical scenes and in the other, planetary vistas, but they were done by the same artists who use much the same color palettes, and make everything look slightly shiny. Even most of the music is the same. By that I mean, uninteresting, suitable for folks my parents' age or older. Lots of Beatles, lots of Crosby, Stills & Nash, lots of toned-down rap.

And, of course, Celine Dion, whoever she is.

There was a red and yellow and blue macaw with a beautiful brass cage just outside our stateroom door. His door was open, and he was sitting on a bar outside, eyeing us as we approached.

"Welcome aboard!" he squawked. "Welcome aboard!"

A steward came hurrying around the curve of the deck, pushing a trolley exactly like the ones we use at the hotel back home, piled with our luggage.

"Sorry, sorry," he said. He was a small man, possibly Japanese but more likely a mix of races, which Dad says is getting a lot more common than when he was a kid. He likes that, because he is mixed race himself and apparently it was a bit of a problem for him when he was young. I won't say we don't have *any* racism on Mars, but it's usually not a big deal for just that reason. So many of us are more than one race. Most of the racism we do have is brought by Earthies.

"I'm running a little late. We've got a large complement of passengers this trip because of . . . well, you know why. My name is Peter, and I'll be your steward on the whole voyage. Anything you need, anytime except from eleven in the evening to six in the morning, just ring and I'll be there. On the late shift, ring for the deck steward."

Dad introduced us all as Peter unlocked the door. Throughout the voyage he never missed our names once. He held the door open for us, and we entered our new home for the next six days.

I hadn't known what to expect. Mom had of course booked at the last minute, and had taken what she could get. Which turned out to be a two-bedroom suite with a large living area, not bad at all. Far from the most luxurious suite on the ship, but a long way up from economy class. The furniture was comfy though unremarkable. There was a small wet bar and a fridge with liquor, which Dad kept the key to. There was only one small bathroom—shower, no tub—and I imagined it would be cramped for the four of us, but we'd have plenty of spare time.

Peter pressed a button, and the airtight shutters drew back very quickly from a wide picture window. We all went over there and could see already that Mars had gotten smaller. I felt a lump in my throat. Sure, it sucks, but it's home . . . and I wasn't looking forward to getting to a planet which, truth be told, sucked a lot more.

"May I ask . . ." Peter was saying, hesitantly. "May I ask, Mr. Garcia, if you have friends or relatives at risk in the tsunami zone?"

I realized he was talking to me.

"Call me Ray," I said. I'd spent all my life around porters, which are just like stewards only on land, and I wasn't about to let one older than me call me mister. "Yes, we know a lot of people in Florida, it's where my parents grew up. My grandmother is there . . ." I couldn't go on. Peter didn't say anything but left the room quietly.

I went into the first bedroom, where Mom was busy already unpacking our stuff and stowing it away in the various closets and cupboards. I looked around. There was no wide window in here, just a round porthole. There were two folding bunks, like I once saw in a Pullman train car in an old movie. I think Cary Grant was in it. I presumed Elizabeth and I would be sharing the room. All in all, it wasn't as nice as the cabins I remembered from our trips when I was smaller. Now I was a typical Martian teenager, six feet six inches tall, and Elizabeth was about six-two, though she'd never say exactly. Martian girls have some trouble with that, especially around runty Earthie boys. I was pretty sure the bunks were about six feet long, which meant sleeping scrunched up or with my feet hanging over the edge.

Oh, well. I'm sure Dad could tell me lots of stories about the hardships of growing up poor on Earth if I complained about it, so I wouldn't.

That's when our roommates arrived.

THE CRUISE LINE has a policy of not allowing doubling up in accommodations, just as the Red Thunder Hotel does not allow groups of vacationing college students to share a single room. If you'd ever seen a room after a group of them were through with it, you'd know why.

However, when Mom sets her mind to something she is a very hard woman to say no to, and while the rest of us were still running around like chickens with our heads cut off—do they really do that?—Mom was busy getting passage on the first flight leaving Mars not only for our family but for the families of other Red Thunder Hotel employees who had relatives in the tsunami zone.

Others were sharing rooms, too, taking the ship a bit beyond what was the strictly legal complement of passengers, but silly rules are made to be broken, according to my mother. Silly rules, of course, are the ones she disagrees with or that get in her way. The extra souls aboard should have no effect on the ship, which carried enough food, water, and air to make several round trips from Earth to Mars without restocking.

Well, there was the matter of the lifeboats, but even those could handle a few standees if it came to that, which it never had in the history of passenger space travel except for that fire aboard the *Carolina,* which was put out within an hour and everyone was off the lifeboats and back at their dinner an hour after that.

OUR SUITEMATES WERE the Redmond family. I didn't know them very well. The father was a chef. I don't know what Mrs. Redmond did, but the whole family had come to Mars for the high wages.

The most important thing about the Redmonds though, from my point of view, is that they had three children. There was Anthony, age six, and William, age eight. Then there was Evangeline, age sixteen, one year younger than me. She also just happened to be about six-foot-one, with straight, pale blonde hair and a pale complexion, deep brown eyes, and a real stunner.

We worked out a shift system for sleeping. Elizabeth and Evangeline got the room from right after dinner to four in the morning, and the brats and I got it from four to noon. After the first night of them fighting in the upper bunk, I mostly wandered the ship while they were pretending to sleep and caught naps during the free hours between noon and eight, much to the annoyance of the maids who wanted to make up the room.

And, okay, I admit it, I wasn't actually wandering all that time. During the times that Evangeline was awake, I might have been sort of following her around.

It started as soon as they moved into the suite. Mr. Redmond was so apologetic that I was embarrassed for him. He kept thanking Dad and Mom. They just said, think nothing of it. The brats were running around like hurricanes, smearing the big window with their greasy fingers, knocking stuff over, and making it as awkward as possible for their mother and father to gracefully thank my mother and father.

It was a bad scene, all around, and I could immediately see that of all of them, Evangeline was taking it hardest of all. She blushed furiously every time one of the little terrors did something noisy or rambunctious and did her best to corral them and make them shut up, which would last until she turned her back. Those kids were into everything. So it was *What's in here?* and *How long till we get there?* and *Stop hitting me!* and *I didn't hit you!* and, of course, always, *Mom, Mom, he hit me!* pretty much nonstop. And each time Evangeline would cringe.

I hate this class business, but Dad says there's no way to get away from it. He was on the other end, growing up, not having any money, unable to go to a good school.

Working class.

Dad doesn't talk about it a lot. I know it annoys him to think back about it, he'd prefer to focus on the future, but I know it was also hard to have a rich and beautiful girlfriend. I think he wasn't sure of her love for a long time. I think sometimes even now he's not sure of it, though they've been together for years and years.

Evangeline's family was working-class, no doubt about it, and it clearly bothered her. She went to Nelson Mandela High School, which I'm told is a fine place, certainly better than most public schools on Earth. I know they have a better basketball team than my school does; they beat us every year. Well, they have a larger enrollment. Basically, they have everybody who doesn't go to one of the private academies that the more-well-off Martians, like my family, can afford.

Money's a bitch. I'm sure glad we have it, but it doesn't bring people together, except within their own class, and that's not good, is it?

It's especially bad when you think you might be falling in love, and the girl you want to be with is so ashamed of her baby brothers she can hardly bear to look at you.

I'd have to talk to Elizabeth about it.

EVEN FOR A trip as short as Mars to Earth, you get into a shipboard routine very quickly. Pretty soon, it seems like you've been doing it all your life.

Memorial and prayer services replaced the normal shows for the first twenty-four hours. But you can only mourn so long, so normal entertainment was resumed fairly quickly. The comedians in the lounges even found they were getting more than the normal amount of laughs, though the audiences were smaller. Not all the passengers were going back to look for survivors, of course. The rest maintained a respectful distance from the emergency passengers at their dinner tables, but they had paid a lot of money for their tickets, and you couldn't expect them to give up their merrymaking just because some people had died on Earth.

But how many? That was the question. We knew we would not be likely to know much about specific survivors until we got there, but we'd expected to learn more about the scope of the disaster in the first day or two.

It didn't happen.

That was almost as shocking as the disaster itself, in some ways. We live in the information age, we're used to a steady stream of it. Sure, in the first hours after a big event the news is dominated by rumors or flat-out inaccuracies, but usually the true story begins to emerge fairly soon.

We were learning some things. No tsunami can keep helicopters and airplanes out of the air. But governments can.

Many of us were gathering in a Starbucks near the observation lounge that had been converted into a meeting place that was more or less restricted to those of us "going home" to see about our loved ones. We found it was better to sit together and watch the news on the multiplex screens on the wall rather than explore in the isolation of our personal stereos. The coffee was better, too.

It was certain that at least half a million people were dead. There were rumors that the various governments involved, in particular the United States government, were suppressing casualty figures while they frantically tried to find a way to cope with the situation. There was no question that it would be handled, in time, that all the bodies would be gathered up and disposed of—there were rumors of mass graves, of vast funeral pyres. There was no question that all the debris would eventually be bulldozed out of the way and burned or recycled.

One big question was, who was going to *pay* for all this? And another question: What are we going to do with the survivors who have lost everything, including the clothes on their backs? Until somebody had a better idea of the answers to those questions, those in power were trying to limit knowledge of just how bad the problem was. That was the buzz on the wires, anyway. And that, of course, just made the rumors buzz all the louder, and made them more and more dire. I heard a reputable newscaster speak of 20 million dead. Then I didn't hear from him again.

First, of course, there was the matter of digging in rubble for people who were trapped, and of flying in food and water. That had been easier in highly localized disasters, like Islamabad and New Delhi. This one was spread out over such a vast area that much of it was still chaos, and likely to remain that way for quite a while.

We all watched tape of the wreckage from the Everglades to Cape Cod taken from aircraft, until they stopped showing it. "Out of respect for the dead," was what the United States President said, but there were other opinions. Very little was coming from the ground. People would make their way out of the zone of destruction and post their personal tapes and someone would pick it up and it would be all over the cybernet for a while, then mysteriously vanish. Newscasters were reporting that big parts of the net were being shut down, those that weren't already crippled by the wave itself.

The net is mysterious in many ways to most of us. We experience it quite simply: Step One: we put on our stereos. There is no step two. Putting on your socks is quantum physics compared to entering cyberspace.

But that's because it's evolved over the years. Mom and Dad tell me of when they were very young, and you used equipment so large it had to sit on a desk. You had to plug it in, or if it was battery-powered, you used a battery the size of a book, and had to change it or charge it every couple of hours. Before their time you had to run an actual wire to your computer. The data transfer rate was unbelievably slow. You couldn't send moving pictures. Even before that, you couldn't send pictures at all. People transferred data at the rate of two hundred bytes per second. I'd just as soon chisel my messages onto stone tablets and put them on the back of a mule.

Because it's so easy and invisible, we don't think much about how it works. But it's there, undercover, often underground, in the cellars of big buildings in cities, in broadcast towers in the country, and, of course, the satellites overhead.

Only the satellites weren't affected by the tsunami. Many central routing stations had been flooded, many towers knocked over. The rest of the system, trying to take up the slack in a period when traffic was almost ten times normal because of the disaster with everyone trying to access the same sources at once . . . well, it never completely crashed, but it was now chugging along like a steam engine patched with bubble gum and Band-Aids. There was no hope it would be back to anything like normal soon.

More basic than that, the electrical grid was down for much of the East Coast of America. Even in places where the wave didn't reach, the outages and disruptions had crashed the system. Many places within a hundred miles of the coast didn't have electricity. As for the coast itself . . .

The water had roared up river valleys and surged over floodplains, a term that now had a new definition, as places that hadn't seen seawater in a million years or more were suddenly inundated with twenty feet of it.

We had seen endless footage of it, and like the old footage of the wave of '04, the first thing that often struck you was . . . where's the water? What you saw was a tumbling wave of wreckage, cars and trucks and furniture and walls, surging, swirling, tumbling, breaking apart, crashing together, getting chopped finer and finer. We saw footage of the coastal cities with storm wrack floating at third-floor level, or fourth-floor. Or sixth floor.

The Blast-Off annex was ten stories high. We looked and looked, no longer able to surf cameras on our own but dependent on what coverage there was from helicopter cameras, but never seemed to be able to spot it. We did see a lot of tall buildings in Florida that had fallen over, including a thirty-story condominium tower in Fort Lauderdale, and a few that were leaning, the backwash of the wave having sucked the sand out from under the foundations, many of which were later found to be not up to county building standards.

"Typical Florida," Dad said.

I DON'T WANT to be prejudiced here, and I know that, although America got it bad, the Caribbean got it worse. Some little islands were scoured almost down to the rock. The Bahamas were in terrible shape, survivors coming down from the highest ground many days after, starving and thirsty and injured. There were deaths in Africa from Guinea to Morocco, and in the Canary Islands, and Portugal, and even in England and Ireland. There were some passengers from those places, and we commiserated with them just as they did with us. But most of us were from America, born or naturalized, and that's where we looked the most. And again, though water had surged up the Potomac and the Hudson, though the wave had swept through the financial district of Manhattan and killed many people on Staten Island and in Brooklyn, and the coasts of Connecticut and Rhode Island, the worst damage was in a horrible swath from the Florida Keys to the Chesapeake Bay. And in the middle of that was Daytona Beach.

HOUR BY HOUR we got heavier.

At first it was easy bouncing up forty decks to the dining room in the morning for breakfast, and just a little bit harder for lunch, and just a tad harder for dinner. But by the time of turnaround (which took ten minutes in weightlessness and resulted in the usual quota of scrapes and bruises) we were up to .75 gee, and breakfast was getting to be a bit of a slog. At lunchtime I was breathing pretty hard by the time I reached the seventieth deck, and even coming down wasn't a walk in the park.

About the only consolation: Mom was looking a bit haggard, too.

By breakfast the next morning I was starting to get a bit worried about Dad. He was covered in sweat and almost too tired to eat by the time the waffles and eggs Benedict and bacon was set before him.

"Which is part of the problem," Mom said quietly, as she dug into her oatmeal. Dad glared at her but didn't say anything. Mom isn't a nagger, I'll give her that, at least not where Dad is concerned. She'll say something like that once, then not mention it again. "He can dig his own grave if he wants to," she once told me, when she was particularly angry about how Dad would slack on the daily exercise.

Any Martian with any sense will be under a doctor's care during a return trip to the Earth. Dad has sense; it's just that he's like me, he hates to exercise, and since he's an adult without Mom cracking the whip over him, he can get away with it. Last time we went to Earth he worked hard for three months before we boarded ship. This time caught him off guard, and his heart didn't like it.

The *Sov* didn't have anything like a fully equipped hospital, designed as it was for trips never taking longer than eight days. But there were two doctors on staff, and three Martian doctors going home for the emergency. We visited every day, as a family, as it was a bit of a cattle call with all the people needing to be monitored. So Mom and Elizabeth and I all got to stand in the diagnostic machines and get a clean bill of health, and we all—plus everybody else who might happen to be standing around—got to hear the doctor tut-tut the way some doctors do and tell Dad he had only himself to blame for his shortness of breath. He wasn't a Martian doctor; a Martian would have been more understanding.

"You're basically quite healthy for a man of your age, Mr. Garcia," the doctor said on our visit shortly after turnaround. "But you need to lose about twenty-five pounds, and you know that will feel like sixty extra pounds when you get home. You don't need to worry about your heart right now, but if you keep up this way for another ten years, you will. For now, I recommend you take it easy and be sure to get plenty of fluids when you get to Florida. Heat exhaustion is your chief peril."

What an asshole. Dad stood there and took it, and the next morning he had a bowl of cereal and spent an hour in the gym.

CLOSE YOUR EYES. *Be very quiet. You are getting very sleepy. I want you to imagine that your arms and legs are getting heavier. Heavier and heavier. Imagine yourself lying in a warm bed (forget about those two brats running around the room) . . . okay, imagine a bubbling brook, surf lapping gently on the beach. You're getting heavier. Your eyelids weigh five pounds. Your face weighs ten pounds. Your arms weigh a ton. Your head weighs ten tons. Now sleep, sleep, sleep, and it will all go away . . .*

Now wake up!

Too bad. It wasn't a dream after all. You swing the iron diver's weights on your feet over the side of the bed, only there are no weights there, sit for a moment while your chubbier identical twin settles himself on your shoulders with his hands holding your cheeks to pull them downward, struggle to your feet, and thud your way across the room under one full gee of deceleration. You go to the window and press your forehead to it and look down at the Earth, which looks like a blue-and-white beach ball. It would look a lot prettier if you could forget that it would pull at you just as viciously as this deceleration is pulling at you, they aren't going to ease up on it just for a bunch of Martians who would really appreciate it.

You singin' dem One Gee Blues, as the great Martian folksinger Spider Anson laments. *Oh, Lord, why won't you lighten up?*

I met Peter the room steward on my way out that last morning. He looked sympathetic, which is more than you could say for most of the Earthie passengers, who liked to pretend they were enjoying the returning weight.

"Anyone in here need a wheelchair today, Ray?" he asked.

"I'm fine, but if you could get one for the dude on my back I'd appreciate it."

He'd probably heard it before, but he laughed anyway. I made a note to remind Dad to be extra generous tipping Peter.

I made it five decks up the stairs, thought about the twenty-five still to go, and mentally told my mother what she could do with her lousy stairway rule. I got on the elevator for the first time . . . and was horrified to find myself graying out just a little bit as we accelerated up toward the dining room. It made me a little sick to my stomach. I'm not sure what it was all about. I had a clean bill of health. But I skipped the regular breakfast and went straight to Starbucks for a coffee and a biscotti.

There had only been a few people in wheelchairs the day before. Today there were dozens. Some of them would stay in the chairs until they returned to Mars, permanent residents whether they wanted to be or not. The body adapts, and that's not always a good thing. Past a certain age, what you lose you are unlikely to ever get back. I tried to look on the bright side. At least I was walking. I could probably even do a few chin-ups, though not with one arm.

I joined Elizabeth and Evangeline at a table with a big double latte. They were thick as thieves, and even more so today for some reason. They had some shopping bags on the floor beside them.

"What up?" I asked.

"Breasts," Elizabeth said, and Evangeline giggled.

"How's that?"

"We've been shopping. Got some support shoes." She took a pair of brown, businesslike hiking boots out of the bag and plopped them on the table between us, almost upsetting my drink. "You might want to do that, too. Those deck shoes aren't going to do you much good where we're going."

"Good idea. You think they sell anything on the ship to deal with water moccasins?"

"No, nor water-purifying tablets, nor chain saws, nor emergency flares, nor electric hovercraft. We'll have to get all those things when we get there, if they aren't already sold out. But they have figured out the one item Martian girls are likely to need and probably didn't bring with them because they don't own one." She reached into another bag from Victoria's Secret and brought out a pink bra.

The three of us broke up laughing.

"I swear, I don't know how Earth girls put up with it," Elizabeth said, reaching a thumb under her blouse and hooking it under a bra strap. I realized both girls were wearing them. You could hardly tell . . . but I guess I could have told if they weren't. "I've got to get something more practical; these things cut into your shoulders something fierce. Why do they make the straps so skinny?"

"Sexy," Evangeline said.

"You think so? Ray, you think that's sexy?"

"You're asking the wrong dude. I don't know from bras."

"Aw, come on," Evangeline said, and nudged me with her elbow. "How about this one?" She lifted her blouse and displayed a fetching blue number, and created a bit of a stir among the few Earthies in the place. We Martians are easier about dress than Earthies are. We spend most of our lives indoors, have to wear insulated and heated air bags when we do go out, so clothes are for decoration first and modesty second. There are in fact no laws concerning nudity on Mars, just rules about where it's appropriate. Earth boys get a big kick out of that when they go swimming.

"It suits you," I admitted. What I didn't admit was that by its very novelty it was turning me on quite a bit. More, in fact, than her bare breasts would have. After all, I'd seen her naked when she came out of the shower in our cabin.

"Well, it's a new one for me," Elizabeth said. "I didn't have boobs when we left Earth. Now I feel like I've got too much of a good thing."

"I doubt the Earth boys will think that," I said.

"Count on it." Evangeline laughed.

"The saleslady tried to sell us *girdles,* if you can believe that," Elizabeth said. "I said no thank you. I said, my butt's behind me; if it's gonna go south, at least I don't have to watch it sag."

Evangeline thought this was the most hilarious thing she'd ever heard, and soon Elizabeth and I did, too.

5

★ ★ ★

WE CAME IN at night. I saw the lights of Las Vegas, Lake Mead, Boulder Dam, then it got too dark to see much. I got a glimpse of the sprawling runway lights of the Area 51 North American Continental Spaceport, and then we were down, and taxiing, and pulling up to the gate.

Customs took four hours.

The whole time we were covered by at least three soldiers of the Homeland Security Enforcement Corps in their black uniforms and black Darth Vader helmets, who were almost as well armored as American football players and carried weapons that looked able to shoot down combat helicopters and surely would have atomized everybody standing there if they were ever fired.

One by one we were shown into private rooms and matched with our luggage, which had already been MRIed and chemically analyzed and scanned for microelectronics and peed on by dogs.

My stereo was taken from me and I watched as they plugged it into an analyzer and started running exploration programs to see what was inside. I'd known this was going to happen, so I'd cleansed all the stuff that was illegal on Earth, or in America anyway, and archived it back home.

A customs officer behind a thick shield of Plexi told me to open both my bags and unpack them. I did, item by item, was told to unfold all the clothes and lay them flat on a conveyor. All the other items went through another conveyor. Then I was told to strip and put my clothes on the first conveyor and lie down flat on a third conveyor, which fed me into a tube and out the other end. When I came out I was in a small room with a rack of disposable paper hospital robes.

BY THE TIME I was allowed into a room with hundreds of men wearing paper coats and boots just like mine, I was beginning to wonder how much all this cost and how much extra security it provided. I saw Dad standing by another long conveyor so I joined him and asked him.

"Who knows?" he said, with a tired shrug. Hours of standing around had taken a lot out of him. He looked like his feet were sore. "Last time through it was rough, but nothing like this. They seem to have found another dozen things to be afraid of since we were here last."

"Technology's gotten better, hasn't it?"

"Sure, on both sides," he said. "The bad guys . . ." He chuckled. "The 'evil ones,' whoever they are this year, are better at what they do, and so are the Homelanders. It seems like every year the people of Earth are willing to accept less and less risk and more and more police."

The last conveyor belt in this particular circle of Hell cranked into operation and started delivering our possessions. The clothing we'd been wearing was hanging from a moving rack.

"Just like the old dry cleaners," Dad said.

At the same time the bags were appearing through a small door. They looked the worse for wear. Some were sprung open, everything inside spilling all over the place. Some looked like they'd been examined by an elephant.

There was suprisingly little grumbling. The Earthies just sighed in resignation, and we Martians expected no less from Earthies. That's not to say it went smoothly. There were arguments, and one degenerated into a fistfight. There were no Homelanders around to break it up, I guess that at this point they figured we were officially decontaminated and no longer their responsibility. A regular security cop watched until both the fighters were pretty exhausted, then moved in to break it up.

When I got my shirt I saw that a bottom seam had been ripped open. Damn, they probably got all my microfilm and illegal drugs. Like all my other stuff when I tore it out of the plastic wrappings, it had a chemical smell I didn't want to think about. I figured I was now louse-free, and who cared if my shorts glowed in the dark? I got my suitcases and opened them to check if everything was there, but who could tell? It was just tossed in, mashed into place, and forced shut.

I never did find my other sock.

I'M AT A loss to describe Mom's reaction to all this when the family was finally reunited. If she'd been any angrier, steam would have come out of her ears.

Dad was relieved to see her. They were a little later than us getting through the process, in fact they were some of the very last women to come out of the dressing room, and Dad muttered to me, "I hope she didn't get herself arrested."

She didn't, but Elizabeth told me later it was a close thing. That was much later, when we could laugh about it, sort of. Nobody was laughing that night.

Some women would have been shouting, ranting, lashing out at everybody in sight. You know the type. I've seen a million of them at the hotel, and men, too.

I've never been treated so shabbily in my life!

Do you know who I am?

I demand to speak to the manager at once!

Mom didn't say a word, though it looked like you could fry an egg on her forehead. In fact, it looked like someone had tried. Her hair was a wreck, and so was Elizabeth's. Both of them were proud of their long, thick manes of hair, and had just had theirs styled aboard ship. It looked like somebody had gone though both hairdos with a dirty garden rake.

I take it back. She did say one thing.

"I don't think I'll ever feel clean again."

"Ditto," Elizabeth said.

We rented a little cart that held all four of us and our luggage. Dad let me drive it along a long hallway that took us to the departure gates for internal flights in the United States, and without much trouble we boarded a subsonic plane for Orlando.

It was after two in the morning, local time, when the plane finally took off. Dad was asleep almost the moment he landed in his seat. I was sharing a row with Mom, and I looked at her cautiously. She had piled her hair on top of her head in a way that looked okay to me but probably didn't satisfy her much. She seemed calmer, until you looked at her eyes.

"So, what do we do when we get to Orlando?" I asked.

"Play it by ear," she said. She gave me a tight smile and squeezed my hand, then went back to brooding.

I would have hated to be the next person who got in her way. In fact, I resolved not to be that person. Come to think of it, that's sort of the way I'd lived my life so far. All night long she kept muttering words like police state, fascists, and Nazis. I didn't disagree.

I SPENT THE night brooding on a problem less futile than trying to figure out how to get back at the Homelanders, one that probably had an actual answer.

What had hit the Earth in the middle of the Atlantic Ocean?

At first everybody assumed it was some sort of asteroid. Most astronomers shook their heads on that one, but for a while everyone accepted it anyway. It was easy enough to find a couple talking heads with Ph.D.s to say it was an asteroid.

Then people began adding up what we knew about it.

It had been going at around 99.999 percent of the speed of light. That was a big problem right there. Nothing that size had ever been observed traveling even remotely that fast. In fact, the only things humans had ever observed traveling that fast were subatomic particles and starships. And we observed starships from the inside, which was different.

Out at the far "edges" of the universe—and I put that in quotes, because the universe has no edges, and from any point inside of it you appear to be at the "center"—galaxies have been observed moving at maybe .9c relative to us. But that's the problem, the word relative. From the point of view of a person on one of those galaxies, it was *us* that was traveling at .9c, away from *him*.

There are systems in place ready to fire nuclear bombs at any asteroid that we detect on a collision course with the Earth. But with an object going this fast, what are you going to do? How are you going to detect it?

Imagine an airplane coming at you at a hair under the speed of sound. You can see it, but you won't hear a thing until it's on top of you, because the sound is traveling along just a little bit ahead of the plane in the atmosphere. It's the same with whatever hit Earth. It was traveling so close behind whatever light it emitted that by the time you can detect it, it's far too late to react.

Radar? Forget it, radar is even less use than emitted light in detecting something like that. The radar has to reach it and then bounce back.

Okay, somebody said. We've never detected an object like this before . . . but maybe that's why! Say it had passed harmlessly between the Earth and the moon, maybe a hundred thousand miles away. Would we have even *noticed* it? Remember, it's not leaving a vapor trail or anything. Is it leaving any sort of trace of its existence at all?

Hmmm . . .

There is the matter of its mass. Not its inertial mass, but the relativistic mass. It gets a little confusing, and my physics knowledge doesn't go much beyond the basic concepts of relativity and quantum mechanics. A basic principle is that, the faster an object moves, the greater its inertia. If I were to toss a bullet at you, it would bounce off your chest. But if I fire it out of a gun, it has lots of inertia and can blow right through you. That's because you've put a lot of energy into it: Newton's First Law.

Einstein changed that. He found out that your actual mass increases as your velocity increases. You don't notice it except at very high speeds. But the reason a physical object can't ever reach the speed of light, no matter how much energy you put into it, is that its mass would become infinite, and you can't have infinite mass. Not even a black hole has infinite mass, just great density.

Confusing, huh?

Anyway, all that moving mass, even if it's going by so fast you'd never spot it, has perturbing effects on the objects it passes. It's not going to shake the Earth or the moon out of their orbits, but if it passes close enough to a small satellite, it ought to give it a tug. Not a big one.

Extremely tiny, in fact, but there were enough man-made orbiting objects the killer asteroid must have passed that scientists were looking for those tiny orbital wiggles that might tell us more. Right now there were too many unknowns in the equations, but we're pretty good at detecting very tiny effects these days. That's how we first detected gravity waves, which caused a two-mile laser beam to expand and contract less than the width of one proton.

The verdict on that was far from being in yet. To me, it seemed entirely possible that the universe was lousy with objects like the one that had grazed the Earth. There might be hundreds of them passing through the solar system every day, and we'd never know it, even if they came equipped with headlights and had them on high beam. The chances of a collision with anything were small. The most likely object they might hit would be the sun, which we'd never notice, either. The chances of one hitting the Earth would be even smaller.

Which did sort of present a problem, at least to a suspicious mind.

I have a suspicious mind.

One had hit the Earth. *Something* had hit the Earth.

Which brought up the second theory. The only large objects we *know* of that approach the speed of light are . . . starships.

And a lot of people just didn't want to go there.

I won't even mention the second, third, fourth, and nine hundred ninety-ninth theories about what the object was, nor their almost infinite variations. The nature of the cybernet, since the time we were calling it the internet, is chatter, and anybody can do it. Crackpots breed like lice on the web. You can find support for absolutely any proposition on the web. Naturally, the big impact had generated a lot of noise.

I take it back, I *will* mention the third most popular explanation for what it was: The Wrath of God. Actually, some polls put it in the number two spot, with a bullet.

Most of the Rapture people had already packed their bags, those who hadn't already packed when Tel Aviv and Cairo were bombed. Figuratively, of course, since they expected to be Raptured physically out of their cars and clothes and lifted straight to heaven while the rest of us remained on Earth to duke it out with Satan. (What about us Martians? I'm hoping we can sit on the sidelines and wait till it's over.)

Plenty of other religions saw it as God's revenge for one thing or another. Many Muslims thought it was September 11 on a bigger scale, and thanked Allah.

Personally, I discount all supernatural explanations until more data is in.

But if it was a starship, that meant one of two things:

Aliens, or one of ours.

Which is where the various governments of Earth were pretty much united. They *really* didn't want to go there, in either case.

Aliens? What can you say? We haven't encountered any so far, but not many of our starships have come back yet, and space is vast. It seems almost beyond question that there are other intelligences out there, and if we can find a way to get to the stars, I'm sure they can, too.

But like I said, with aliens you got nothing but questions, all of them unanswerable because we don't have the faintest notion how aliens would think.

Why would our first contact with them be an attack? Why not land at the United Nations and say howdy-do?

Well, maybe they've been watching us and seeing how warlike we can be. Maybe they wanted to get our attention. They sure got it, if they're out there, but why not show up afterward and tell us about it. Otherwise, what's the point?

Answer: We don't know. They're aliens.

That's the answer to *all* the questions about aliens. We don't know. So there's not much point in worrying about it until they show themselves.

But if it was one of ours, the possibilities multiply.

One theory floating around the net was pretty simple. Starship arrives at Planet Mongo, lands, explores, finds it's not worth staying, and heads home. Somewhere along the way an alien virus kills everybody on board. The autopilot keeps it on course. When it gets to Earth, there's nobody alive on board to slow it down.

Could happen, I guess, but a lot of experts doubted it. More likely the autopilot would turn around at the halfway point and the ghost ship would automatically take up a parking orbit around Jupiter, where all starships have departed for fifteen years, by international agreement. On the other hand, there was nobody with the authority to mandate what kind of electronics and programs an interstellar vehicle shipped out with. Some of the countries that sent out ships back when it was a point of national or religious pride were pretty poor; they might have cut corners.

You can come up with a hundred accident scenarios without breaking a sweat, and I'd read dozens of them in my spare time aboard the *Sov*.

Then there was the scariest possibility of all.

Maybe it wasn't an accident.

SOMEWHERE IN THOSE nightmare scenarios I guess I drifted off to sleep. Weak orange morning sunlight was in my face when Mom shook my shoulder, and I looked out to the east as the plane descended into Orlando.

The sky was black with smoke.

6

I HAD MEANT to look at Disney World and all the related attractions as we flew over them, to see if I could spot the final landfall of *Red Thunder* in one of the vast parking lots. There was some kind of monument. But I kept looking at the smoke as we descended into a sooty black layer of air.

As far as the eye could see—which wasn't all that far, that awful morning—columns of smoke rose into the air. At some point they reached winds in the upper atmosphere and swirled and merged into a thick layer. Soon we descended into it, and the morning darkened. By the time our wheels touched on the runway it looked like twilight, not morning. The sun was an orange ball near the horizon. You could look right at it.

We were going into *that*?

I realized I didn't have much of an idea just what we were going to do when we got off the plane. Last time I landed in Orlando I got on a train and was in Daytona Beach an hour later. Somehow I didn't think it would work that way this time.

Mom and Dad hadn't told me much about their plans. I'm not blaming them; I hadn't asked. Now I was kicking myself because I realized I'd been acting like a little kid, letting the parents handle everything. I hated it when they still treated me like a kid. I hated it even worse when I gave them an excuse to do it. I resolved to get more involved in the family. Not going to be easy, I realized, because I'd spent the last four or five years distancing myself from them.

Uncle Dak was waiting for us as soon as we got off the plane. Dad gave him a bigger smile than I'd seen from him in days, and they hugged each other, then Dak hugged Mom. He was going to hug me and Elizabeth, but pulled back, looking alarmed.

"My god, you guys are sure growing 'em tall on Mars. This can't be little Ramon and Elizabeth?"

"Ray, Uncle Dak," I said, and took his hand. He was fairly tall himself, for an Earthie—and I'd have to remember not to use that term too freely while I was actually here—but I had three inches on him.

"And Elizabeth, holy sh—you must have to beat 'em off with a stick. The fine young men, I mean."

Elizabeth shook hands solemnly, and Uncle Dak seemed to remember why we were here, because he dropped the glad-handing immediately.

"No news since we spoke, my friends," he said. "It's a fu—it's unbelievable over there. Worst thing I ever saw."

Uncle Dak was the same age as Dad, still skinny as a rail, with long-fingered hands, dark skin, and a forehead a lot higher than I remembered. The hair he had left he wore naturally kinky and short-cropped, against the current fashion for trendy Africans worldwide. There was a lot of gray around the temples.

Dak was introduced to the Redmond family, and we set off down the concourse, past long rows of slot machines and shops and restaurants and a chorus line of dancing Mickey Mouses. After about a mile Dak started to look concerned.

"Dude, you want me to get y'all a cart?" he asked.

"I might as well get used to it," Dad said, huffing and puffing.

"Is that a yes or a no?"

"Get used to walking, I mean. In one gee."

"Like God intended," Dak said, with a grin. "I told you you'd regret it, living the soft life on that damn place."

Dad gave him a dirty look. I knew there was some sort of history there, but I didn't know much about it. Dak and Dad had been best friends for some years when they were my age, and for a while after they got back from their first trip to Mars, but they hadn't actually gotten together since my family moved to Mars. I don't think they even talked on the phone anymore, which was why I was a little surprised to see him waiting for us.

"So how is your father?" Dad asked him.

"Retired to California, two years ago. Sold the speed shop, got good money for it. He still tinkers with the cars out there, but mostly he putters."

"Putters?"

"In the garden. Yeah, I know, the man knows bupkis about plants, he used to could kill a lawn just by walking over it, and he's not doing much better out there in the golden west, but he seems to enjoy it. Christmas, he FedExes me a box of oranges from his trees. I figure they cost him about fifty bucks each, and they ain't as good as the ones they grow here and sell for five bucks a pound. Or used to. Who knows what they're going for now?"

Everybody knew the American economy was in the toilet, and had been for over a decade. All the bills coming due, Mom said, and nothing to pay them with. According to Dak, the tsunami had hit the financial world almost as hard as it hit the beaches of America.

AFTER WE PASSED out of the security zone we reclaimed our luggage and stepped out into the pleasant air of Florida.

I'm kidding. It was ghastly.

Even in the wintertime Florida can be blistering or, even worse, smothering. Consider that I'd spent most of the last ten years in a totally temperature-controlled environment. It hit us like a hammer. Ninety in the shade. Temperature *and* humidity. In five minutes my shirt was sopping.

There was a long line of people just outside the entrance, and I figured we'd have to join that one, too. In fact, I was headed that way already, just like a docile American, when Dak called me back.

"No need, Ramon. . . . sorry, Ray. That's for weapons."

"Weapons?" I'm pretty good at feeding the straight line sometimes.

"Folks who feel naked without a piece. They can't bring 'em on airplanes, so they send 'em ahead."

I looked at people retrieving packages, mostly small ones but a few long and thick. Some of them unwrapped them right there on the sidewalk and stored them away in shoulder holsters or purses.

"Does everybody go armed now?" I asked him.

"Pretty much." He pulled back his light windbreaker and showed me a big ugly lump of metal stuck into his waistband. He grinned at me. "You gotta remember, Ray, you ain't on Mars anymore. You in America. Worse than that, you in *Florida*."

THE ROAD AWAY from the airport was lined with stores that all seemed to have the same name: GUNS! Okay, there were a few liquor stores, too.

Dak had taken us to a rental agency, where we picked up a vehicle large enough for the nine of us and Dak. We loaded it with our stuff and he punched in a destination and the vehicle moved automatically onto the web of autoways that crisscrossed and ringed Orlando. The adults were in front, Dak and Mom and Dad reliving old times, the Redmonds mostly staying quiet. Elizabeth and Evangeline were talking to each other, and the brats were busy plotting the downfall of human civilization, leaving me with not much to do but look out the window.

Naturally, there are no road signs on the autoways, since no manual driving was allowed, but it seemed to me we were going in the wrong direction. I've got a pretty good navigator in my head, but it's not much use in strange terrain when you can't see the sun. So I opened a GPS window and confirmed my hunch: We were heading west on State Autoway 528, not north on Interstate 4. Looked to me like we should have been going north on 417 . . . but what did I know?

We took an exit that had an animated arch over it, advertising the twenty or so theme parks in the Lake Buena Vista area. A few minutes later we were pulling up to a fanciful hotel that looked like a log cabin garnished with lollipops.

"Here we are, kids," Dad said. "This is where you get off."

I turned around and watched the brats tumble out along with their mother. Good riddance. I hoped the hotel would still be there when we returned. Then I turned back around and saw that Dad was looking right at me.

"No fucking way!" I shouted.

"Language, Ramon."

"My name is Ray, Dad, and there's no fucking way I'm staying behind."

"Ray, we've discussed this and—"

"Dad, I'm seventeen. Mom, you guys can't do this to me."

"What about me?" Elizabeth wanted to know. "Are you dumping me, too?"

"Ray, Elizabeth," Mom said. "This is going to be dangerous. Dangerous, and very, very ugly. We have decided it wouldn't be responsible to take you into this mess. You can stay here with Mrs. Redmond and her kids."

"Mom!" I was horrified to hear a note in my voice I'd tried to stop using when I was about twelve. Not satisfied with that, I went on with another childish argument. "This isn't *fair*. If you were going to strand us here, why the hell did you drag us along in the first place? Why not hire a babysitter and leave us back home?"

"Ray, you're just going to have to accept this."

"I don't think so," I said.

Dak muttered something. I saw him grinning in the rearview mirror.

"You say something, Dak?" Dad asked, dangerously.

"I said, 'Told ya.' And I did."

"You stay out of this. You don't have any kids."

"You're right," Dak said, not seeming to take offense. "But if I did, I'd hope they had the sort of balls Ray has."

"Dad," I said, with no idea where I was going. Then I had it. "If you leave me here, you'd better tie me up. Because I'll follow you."

"Oh? How?"

"I'll . . . I'll get a taxi!"

"And how will you pay for it?"

"I've got money." Not a lot. There was a trust fund for me that I would get when I turned eighteen, but my allowance was fairly generous, and I'd saved up a bit. Frankly, there's not a lot of things I wanted to buy on Mars, after Dad bought my airboard.

"How much cash?"

That's when it sank in. Cash? *Cash?* What would I need with cash? It's practically obsolete back home. You pay for things with credit and a retina print. I had a stack of Martian redbacks back home in my closet. Why bring them?

Because if you're under eighteen a parent can shut down your savings account and/or line of credit in two seconds and not even have to get out of his chair. Isn't modern banking wonderful?

We glared each other down for a while. I knew the money business was a fight I couldn't win, and he knew it, too.

I'll give him one thing. He didn't look happy about it.

"I'll hitchhike," I said.

"No, you won't," Dak said. "Manny, this is—"

"Stay out of this, Dak."

"No, man, I'm just saying. This is Earth, remember, and it's scary times. There's looters and rednecks and all kinds of nuts out to settle scores. Just plain maniacs. Ray, this ain't going to be no trip to no ski resort."

"He won't have to hitchhike," Elizabeth said. "He can go with me."

"You're not going anywhere, Elizabeth," Mom said, sharply.

My sister and I got along pretty well. I'd gone through a hell-raising stage, getting in small trouble here and there, rebellious, defiant, but mostly I was good, I didn't do illegal things, and if I wanted to do something Mom and Dad wouldn't have approved of, I just did it and made sure they didn't find out.

Not Elizabeth. As far back as I could remember she had been the perfect daughter. About the worst thing I ever saw her do was cover for me when I'd done something bad, and never a word of reproach from her except to make me promise never to do it again. Usually, I didn't. We were close, until we got into our teens, when boys and girls turn to different interests.

Elizabeth was the dream child. Beautiful, smart, obedient, helpful, cheerful, courageous. I couldn't count the number of times I'd seen her stand up for younger or weaker kids against bullies. Sometimes that child was me, before I got my growth. I can't think of any major faults she has, unless it's to resist everyone's attempts to call her Liz or Liza or Beth or Betty.

In short, if a neutered house cat had suddenly growled like a Bengal tiger I could hardly have been more surprised. I looked back over my shoulder and saw something I'd hardly ever seen before. My big sister was angry.

You wouldn't have known it unless you knew her as well as I did. Her face wasn't twisted up, she wasn't glaring at anyone, just looking at Mom calmly, but with absolutely no give to her. It was the way she looked when she saw an injustice, and the look meant, to anybody with any sense, that they'd better retreat to the bunkers because a world of hurt was about to descend on them.

"Elizabeth, be reasonable," Mom said.

"I am being reasonable, Mother." Not Mom. I smiled. This was the equivalent of Elizabeth calling me Ramon, which she never did, except when I'd screwed up big-time.

"This is not open to discussion," Mom said.

"If that's the way you want it," Elizabeth said, calmly. She opened the car door and got out. "Are you coming, Ray?"

I piled out after her, so Dad got out, and then Mom. I could see Dad working to control his anger, and I could see the wheels turning in Mom's head, figuring the angles, what arguments to use, which angles to try. She was looking increasingly frustrated. She had forgotten one crucial fact, probably because she'd never really had to face it before.

Elizabeth was happy to point out the flaw in her reasoning.

"It's really very simple, Mother. I am nineteen. You don't control my money anymore. You should either have left us at home—in which case I would have bought tickets on the next ship out—or discussed this on the way here. I'm on Earth now. I intend to rent or buy a vehicle of some sort, and hire a driver, and take off for Uncle Travis's place as soon as you are gone. If you leave Ray here I'll take him with me. Look for us in your rearview mirror. I don't know how you can stop Ray from going. You can't tie him up, you can't arrest him. About the only option I can see is for you to give him such a guilt trip he'd probably end up hating you. Did I miss anything?"

Anybody else, this speech would have a high raspberry factor. You know, a Bronx cheer, *phooey on you*. Elizabeth simply laid it out there as if it were the most reasonable thing in the world, I'm resorting to this more in sorrow than in anger. And you know what? I believed her.

Apparently Mom did, too. She sighed.

"Get back in the car, kids."

"Kelly, I don't think . . ."

"Manny, darling, if you have a better idea, let's hear it. I think she's got us backed into a corner."

He looked like he was about to get angry, then gave it up.

"Look at it this way, Dad," I said, taking a chance. "If Grandma had put her foot down when you decided to build *Red Thunder,* none of us would be here."

"Don't push your luck, young man. That was different."

Sure. It's always different, isn't it?

That's when Evangeline spoke up.

"I'm going, too."

WE ONLY WASTED about five minutes arguing about that one. Mr. Redmond tried, but his heart wasn't in it. So we waved good-bye to Mrs. Redmond and the brats. There were some tears, but not from Evangeline. She didn't have any more use for the brats than I did.

Soon we were hurtling down the autoway again. Elizabeth was wedged between me and Evangeline in the very back of the bus. I turned to Elizabeth.

"Thanks for what you did," I said.

"No need. It wasn't fair."

"I was . . . sort of surprised. Not you standing up for me, you standing up to Mom. You don't do that a lot."

She thought about that for a while.

"Elizabeth the compliant little mouse, you mean?" she asked.

"You know I don't think of you like that."

"A lot of people do. I don't mind. Uncle Jubal told me a story a long time ago that you might consider the next time you find yourself about to get into an argument." I saw Evangeline's face perk up at that. To most people, Jubal Broussard was a semimythical figure, the most famous person in the world that nobody ever saw. The general impression people had was that he made Einstein seem about as bright as Spongebob Squarepants. Naturally, Evangeline was all ears. She didn't know that Uncle Jubal is just a simple country boy, mostly.

"He told me about this boy who grew up and never talked," Elizabeth went on. "When he was two, his parents were just a little worried. They figured he'd talk when he was ready. By the time he was four they were going crazy. He didn't speak a word. They took him to doctors, who couldn't figure it out.

"He got older, and never talked, and they eventually resigned themselves to it.

"Then one day his mother was making breakfast, and she burned the toast. She was in a hurry, so she put the burnt toast on his plate beside the grits and scrambled eggs and catfish. The boy took one look at it, and he said"—and here Elizabeth dropped into a pretty good imitation of uncle Jubal's deep-bayou fractured Cajun dialect that's like no one else's in the world—" 'I cain't eat dis toas', me! Dis toas' is *boint!'*

"Well, de boy mama, she jus' 'bout lost it rat dere. She jump up and down and she shoutin' *hallelujah,* she shoutin' *praise de lawd!* Den she stop, and she look at her boy, her, and she axe him, 'How come you never talk before?'

"An' he say, 'Up to now, everything been *okay.'* "

After we'd stopped laughing, I thought about it.

"You're saying, save your energy for the fights that matter?"

"Ray, you waste a lot of time and energy bitching about things you can't change. Or worrying about trivia. You say you hate living on Mars, but you've never done anything that will lead you away from it. You just coast a lot. You're smart, but I've never heard you say anything about what you want to do with your life."

"Maybe I just haven't shared it with you," I said, stung by her words. But what stung the most was, she was right. "Anyway, you haven't told me what you plan to do with your life, either."

"That's because I haven't come across it yet. But I know that when I do, I'll be ready." She can be maddening sometimes, because she can say things like that, and you just believe her.

The traffic slowed, and slowed, and slowed again and then came to a complete stop. We didn't move again for two hours.

7

"NOW YOU'RE SEEING the *real* Florida," Dak said, as we inched forward along Autoway 4, along with hundreds of others. It turns out that one reason the traffic was flowing so well in Orlando was that a great many people were out of town.

According to Dak, they were going in two directions. A lot of people were going east, like us, trying to get through the Red Line, which defined a zone that, in Florida, stretched as much as twenty miles inland. Basically, the part of the Eastern Seaboard that had been submerged by the wave was barricaded, off-limits to anyone but authorized personnel.

"Lot of other folks are heading west," Dak said, moving us forward twenty feet and stopping again. "Mostly young people. Rumor is, the press gangs are moving west, too. Next stop, Orlando."

I hadn't been paying much attention to that part of the story. With my Martian passport, I was immune to the press gangs. Plus, I was probably too young, though there was another rumor that they were going to start drafting people as young as sixteen into the Florida National Guard.

"The U.S. Army is stretched too damn thin," Dak said. "All over the world, one war or another. We can't just pull 'em out, or that's what the President says. So the Guard has to take up the slack. Lots of folks would volunteer, I'm sure of it, but the fact is once they got you, even if you signed up to help the tsunami victims, you don't get out till they *say* you get out, and they haven't been sayin' that much for years now. Army's done turned into a career for a lot of folks didn't have no intention of being no soldier."

Good information was hard to come by. It was amazing, when you thought about it. Sure, the power was out in the Red Zone, and would be for a long time yet, but there was what people were calling the Yellow Zone, and a lot of people lived there. Problem was, it was getting harder and harder to talk to them. Messages weren't getting through.

More rumors. The government had turned on its big, its *really* big computers, the ones it was rumored to have—see what I mean?— that could monitor every byte of the zillions and zillions of gigabytes that flowed through the cybernet every day, and pick and choose what got through and what didn't.

But why?

"Cover their asses," Dak said, confidently. "Manny, Kelly, it's lots worse than anybody's been admitting. I've been along the Yellow Zone, thinking about trying to get in, and . . . well, you'll see when we get there."

"But they can't cover it up forever," Dad protested.

"Of course not," Dak agreed. "Shit, eventually folks gonna be able to get in and see it with their own eyes. But they let it out a little bit at a time, maybe they can salvage a little bit of the economy. Hope you folks got out of the dollar."

"Long time ago," Mom agreed. "The trouble is, what do you put it into? In a worldwide collapse, no currency is likely to stay very stable. When the claims start coming in, I don't know how many insurance companies will be able to stay afloat."

"They already failing," Dak said.

THE BARRICADE AT the edge of the Red Zone was manned by National Guard, not Homelanders, and most of them didn't look any older than I was. They were dressed in jungle camouflage and heavy body armor and the military version of stereos, which were three times as bulky as the civilian version. They carried the usual arsenal of weapons and unidentified but probably lethal gizmos, and they held them at the ready, covering each other, as if they expected armed terrorists to leap from one of the family wagons at any second. Come to think of it, I doubted the terrorist part, but it was a sure bet most of these people were well armed.

They were not happy campers. It was a day for Bermuda shorts and tank tops, not Kevlar and khaki. The soldiers were pissed off about the duty, and the people in the cars were frantic with worry about their loved ones in the Red Zone.

They directed us to a parking spot alongside dozens of others. It looked like it would be some time until they got to us. We all got out of our cars and stretched our legs, just like everyone else was doing. I felt every foot per second per second of the brutal gravity.

Some of these folks had been coming out here every day since the wave and getting the same runaround. Still far too dangerous to let the general public in. Show a press pass from an "accepted" media outlet, or papers from an authorized relief agency. Give us a verifiable phone number for someone living in the Yellow Zone that you intend to visit, and hope that he's got power so he can take the call and okay you.

Otherwise, turn around and get your butt back to Orlando.

Which is what was happening to about 90 percent of the cars out there. I could hear heated arguments and see angry citizens shouting and making obscene gestures at the soldiers, who reacted either with weary boredom or some quick and startling violence. No shots were fired, but one guy got a rifle butt in the face and quite a few kicks while he was down. The officer in charge watched while his soldiers tossed the bleeding and unconscious guy into the backseat of his car. His wife burned an inch of rubber off her tires in her hurry to get out of there.

"Florida, huh?" I told Dak, as we watched.

"This is bad even for Florida," Dak said, softly. "Tempers are fraying, my man. Listen, you hear shooting, you hop back in that bus, right? It'll probably stop the lead most of these citizens carrying. Not those military guns, though."

"Then throw myself over the women and children, right?"

"Heck, no, throw yourself over me, 'cause I'll already be in there." He grinned and patted my shoulder. "Don't worry, it'll be all right."

After about an hour a team of three soldiers approached our vehicle and asked us for our papers. While we were getting them all together one of the guardsmen came over and looked me up and down. He was a huge mix of muscle and fat, his face burned a bright pink and his eyes showing about as much intelligence and compassion as your average lizard.

He nudged me with the barrel of his rifle. Pissed me off something terrible, but I know a *little* about choosing my fights, so I didn't kill him.

"How old you are, boy?" he wanted to know. Or at least I think that's what he said. He had a very thick accent. His intention was clear though. If I'd been an American, I'd have been slapped into a uniform and handed a gun in about two seconds.

"He's a Martian citizen," Dad said, holding out our four passports. Lizard boy grinned and poked at me with the rifle again.

"Fuckin' red boy, huh? My old man says the gummint be wastin' all our money on that Mars shit. He say we oughta bring all y'all rich folks back down here where God-fearin' folks live and put y'all to work." He grinned, showing at least three teeth, none of which had any close neighbors.

I thought about explaining that the gummint hadn't spent much money on space since before I was born, except for orbiting weapons platforms. I considered explaining that the vast majority of the infra-structure on Mars was paid for and built by Earth corporations, that the whole space travel and space tourism industry provided thousands of high-tech jobs to Earthies and over a billion dollars in taxes to Earth governments every year.

Or I could ask him what it was like to fuck his mother.

While I was thinking over these options Mom stepped forward, still digging our papers out of her shoulder bag, tripped over her own feet, and fell. Dak, who was closest to her, grabbed at her arm but missed, and all our papers and some money scattered all over the hot asphalt.

Everybody but the soldiers scrambled to help her up, but she waved us off, preferring instead to move around on her hands and knees, gathering our papers and the other items that had been in her bag. Lucky for us there was no wind or our entire identities would have ended up in some swamp somewhere, and we'd probably have ended up in some camp for un-persons. I got down and helped her, grabbing at hundred-euro notes, van rental papers, insurance agreements, vaccination certificates, Homelander clearance cards, lipsticks, tissues . . . it was amazing what all she had in there.

Dak and Dad helped her to her feet and she shuffled all the papers together. Somehow, through some odd mix-up, a couple of bits of currency had gotten mixed up with the other stuff, just the corners peeking out. She handed it all to the soldier.

"Is there some problem, Officer?" Dak asked. "We were assured we'd be able to get through to DeLand."

"Don' call me officer," the lizard said. "Corporal, me. Corporal Strunk." His pink and peeling and sweat-coated brow was twisting with the unaccustomed effort of thought. I think he was trying to add the numbers on the corners of the bills and having a tough time of it.

"DeLand is only another twenty miles," Dak was going on, smiling big. "We have the phone number of our friend. Maybe you've heard of him. Travis Broussard?"

It took a little time for the words to penetrate Corporal Lizard's mathematical fog, but finally he frowned even deeper and looked at Dak.

"Broussard? The rich guy?" I held my breath. This idiot had already expressed a certain distaste for the rich. I hoped it only applied to rich Martians.

"That's the dude. Here, look, we got his picture." Dak held out a snap that clearly showed him and my father and mother and uncle Travis. Also myself, at a considerably younger age.

I'd have bet he wouldn't have known Travis Broussard from Sir Isaac Newton, but I would have been wrong. Uncle Travis is one of the richest men on Earth, and though he doesn't try to play the celebrity, there's nothing he can do about it. Even a dimwit like Corporal Lizard had heard of him, and he was apparently impressed enough not to want to risk offending him if it came to that.

Which was a good thing, I later learned, as Mom had been trying to contact uncle Travis for the last hour and he wasn't answering his phone.

Or maybe it was just the money. When he handed the papers back to Mom the money was missing. He jerked his head once in the direction we wanted to go and moved on to his next victim.

"Getting to be more and more like the third world every day down here," Dak said, shaking his head as we drove away.

THE ROAD WAS clear for a few miles. We were paralleling the coast, about twenty-five miles inland. There was almost no traffic, and other than the columns of smoke to the east, no sign that just over the horizon was the biggest catastrophe of all time.

Dak was driving, of course. He used to be a professional race driver, making anything on two or four wheels go very, very fast. He showed no tendency for speed today, though. We started bumping over rough road.

"Tank tracks," he said. They had torn up the road considerably, cutting gouges out of the asphalt surface that probably dated back to the twentieth century and hadn't been in all that good repair for quite a while. We traveled through a few miles of this, then began to see the tanks themselves, great big black monsters with stealthy radar angles and giant cannons and turrets. The soldiers lounging around them were not National Guard slobs, but regular Army. They watched us go by with no particular hostility. A few even waved at us, and Dak honked back.

"Tanks?" Mom asked.

"Just the thing to turn back another tsunami, huh?" Dak said, dryly.

"What's the point?" I asked.

"No very good point, far as I can see," Dak said. "But the military commanders are really hyped on this alien invasion, warning shot deal. A lot of them are expecting another barrage any minute."

"They're worried about the refugees," Mr. Redmond said, surprising us all. Not the idea, but the fact that he'd spoken at all. Mr. Redmond was not a man to put his thoughts forward, at least not around us.

"Think so?" Dak asked.

"From what I've been hearing. Not on the net. Nothing is coming out through the net. But *people* are getting out, and stories are getting out by old-fashioned word of mouth. Of course, you can't believe everything you hear, but if a tenth of it is true, they've got good reason to be worried."

"How come?"

"Riots. There have been some big ones in Miami and Savannah."

It turned out Mr. Redmond had learned a lot more than we had. He wasn't forthcoming at first, but the more we questioned him the more we learned. All of it subject to the caution he kept repeating: By its very nature, this is all rumor. Some of it will be exaggerated. Don't believe everything you hear.

Around then, all our stereos went dead.

AS WE APPROACHED the high stone wall that surrounded the old part of Rancho Broussard we passed a small area where the ten-foot, well-maintained electrified fence took a jog to the left, then right, right again, and left again, cutting out about half an acre that had no fence around it at all. On that little plot were the two ricketiest, most ramshackle structures I'd ever seen. Both of them were "mobile homes," one of them a double-wide with what passed for stained-glass windows cut out of it. It was just colored cellophane taped to the glass. There was a big wooden cross on the roof.

But you could hardly see the buildings for the forest of signs, hand-lettered with house paint on plywood, that sprouted like a colorful crazy quilt along the roadway. The biggest one said:

NEVER MIND THAT
HEATHERN OVER YONDER!
JESUS IS YOU'RE LORD!
COME AND WORSHIP!

"The Holy Reverend is still there, I see," Dak said, as he turned into a driveway next to it.

"You're kidding," Dad said. "The same one? He's still alive?"

"Far as I know it's the same dude. I thought he was older'n dirt when we first started coming here."

The Holy Reverend was the source of one of the most-told stories in our family. He had briefly converted to a belief in space aliens after inadvertently viewing one of Uncle Jubal's early bubble experiments, but had since gone back to Jesus. It's a pretty funny story; Dad covers it in his book. He and Travis hadn't gotten along too well before that, and after that the Holy Reverend thought Travis was the Devil himself. I thought Travis hated him back, but Mom said no.

"The funny thing is," she told me once, "Travis owns the land the church sits on. The Holy Reverend doesn't have two dimes to rub together. Travis pays the taxes and even contributes anonymously. He likes the old coot."

We came to a stone guardhouse and gate. A heavily armed man came out, smiling, waving at Dak. Dak stopped the vehicle and told us to roll down the windows. The guard asked all our names, paying particular attention to Mr. Redmond and Evangeline. I couldn't help noticing the whole process was nothing like the wringer the Homelanders had put us through. We were known to the guard of course, and I knew that Uncle Travis didn't really want to live in a guarded compound at all, but he had no choice. He can handle himself, he's quick and accurate with a gun, but he wouldn't stand a chance in a determined kidnap or murder attempt, both of which had been tried more than once. But he instructs the guards to keep the fascist stuff to a minimum, be polite, and only shoot to wound if at all possible. If you knew my uncle Travis, you'd find this an amazingly liberal attitude.

We drove through virgin piney woods and pulled to a stop on what had once been a basketball court. Dak shut off the engine, and for a few moments nobody spoke. Then, amazingly, my mother began to sing.

" 'Seems like old times . . . ' " Mom used to be a killer karaoke bar performer, according to my father, but you had to get a few drinks into her. It's the one thing I know of that she's shy about, and I don't know why, because she has a soothing contralto voice that is one of my favorite childhood memories, back when she was singing me to sleep.

Dak and Dad laughed, and I knew why. I'd seen plenty of pictures of Rancho Broussard back in the days when Uncle Travis was a drunk rotting away in it and Uncle Jubal was a retarded (so everybody thought) idiot savant tinkering in his big prefab metal barn and supporting them both with his crazy inventions.

It was a ranch-style rambler that sprawled through the wild tropical plantings that hadn't been trimmed back in years and almost concealed it completely. The basketball court had been cracked and weed-choked, the swimming pool empty except for leaves and sludge.

It looked pretty much the same today. It had looked pretty much like that the last time I visited, years ago.

After a while my eyes began to pick out differences. There were actual nets in the basketball hoops. The concrete was still cracked, but it looked like somebody had hit the plants growing there with a weedeater.

The pool was still empty, Travis preferred to swim in his little lake. But it was reasonably clean, and there was stuff down there wrapped in tarps.

The house was still almost concealed by growth, but it had been painted at least once. Travis figured that cutting the lawn once a year was about enough, same with trimming the bigger plants. He liked the wild look.

It was a nice house, but not what you'd expect from a multibillionaire. It was not as imposing as the McMansions of his new neighbors, and you just knew that if those folks ever got a look at it, they'd crap their pants. There goes the neighborhood! Never mind that he was there first.

Dak and Mom and Dad marched right up to the sliding glass doors that led from the patio to the main room but they weren't locked, as always. We walked in.

"Travis, are you decent?" Mom called out.

"Dressed, maybe, but never decent," Dak said.

We didn't get an answer for a moment. The room was clean, and the disorder was under control.

"Nobody home," Dak said.

"Nobody but us ghosts," came a voice, and we all jumped. A big wall screen came to life, and Travis's face appeared on it, sweaty and grease-covered. "I'm glad to see y'all made it. I'm over in the warehouse. Got some food here, too. Come on over." The screen went blank.

We all trooped outside again and walked through the muggy Florida heat and crushing Earth gravity toward Jubal's old barn.

This was one of two things that had really changed since the voyage of *Red Thunder.*

There was a big iron fence around it, and a lot of big signboards that were turned off now, but on visiting days showed old films of *Red Thunder* and her crew, the famous footage of the takeoff that melted the barge the ship was sitting on. There was a little concrete-block building where the volunteer docents hung out between tours.

Uncle Travis bitches and moans about the building being declared a National Historic Site, and even more about being required to open it to the public one day every week, but I think he is secretly pleased. Or at least he realizes that the building *is* an important part of the human scientific heritage, right up there with Edison's lab and the *Apollo 11* launch pad.

The other building was the same type, a poured-concrete foundation and steel beams and sheet metal, but in the large economy size, maybe five or six times as big as Jubal's old digs. It was windowless and painted a pale green. Massive air conditioners throbbed as we made our way along the concrete path to a human-sized door set close to a giant garage door. This was where Uncle Travis kept his toys.

I don't know how many billions of euros Uncle Travis had. Some people say he was the richest man in the world. Travis laughs when he hears that, but he doesn't deny it. He gives away several billion euros every year and he told me he doesn't figure he'll run out before he dies. Compared to other billionaires he doesn't spend much money on himself. All you had to do was take a look at Rancho Broussard to see that. He has a house on Mars where he stays when he comes to visit (not often enough), and a working ranch out in Montana somewhere, and that's it. What he likes, his only real luxury, is fine machines, many of which will go very, very fast.

Do I need to say he had been my favorite uncle when I was here last time? Uncle Jubal was fun and a genius and a great man . . . but Travis was a pilot and an astronaut and a race car driver, and when Mom and Dad weren't around he let me sit on his lap and steer his '65 Shelby Mustang around the dirt road of the ranch. What boy could ask for more?

He takes good care of his toys, too. He has a hangar somewhere to keep his airplanes. This building was where he kept his land vehicles. It felt great to go through that door. I could still use a shower, but feeling the sweat drying out was a lot better than feeling it dripping down my ribs.

There were several hundred vehicles in there. My favorite was a Rolls-Royce that had been converted into a pickup truck. Uncle Travis actually used that one to haul things around the ranch, at the infrequent times he was actually hauling stuff. Nevertheless, it was sparkly clean, like all his vehicles. He had a full-time staff whose job was to keep everything polished and tuned up.

Of the big stuff, I guess the most impressive was an M1A1 Abrams tank. He'd let me drive that once, too, and even fire off a blank round.

But the center of interest today was a long, wide, brightly painted thing I hadn't seen before. It looked like a squared-off boat with wheels on it, six of them, two in front and four in back, on two axles. It had high roll bars and a white canvas awning stretched over them. The side facing me had huge lettering spelling out DUCK TOURS in a racing motif, and a picture of Donald Duck water-skiing. But as we approached, one of Uncle Travis's assistants came around the back and started spraying it with olive drab.

"It's called a Duck," came a voice, and Uncle Travis's head popped up near the back. "Spelled D-U-K-W, for some reason known only to the United States Army. Built in 1943 for amphibious landings, only they tended to sink in high waves." He bent over again, and we heard the engine start up. It revved a few times, a deep-throated rumble like a marine engine. He stood up again, grinned at us, and shut the engine off.

"I replaced the standard engine with something that has a little more authority. It should get us where we're going. How y'all doing?" He moved to the side of the thing and vaulted over the edge, which I winced to see, because the side was about seven or eight feet high, and I knew that doing that myself would practically kill me. It didn't do him any good, either. He landed a little harder than he would have liked and stood stooped over for a minute.

"Be careful, old man," Mom teased him, and helped him up and put her arms around him. He held his hands out to his side and grinned down at her. "Is that all the hug I'm going to get, after all these years?"

"I'm filthy, hon. And not that old."

"I love you anyway, and you think I'm going to get through this without getting filthy, too? Kiss me, you fool."

Uncle Travis grinned even broader, put his arms around her, and kissed her on the forehead. Then he hugged Manny and Dak and Elizabeth, was introduced to Mr. Redmond and Evangeline, then was facing me.

How's the weather up there? Earthies love to say that, and I'm pretty sure he thought about it, him being a good eight inches shorter than me. But he just looked me in the eye and shook my hand, firmly but not a knuckle-breaker, though I don't doubt he could have thrown me over his shoulder if he wanted to.

So I returned the favor, and didn't tell him how much older he looked.

Not that he looked bad. His hairline had receded, but he still had more hair than my dad, though all of it was white. His face was lined and leathery from the sun, with a few little white spots where skin cancers had been frozen off. It was a strong face, with a twinkle in the blue eyes, and at the right angle he looked a little like that old action film star. What was his name? Bruce something. Dad liked his movies.

"So you talked them out of it, huh?" he said to me. It took me a second to understand what he meant.

"Oh. No, actually, Uncle Travis. That was Elizabeth." I felt stupid as soon as I said it, the poor little brother. "She's older, she can do what she wants."

"I'll bet she can. Just like her mother."

"Only quieter," Dad said.

"Quiet can get the job done, too. Sometimes better than noise. Not everybody's cut out to be an in-your-face asshole like me. Come on, I'll show you what I've got done so far. I need more ideas on what to bring along." He stopped and put a hand on my shoulder. "And you can stop calling me uncle, Ray, unless you really want to. Call me Travis."

"Okay, Travis." It sounded odd, but I liked it. I wondered if I could start calling Dad Manny someday.

Nah.

There was a ladder alongside the Duck that Travis could have used if he hadn't been so macho as to risk breaking an ankle. We all trooped up and inside.

It was quite nice. The Duck had originally been a war vehicle, sold as army surplus, then refurbished and put to work puttering around in the Halifax River—which is not really a river, to my way of thinking, but a salty strip between the barrier island and the mainland, but they do things differently in Florida—with a dozen or so tourists. It could launch itself on any boat ramp, or simply slosh through marsh to the water's edge and into the drink.

Travis had pulled out a few rows of seats to make room for all the gear he planned to take along, and there was still enough seating for all of us, plus a little tent he'd arranged in the back with a cot inside where we could take turns taking naps.

"I planned to restore her to factory condition when I got her, years ago," he said, "but I never got around to repainting, and eventually I got to liking the silly thing. But I decided we didn't want to look like a bunch of goofs out there. I hear it's pretty hairy, some places. We want to be taken seriously."

"Too bad," Dad said. "The paint job sort of reminds me of the old *Red Thunder*." The old ship had been outrageously painted by a guy called 2-Loose La Beck, a friend of Mom and Dad, in a style that has been called "Barrio Krylon Heroic" by art critics. You can see the same style on railroad cars and schoolyards from Los Angeles to Miami.

"Me, too," Mom said. "But you're right, we should keep a low profile this time." They shared a wistful look.

They discussed various aspects of the plan, the parts that could be anticipated, at any rate. Up to a point, it was easy. Travis had been as far as he could, up to the area the media were calling the "debris line." That was where the wave had finally lost its momentum and started its long retreat. That was a few days ago, and he didn't know much beyond that, except that main roads were being cleared and that, beyond the cleared roads, anarchy reigned in many areas.

I was listening when Elizabeth approached me with Evangeline trailing behind, grabbed me by the arm, and said, "Let's go."

SHE TOOK US out the back door and down a path to the shooting range.

Nothing fancy about it, at first glance. Just an open field with a high ridge of earth at the far end, and some old plywood cutout human forms. All the figures had old, faded pictures of Osama bin Laden pasted on them.

There was a bunker/blockhouse that Elizabeth opened with a key and we went in. Evangeline looked like she didn't really want to be there. It's a common enough attitude among Martians.

The room was a temple to the Second Amendment. That's the part of the United States Constitution that . . . well, I can quote the whole crazy thing, it's not very long:

A well-regulated Militia being necessary to the security of a free State, the right of the people to keep and bear Arms shall not be infringed.

Uncle Travis . . . sorry, *Travis* feels this should be tattooed on the trigger finger of every American citizen. Mom would like to melt down every gun on the planet and cast them into a giant iron statue of a four-year-old with the top of its head accidentally blown off while Daddy was cleaning his guns. I once heard them get into it.

The rule was written for an agrarian democracy!

Guns don't kill people! I kill people! And I'll take the responsibility for it!

So you'll fight for the right of every pissed-off, drunken husband to walk into a courtroom and kill his wife, the judge, and anybody else in his way?

People kill people with knives, too!

Knives don't go off when they're "unloaded!"

And like that. They are civilized arguers, they never stay mad at each other, but when they really get into it you want to wear some serious body armor.

Myself, I'm not sure I get it. A well-regulated militia? Sounds like you ought to at least put them into a uniform before you hand them a bazooka. So why does that mean all those people getting off the airplane today get to pack? On the other hand, I guess the militia is Corporal Lizard, right? The IQ of a palmetto bug but not nearly as attractive, and with a bad attitude about people from my home planet, too. But what do I know, I'm only a dumb heathern red boy. And, being a boy, I'll admit that I kind of like guns. Not that I'm anxious to carry one, like Travis, but shooting is fun.

There were maybe a hundred weapons in the blockhouse, and these were just Travis's "working" arsenal. Nothing expensive or very fancy or collectible; those were all away in a much more secure place in the house itself. These were just the things the *padrone* of Rancho Broussard fired to keep his hand in. There were rifles and shotguns, and revolvers and automatic pistols.

I took a Winchester .30-06 (thirty-ought-six) rifle off the shelf, checked that it was unloaded, and a Mossberg shotgun, ditto. Elizabeth stuffed a Glock 9mm into the waistband of her jeans and picked out a smaller shotgun, which she handed to Evangeline, who looked at it like it was a snake about to strike.

"Uh-uh, I don't want that thing."

"Honey," Elizabeth said, "do you want to be the only one aboard who's not armed?"

"What? I mean, no . . . but . . ."

"If you don't want to carry, I'd advise you stay right here."

"But I don't want to *shoot* anybody!"

"Nobody does. And I don't expect we will. But think about this, spacegirl. Worse comes to worst, do you want to be the poor helpless one lying down at the bottom of the Duck and depending on everybody else to save your ass, or do you want to be at least able to fight back?"

It was clear from the look on Evangeline's face that crouching in the bottom of the Duck in such a case didn't sound all that bad to her, but I'd picked up on the fact that Evangeline idolized my big sister as a sort of . . . well, big sister.

"It's just in case, Evangeline," I said. "But Travis won't take you along unless he thinks you can handle yourself. He doesn't believe in helpless females, and neither does my mom or Elizabeth. Remember, this isn't Mars. This is Earth, and even worse, this is America, and even worse than that, this is Florida. The people down here are trigger-happy enough even in the good times, and this isn't a good time."

She still looked dubious, but took the little shotgun when Elizabeth handed it to her. I showed her how to break it open and look down the barrel while my sister was gathering various types of ammo, then we went out to the range.

Elizabeth took her stance and put a group right into the nearest Osama's chest, nodded in satisfaction, and looked at me.

"Ray, why don't you show Eve how to load that elephant gun?" she said, and rolled her eyes where Evangeline couldn't see.

Well, the best way to teach somebody how to shoot a long-barreled gun is to stand behind him or her—and in this case, very definitely her—and show how it's done. This involves putting one's arms around the student, in an objective manner, of course, resting one's chin on the student's shoulder, purely to be able to experience the sightlines of the weapon, adjusting this and that with one's hands, nudging the student's legs with one's feet to achieve the proper stance . . . smelling the student's shampoo and some other fragrance she was wearing, feeling the brush of a hip or an arm or a hand . . .

Luckily, the gun went off before I did. The first one startled her, but the kick wasn't too great, and soon she was firing off rounds pretty confidently and we switched over to a little more authoritative rifle and tried to actually hit something. She was deadly at ten feet, not so great farther out.

We spent about half an hour at that before Travis and all the rest joined us. He put us all through refresher courses, and I could see clearly that he'd love to leave Evangeline there at the ranch, but he respected grit and gameness, and if she was up to it, so was he.

He nodded when he saw what Elizabeth planned to take, and handed out weapons to Dad and Mom and Mr. Redmond according to their preferences, but he frowned when he looked at my Winchester.

"Best to take something with a magazine," he said, and found me a semiautomatic with a thirty-shot clip. "Something happened to this one, I've been meaning to fix it. Funny, you squeeze the trigger once and you get one shot, but you hold down the trigger and it just keeps firing until it's empty. Craziest thing. Keep it in mind."

"Even crazier," Mom said. "This one seems to have the same flaw." She pointed her rifle at an Osama, who quickly became a pile of splinters. "If I didn't know you were such a good citizen, Travis, I might suspect you'd done something to them that isn't strictly legal under Florida's gun laws, such as they are."

"Unconstitutional, every one of them, but I wouldn't dream of breaking the law, you know me. I just hole up here like the crazy hermit that I am and let the world go to hell by itself."

When we were all checked out on the weapons, Travis led us all back to the big house, just in time to meet a delivery van that started unloading hot food, first, and boxed supplies later. There was Chinese, and barbecue, and big sloppy Cuban sandwiches, and pizzas the size of truck tires. Nothing healthy anywhere in sight.

"Still just as good a cook as ever," Mom observed.

"Enjoy it. It may be MREs for the next few days."

It was good stuff. Some of the best barbecue I ever ate, and the pizza wasn't bad, either, though I wasn't sure what all the stuff on it was, nor in the Cuban sandwiches.

Dad fell asleep at the table. Luckily, he didn't fall forward into the food, but he just sort of drifted off and his chin rested on his chest. Travis and I helped him out of his chair. He woke up, more or less, as we put his arms over our shoulders and took him from the table, staggering like a drunk and muttering, "I'll be okay, I'll be okay, just a little nap is all I need." We got him into one of the guest bedrooms and stretched out, and decided to let Mom undress him, if she wanted to. Then we stood over him and looked down for a minute.

"I hope you know what a great dad you've got, Ray," Travis said, softly.

"I guess so," I said. "I don't really know him that well. I don't know why."

"You should try harder. No reflection on you, I know how it is. But he's one of the best men I ever met. You read his book?"

"Yeah. Quite a story."

"He didn't tell the half of it. When we found the American ship, blown to bits by that half-assed engine Jubal warned them about . . .

"There he was, Manny, your father, puking his guts out, I wouldn't let him go over with the girls because he wouldn't be any use. Then somebody *had* to go over, and it couldn't be me, and I sent Manny. Hardest thing I ever did, landing that VStar in Africa was *nothing* compared to that . . . but it was nothing, *nothing*, Ray, compared to what your father did. I saw him, suiting up, and I don't think I've ever seen anybody so scared. He didn't put that part in his book. How his hands were shaking and he kept throwing up until somehow, he just *stopped*. Stopped puking, stopped shaking, walked into that air lock and out into space." Once again he looked away into a distance much farther than the walls around us. "I'd do anything for him, Ray. Anything at all."

I haven't had a lot of "man-to-man" conversations with my father. For one thing, I don't think either of us are very good at it. But we did have a pretty good talk once. It was only about a year ago, on the twentieth anniversary of the *Red Thunder* flight, and he'd just finished the last of a dozen interviews and said his face was hurting from the artificial smile he'd had pasted on all day long. He fixed himself a big drink and let me have a little wine. We were in his office at the hotel, and Mom and Elizabeth were already gone. He said he was glad that was over, at least for the next five years. I asked him why he hated it so much.

He waved his hand with the drink in it at the office.

"It's all this," he said. He paused for so long I thought that was going to be all, but then he sighed and looked at me.

"They compare us to Charles Lindbergh. Neil Armstrong. Christopher Columbus, for crying out loud."

"But . . . what you did was as important as what they did, wasn't it?"

"What we did was important, there's no point in denying that. But those men, they . . . they were *great* men, Ray. They worked hard to get the chance to do what they did. What I did, what we did . . . it just sort of fell into our laps. It was nothing but luck, being in the right place at the right time. Travis could have gone himself, without any of us, if he'd found that first bubble himself. I mean, I literally stumbled on it. I've felt like . . . like an imposter ever since." He gave me a wry grin and sipped at his drink. His eyes were far away.

I thought about it a while. I could just say "You're not an imposter" and leave it at that. But what he had said didn't make sense to me, and I wondered how I could convince him of that. Probably no way, but it was worth a try.

"Columbus was pretty much a loser, wasn't he?" I said.

"What do you mean?"

"Well, he was a big deal for a while, but in history class these days he doesn't come off so good. Sure, he was an adventurer and an explorer. But he and the ones who came after him enslaved and massacred the natives of the New World." I looked around the office. "Don't see any slaves in here."

Dad laughed.

"Just wage slaves," he said. "I wonder what would have happened if there had been natives?"

"We'd have bored them to death with appearances on every television show on Earth, or put them in zoos. Or married them, like Pocahontas. Anyway, there weren't. And from what they told us, Columbus was one lucky fool. Luckier than you. His whole trip was based on the idea that the Earth was a lot smaller than it actually is. He thought he could get to the Orient—which is what he was planning to do, and come to think of it, he died still believing he'd landed in China—by sailing west. If the Americas hadn't been there, he and his whole crew would have starved to death."

He smiled, but didn't say anything.

Okay, reality check number two.

"Lindbergh? Gimme a break. Well-known Nazi. His flight was nothing but a stunt, the Atlantic had already been crossed by air; who cares if he did it solo? He was a media creation, just like you think you are."

His smile got bigger, and he shook his head a little.

"Neil Armstrong . . . well, there you got me. He's a hero in my book. His trip was important, he worked for it, he deserved everything he got. Which, apparently, he didn't want! After he got back he buried himself in Ohio and avoided publicity like the black death. Never tried to cash in on his fame."

"I did. Big-time."

"I'd say small-time, from what I know. And so what? Don't you think I know I wouldn't be where I am today if you and Mom hadn't . . ."

"Sold out?"

"Sold out what? Cashed in, sure. And what's wrong with that? Your book was a historical document. Somebody should complain that you made money off it? Quit kicking yourself over it, Dad. You made one giant leap for mankind."

He actually laughed then, and shook his head.

"Okay, son, you've convinced me."

I could tell that I hadn't, not really, but the look that passed between us was far more important to me. I'd somehow managed to convey to him that, no matter what he thought of himself, I thought of him as a hero. And that that was all that really mattered to either of us.

God, why can't we have more moments like that?

TRAVIS AND I left the bedroom and I thought we were done, but he put his arm around my shoulder and pulled my head down nearer to his level.

"I have two words of advice for you, Ray," he said. "You want to hear them?"

"I guess so."

"Don't go."

I didn't say anything.

"Where we're going, it's no place for a kid, Ray. Now don't take offense, I didn't like being called a kid when I was seventeen any more than you do. But it's a fact. You're a kid. Your sister is almost a kid, too, and she's sure too young and innocent for the Red Zone. Don't even get me started on Evangeline, she's got absolutely no business here. But there's no shame in staying here at the ranch, my friend."

"I've got to go, Travis."

"I know you feel that way, but you don't. Not really. We're going to be seeing some things that will stick with you for the rest of your life, and nothing good will be accomplished by that. We may end up having to do things . . . well, whatever we have to do. You don't need that, either."

"Are you saying you won't take me?"

"I never said that. I think you're old enough to make your own decision. I just think you're making the wrong one."

"What about Elizabeth?" I asked, and I'm afraid I sounded a little petulant, even to myself. "I'll bet you won't ask her not to go."

"You're wrong. I'm going to advise her to stay here with Evangeline. What do you think my chances are?"

"Zero."

"Yeah, that's what I figured. I'll ask anyway. So. What do you say?"

"I have to go," I said.

"So be it." He patted my shoulder and walked away.

It was probably the best advice I ever got. But I didn't take it.

8

★ ★ ★

IT DIDN'T TAKE long for us all to get a taste of what Travis was talking about, and we got it from the man himself.

"Listen up!" he shouted from the front of the newly painted Duck. We were all seated under the big canvas tarp with the sun just struggling to make itself seen through the thick haze to the east.

"There is only one way this thing will work, and that is absolute obedience. Right now this silly little vehicle is a truck, but before we get where we're going it will be a boat, and we will all behave as if it is a boat at all times. A boat has only one captain, and that captain is me.

"Boat captains do not hold elections nor do they conduct polls, except at their own discretion. I may ask you for advice, but once I have received it, my decision in all matters is final, and my orders will be given accordingly, and they *will* be obeyed. We don't have a brig on this vessel, so flogging will be the punishment of choice. Does anyone have any questions?"

"No, sir, Captain Bligh!" Mom replied. Travis looked at her and smiled with one corner of his mouth.

"You will all be allowed one smart-ass remark per day. That was yours, Kelly."

I could see Mom struggling not to laugh, but she kept her mouth shut.

"This is your last chance to bail out," Travis went on, unsmiling. "I won't ask for a show of hands, but I'm about to start this thing up, and anybody still aboard when I get moving has agreed to abide by my orders until we get back, or until you decide to jump ship. Believe me, I won't think any the less of anyone who gets off now." He was staring daggers at Evangeline, who squirmed uncomfortably. I had an idea she'd been subjected to a much stronger argument than Travis had given me. But she didn't move. He shifted his gaze to Elizabeth, who sat calmly. Then he glanced at me, shrugged, and turned away. He pressed the starter button and the engine instantly roared to life.

We were on our way.

THE ROAD DIPPED down to the lake. Travis did something with the gears, and the Duck eased in and I felt the wheels coming free of the ground. Soon we were afloat, moving at a steady five knots, according to Travis.

"They lost a lot of these things on D day," Travis told us. "Can everybody aboard swim?"

Elizabeth swims like a porpoise; she won medals on the school swim team. As for myself, I'm not elegant or quick, but I get there eventually.

"Good. Now, this is all the shakedown cruise we're going to get, so everybody look around for leaks."

I did, like an idiot. Then I asked, "What are we going to do if it leaks, Travis?"

He tossed me something. I grabbed for it, and naturally I reached too high. It would take a while to get my reflexes adjusted to Earth gravity, where things fall too damn fast. It hit my wrist and fell into my lap. It was a piece of bubble gum.

"You walked right into that one, Ray," he said. I tossed it back at him.

"Got something else for you guys," he said, and dug around in a backpack he had carried aboard. He came out with a handful of thin black leather wallets. I opened mine and saw a shiny gold badge that said VOLUSIA COUNTY DEPUTY SHERIFF.

"Badges?" Dak said. "Badges? We don'—"

"—*need no steenkin' badges!*" Travis, Mom, and Dad finished with him, and laughed. I looked over at Elizabeth and Evangeline, but they just shrugged. Normally I could have googled the source in about three seconds, but none of our stereos were working, nor would they until we got back to Orlando.

"Are these any good, Travis?" Mom asked.

"What do you mean? Why wouldn't they be? I'm a deputy sheriff, and I'm authorized to deputize other people in an emergency."

"I thought that was honorary."

"Let's not harp on technicalities. Oh, speaking of technicalities, all a y'all raise your right hands."

We did.

"Do y'all solemnly swear to do any dad-gum thing I order y'all to do, and to uphold and respect the laws of Volusia County, the great state of Florida, and the United States of America, such as they are in the present state of emergency, and as long as they don't get in the way of doing what we set out to do?"

We all agreed, more or less. Dak was looking down at this badge in his hand and shaking his head.

"Damn. I'm a cop!"

WE HELD A democratic vote to name the Duck. Final results:

Donald 3 (Dad, Mr. Redmond, and Dak)

Daffy 3 (me, Elizabeth, and Evangeline)

Daisy 1 (Mom)

Uncle Scrooge 1 (Travis).

And the winnah is . . . Scrooge! Well, he warned us, didn't he?

We came up out of the lake on a narrow country lane. *Scrooge* handled this as adroitly as it had handled getting into the water. Travis said the thing could go fifty miles per hour on a good road, but we probably would never get a chance to open her up. It was quite a nice vehicle, actually, over thirty feet long and eight feet wide. The seats were comfortable, the ride was okay. It had only one drawback, and that was the lack of air-conditioning. As the sun rose the stifling, moist Florida heat closed in on us.

We were all dressed in Banana Republic safari stuff, supplied by Travis, of good quality but far too heavy for the humidity. I understood the logic. This wasn't a pleasure trip, we needed the soldierlike garments. But I wished for a light cotton aloha shirt, maybe one with blue parrots or something, like Travis usually wore. Within half an hour we were all drenched.

Come to think of it, *Scrooge* had a second drawback: no windows. Before long we were swarmed by the kind of mosquitoes you think might actually pick you up and carry you away to devour at their leisure. The only thing I know of worse than being covered in sweat is being covered in sweat and bug dope at the same time. It smelled bad, it was oily and sticky, and many of the mosquitoes seemed to regard it as little more than an interesting sauce for the steaming human hot dogs they were feasting on.

No question, the worst thing about Earth was Earthies. The second worst was gravity. And coming on hard on the rail was bugs. I *hate* bugs.

THERE WAS AN actual boundary to the Red Zone. Starting about seven miles from where the coast used to be, there was an actual wall, from just a few feet high to as much as ten feet, depending on the vagaries of the mostly flat landscape. It was composed of cars and wrecked houses and smashed mobile homes, so common in Florida. It was composed, in fact, of just about anything human beings used in their homes and on their jobs, as if it had all been tossed into a blender, churned on the high setting for a while, and then poured out in a line that cut right across the road we were on.

On either side of the road we saw groups of people, some in uniform, some civilians, some with heavy equipment, some with cadaver dogs, some simply moving wreckage by hand. The operation was at the point all catastrophes like this eventually reach, where some hardy souls are still holding out hope to find living people buried in the debris.

"You can't argue with people like that," Travis told us, "because one in a million times a survivor *is* recovered even this long afterward, and the media jump on the story and write endless pieces about the 'miracle.'" He stopped himself when he saw Mr. Redmond's face, which was leaking tears. We hadn't talked about it much, but Mr. and Mrs. Redmond had about a dozen relatives in the area, in *residential* areas, the debris of which we were looking at right then. It was questionable if any of them had made it to high ground or a strong, multistory building.

"I am such a total asshole," Travis said. "I should give asshole lessons. Jim, I am so sorry, I didn't mean . . ."

"That's okay, Travis," Mr. Redmond said. "We understand the realities here. We're just praying they got to a safe place."

"I'll pray right along with you," Travis said.

There was a big refrigerator truck with a generator humming, and beside it a row of yellow body bags. Some of the rescue and recovery workers waved at us and we waved back. Then Travis got moving again.

The road had been bulldozed ahead of us for about half a mile. To each side was . . . it's hard to describe what it looked like. It had been a residential neighborhood and there were houses standing here and there, mostly made of brick, but with all the windows broken out and draped with garbage rotting in the sun. There were some wooden houses more or less intact, but knocked off their foundations by the force of the waves. Instead of the normal grid you'd have seen before the waves, neat little houses and trailer parks all in a row, it looked like somebody had taken a lot of little Monopoly houses and shaken them in a jar and dumped them out on the board. Power poles leaned in every direction. Cars were on their sides or on their roofs or piled up by the force of the water. And over everything, filling all the cracks, was the endless wreckage and mud washed in from locations closer to the ocean.

Before long we came to a roadblock. There were maybe a dozen men and women there, in different uniforms. There were Florida National Guard, regular United States Army, and one Homelander. There was a guy in the ragged remains of a blue police patrolman's uniform, looking like he hadn't bathed or slept since the wave hit. A guy in a white MP helmet, maybe about twenty-five years old, turned his rifle in our general direction, but pointed at the ground, and held his hand up. Travis stopped.

"Everyone down from the vehicle, please," he said, motioning with his weapon. Travis lowered the ladder and we eased ourselves out and down to stand in the mud.

"Deputy sheriffs, Sergeant," Travis said. He was shrugging into an Eisenhower jacket as he spoke, which struck me as the height of insanity.

"And what is the purpose of your visit, sir?" the guy asked.

"Rescue and recovery, just like you. Is there a problem?" He pulled an Army cap over his head, and I saw it had two gold metal stars pinned to it. There were stars on each of his shoulders, too. I thought it was sort of pretty, and I wondered if I could wear some stars, too.

The soldier saw it, and his eyes got very large. He snapped to attention and saluted.

"No, sir, no problem sir."

"At ease, soldier," Travis said, easily. "They put me out to pasture years ago, I'm retired, and I'm not here to screw up your patch."

"Yes, sir, General Broussard, sir." He must have recognized the famous face, because Travis's name wasn't anywhere on the uniform.

Travis started questioning the sergeant about conditions up ahead, and the other soldiers gathered around respectfully, offering information, except for the Homelander, who as usual stayed behind his black plastic mask, aloof and above it all, a law unto himself. I wondered if those black uniforms were air-conditioned, or if a requirement for Homelander service was the ability not to sweat.

A lieutenant of some sort came up soon in an amphibious Hummer, saluted, and joined the conversation. Everything seemed to be going well between Travis and the soldiers, but the lieutenant was looking suspiciously at the rest of us.

"Look here, General," the lieutenant finally said. "I'm not going to try to stand in your way if you want to go farther, but I don't know if I can take the responsibility for the rest of your party. My orders are, nobody but authorized personnel goes in, and anybody who comes out can't go back. Tomorrow or the next day we're scheduled to start moving in and get the rest of the survivors moving inland toward the refugee camps, but a lot of them don't want to go. I'm afraid it could get ugly."

"I'm sure it might, Lieutenant," Travis said. "It's a dumb idea trying to get Americans to give up what's left of their homes. They don't want the government putting them in camps, no matter what they call them, unless they have absolutely nothing left. I expect some of them will resist."

"Between you and me, sir, I agree, but orders are orders. Personally, I don't intend to shoot any citizen who hunkers down in his house."

"I'm glad to hear it. Meantime, I won't bullshit you. We're on personal errands, and I'm using my political weight to get special consideration." He flashed a big grin at the lieutenant. "I'm willing to take personal responsibility for these people, who, though it may sound ridiculous, *are* in fact legally sworn deputy sheriffs. It would, in fact, be a felony for them to display those badges if they weren't. If the phones were working I'd call up the governor, who I believe is in charge of this part of this fiasco, technically, though we all know who's *really* in charge"—he glanced at the Homelander—"and I guarantee you he'd say let that idiot Broussard do whatever he wants to do, so long as you keep him out of my hair. So what do you say, Lieutenant?"

The lieutenant looked a little stunned—people often do when dealing with Travis—but he finally smiled.

"Well, since you put it that way."

We were climbing back aboard when the lieutenant took another look at me.

"How old are you, son?" he asked.

My mouth was living a life of its own.

"Seventeen, sir . . . that is . . . uh . . ." Oh, brother. Now I'd stepped in it, now I was screwed. But Travis put his arm over my shoulder and smiled again.

"That's Martian years, right Ray? In Earth years he's . . . oh, about twenty."

"That's right, General." I saluted. Travis gave me a droll look.

"Okay," the lieutenant said. "It's on your head, General. This spot where we're standing, this is the last outpost of law and order in the United States. Beyond that, there's pockets of reasonable order, mostly vigilante law. The rest is anarchy. Bear in mind, just about all the prisons survived the wave, there was time to get the inmates up on the top floors but nothing to feed them with afterward and all the guards took off to see about their families, so those folks are running around out there, along with the bad guys you'd normally run into. They've probably just about drunk up all the liquor that survived the wave by now, and I don't know if that's good news or bad news. They might be starting to feel some pretty bad hangovers about now . . ."

"Thanks for everything, Lieutenant," Travis said, and sat in the driver's seat and started the engine. We pulled away from the little knot of troops and into the real chaos.

JUST DOWN THE road Travis stopped *Scrooge* again and walked to the back and rummaged in a box. He started passing out things. We each got a military helmet like the regular Army troops were wearing. He told us we had to wear them from now on when we were moving in *Scrooge,* as the ride was apt to get rough from here. Wearing them when we got out was up to us, but he'd advise we keep them on. He said Kevlar vests were available for those of us who thought we could wear them without dying of heatstroke. Nobody put them on, but we kept them handy. Then he gave us each a little white bundle, which turned out to be jars of something called Vicks wrapped in cloth surgical masks.

"The trick, as I understand it," he said, "is to rub some around your nostrils, your upper lip, and work some into the mask. I don't know; I've never had to try it. It's recommended by coroners for people attending autopsies of bodies that have been dead a while. They say gasoline works pretty well, too. It deadens the sense of smell, and it damn sure smells better than a decomposing body."

Even predisaster Florida has its own distinctive smells, not all of them pleasant. Mold and mildew are strong themes, and other things associated with a hot, wet climate that can rot things pretty fast. There are smells associated with swampland that I don't mind. The cities have their own distinctive smells.

After the wave, all those things were intensified. There was also the smell of salt water, still lying in pools here and there on the saturated ground. There was the constant smell of smoke, of course, and the smell you get after a house fire that has been doused by the fire department. Those were the easy ones.

Then there were the miles and miles of broken sewers and septic tanks that had been uncovered by the receding water. Many of the mobile homes or modular homes or trailers and recreational vehicles used propane, and many of those that hadn't burst and already dissipated were leaking slowly. Propane has no odor, but the stuff they mix in with it does, and it's not pleasant. We smelled all these things in various strengths as we went down the road, depending on which way the wind was blowing. And there was the smell of rotting flesh, distant, not yet overpowering.

It was about an hour later when we saw our first body.

It was lying in the road, directly in our path. The bulldozed path was too narrow for us to go around it. Several of us stood up, to get a better look. I wished I hadn't. He was dressed in black leather and most of his head was missing. I sat back down, and Elizabeth, sitting next to me, leaned over the side and quietly vomited.

Travis and Dad stood up and walked out onto the flat hood of *Scrooge*, looking down at the corpse. I heard a sound off to the left and saw a guy coming down a partly cleared suburban street. He was bald up to the top of his sunburned head, limping slightly, wearing gold-rimmed glasses with one lens missing. He was filthy, and looked exhausted. He carried a shotgun cradled in his arms.

"Afternoon, friend," Travis said. "Looks like you've got a dead one here."

"Yeah, I popped that one about this time yesterday. That's his motorcycle over there." He gestured to a burned-out wreck that used to be a Harley.

"What'd he do?"

"Came roaring up, drunk, firing away. We waited till he stopped to reload, and I shot him." He made another gesture, and two more guys appeared from behind bits of wreckage. They also carried shotguns, and they weren't smiling. But they weren't pointing them at us, either.

"Seems hard, just leaving him there like that. Couldn't you bury him?"

"Mister, it took me two days to find my way here to my neighborhood. One of my daughters is dead, and one was medevaced out and I don't even know if she's alive because the fucking phones don't work. I've spent five days digging my neighbors out of the ruins of their houses and only found one alive, and he died later. We've buried fifty on this street, and we've got a long way to go just on recovering bodies. After you've wrapped a six-year-old in a tarp and put him in the ground by his swing set . . . well, mister, I plain don't have the time and energy to bother with roadkill like that piece of shit. You want him buried, *you* bury him."

"I get your point," Travis said. "And I'm sorry for your loss."

"Fuck your . . ." He stopped and ran a hand over his bare head. The hand was wrapped in dirty bandages. "Sorry. We had a band of inmates on motorcycles come through just before I got here. They . . . never mind. We're armed now, and we don't fuck around. We're going to hoist that piece of garbage up on a lamppost when we get the time, as a warning." I thought he meant the biker, but he pointed to the burned Harley. "I think they're getting the message. Other neighborhoods have been hoisting other things up on lampposts, if you get my meaning."

"I do indeed, sir. And good luck to you."

"Same to you. Where are you going?"

"All the way to the ocean."

The man laughed, though it wasn't much of one. "Good luck to you, too. You're going to need it."

He went away down the street and the two guys set up for a cross fire ducked back behind their shelters. Travis was looking down on the dead man.

"Well"—he sighed—"I'm not going to just run him over." He jumped down to the ground. In the seat ahead of me Dad started to get up. I put my hand on his shoulder and pushed him back down as I went by him. I heard him saying something as I went by but I didn't look back.

I joined Travis and we each took a boot. I had thought the blackness around the remains of the dude's head was dried blood. It was flies. They swarmed up as we pulled him, like they were angry at us. There's some big flies in Florida.

We got him off to the side of the road, and I walked on a few steps away from *Scrooge* and puked. I don't throw up as easy as Elizabeth does; it's a gut-wrenching, exhausting business for me. It took a few minutes. When I straightened up I saw Travis wiping his mouth. He gave me a faint grin.

"Join the club," he said.

"I thought . . ."

"What, that I'm tough? Nah. I've never seen anything like this. I was never in combat, I was a flyboy, out in space. But the guys who have seen it have told me that . . . not that you get used to it, you don't ever want to do that, but that it gets easier."

And it did. I didn't puke again. I think the puking part of you gets numb, you switch into another gear or something, or you store the sights and smells away in some other part of your mind. That's what I did.

I got back into *Scrooge* and sat by my mother. She put her arm around me and hugged me tight. It felt good.

TRAVIS HAD PICKED up a soggy booklet with a bright orange cover from the ground before we got moving again. Soon we were seeing them by the thousands. They were air-dropped leaflets advising people what to do, in the simplest and starkest possible terms.

There was the obvious stuff: boil all water, even if you're only going to wash in it. Sewage had contaminated everything, typhoid and cholera were distinct possibilities, as well as dysentery. Sterilize cans before you open them. Basic first-aid instructions, in English and Spanish, with simple illustrations.

I wondered if everyone was taking the time to boil their water. I hoped so, but there was so much to do, and quite a few Americans couldn't read. Maybe the pictures would be enough. And there was plenty of firewood around.

The authorities were now advocating cremations rather than mass burials for bodies that couldn't be gotten to reefer trucks before they got too ripe.

Travis asked Mom to read the booklet aloud to the rest of us. One part of it stands out in my memory.

"They say here that, if possible, you should pull some head hairs from a body before you burn it. Get the roots, it says. Put the sample in a plastic bag and write on it where you found the body, age, race, and sex if you can tell, and how you disposed of it, and give the baggie to your 'neighborhood disaster coordinator,' whatever that is."

"Maybe that guy we talked to back there," Dad said.

WE PULLED UP to a knot of cars strewn across the road. There was a gap, but it was too narrow for the broad-hipped *Scrooge* to get through. Travis pulled up close and nudged one of the cars with the nose of the

Duck and it moved a little, then jammed tight. He turned off the engine to conserve fuel.

"No good," he said. "I wish I'd had time to install some sort of 'dozer blade on the front of this thing, but I figured it wasn't worth the extra time. And I can't push too hard on stuff like this or it might poke a hole in the hull."

So no bulldozer, but we did have two big Earthies and six game but gravity-lagged Martians. We also had a powerful vehicle, chains, and block and tackle. Combine that with a lot of sweat, and you can move a lot of things.

The rest of that day was spent moving cars, mostly. We'd attach a heavy chain to one and then to *Scrooge,* and Travis would tug it out of the jam, then another, then another. Sometimes we had to loop the chain around a fire hydrant or street sign embedded in concrete to get it to move sideways. After we'd cleared a path we Martians would take turns walking ahead of *Scrooge,* our job being to kick most of the loose lumber out of the way, being sure there was none with nails poking up.

We saw bodies here and there, mostly so tangled up in the wreckage you could hardly tell that's what they were.

We came to a big stack of cars, three high. I climbed up and looked inside. Nobody there. I looped the chain around the doorposts of the top car, climbed back down and stood well back—Travis had warned us the chain could snap, and pop like a whip—and Dad reversed *Scrooge* and the car toppled off the stack and was dragged back out of the way. I climbed back up again and looked inside. Bad idea. There were six people in there, looking about what you'd expect corpses to look after seven days in hot weather. If you have no idea what that would look like, good for you. Try to keep it that way.

I controlled my stomach, hooked up the chain, and got down again. Dad dragged it off and over to one side, and I never looked at it again. Just another day's work.

WHEN THE SUN reached the horizon in the west, we had gone two hard miles into no-man's-land. We had about another two miles to go to reach the ocean, and they promised to be harder.

The battery-powered GPS map showed an elementary school off to the south, two streets over, and by standing up on one of the roll bars with the tarp rolled back I was just able to see it, on a low rise. It was a one-story sprawling brick building like a hundred others in that area, with two larger buildings that were probably an auditorium and a gym at either end of the classrooms.

Travis turned off on a cleared street going south and we were immediately approached by four men with rifles, this time pointed right at us. They wanted to know our business. They were reasonably polite about it, but the rifles never wavered. We told them we were headed for the beach to check on our relatives. They examined our papers, compared pictures with faces on passports and drivers' licenses. Travis's major general's stars didn't exactly impress them, but did calm them. They pretty much ignored all our silly little deputy sheriff badges. Finally, they all lowered their weapons.

"The baseball field over there is pretty clear," the leader told us. "There's a tennis court, too, you could park that thing there. We buried all the bodies we could find lying around here, and the ones in homes, but we haven't got into the school itself. I wouldn't go over there, if I was you. We're fixing to start tackling that tomorrow. I'd rather cut off my own right arm than go in there, but the government hasn't showed up, and it's getting to be a health hazard."

"We won't disturb them," Travis assured them, and we were waved on.

There was enough room to park *Scrooge* on the tennis court, and we were almost a hundred yards from the building. It was getting dark as Travis turned off the engine, and we all climbed down. He pulled the tarps off the supplies in the very back of the Duck and began tossing items over the side. After a short time of confusion we managed to get a large inflatable tent set up, not much different than the instant tents we used on Mars except not pressure-tight. There was a folding picnic table and gas grill, and boxes of canned food and bottled water, and even a cooler full of ice. It was all high-end camping stuff, brightly colored and sturdy.

The Coleman lantern reflections on the few unbroken windows in the schoolhouse looked like the wandering ghosts of all the dead children inside.

Don't go there. Both literally and figuratively, just don't go there.

I lost track of how many hot dogs I ate. We were all like that, slapping one dog onto a bun and slathering it with mustard and slopping on the fiery chili even as we were cooking the next one. I'd eaten very little during the day and thrown up most of that. The good honest smoke of our fire smothered the less pleasant smells around us, and we ate like ravening dogs, all conversation ceasing, very little sound at all except the crackling of the fire and the snap of soda can pop-tops. I know it will sound odd to say this, but it was a very good time. Simple pleasures, good company, hearty appetite. The day's worries behind us, tomorrow's horrors temporarily put on hold. I wondered if it was something like what soldiers experience on the battlefield after surviving a day of fighting.

What it wasn't like was camping out on Mars, except for the shape of the tent. Martian Boy Scouts have mostly different merit badges, though we do learn to tie knots. It did take me back to my earlier boyhood, though, when my family camped out from time to time before we emigrated.

We finally all sat back, cross-legged on the cool concrete, stuffed probably more than was wise.

"This would be the time when we'd tell ghost stories," Dad said, and looked at me for a moment. I knew our minds had gone down the same path.

"Let's don't," Mom said, and everybody agreed, including Dad. "I can't see that it's a good time for telling jokes, either. What else is there to do around the campfire?"

Surprising us all, Evangeline began to sing. Up to then she'd been so quiet you hardly knew she was there, though I sometimes saw her whispering to Elizabeth, as if afraid that we'd all laugh at her if she spoke aloud. But her voice was clear and confident and sweet, contralto, and she had either had some training or was one hell of a natural talent. The song was "Tenting Tonight," which I didn't know, but later learned was quite old. They sang it during the American Civil War. When she got to the chorus Elizabeth joined in, and soon we were all doing it, letting her carry the verse.

When she was done we were all smiling and clapping, which was something of a mistake, because when we stopped the darkness and deathly silence closed in even more than it had before. We all felt it, like a damp blanket spreading over us. The wind picked up a little, and sang though the broken glass of the schoolhouse.

The best thing to do for that, we silently agreed, was to sing more. It turned out Evangeline knew a lot of songs suitable for campfires. Not all of them made a lot of sense for the situation—I remember singing "All You Need Is Love" and thinking these people here needed a lot more than that—but who cared? It was the sweet music that mattered, not the words. Words couldn't do anything to help us deal with this awfulness, we'd already tried words in every combination we could think of, and they just didn't cut it. But music could.

Eventually the tunes turned into yawns. Travis showed us how to put the side flaps down on the Duck awning, so there were two places to sleep. Amid some grumbling about what a fuddy-duddy sexist pig Travis was, the women were bedded down on the folding seats in *Scrooge* and the men in the tent outside. When the girls were out of the way Travis revealed he was an even worse pig than they supposed; he set watches throughout the night, but not for the girls. I was sure he'd cut me out of it, but he didn't. In fact, he asked me if I was up to standing the first watch. I was tired, but not sleepy, and I said sure.

"If you feel yourself drifting off," Travis said, "shoot yourself in the foot. That usually wakes me up." He tossed me a rifle and watched as I checked it out, then Dak and Dad and Mr. Redmond climbed into the tent.

I SAT ON a camp chair and, naturally, about fifteen minutes later I almost fell off. Oh, great. Bitch every time somebody treats you like a kid, Ray, and then when they give you a really adult responsibility, you fall on your stupid ass.

So I stood up and started walking around *Scrooge,* taking my time. Never has an hour and a half passed so slowly. I learned a new definition of boredom, I learned how hard it is to stay alert for even ten minutes when you're exhausted, and then the tiger came.

Tiger? I hear you cry. *In Florida?*

What happened was, I heard a sound. It wasn't a roar or even a purr. It wasn't a snapping stick or a squishing footstep. Maybe there was no sound at all, maybe my brain invented a sound when my poor pitiful at-rophied monkey nose smelled something wrong, wrong, *wrong*, and from deep in my brain something let me know that trouble was approaching.

Predator!

So I snapped on my flashlight. I'd kept it off, mostly, to conserve the batteries. I fanned the beam around, and at first swept right over it, then it registered, and I moved the beam back and there it was, squinting in the glare, just sitting there and watching me, looking like he was decid-ing whether to go for the throat or rip out my guts.

Decisions, decisions.

Instantly, my mouth went dry, every hair on my body stood on end, and my heart began to pound. Those old fight-or-flight hormones were still in working order, and they were saying *flight, flight, flight!* But that old monkey brain isn't always right, and I retained just enough of my ability to think to realize that turning and running wasn't the deal here, that he'd have me in a second.

And you know, for a few seconds there, I entirely forgot I had a rifle in my hands.

When I remembered it I felt a little better, but not what you'd call confident. It wasn't a peashooter, but I was far from sure that one slug would take him down, and I thought one shot was all I was likely to get. One leap and he'd be all over me. He was *that* close.

He yawned. He got up off his haunches and started walking toward me. And I fired the rifle, into the air.

I don't know why I did that. Waste what might be my only shot? But I did, and the tiger jumped, and melted away into the darkness and it was like it had never been there in the first place.

SHORTLY, THAT VERY idea was being debated.

"A tiger?" Mom asked, peering down at the men gathered around me. I looked up into three female faces between the awning flap and the edge of the Duck.

"In Florida?" Evangeline asked.

"You sure it wasn't a Florida panther?" Travis asked. "I hear they're making a comeback."

I sighed. "Orange with black stripes?" I said. "Big white teeth? Triangular pink nose? About eight hundred pounds? Is any of this ringing a bell?"

"Settle down, son," Dad said.

"I got no problem with it," Dak said. He was fanning a big high-intensity light all around into the darkness. There was no sign of the tiger. "I mean, I got a *big* problem with him being *out* there, but there's plenty of tigers in Florida. I've seen 'em myself. You got your zoos, and you'd be surprised how many private citizens own big cats. Probably somebody's pet, just a big dumb kitty cat never hunted in his life."

"Okay," Travis said. "It doesn't really matter, Ray."

"It matters a lot to me. I know what I saw."

"Okay, you saw a tiger. Anyway, your watch is over. I'm going to set up some more lights, that'll probably keep it away. Meantime, you get some shut-eye. We've got a hard day ahead of us. Everybody back in the sack. You gals doing okay up there?"

"It's not quite five-star," Mom said, "but we'll manage, if you just get the spa and shower working."

"First thing in the morning," Travis agreed.

I climbed into the tent, seething, feeling sure nobody believed me. They all thought I'd fallen asleep and had a nightmare. Hell, by the time I got stretched out on the air mattress I was beginning to wonder myself.

One thing I was sure of, though. It was going be tough getting to sleep thinking about that thing prowling around out there.

Two minutes later, I was a goner.

SIX HOURS LATER the sun was coming up, somebody was shaking my shoulder and shouting. I struggled up and stared at Travis, wondering who he was for a moment, and why had he poured molten lead into all my joints? I was hurting in muscles I didn't even know I had, and my back was on fire and my ankles had swollen up like pink apples. This must be what it feels like to get old, I thought, and if so, I didn't want any part of it.

"You're wet," I told Travis.

"Went for a swim with your tiger," he said, and grinned at me. "Rise and shine . . . no, don't hit me! Breakfast is cookin' and time's a wastin'!"

I got my boots on and struggled to my feet and finally identified the sound I'd been hearing. It was rain pouring down on the top of the tent. There's this about Earth weather. No matter how bad things seem, they can always be worse if it's raining. Travis handed me a poncho. For some reason a heavy shower doesn't seem to cool Florida off much, it just adds mugginess to the already stifling air.

Everybody was gathered in *Scrooge,* so I made my way painfully up the ladder and into the most heavenly aromas I had ever encountered. There was bacon, and eggs, and waffles, and toast smeared with wonderful cherry jam or orange marmalade, and big mugs of coffee, all being turned out by Mr. Redmond from propane appliances set on the dashboard. I loaded my plate and sat down with it balanced on my knees and ate like I'd never eaten in my life. By the time I had polished off a second plate I felt a slowly reviving interest in living.

It took a while in the rain, but finally we had all our gear stowed away and battened down.

The rain, falling on the flat Florida ground, didn't have its usual channels to find its way to the sea. All this part of the state, and much of the rest of it, was artificially reclaimed from swamp. All the sewers were clogged, backed up, going nowhere. Little pools and lakes were forming and the streets were turning into streams.

I had hoped that at least the rising water would float away some of the wooden wreckage, but no such luck. Oh, it took some of the larger pieces, but mostly it just jammed everything together, making choke points that were almost impossible to get through.

We slogged on, this time in water that varied from ankle deep to knee deep, and was filled with the vilest things imaginable. Dead cats, dead dogs, raw sewage, the rotting contents of refrigerators and freezers, and the occasional human body. If the water got a little deeper, *Scrooge* would float, and we might have a chance of motoring our way around the worst jams. If it got shallower, it would be easier to see the wreckage we had to move out of the way or risk a flat tire. But it didn't do either, and all morning we found ourselves dealing with the worst of both worlds. Travis cursed the poor, faithful Duck every time he felt the wheels lift off the pavement and spin, then settle back down.

"Should have brought a stinking bulldozer!" he shouted every ten minutes or so. "Should have brought dynamite!"

"Should have brought a team of elephants!" Dak shouted back.

"We could have hunted Ray's tiger on them!" Elizabeth said.

I was resigned to it by then. At every opportunity everyone but Mr. Redmond hit me with something about tigers.

Watch out for that tiger, Evangeline!

Is that a dog barking, or do you think it might be a tiger?

Hold that tiger, hold that tiger, hold that tiger!

Ha. Ha. Ha.

Oh, well. I guess we all needed *something* lighthearted by that point, and I might as well be the butt of it. There sure wasn't anything in our surroundings to make us happy and gay and get us through the day. I kept my mouth shut and endured it.

Then one of *Scrooge*'s tires blew out with a sputtering sound. That was because the puncture was underwater. It could have been one of the tandem pair in back and we could have slogged on, but of course it had to be the right front.

I waded back to look at it. There was a plank with several nails deeply embedded in the rubber. Naturally, it was on the side where it had been my responsibility to clear the path. I must have stepped right over it.

Nobody said anything to me about it. It took an hour to get the tire on, and when that was done no one was laughing or making jokes anymore. We carried on, checking our position once an hour, and finally heaved up onto semidry land at a point that was as close as we were going to get to the home where the Redmond's family had lived. There was a big Walmart, and smaller stores, and no people in sight.

We stopped, and everybody climbed out onto the hood or stood on the seats and looked to the north. Travis was peering at the screen of his GPS.

"It says 1.45 miles from here," he said, and pointed. "This is as close as this road gets." We all stared silently. Calling what we were on a "road" was more than generous, though it had been a six-lane main drag before the wave. Some of the palm trees that had run down the center were still standing, but most were leaning sharply or pulled out of the ground by the roots. On each side of us strip malls were visible under heaps of trash, a few signs intact. Advertising signs on poles set deeply in concrete were still there: McDonald's, Gap, Infosys, Jill's Crab Shack. The concrete block buildings were mostly still standing, but all

the glass was broken out of the windows and the contents of the buildings had come gushing out as the wave hit, and again as it receded.
There were side streets leading off in each direction in the familiar flat
grid pattern, but these were far too choked for any vehicle to get
through. No, it was clear that the only way into that mess, for now, was
on foot. Which, of course, is just what Mr. Redmond proposed to do.

"Jim, I advise against it," Travis said.

"I know the advice is well intended," said Mr. Redmond, quietly.
"But if I don't go, there wasn't much point in me coming here in the first
place, was there?"

"Well, I don't know about that. Your relatives are probably in a shelter somewhere, back the way we came. When these damn stereos start
working again, I imagine they'll have lists of the survivors and the . . ."

"And the dead. We know they're probably dead, no need to tiptoe
around it. But what I came for was to find them, and right now this
looks like our best bet."

"Jim . . ." Dad said, and then paused. "I'm not quite sure how to put
this. You're a great cook, and a good man, but are you sure you're up to
this?"

Mr. Redmond smiled for the first time in a while. It wasn't a happy
smile.

"Manny, thank you for your concern, for the loan of the money. For
everything you've done. But before I settled down and perfected my
trade, I had a few little adventures myself. I'm no Navy SEAL, or com-
mando, but Uncle Sam sent me some places that looked a lot like this,
after the bombers were through, and they were full of guys a lot scarier
than some drunk piece-of-shit biker gangs. I came back alive, and I
reckon I can get through this, too."

"At least leave Evangeline with us," Mom suggested.

"I would, I promise you, but she'd only sneak away first chance she
got. We talked it over. I'd rather have her by my side, keep an eye on her."
He held his hand out to Travis, who shook it firmly. "Thanks for the loan
of the weapon, General," he said. "I'll do my best to return it to you."

Travis gave him a walkie-talkie, and they checked the batteries and
channels.

"The range is supposed to be five miles," Travis said, "but I've not tested it, so I'm not sure. Call us every day at noon, okay? We'll have our ears on. And I don't know if we'll be able to wait very long on our way back out, but I promise that we'll be here at noon one day. I don't know what day that will be."

"It's okay. We'll try to be here every day. If we get our business done before you do and we get tired of waiting, we'll hike out."

"Go to the ranch. You'll be welcome there."

There were hugs and kisses all around, and I was surprised at the ferocity with which Evangeline embraced me. Her tears were hot on my cheek as she turned away and followed her father into the chaos of the Wal-Mart parking lot, picking their way through the jumble of cars. Soon the rain, which had slackened for a while, came pouring down again and we lost sight of them. I sat down beside Elizabeth, who was crying quietly.

"That's got to be the bravest thing I ever saw," she said.

"He's got guts," I agreed.

"No, idiot! Her! I talked her ear off, 'Stay with us, Evangeline, you don't have to go, you're not up to this.' And the thing is, she knows that. She is so scared she can't see straight. But she felt she had to stay with her father."

Dad had been listening, and he turned around and looked at us.

"Real courage is going ahead and doing what you know you should do, even when you're terrified," he said.

I thought of what Travis had said about Dad, how scared he had been when he made that spacewalk to save my mother and a lot of strangers. I realized that, if he hadn't made it, I wouldn't be alive. I'd never have been born. Courage counts for something.

"So you think she did the right thing?" Elizabeth asked.

"I don't know what the right thing is," he said, with a wry smile. "It's different for everyone, and different situations call for different things. It might have made more sense if we'd all stayed back in Orlando and let the professionals handle the rescuing."

"I couldn't have done that," I said.

"No, but we might have done more good joining the volunteer teams clearing the debris. What we're doing is selfish, you know. There's people all around us who need help, maybe more than Grandma does. But we're driving right past them. Is that courage? Or self-interest?"

"You tell me," I said.

"I don't have the answer. I don't know if there are simple answers to questions like that, in situations like this."

WE WENT AROUND huge pools of crude oil, some burning, some just soaking into the ground and killing all the plants in sight. We passed spills of other stuff, too. Chemical factories had been hit, and the landscape was littered with barrels of who-knows-what, many of them cracked open. Some of them smelled something awful.

But the worst came a few hours before dark.

It had stopped raining but the sky was still cloudy. It was getting hard to see. I was taking another shift out front, clearing dangerous debris, being extra, extra careful not to miss another board full of nails, feeling more dead than alive. I looked up . . . and the ground was covered with swollen, pinkish gray bodies. Thousands of them, uncountable thousands.

At first my mind just couldn't wrap around it. Naked? Thousands of naked dead people? I couldn't come up with any way for that to make sense.

It was pigs. Hogs, swine, whatever you call them. These were massive porkers, a thousand pounds easily.

"Get back up here, Manny, Dak," Travis called down. "Jesus, get up here. No way I'm going to ask anybody to move that."

"What *is* it, Travis?" I asked.

"Pig farm," he said. "Or pig factory, really. They raise the damn things in big sheds. *Damn!* All the things we've seen, and *this* is about to make me throw up. Come on, you guys, get up here!"

We did, and Travis slammed *Scrooge* into gear with a vengeance. We plowed into the horrible mess and must have had a bit of luck, because though we skidded around and bumped and swayed, we got through it without a breakdown.

FOR A WHILE it looked like we'd be completely stymied by US 1, an elevated autoway that followed the shore all the way through the city. Most of the concrete pylons holding the roadway up had withstood the force of the wave, but the backwash had turned these vertical posts into the teeth of a comb and gathered the debris rushing back toward the sea into an impenetrable mass.

But we were close enough to the ocean now that we had begun to encounter more rescue and recovery parties, working their way inland from ships offshore. They had cleared an access road on the west side of the highway. We talked to some of them, and they said there was a way under the autoway about six miles south, which was a bit of luck since that's the way we needed to go, anyway.

We passed several blocks that had been bulldozed and crushed flat enough to erect tent cities. They were full, and covered with Red Cross tents and soup kitchens with long lines of shuffling people. Fires were burning in oil drums. A few children played with salvaged toys, but most of the people we saw had what Dad called the thousand-yard stare of the dispossessed. It was an expression we'd all grown up seeing count-less times on the stereo, mostly from third world countries where there was a revolution or a famine, or sometimes both. But we'd seen it on Indian faces, and Pakistanis, after the bombings of New Delhi and Islam-abad, and on Jewish and Arab faces. Some news writer had termed that look "The Face of the 21st Century," and the term had stuck.

Seeing them shook me more than the dead bodies had. These were living people, but most of them were shuffling like zombies. That's what happens to you when you lose *everything*. These people had gone, in the space of a few hours, from being citizens of the United States of America to faceless refugees with nothing but the clothes they stood in, and those clothes came from air-dropped canisters filled with the donations of peo-ple from all over America and the world.

Florida was no stranger to disaster. Hurricanes had pounded it countless times. Help was always on the way. Sure, it stunned you, and you mourned your losses, and you buried your dead, and you scrounged around for family keepsakes. Then the President declared a disaster area, government agencies arrived with portable housing, the insurance com-panies came in and started writing checks, you applied for an emergency loan, again from Uncle Sam, and you pulled up your socks and rolled up your sleeves and got to work, rebuilding.

Not this time.

"God, I hate to see Americans like this," Travis muttered, as we moved slowly through the survivors and soldiers in the gathering dusk. "Hate to see *anybody* like this, sure, but . . . I always figured we could handle the worst case. You know, a major city American city getting nuked. We've been waiting for it to happen since 1947 or so, then since September 11, and so far the worst they've managed is big fertilizer bombs. But say New York got hit, or LA. Millions dead . . . but a few days later the hospitals are in place, the people are getting food and water. A week later . . . I think I was wrong, you know? It would have been a lot worse than I figured. And *this*. This is about as close to a total nuclear exchange as you could get. Miami, Jacksonville, Savannah, Charleston, Chesapeake Bay, Washington, Baltimore, Atlantic City, New York, Cape Cod . . . I remember orbiting over the coast, all those billions of lights, millions of people."

I knew not all those places had been hit as hard as where we were, but some of them had been hit very hard, indeed. Most of the government offices had been moved to Chicago, as Washington still had no power. The financial district of New York might or might not be functioning again. And all those cities and small coastal towns, and cities far up the eastern rivers.

I was a Martian, that was my country, though technically it wasn't a country at all. But I was Earth-born, America-born, Florida-born. They felt like my people, too, much as I may complain about them. The Brotherhood of Man, I guess.

But I could hardly imagine what Travis must be feeling. He was an American to his core, almost to a fault, as Mom sometimes said. Not "my country, right or wrong," not that sort of idiot, but a deep believer in the core values of America, and a deep hater when those values were violated. He didn't like American adventurism, which had occupied America for quite a few years now, but if you attacked his beloved country, look out. You wouldn't want to get in his way.

Looking around me, I wondered how long it would take America to recover from this blow. Or if it ever would.

IT WAS ALMOST completely dark when we reached the Halifax River, which used to be a broad expanse of water separating the mainland of

Florida from the long barrier island where the Blast-Off Motel was. The main way we could tell we were there, aside from what the GPS was saying, was the large number of boats. Just about every one of them was capsized, on its side, or stove in. They were piled up like a rich kid's toys on the edge of a very dirty bathtub. Everything from one-mast sailboats to multimillion-dollar motor yachts, all equal now, all nautical junk.

We found a wide concrete pier that was relatively free of debris and drove out to the end. In the failing light that leaked through the overcast there was very little to see but a stretch of black water and, maybe half a mile away, a few fires. Most of them looked pretty small, maybe no bigger than the drum fires of the homeless we'd just seen. One was a little larger.

One of the soldiers had told us that none of the six or seven bridges over to the barrier island was passable. There were plans for a pontoon bridge, but no one knew when it would arrive. There were just too many places that needed them, and too few bridges. Most of the ones the Army had were in use in Indonesia or Nigeria. Just not enough equipment to go around, from planes to boats to bulldozers to choppers, he had said. He didn't sound happy about it.

We all got out. Dad and Mom and Dak were trying to orient themselves; this had been their hometown, their old stomping grounds.

"That's it for tonight, friends," Travis said, turning off the headlights.

Mom was working at the GPS screen and Dad had a pair of night glasses, scanning the island.

"I recognize three hotels over there," he said, breathing hard. "One of them seems to be missing, and there's a lot of heat coming from that area. Maybe a pile of rubble. Wait a minute, I think I have the Tropicana . . . yeah, that's it. No lights, can't see anybody moving around. And moving down the beach, I think it's about a quarter mile, Kelly?"

"About that. Can you see it?"

Dad stopped scanning, looked for a moment. Then he dropped the night glasses, rubbed his eyes, and pointed at the largest fire.

"That's it. It's still standing, but I think it may be burning."

9

★ ★ ★

HOPE IS A tough thing to stretch through a night that long.

Breakfast wasn't too appealing because the wind had shifted during the night. It had been coming from the land, which was bad enough, but now it blew in over the Halifax River, which was even worse.

The river was choked with floating bodies. They came in all lengths, but were all large and round, having swollen in the heat until they stretched their clothes.

Travis eased *Scrooge* into the water and as soon as it was afloat it became clear that somebody was going to have to stand out on the hood and move the . . . debris. Not just bodies, of course, the great majority of the stuff choking what had once been a clear blue strip of water was the remains of homes and other such wrack and ruin. We didn't dare try to drive over a large piece of a wall, or part of a roof, so we had to shove it away with a pole we had found on shore.

Dad took the first shift. After about five minutes he leaned over and brought up breakfast. He stood with his hands on his knees for a while, Travis letting the engine idle.

"You okay, Manny?" he asked.

"I've never been less okay in my life. But, yeah, we can go on. Travis, take it *slow*, okay? I can't bear the thought of running over one of these people."

"You got it, my friend. All ahead, extremely slow."

And that's how we did it. It would have been slow in any case, but with all the obstructions and the time we took to gently pole the corpses out of the way, a trip that would have taken maybe ten minutes under normal conditions took us a full three hours. I kept thinking that human beings shouldn't have to do what I was doing. Nobody should have to pole their way through the River Styx, Hell on Earth.

Finally, *Scrooge* began lurching and tilting, and we were moving up onto land again. Mom and Dad were looking at the GPS map and comparing it to the reality, and pointing out just how much of the barrier island had been swept away.

"It's a whole different landscape," Dad said, staring around in wonder and horror. "It looks like the wave just sucked half of it away."

We made fairly good time on our way over the remains of the three or four blocks to the hotel tower. Then we came to a pile of junk that looked like it wasn't going to be moved short of dynamite.

"Let's get out and walk around it," Dad said. It was easy to see that he was very afraid of what we'd find when we got there.

"You guys go," Travis said. "I don't want to leave the Duck alone. I'll see if I can find a way around. And don't forget your guns."

Mom and Dad and Dak got down, and handed me my rifle. Travis turned away and soon had driven around another heap of trash and was out of sight. The sound of the Duck engine, never very loud in the first place, faded away, and it got very quiet. Right where we were standing, normally the traffic would have been thick. Now, the cars that remained were topsy-turvy, including some that were buried in sand almost up to the roof. We stood there and listened, hearing nothing but seagulls, trying not to think about what they were feasting on, then moved cautiously through small gaps in the wreckage until the Blast-Off Tower came in sight.

It had been burned, but it had not been consumed.

There was an ugly black scar up the northwest side of the building, not far from the swimming pool, which had at least four cars in it. All the windows up to the fifth floor had been broken out. Furniture and rug scraps were hanging out of some of them.

The best news of all: Plywood storm shutters were in place around all the top floor rooms on the side we could see.

"Should we shout?" Mom asked.

"I don't know. Maybe she's moved on . . ."

A bullet hit the concrete about ten yards to our left and went whanging off into space. All of us hit the ground.

"Find some cover!" Dad was shouting. I noticed he was trying to shield Elizabeth with his body. I looked around for Mom, and saw Dak pulling her toward an overturned car. She was reaching out to me. I did some world-class scrambling and hunkered down behind a car, breathing hard.

"Is everybody okay?" I heard Dad call out.

Everybody said they were okay. Somebody shouted from the top of the building. It sounded like a woman, or a young boy.

"Who are y'all? If you don't mean us harm, then just keep moving. But if you want trouble, we got that, too."

"I'm Manny Garcia. That's my mom's hotel you're in. Who are you?"

"What did you say? Stand up so I can see you."

"You won't shoot me?"

"Mister, if I wanted to shoot you, you'd be dead. We don't want to hurt nobody don't ask for it."

Dad put his gun down on the ground and stood up from behind the wrecked car where he was crouching with Elizabeth. He held up his hands to show he was unarmed.

There was no sound for a while. I risked a look and saw a blonde head and shoulders and the barrel of a gun sticking out over a barricade of sandbags, way up there at the top of the tower. Then a second head appeared, this one gray.

"Manny?" Grandma called out. *"MANNY?"*

IT WASN'T EASY getting into Fortress Blast-Off, and that was no accident. There were fire stairs on each end of the tower, but one was partially collapsed. The other was blocked with a plywood wall at the second floor. Grandma said there were booby traps in that stairway, and it would take a few minutes to get through them.

Travis pulled up in *Scrooge* and we all went inside. The walls were crumbling, the floors were inches deep in sand and grit. Clothes still hung in the closets. There were big heaps of seaweed and the smell of salt water and dead fish. We went down to the stairway and waited.

Ten minutes later Grandma burst through the door and flew into Dad's arms. Mom moved into the embrace, then Elizabeth, and finally Grandma got an arm free and beckoned to me so I joined in, too. There were a lot of tears and a lot of joy, and I was grinning like a crazy person.

Then we trudged up the stairs, having to stop once while Dad got his wind back. Grandma seemed as spry as ever, wiry and burned even browner than usual. She's originally from up north, it was Granddad who was the Hispanic in the family. She was filthy, and her clothes were dirty, but so were we.

Finally, we made it to the top floor, and I was huffing and puffing, too. It was brighter up here. All the room doors were open, and the carpet and walls were dry. There was an odor of some disinfectant. The storm shutters had been made years ago with the idea of protecting the top floor from hurricane damage. Grandma and Aunt Maria could batten the whole thing down and ride it out up there.

The shutters were still there, but moved aside to allow some cooling breeze in. It was a fortress atmosphere, and no surprise: That's exactly what it was.

"First few days, everything was cool," Grandma was saying as we moved along the corridor. A couple of small children stood in the door and stared at us as we passed. They could have used a bath, but they had none of the hollow-eyed, lost look of the kids we'd seen in the soup lines.

"We had about 150 people up here on the top floor when it hit. We heard a little shooting, before. There's a story going around that the Dolphin was insisting on registered guests only, and some people didn't react well to that."

"It's hard to believe," Dad said.

"I know what you mean. What sort of people would do that?"

We had arrived at the far end of the hall, the end facing the sea, and we started up one more flight to the roof. We came out into the overcast day and looked around the roof. There were maybe thirty or thirty-five people up there. It looked a little like the refugee camps we had passed, but different. I mean, the people were filthy, and they had a sort of aura of shock still clinging to them, but they didn't seem lost. I later learned that, unlike most people who had lived or died on the ground, most of these people hadn't lost any loved ones. Most were registered guests, here from somewhere else, and their biggest worry was getting the news to their loved ones in Ohio or Alberta or Norway that they were okay. There were a fair number of children—the Blast-Off had always been child-friendly—the kids liked the spaceship theme.

Canvas had been strung to provide shade, which we didn't need at the moment. There was a big gas grill with several big pots simmering on it, attended by a man and a woman. The man wore a white chef's hat.

Grandma took us over to the railing, which had been backed up with a wall of sandbags four feet high.

"We'll never know about the Dolphin," Grandma said. She gestured to the north, where there was a huge pile of rubble. I realized it used to be the twenty-story Daytona Dolphin Hotel, one of the most luxurious in the area.

"We heard it go down. We were . . . we were hunkered down, of course, down below, but even with the sound of the wave, even then, there was no mistaking that sound. The most awful thing I ever . . ." She stopped, and gripped the railing hard. Dad put his arm around her and hugged her close. "Screaming," she said. "We could hear screaming, even over the wave. Or maybe that's just in my dreams. I don't want to have dreams anymore. I'm all through with dreams."

We all gazed out over the destruction. North and south, the relatively undamaged pinnacles of the big hotels and condos and apartment buildings. In between . . . nothing but piles of stuff, plumes of smoke here and there.

East, the river we already crossed. Enough said about that.

To the west, the beach was a lot closer than it had been a week ago, but it was no longer a thing you'd want to put in a tourist brochure. Boats and cars and flotsam and jetsam washed back and forth in the low surf. Farther out, unidentifiable objects tossed and rolled. Beyond that, an amazing number of boats and ships. Most distant was an aircraft carrier. I could see helicopters coming and going. Closer in, fishing boats and large private power boats.

"I don't think a single private boat on the Atlantic Coast survived the wave," Grandma was saying. "These are all people who came around from the Gulf. All the Gulf Coast, all the way around to Texas. They say it looked like Dunkirk, coming around the Keys. The largest private flotilla ever assembled, they say. Mostly volunteer."

If my stereo had been working I'd have googled Dunkirk. Later I learned it was a big evacuation from France during the Second World War.

"Everybody wanted to help, naturally. People are like that, after a disaster."

"Americans will always come through," Travis said.

"Shame on you, Travis," Grandma said, with some heat. "All people are like that. We even met a family from Mexico who came to help. We don't have any news, so I don't know what's going on in the world, but I'll bet you a thousand worthless dollars everybody's doing everything they can, *everywhere*. All those islands, Cuba, I don't even know who all got hit."

"I won't take that bet," Travis said, "and I was out of line, I'm sorry I said it. It's just . . ." He waved his hand all around. "I wonder how America is ever going to recover from this."

"If it's this bad all the way to Long Island, like I been hearing, I don't know, either. I mean, I guess California will get along okay, Illinois, Texas. But I don't know how Florida is ever going to recover."

Nobody had anything useful to say about that. Time would tell.

"Anyway, all those folks trying to help, and they haven't been able to do much good. Not here, anyway. I don't know about other places, I've had my own wars to fight. You'd be amazed how quick it can come down to us against them. Family against everybody else."

AT FIRST SHE didn't talk about the wave itself hardly at all. "It came up to the seventh floor," was all she would say.

We were sitting under one of the canvas shelters, a light drizzle coming down, while Jorge, who had been the restaurant cook—and I guess still was—served us a hot breakfast. Grits, powdered eggs and potato flakes, and Spam. Sounds dreadful, but Jorge made the eggs special with peppers and salsa, and the potatoes had melted cheese.

"It took a long time for the water to go down," she said. "Hours. A couple hours, I don't know. We went down, floor by floor, watching everything get swept by us. We saw a few people still alive, holding on to wreckage. We tried throwing them ropes, but we never reached anybody. One man, saw he was about to be swept out to sea, he tried to swim for it. He got about halfway to us . . . the water pulled him away, then it pulled him down. We never saw him again."

She had to stop for a while. She did that a lot. Nobody pressed her.

When the water receded enough that they could wade, they ventured out and started searching. They pulled three people from the wreckage, all of them injured to one degree or another. One of them died later. Considering everything, they felt they'd done a pretty good job. They had set up an infirmary in one of the top-floor rooms and done what they could with the first-aid supplies. One of her guests was a nurse, so the injured were getting pretty good care.

"Is that where Aunt Maria is?" Dad asked, at this point. "I know she was sick . . ." He stopped when he saw the expression on her face.

"Maria didn't make it, Manny."

"What . . . I thought you said . . ." He couldn't make any sense of it. Grandma put her hand on his arm.

"It was on the third day," she said, quietly. "You know her heart was bad. What happened, after the wave hit . . . she just lay down in her bed and never got up again. I think she had several heart attacks. It was just too awful for her."

I had liked my aunt Maria when I was a child. She always had sweets she had baked for us. She liked to cook, and she liked to eat, and she had always been overweight, a tubby little brown woman with a Hispanic accent who spent most of her days sitting around the pool with her old friends, telling lies about the trip over from Cuba, many years ago, chattering in Spanish. She had worked hard all her life in the old motel, until Mom and Dad made a lot of money and bought it and expanded it, and she and Grandma could hire help to do all the hard work they used to do. She had loved the life of a well-off innkeeper, though she hardly ever bought anything. "I don't drive, and I don't need no fancy clothes or jewels," she told me. She never had any children of her own. "I'm saving it all and it will go to you niños when I'm gone."

I looked at Mom. "I didn't know Aunt Maria was that sick," I said.

"I guess I didn't, either, Ray," Mom said. "Betty, why—"

"It's complicated. She made me promise not to make a fuss to the family. She wanted to wait until she was better, then let you know."

Dad was still in shock, so Mom asked the question.

"Why didn't she get a transplant?"

Grandma sighed.

"I spent the last year convincing her. She was traditional, you know. Catholic, and superstitious. She didn't want somebody else's heart in her chest. Didn't seem right, she said, somebody else had to die for her to get a heart. As for getting a cloned one . . ."

"Oh, god," Dad said.

"Yeah. For one thing, they're illegal in the U.S., and on the one hand she could talk all day about those crooks in Tallahassee and Washington, part of her thought that if they said it was bad for you, it was bad. And the Church is against it. And we'd have had to travel. She doesn't like . . . she didn't like to travel much anymore. 'The trip from Cuba, that was enough for me,' I heard that all the time.

"But six months ago I finally persuaded her. We flew to China, they started the culture. We were due to go back next month, get the operation done. So, Manny, somewhere in Hong Kong a little piece of Maria is still alive. Her heart. I've been wondering what I'm going to do with it."

Dad was silent for a while.

"Where is she now? Where is Aunt Maria?"

Grandma looked at him sorrowfully.

"Manny . . ." Of course. I had realized it as soon as I heard she was dead, but it was harder for Dad. He grew up with her.

"That's what we've been doing. That's why we're all so dirty. Every day, out into the mess. Drag the bodies onto bedspreads, wrap them up, take a hair sample, put it in a baggie. We've got a pile of wallets and watches, a room full of clothes. We don't undress them anymore, they're too . . . it's nasty, and too much work. Nobody's ever going to know exactly how many people died out there. We say a little prayer and we set them on fire, and we go away. And we come back here and eat a meal of Spam à la Jorge, and go to bed and sleep like the dead."

SINCE DAY ONE they had been waving a sheet with a red cross painted on it every time a helicopter or a low-flying plane went over. So far, nobody had landed. Grandma was pretty angry about that.

"A few of these people, we don't get them to a hospital soon, I don't know if they'll live. I thought somebody would have showed up to medevac them out by now. I don't get it."

"They'll probably be here soon," Travis said. "They're making progress. What I heard, hospitals all the way to Ohio are already full of people. Not much elective surgery going on. If you aren't bleeding, they say you need to take care of yourself."

"Some of these people are bleeding."

"What can I say? There's too much work to go around. But the European ships are starting to arrive in force. South Americans. Some African nations. Cruise ships mostly rode it out, they're converting them to offshore hospitals. Something will happen in the next few days. I hope."

"Meantime," Dad said, "I want to get you out of here."

There was a long silence. Sometimes I think I understand Grandma better than Dad does, because what she said next didn't surprise me.

"I'm not going anywhere until all these people can come with me."

THE ARGUMENT WENT on for a while, but eventually it was only Dad who was arguing that Grandma get into the Duck and get out with us. Travis and Dak didn't contribute at all. Both of them seemed willing to stick it out as long as it took. Mom dropped out early, and so did Elizabeth. As for me, I wanted to go home more than anything I'd ever wanted in my life, but I knew deep down that you couldn't just ask Grandma to leave everything that had ever been important in her life, even if it was in ruins. She needed a little time.

But far more important, the people who had stuck with her after the water subsided had become a family to her, and she intended to stick with them until they had a place to go.

The only reasonable plan Dad came up with was to ferry everybody over to the mainland in groups, where they could join the refugee camps.

Travis spoke up for the first time, saying he was far from sure he had enough gas for that. He knew we had enough to get back out of the Red Zone, but thought there was a fair chance we'd be hoofing it the last miles back to Rancho Broussard. *Scrooge* was not a fuel-efficient vehicle.

"How about the gas in the generator here?" Dad asked.

"How about it, Betty," Travis said. "Didn't you say that was a diesel generator?"

"That's right. We've rationed it, and we've got enough for about another week."

"Unfortunately, the Duck won't burn diesel. What about water?"

"We're okay there. We're not heating what was in the water heater tank, and we've been throwing our sewage over the side. Preferably when there's some bad guy drunks down there. As long as we don't shower or bathe, we're good for another week." She rubbed at her dirty face, absently. "I'll admit, I got weak, we all get a pint of water once a day to wash our faces. Turns out that's a morale-raiser. I was about to do that when you guys arrived."

"How about this?" I said. Everybody looked at me. Damn. I hated that. "You said you have some people who shouldn't be moved. That doesn't make sense to me. Seems to me that if they're in bad shape, the best thing to do is take them to the mainland. They had a tent hospital over there."

"Not much of a hospital," Elizabeth said.

"Well, with all respect to your nurse, they probably have more stuff over there than we do here. How about it, Grandma? Are any of them in danger of dying?"

"I can answer that," somebody said. We all looked at a young black woman who spoke with a Haitian rhythm. Grandma introduced her as Elaine, the nurse.

"I've got three patients whose wounds are infected. I cleaned them up as well as I could, but some of them were lying in filthy water for a couple days. They need more help than I can give them, and they need it fast."

"Travis," Grandma asked, "can that crazy-looking thing make it to the mainland and back, and still have enough gas to get y'all home?"

"*Us* all home," Dad said.

"This is still my home, Manny, until all my guests are taken care of."

"We should be able to make one crossing," Travis allowed.

"Then let's do it."

TRAVIS AND DAK handled the ambulance ferry duty. We all helped manually operate the window-washing equipment on the side of the hotel to get the people to the ground, which was hard work but not nearly as hard as carrying stretcher cases down all those stairs. We all stood together and watched *Scrooge* roll off and lose itself in the heaps of debris.

Down there on what used to be the pool deck, thinking about the long walk back up the stairs, I noticed the big black scorch mark on the side of the building and remembered the night before, when we all worried the Blast-Off was on fire. I asked Grandma about it.

"Lots of bad boys out there," she said, looking up at the scorch. "We've been fighting a running battle with them since about Day Two."

"Who are they? Convicts?"

"Some of them. A couple boatloads rowed over early on, looking for loot. Hotel safes, luggage, cash in wallets, they'd take anything they could find. Street gangs, too. The bad survived along with the good.

"Later on, everybody started getting real hungry and thirsty, good *and* bad people. Some of them drank standing water, and now they're regretting it. Not much we can do to help the sick ones, and it breaks your heart.

"These people"—and she gestured up at the roof—"these people, we started out about half paying guests and half people who ran in off the streets when the alarms went off. It wasn't a huge rush, at first. You know how it goes. Don't believe it at first, then a building panic, then everybody's in their cars and in about five minutes there's wrecks on all the bridges, nobody's going *anywhere*. More running around, and then the pictures start coming in from the Bahamas.

"By then I was sort of organized. I got Mario and Hugo and we stood by the door with guns. 'Everybody's welcome!' I was shouting. 'Only don't trample each other! You have plenty of time to get to the top.' Couple of shots in the air and a good look at Mario and Hugo calmed them down. But first I sent everybody to the pantry in the restaurant, had everybody carry up a box of canned food.

"So you got people thinking it through and people who panic. Some guys came back and made a bunch of trips with food. Other people carried up big boxes of frozen steaks and chickens and veal and ribs, whatever they could grab. Saw one big fellow about to bust his gut humping six big boxes of ice cream up the stairs. Ice cream!

"There were three waves, each a little smaller. It was so *noisy*, Ray, you have no idea! Like a giant garbage grinder, everything crashing against everything else . . . and we still didn't know if the building was going to hold up, it just *lurched* when that first wave hit. It's a little off kilter now. I noticed that a beach ball, if you put it on the floor, it rolls into the southeast corner of a room now, water pools there if you spill it. But it seems solid enough.

"So after, there were three schools of thought. One group thought we ought to just sit tight and wait for the authorities to come rescue us. And eat my food and drink my water while we waited. Another bunch thought we all ought to leave and make our way inland. Safety in numbers, I guess. A couple guys appointed themselves leaders, and there was a fistfight, and I had to fire a couple more shots. Then there were those who didn't want to sit and wait for help and didn't want to wait until the leadership business was sorted out, either one. Those were the folks who had loved ones in other parts of the city. Some of those just took off on their own, which is a shame, because those that waited just a little longer, I sent them off with at least a bottle of water to drink.

"I never did see any of those folks again."

She stopped talking then. Just sort of ran down. I realized that Mom and Dad and Elizabeth were standing beside me. I hadn't heard them come up. Dad made a gesture to me, afraid to speak himself, I think.

"So what did you decide on?" I asked.

Grandma shook herself and looked around. Her shoulders sagged, and she looked older than her years for once.

"Everybody was free to go, of course. But nobody was welcome to stay and freeload, except the sick and injured. I still don't know if we all should have left. Maybe we could have got the stretcher cases over the water and out of the . . . what did you say they're calling it? The Red Zone? And if you think the river is choked now, you should have seen it right after the wave, before a week's worth of tides.

"I don't know. But in my heart I knew I had to stay, because there were people *hurting* out there. When the water went down for the last time, we could hear a few of them screaming.

"So, anybody who wanted to stay at the Blast-Off had to go on the rescue details. I'm not saying there was a lot of argument about that, at least not after the first twenty-four hours, when anybody could see that no help was coming anytime soon.

"It was scary at first, going down there. Remember, we didn't have a very clear idea of what had happened. So there we were, cut off, no communication until about Day Three, when somebody dropped some leaflets. All the time we were on the ground we kept looking and listening for that next wave.

"But you get used to that. Pretty quick, in fact. After you've pulled your first dozen bodies out of the shit, you start to wish another wave would come. Your whole world has turned into a toilet, literally, the *stench*, even before the bodies started to swell up and pop in the sun . . ."

Once again she seemed lost in the past, and I thought she wouldn't go on. But she did. In fact, she even laughed for a moment.

"Those idiots saved the steaks? Turns out it was a good thing. I mean, that first day, we ate well, and brother, we *needed* it. You know the kind of people we get. Lot of retired people. My age and older. Some of them pretty out of shape. None of them shirked. In fact, I had to make one old guy stop working when his wife came to me and told me about his heart condition.

"Some people couldn't eat at first, of course, or couldn't keep anything down. But hunger gets everybody soon enough. We didn't have much steak or chicken left by the time it was getting too ripe to take a chance on. Since then it's been rice and beans and Spam and creamed corn."

"What on Earth were you doing, stocking Spam, Mom?" Dad asked. "I don't remember it on the menu at the restaurant."

"Oh, silly old me, that was hurricane supplies, Manny. We didn't have any canned meat at all in the restaurant, as you well know, except a lot of tuna fish. We even have mayo, but no bread to put it on. No problem, though. Jorge had his spices and his pots and pans. You'll be amazed at the stuff he can whip up. Although I hope I never eat another bite of Spam in my life."

She smiled briefly again, then went on.

"I think it was about Day Three things began to get edgy. Three or Four; it got sort of hard to keep track. That's when the bad guys really started rampaging. At first it was just liquor and looting. We steered clear of each other. Then they started to get bolder. And hungrier. And some of those boys were just plain ornery in the first place.

"We had to give up the rescue operation and sort of pull up the drawbridge. So we boarded up and decided to just stay here until the food and water ran out. I figured that if we had to make a run for it, if help *still* hadn't come, at least we'd be healthier and better fed than those we came up against.

"But then it got really hard."

"What do you mean?" Dad asked.

"Remember fallout shelters? You dug a hole and stocked it with food and water for a few months. What do you think is the biggest problem having a fallout shelter?"

"Having the only one in the neighborhood," Mom said.

"What could you do? After the wave we took people in. Anybody who showed up. I still thought help would arrive in a few days, but I think I'd have let all comers in, anyway.

"Then there was a time when people were leaving, trying to find their way home. Others were staying, in other hotels, in condos. And food started to get scarce. That was bad enough, you hate to turn away hungry people. The last few days, hungry, thirsty people have been showing up downstairs, begging for food and water. Some of them are already sick from drinking bad water. I guess Americans just aren't used to the idea that water can be deadly, this isn't the third world. Yet, anyway.

"I've had to . . . ration. There's just no way I can turn away a woman and her three children without a drink of water. So, I've been handing out two liters of water and a bowl of rice to most of the people who show up. It's meant cutting our own rations, but what the heck?

"Still . . . I don't really know how long we can hold out. Does anybody know *anything*? Manny? Kelly? Did anybody give you any indication of when we might see some food and water delivered out here?"

Mom shrugged, helplessly.

"Nobody we talked to really knew anything. Everybody seemed to be digging in for the long haul, though."

I was angry, because I couldn't figure it out.

"Why don't they leave?" I asked. "I mean, there must be boats somewhere they could fix up. Make a raft, or something?"

"Some people have done that. I understand there's a sort of water taxi with a Boston Whaler people are rowing back and forth. But I don't think you realize how many people survived out here, Ramon. There's a lot of tall buildings along the coast, and most of them survived. The crossing is no picnic, either, which you know. Falling into that water is not something you want to do.

"But part of it is some kind of syndrome, I guess. Shock, grief, and sheer exhaustion. These people are dehydrated and weak, and a lot of them just sit there and moan, until thirst drives them to get up and look for water. They need food and water, first, and then they need medical help."

I remembered what I'd asked about at first, which was the bad guys, the ones who were responsible for the fire we saw last night.

"So people are pissed at you?" I asked. "Because they don't think a bowl of rice is enough?"

"No, the bastards who tried to fry us last night are guys who already had a grudge against us. The rats and cockroaches that come out of the swamp after a hurricane, only a lot more of them this time, both the lowlifes who were on the street and survived the hit and the inmates who didn't drown in their cells. Ask yourself this. You're the warden at a big penitentiary, like Raiford, and you hear the government telling you the biggest wave anybody's ever seen is headed your way. Now, I don't know for sure, but I don't think a lot of high-security pens are located very close to the ocean, beachfront prices being what they are. But there's bound to be some, we've got so damn many prisons in this country.

Then you got your medium-security places, and your city jails. If you're the warden, and your jail is only two or three stories high . . . what are you going to do?"

It was a tough one, I had to admit. Pick and choose? Let the ones go who were in for drugs or embezzlement, keep the ones who were murderers locked up? And what about the criminally insane?

"There was this dude calls himself 'The Humongous'—which is a laugh, since this dude is six-six, maybe 120 pounds he's so eaten up with the speed. We'd heard from the survivors at the Sea Breezes that his gang had raped about a dozen women there, and killed one of them and two men. So we were ready for them when they roared up on their big hogs.

"I was on the fourth floor with my bullhorn. I told them to get their sorry asses off of my patio. They laughed, and headed for the stairs. So I started putting rounds through their gas tanks. That got their attention. They fired back, but this was . . . Day Four? Day Five? Whatever, by then they still had plenty of guns but were having trouble finding ammunition. They fired a few rounds, but when they saw they wouldn't be able to get at us without being in my field of fire for way too long, they hightailed it.

"We didn't see them here again until last night. They're pretty cowardly, they only operate in gangs, and only when the numbers are in their favor. They managed to stack a lot of lumber against the side of the building and we didn't hear them. It gets *dark* out there at night, now, and we don't waste power to run any lights down there. Have to change that. Anyway, they poured gas on it and set it on fire.

"Big mistake, tactically. When we saw the light, we could see *them*. I'm afraid I got a little angry. I didn't see any bikes around this time. So I shot at Humongous. I was aiming at his arm, a pretty thin target from the roof, let me tell you. And the little turd moved at exactly the wrong moment . . ." She stopped. She took a deep breath.

"I think I killed him, Manny."

"Jesus Christ, Mom," Dad said. "He was trying to burn you out. If you'd tried to escape, he'd have killed you. If ever there was a justifiable homicide . . ."

"I'm not worried about the legal part, Manny. You see any cops around here? And you think any of my people here would testify against me? I'm not even sure I killed him. His pals dragged him off, and it was too dark for me to tell much. But I know I got him in the chest, and if he is alive, he'd better get to a hospital real quick."

"In any case," Mom said, "it's over and done with, Betty. There's not one of us here who wouldn't have done the same thing."

"That's not it. I know it was justified. I know if I hadn't done it, somebody else would have, either vigilantes, or the Army if they ever get here, or the cops would have arrested him, and there's plenty of witnesses to the capital crimes he's committed . . . and I have a feeling that order's going to be restored here a lot quicker than law, if you know what I'm saying."

"I'd guess there's going to be some quick trials and speedy hangings," Dad said. "And that's my point, Mom. That's already started. On our way here we saw some of it. By now there may be a bad guy hanging from every lamppost that survived the wave. What you did . . . it doesn't even compare."

"It doesn't have to!" Grandma shouted. "I know it was an accident, and even if it wasn't, I know it was justified. It's *me*! It's *killing*! I've never done it, I never wanted to, and I don't like it, even a bastard like . . . whatever that pathetic man's real name was. I was hoping I could get through this without having to kill someone. I'm good, you know that. A good shot, I mean. I figured that, came to it, I could always put a round through a shoulder or a kneecap. Something with some stopping power. I know I could have done that and never lost a minute's sleep."

She *was* good. She was way more than good. Grandma had won a lot of trophies, and even went to the Olympics one year. If you asked her to shoot that fly sitting on that can over there thirty feet away, she'd ask you if you wanted a head shot or if just cutting off a wing was enough.

"I've always liked guns and shooting. But I never hunted after one time when I killed a deer. I'm a shooter, I'm a *markswoman*, and I'm proud of it. It's the discipline I like . . . and the sense of assurance you get when you know you can protect yourself. But I'm not a gun nut. Am I, Manny? I mean, I own a couple of handguns, and six target rifles, but I don't have a shotgun. . . . No, wait a minute, I think I do, that one I bought for skeet shooting. But I haven't used it in years."

That was true. Grandma had tried skeet for a while, decided it was too easy. Shotguns? Why not use a flamethrower? she said.

"That makes . . . eight guns. No, nine. Does that make me a gun nut? Does that make me a killer?"

"No, Mom," Dad said, gently. "By Florida standards, I think that qualifies you as unarmed."

"It's right there in the Florida law, Betty," Mom said, solemnly. "Less than ten firearms means you're a bleeding heart liberal."

Grandma laughed, but there was no humor in it.

"But I'm not a killer. I'm having a hard time dealing with it. And if this doesn't end soon, I may have to do more of it."

"We're here now, Mom," Dad said, patting her back. "You won't have to shoot anybody else. If it comes to it, *I'll* shoot them."

"Me, too," Elizabeth said.

"Damn right," Mom said.

I felt I ought to say something sufficiently bloodthirsty, too, but Grandma smiled, shaking off her momentary weakness.

"Anyway," she said, sniffing and wiping her nose, "you have to be prepared. I'd already strung a hose to the pool. It's still down there, under all that floating crap. One of my people, Jerry, is an engineer, and he managed to hook the pump into the fire-fighting system. We weren't thinking arson, we were remembering seeing three other buildings go up. So we just soaked it down from a hose on the sixth floor and pretty soon it was out. We heard them driving away, and it didn't sound like there were many bikes left. I hope not, anyway. I hope we've seen the last of them."

10

★ ★ ★

TRAVIS AND DAK returned that afternoon with no real news. The military were getting information over their own radio system, but they weren't passing it on.

"I tried chatting up a few of the officers," Travis said. "My name still carries some weight. Didn't get anywhere. Some of them acted a little scared, though."

"Scared of what?" Mom asked.

"Rumors floating around, no idea how reliable they are, probably not very. Stories about civilians attacking food convoys, riots here and there. Troops firing on crowds. Nobody understands why there haven't been airdrops, more choppers to bring out the seriously wounded. Hell, to bring out everybody."

"Myself, I don't think most people have grasped just how big this is," Dak said. "People stuck in here, they just know it's bad as far as they can see."

"What are you saying, Dak?" Dad asked.

"I'm saying there just ain't enough choppers, and there ain't enough big cargo planes for the airdrops or the evacuation flights. We heard that's happening some places. But it's two thousand miles of coastline, and the river estuaries up to a hundred miles inland, all of that got hit hard. I'm saying they just ain't got around to us yet."

"So be patient, right?" Grandma said.

"Not much else we can do."

THE NEXT MORNING we woke up to the roar of airplanes. I ran out onto my balcony and was in time to see a flight of three olive green cargo carriers flying fairly low and slow, north to south, right over the beach. As I watched, something fell out of the open cargo bay in the back of one of them, a bright orange cylinder. It quickly sprouted an orange parachute and began drifting to the ground.

By the time I reached the roof Elizabeth and Grandma were already there, along with a dozen of the residents whose names I didn't know yet. There was excitement, some cheering, as more chutes opened. We all watched as one hit the ground about a block away from us.

"I'm going to check it out," Travis said.

"I'll go with you," I said, immediately. Travis looked at me, then at Dad. Dad hesitated a moment, then nodded.

"Me, too," he said.

So we hurried down the stairs, each of us armed and with a canteen strapped to our belts, and I noticed it was easier than it had been the day before. Even Dad was moving a little better.

The delivery had landed about twenty yards from what had been Atlantic Avenue, on a stack of debris. There were three men there already, wrestling it down toward the meandering north–south path that had been cleared in the wreckage, and that made travel possible at all.

One of the guys took out a huge hunting knife when he saw us, or maybe he took it out and then saw us. I saw Travis's hand go toward his gun. The three guys eyed us suspiciously. Neighborliness was pretty much dead in that part of Florida, and those guys knew that three guns trumped one knife.

"We'll share," the guy said.

Travis smiled at them. "Take it easy. We don't want it, we just want to see what's going on. We'll even give you a hand."

They looked dubious, but then the guy bent over and started cutting the parachute shrouds with the knife. Travis clambered up and helped.

The capsule was two plastic clamshells making a cylinder about ten feet long and four feet in diameter. It was heavy. Travis tossed the shroud ends to me and Dad, and we pulled as the others pushed, and it finally rolled down to level ground. Everyone gathered around it.

It was embossed with the symbol for the International Red Cross. We found instructions for opening it in French, Spanish, Chinese, and about five other languages until we rolled it slightly and found the instructions in English. It opened fairly easily. What wasn't so easy was figuring out what was inside. Travis spoke for us all.

"What the fuck?"

The biggest items in there were nested panels of blue plastic, about three by seven feet. There were other odd-shaped pieces of plastic, too, some white and some blue. Then there were some gallon bottles of a very bright blue liquid. We pulled some of this stuff out, and it finally began to make sense.

"Port-a-potties," one of the other men said. "We got a delivery of about half a dozen do-it-yourself crappers."

Nobody said anything about that for a moment. The disappointment was pretty severe. Then one of the men started to laugh, and there was just nothing to do but join him.

"What's in that cardboard box over there?" one of them asked. Another pulled it out and opened it. There were rolls of white paper in it.

"Well, boys, we got about a hundred rolls of asswipes, too."

We laughed even harder, so hard it hurt.

After that, we were all buddies. They were Wright, who was an accountant, Richard, who did something in the city government—"And will again, if I can find any city government"—and Lou, who was a fisherman who had come around in his boat to help out and search for his sister, ran into something big and hard as he tried to steer into the river, and almost drowned when his boat went down.

We used Travis's pocket radio—badly in need of recharging—to tell the girls back home of our find, and that we were going to walk down the beach a bit and see if anything more useful than toilets had been air-dropped.

The next capsule was already surrounded by a dozen people. We got it down, got it open, and were staring at a whole lot of heavy-duty ten-pound canvas sacks of dry rice.

A couple of people just seemed to snap. There was a scramble, and the rest of them, not wanting to miss out, started grabbing for the bags, too. Without thinking about it, I aimed my gun in the air and fired it. Everyone froze, and Dad looked startled. I kept my gun pointing at the sky and my finger on the trigger.

"Let's try to pretend we're not animals, okay?" I said. "There's enough here for everybody. Why don't we form a line or something? We'll share it out."

There was some muttering, but nobody pulled a gun. I thought it was over, then some guy had to speak up.

"I know who you are. You're with that bunch on top of the Blast-Off. The one with that trigger-happy bitch in charge. Why should you get—"

He didn't finish his sentence, as there was another gunshot and a hole appeared in the broken asphalt a few inches from his foot.

"You go to the end of the line, asshole," Travis said. He held his pistol negligently at his side, but that's where it had been before he fired, too. "That bitch has been feeding starving people. Who have you been feeding?"

The guy didn't have anything to say to that. I looked at him and wondered what he had been before. A troublemaker? Or just a hungry, desperate man looking for someone to blame? Whatever, I figured him for a whiner. Nobody else had complained.

"We're not taking anything," Travis went on. "But we're not going to put up with any shit, either. So let's divvy it up, okay?"

Nobody had any problem with that. We all gathered around and divided it equally. In fact, when more people arrived everyone agreed that each person would get one sack of rice until it was all gone.

"Be sure to boil your water," Travis said to everybody who came by. "And sterilize your cooking pots." When we got to the bottom of the capsule we found small bottles of water purifier with instructions in Spanish. Somebody translated the words, which were simple enough, and we passed them on to new arrivals until it was all gone.

Some of the new people were carrying sacks with silvery MREs, military field rations, that they said had been in the next capsule down the beach. Some swapping was done, rumors were exchanged, and in general people seemed a little more optimistic than they had been.

None of the rumors amounted to much. One I remembered was that the President had been assassinated, and a state of martial law had been declared in Florida and Georgia and maybe the Carolinas.

Who knows?

NOTHING MUCH HAPPENED the next day. Just another typical day in Hell.

ON THE NEXT day, more planes. More capsules dropped. Then a huge hovercraft shoved itself ashore no more than a quarter mile from us.

I wanted to go, but sexual equality trumped me. Mom and Elizabeth went with Travis and Dak, and there wasn't anything I could do about it.

I watched from the roof. A ramp came down and some heavy military vehicles rolled ashore, along with about a hundred people in some sort of military uniforms. I later learned they were part of something called the Asian Compassion Corps, and they'd been waiting offshore for five days while sovereignty issues were ironed out. America, which has had troops posted in other countries for almost a century, and which was currently involved in fighting either five or six wars against terrorism, depending on who was counting, was not used to accepting foreign troops on its own soil. America, which had always been generous with aid to other countries experiencing a natural disaster or the aftermath of war, had little experience in accepting such aid. There were no bureaucratic mechanisms for it. Lots of people in Congress, which had been reduced to a sort of traveling road show meeting in hotel convention centers around the country on a day-by-day basis, were opposed to the whole idea. They even had a name for themselves: the Go-It-Aloners. The GIAs had even blocked the arrival of the units of the ACC for twenty-four hours due to a dispute about what they were going to call themselves. I don't even want to think about how many injured survivors died in that time. Originally they were going to be the Asian Aid Force. The GIAs didn't like that word "force." This was after all the bullshit about what kind of weapons the AAF, later the ACC, could carry. When they arrived at Daytona, each soldier was carrying only a rifle.

These troops were from India, but there were others from Indonesia, Vietnam, China, and most of the smaller countries in the area. In fact, most of the countries in the world that could afford to give any kind of aid at all were doing as much as they could. The British and French were dealing with what was left of the Bahamas, and with the Caribbean islands.

The Indian soldiers of the ACC prepared a beachhead and started unloading supplies from an offshore cargo ship crammed to the scuppers, or whatever you cram a ship to, with the stuff the horrified people of India had scrounged up to give to starving, hurting American children. By that evening many of the isolated residents of what had been Daytona Beach's exclusive beach communities were gathered around a roaring fire wearing brightly colored saris and baggy pants, eating fresh-baked chapatis, and saying "Please pass the curry."

And they were clean. One of the first things off the boat was a desalinization plant of the sort India had deployed to seaside villages all over the subcontinent. In a jiffy, or two jiffies at the most, a simple canvas structure had been erected and there were long lines of people munching fiery Gujarati burritos filled with meat they weren't sure they could identify and didn't want to. I was in that line, and was given a tiny bar of soap wrapped in paper that had TAJ MAHAL HOTEL, MUMBAI printed in gold lettering.

A polite officer in a red turban showed up at the Blast-Off with a truck and five smiling men dispensing chocolate candy to all comers, and carrying what proved to be a cell phone transmitter, which they wanted to set up on our roof. Grandma welcomed them in, and we all watched as they set it up. Almost exactly at midnight one of them gave a thumbs-up, and I put on my stereo, and was connected again.

SO WE STARTED to learn stuff.

Gosh, where do I begin?

First, the President hadn't been assassinated. Not for sure, anyway. If he had, it had happened someplace where there were no cameras to catch the act, and so it didn't count. The best I could determine was that nobody knew where he was, for security reasons, and something that looked very much like him was delivering daily broadcast speeches that were compassionate, defiant, determined, optimistic, worried, reassuring, comforting, and angry, sometimes all at the same time.

Most people seemed to believe that he was alive, but the web being the web, rumors abounded. We had long passed the point where you could rely on anything that was shown on video. It was child's play to morph a face onto a cyberframe and have it do and say anything you damn well wanted it to say. The software came built into your stereo. Until he appeared in public before a large crowd, in the open, all bets were off, and it didn't seem like he was going to do that anytime soon. A tour of the stricken areas had been planned, announced, and canceled at least five times since the disaster, adding to the impression that the government was running around and around in circles without the faintest idea of how to handle a crisis of this magnitude.

National Guard troops from the West Coast had been pulled back from the disaster area and redeployed to contain an uprising in Idaho, where various groups of crazies from white supremacists to millennialists to libertarians had united and decided the time was ripe to overthrow the federal government. Troops were said to be on the verge of retaking Boise.

Martial law had indeed been declared in Florida, Georgia, and the Carolinas. Also in Virginia, Maryland, the District of Columbia, Delaware, New Jersey, New York, Connecticut, Rhode Island, and Massachusetts. The offices of governor in those states had been suspended for the duration, and the governors themselves appointed as Federal Disaster Relief Coordinators for their states, except in Georgia, where the governor had refused and had been arrested, whereabouts unknown. A gun battle had erupted on the floor of the Georgia State Senate in Atlanta, killing three Democrats and one Republican and one page, age fifteen. All police agencies in the affected states had been nationalized.

Some of this just seemed to be formalizing a situation that looked as if it had already existed when we made our way into the Red Zone. To me, military was military, no matter what uniforms they wore, whether they were soldiers or cops, but the American people were deeply disturbed by all this, both the left and the right.

Me, I'm a Martian, I don't know much about government. Maybe we should get ourselves one someday. Mom says so, but from seeing how well they work on Earth I'm dubious.

Then there were the Rapturists.

In various places all over America, but more in the South, huge numbers of people had gathered in churches and stadiums and even in open fields to wait for the Rapture. I googled it and . . . well, frankly, it was almost impossible to believe that people bought into it, but apparently millions did. They thought this was the time of the Biblical Apocalypse. They were waiting for the forces of Satan—an actual army, I gathered, with tanks and airplanes and probably atomic bombs—to attack America. Then they expected Jesus to appear and win the battle, and for everyone to be bodily taken up into Heaven.

Most of those millions of Rapturists thought it was pointless to help out the victims of the wave. Jesus would be here soon, and he would take care of them. At the same time, these were the very people who were most opposed to accepting any international help. They were worried that the forces of Satan would disguise themselves in these foreign armies. That, or the armies *themselves* were the forces of Satan. It didn't help that most of the countries trying to help out weren't Christian.

I didn't pay much attention to the economic news, but Mom did, and summed it up for us. Not frequently; once the stereos came back on she spent many, many hours managing our accounts and assets. But she'd give us reports now and then, and mostly she was smiling.

Bottom line: We weren't broke. We had taken a hit, but almost everyone had, and some were way, way worse off than we were.

"Short of the end of civilization, the end of all economic activity," she told us, "there is nothing that can happen that doesn't benefit someone in the pocketbook."

I asked her who would benefit from something as horrible as this, and she pointed out something so obvious I felt stupid for not thinking of it.

"The people who make modular housing. So I'm putting a lot of our money into the Martel Corporation."

I think I may have actually gasped. I could hardly have been more surprised if she had said she planned to sell Elizabeth into white slavery so she could buy a new dress. She hates the Martels that much.

"I know. But there's something you may not know about them. They've been at work on cheap, prefab structures like the rooms in those awful hotels back home. They can make a cheaper model that doesn't have to stand up to Mars low pressure and temperature and be turning them out by the thousands almost overnight. Better than your standard Red Cross tent, and hook several of them together and you have a house.

"So, the company comes off looking good at both ends of this crisis. Short-term with those damn Martel rooms, long-term with housing that's cheap and goes up quickly and is actually nice to live in.

"Plus, if they're busy putting the things up down here, maybe they won't have a lot of time to plant more of them back home."

Mom's mind works in funny ways, but sometimes you just have to admire how she could manage to get three things done at once.

NOT THAT MOM was having an easy time of it. The New York stock exchanges were shut down, not because they couldn't open up—their data was stored multiple places, so what had happened to Wall Street the place didn't *have* to have affected what happened to Wall Street the institution—but because everybody was afraid to allow trading to begin again. Too many of the stocks traded there had gone belly-up, and a huge number of others were in a sort of financial limbo. Nobody knew what their shares were worth, but everybody thought a lot of them were probably more useful for starting fires than selling for cash money.

Some of the other big financial markets had suspended trading, too, but a few were open, and trading was brisk, according to Mom. She was spending a lot of her time watching quotes from Shanghai, Kuala Lumpur, and St. Petersburg. Futures, bonds, shares, funds, all sorts of things we hadn't covered much in economics class, or that I hadn't paid much attention to, or that I flat out didn't understand.

I saw on my own stereo that gold was at an all-time high, hard to even buy at all, and expected to go higher.

"Do we have any gold, Mom?" I asked her.

"Yes, honey, we have some gold. I bought as much as we could before we even left Mars."

"That's good, then."

"Yes, dear, that's good." I felt like a puppy who had learned sit up but
wasn't quite ready for roll over, so I didn't ask her about any more details.

One of the many things nobody knew for sure was just how much
the damages would add up to and how much of it was insured. I read es-
timates as low as 5 trillion euros, ranging up to 40 trillion. This was *way*
bigger than the entire gross economic product of the EU.

None of which mattered much to me. I'm sorry, I just didn't have it
in me to worry much about the state of the economy of another planet.
My planet had one industry, and that was tourism, and short of total
economic collapse tourism will always do okay. Somebody, somewhere,
will have extra money to spend. Mom agreed with me. She didn't expect
a lot of softness in the tourism business.

Not on Mars, anyway, though Florida was sure going to suffer for a
while.

I hope I don't sound cold. I hurt a *lot*, seeing people who had lost all
their worldly possessions. And I felt sympathy for those who lived in
other places and had lost their money, some of them *all* their money.
But there's only one way to deal with that. You see it time after time in
news coverage after a tornado has swept through, or an earthquake.
They interview the survivors, and they take comfort that at least they're
alive. That's what you had to do. Weep for your dead, recover what you
can, take a deep breath, and move on. You draw closer to your family
and your friends, and you do what you need to do. I didn't know that
before, I'd never faced adversity—wasn't facing it yet—but I felt I had
a better understanding of it. None of the people at the Blast-Off were
despairing, nobody had given up.

TWO DAYS AFTER that a bridge was repaired to the mainland, and an
unlikely visitor dropped by the Blast-Off. He introduced himself to
Grandma as Alberto Juarez. He was Cuban-American, short and potbel-
lied and brown-skinned, bald with a neat little mustache. He was

dressed in a wrinkled lightweight suit, sweating profusely, and carried a briefcase. We were still suspicious of strangers, though we were no longer meeting them with guns, but this guy looked about as harmless as anyone could look.

He was an insurance man.

Grandma laughed when she heard that, and swept her arm around to indicate the chaos all around us. We were standing on the pool deck, which was mostly cleared; but there was plenty of devastation to see, in any direction you wanted to look.

"Well, Mr. Juarez, you look like you could use a drink. We've got a few beers and Cokes left, and we started up our ice machine yesterday, now that we've got some water. You want a cold one?"

"I'd kill for a cold beer," he admitted.

We sat around on salvaged lawn furniture, a table and slightly askew umbrella and four mismatched chairs, none of which had originally belonged to the hotel, me and Grandma and Elizabeth and Mr. Juarez, and all had drinks.

Mr. Juarez savored his, smiled, and then set his briefcase on the table, opened it, and booted it up. His smile went away as he did that.

"I'm afraid I don't have any good news for you, Mrs. . . . ."

"Call me Betty," Grandma said. "Go ahead, tell me how you're getting out of this, Mr. Juarez. Some clause about acts of God? Not covered for floods? Did I miss a premium?"

"Nothing like that," he said. He was uncomfortable. "You're covered, the policy is clear on that. The problem is, you're covered by a corporation that hardly exists anymore. The company is bankrupt, in receivership, technically owned now by a bank that may not even exist itself. That's all up in the air."

"Just about everything is," Grandma said. "Go on."

He sighed.

"The long and the short of it is, you have a legal contract, but good luck trying to enforce it. One day, when this is all straightened out, a court will probably award you five or six cents on the dollar. You will have legal recourse, I imagine . . . or, at least, when this martial law business is over and the courts get running again."

"Save your breath, Mr. Juarez. No use trying to get blood out of a turnip. I found that out way back, when this was a dump and somebody stiffed me for the room with bad plastic. I understand the reality here. I would like to know something, though."

"Anything I can tell you, I'd be happy to."

"Where are you from?"

"I'm out of the Tampa office. I'd have been here sooner but . . . you know. It's been difficult."

"What are you doing here?"

"Excuse me?"

"Your company is dead. You don't have a job anymore. There was no need to come all the way out here to tell me I ain't got shit. I knew that."

The little man drew himself up and looked Grandma in the eye.

"One does what one has to do. It's true I'm out of a job, but I'll find work. A bunch of us from the office came over and have been volunteering in the Red Zone. We've done this before, but not on this scale, of course. I've been to a hundred disaster sites, often we're there before the ground has stopped shaking or the wind has stopped blowing. I don't know what you think of me, or of my company, but I've been feeling deep shame. People are usually glad to see me. I enjoyed that, doing what I could do to help. I can't do that now, but I feel I owe it to as many people as I can locate to tell them the bad news in person. I know it isn't much, but maybe it helps, just a little, to get people to realize just what their situation is, with no false hopes.

"On the other hand, maybe it's a mistake, perhaps it would be better to leave them with something to hang on to. I've been wondering about that."

"No, Mr. Juarez," Grandma said. "I've always believed that bad news should be delivered as quickly as possible. It ain't going to get any better with time."

Juarez shrugged.

"In any case, I feel it is my duty."

Grandma sighed deeply.

"Mr. Juarez, I confess that my opinion of insurance men has not been the highest in the past. I put them just a cut above lawyers and state senators. But you have made my day, and raised my opinion of your profession greatly. It's a pleasure to meet you."

"I thank you, ma'am. As you can imagine, my reception has not always been a warm one. Or at least, not warm in the way I would like."

"No, plenty of folks still like to kill the messenger. Listen, you look real tired. Why don't you stay for supper? We don't have much, but it's well prepared."

He stood and stretched to his full height, which wasn't much, and squared his shoulders to the extent they were squareable.

"I thank you very much, but I have a lot of work to do and must be on my way. I thank you for the beer."

"Looks like you've got enough work for the next few years, Mr. Juarez. It'll wait, and it won't be any worse after a good meal."

He wouldn't be persuaded, but he did accept another can of beer.

"Are you armed, Mr. Juarez?" Grandma asked.

He gave us a wry smile.

"No, I am not, ma'am. I've already been relieved of my stereo and an old watch that was of some sentimental value and which I was foolish to wear. Nobody wanted this obsolete briefcase. And who would bother to shoot an insurance man?"

He bid us good-bye, and I shook his hand before he left. We watched him pick his way along the partially cleared side street, consulting a crumpled paper list.

"Ray, Elizabeth . . . that's why we're going to get through this, in spite of the idiots running the show, in spite of the damn Rapturists. Because there's good men and women out there still doing their jobs."

I could only agree with her. You could say he was on a fool's errand, and if you did, I'd prefer not to meet you. Dad once told me that it wasn't laws that kept the world running, such as it was. It was things like honor, duty, perseverance, and keeping your word. Before long the whole devastated East Coast would be crawling with bureaucrats with papers to fill out, most of them not doing any more practical good than Mr. Juarez, and with considerably less dedication. But one day, it would all be sorted out. You had to believe that.

"So what are you going to do, Grandma?" Elizabeth asked.

"You mean now that I'm busted?" She leaned back in her chair and looked at the sky, and when she looked back she seemed happier than I'd seen her since we got there.

"Kids, number one, I'm not busted. At least, not from losing the hotel. The bank owned a big part of it, and I'll let them try to collect on their insurance. It's not important to me. Number two, as soon as the wave hit, I knew I was out of the hotel business. I was getting tired of it, anyway. I only stayed on because of your aunt Maria, and when she died . . . well, then I was even more sure." She tossed her empty beer can. "Oops! Littering's illegal." She wiped her hands.

"I'm out of here. The injured are in hospitals, there's only twenty or so still living on the top and they're welcome to stay or leave as it suits them. Authority has been reestablished, more or less. There's nothing else left for me to do here. Ray, go find your Dad and Mom and tell them that old stick-in-the-mud Grandma is ready to go, and ask them if they've got a closet or something I can stay in until I figure out what to do with the rest of my life. I always wondered about golf. Do you have golf up there?"

When we realized she meant she was going to Mars with us, Elizabeth and I both dragged her out of her chair and hugged and kissed her. Then we ran off to find everybody and tell them the news.

ONCE IT WAS decided, it didn't take long to get going.

Grandma had managed to take a few minutes to stuff a few boxes of personal items from her residence down on the bottom floor into the elevators full of food and supplies that were headed for the top floor, "just in case we lived." It didn't take long to load that stuff up.

There were six people who asked to hitch a ride with us, people who had been guests at the time of the wave. Since we weren't going to go by water, Travis said okay, but they could only take one suitcase each. One woman changed her mind rather than abandon her vacation wardrobe; everybody else was done packing in fifteen minutes after Grandma said to meet us by *Scrooge* in thirty.

We all piled in, and it was tight, but a few of us rode out on the hood. I was out there, scouting for tire hazards, but by retracing our route we soon found the cleared path leading to the repaired bridge, and in no time we were back on the mainland.

It's amazing what a little time and a lot of hard workers can do. It was difficult to believe that only a few days ago we'd had to blaze our own trail. Now there was a road cleared wide enough for traffic in two directions. Not that there was a lot of it, and what there was was all business: big trucks, bulldozers, cranes on flatbeds. It would be a long time before private vehicles were allowed back into the Red Zone. To each side all was still chaos. The road we drove on was cracked and rutted from the force of the wave, and ten miles per hour was a pretty bouncy pace, but other than getting out of the way of official traffic there was nothing to stop us.

We were at the Wal-Mart by early afternoon. It was a tent city now.

They had bulldozed the big parking lot and turned it into a soup kitchen and hospital, and in the back, big diesel generators powered half a dozen refrigerator trucks. Some of them contained frozen food for the kitchens, and others were full of bodies. The rooftop air conditioners were humming on the big box of the retail store, one of the most welcome sounds I know of in Florida, better by far than pounding surf.

"Good," Travis said. "We'll have a cool place to go to, maybe something cold to drink, while we wait for Jim and Evangeline."

We had made radio contact with them on the first two days at noon, and they'd had no news. On the third day they hadn't answered our calls, and we hadn't heard from them since. But Travis had promised them that we'd be here at noon one day, and it was about 2 P.M. now, so we were facing a twenty-two-hour wait.

They were probably okay. At least that's what I kept telling myself.

As Travis pulled into the lot, looking for a place to park, we drew a lot of stares. It's not every day you see a World War II amphibious DUKW on the streets, even in watery Florida. Maybe we were a comical sight. A lot of people smiled and whistled, gave us the thumbs-up. *Scrooge*, long, low, and waddling, was a vehicle you just sort of liked the minute you saw it.

I was the first one to notice a small boy running behind us. He put on a burst of speed and came alongside.

"Hey, mister, are you Travis Broussard?"

I whistled for Travis, told him to stop. He did, and the kid stopped and looked up at us, breathing hard. He was wearing a ragged Disney World T-shirt and new-looking sneakers. Just a tousle-headed Florida boy in the ruins.

"What is it?" I asked him.

"This guy gave me some money and told me to look out for a bunch of people in a duck. Is this piece-of-crap ride a duck?"

"It sure is," Travis said. "*Scrooge McDuck*, by name, even if it don't quack. Where is this guy?"

"Got any money?"

Travis cocked an eye at him, but Dak reached into his pocket and tossed a shiny gold ten-euro piece into the air. The kid snagged it.

"Highway robbery, dude. Now, you gonna tell us where they are, or do I have to come down there and lay one upside your head?"

"They in the hospital. C'mon, I'll show y'all."

NATURALLY WE WERE worried, but it wasn't bad. Jim Redmond had cut his hand pulling apart pieces of his uncle's house, looking for bodies. It had become infected and was swollen, but the doctors had it under control.

There were hugs all around. Evangeline's hug lasted longer than her dad's, and I didn't mind. Not at all.

We were introduced to Mr. Redmond's father, who was in a hospital bed with a broken leg and arm and various deep cuts. He was pretty deeply drugged, but managed a smile. We met a cousin, Frank, and an aunt, Billie Mae, who had a five-year-old with her. The child wasn't her own, just a stray she had picked up cowering in an overturned car beside the corpse of his mother. Now he wouldn't leave her.

I never did get all the names and relationships straight, we weren't there long enough to really talk to them all. The Redmond clan was large and complicated, and the news was not all good, not by any means. Of the nine people Jim and Evangeline knew to have been in the wave zone, these were the only ones he'd found, and counted himself lucky to have done so well . . . if you can call three out of nine good news. Of the others, four were on the confirmed dead list, and two were still missing.

What do you do? Rejoice over the living? Weep for the dead? You do both, and it isn't easy, it tears you apart. They all kept breaking down, thinking of those four bodies in reefer trucks somewhere. Then they'd embrace, happy to be alive and happy that not everyone had died. We were all included, we were all family now.

Finally, I couldn't take it anymore, broke away from the group, and wandered out of the hospital tent. The little guy who'd led us to the hospital was hanging around outside, playing with a yo-yo. I reached into my pocket and grabbed all the change I had in there and dumped it into his hand.

"Thanks, mister."

"What can you buy with that around here?"

"Not much," he conceded. "But I'm saving up, for later."

"How old are you?"

"Ten. Are you really a Marsman?"

"We prefer to call ourselves Martians, Earthling."

He laughed. "Cool. I've never met a Martian before."

"Where is . . . I mean, who's taking care of you?"

"They got me in the orphan cage until my mama shows up. But I busted out."

I wasn't going to touch that. The kid, whose name turned out to be Dustin, took me to the "orphan cage." It was a large area of the lot surrounded by a chain-link fence. Inside was a lot of brightly colored plastic play equipment, castles and playhouses and the like, and the fence had been painted gay colors with childish artwork pinned to it; but it still looked like what it was: a cage for children. A few children were on swings, and some others sat around a teacher who was reading them a story, but there was not the activity you expect from kids who ranged from toddlers to a bit older than Dustin. Mostly they sat listlessly or stood at the fence watching for their parents.

"You're leaving here soon, aren't you, Mr. Martian?"

"I'm Ray. Yeah, I'll be going soon."

"You see my mama, tell her I'm here, okay?"

"You got it." We exchanged numbers, he writing my info on a forearm already covered with notes like that. Then I shook his hand and got out of there before I lost it.

EVANGELINE AND HER father joined us at *Scrooge* as we prepared to shove off again. They were going back with us. Jim Redmond had a job, and Evangeline had school. The rest of his family were taken care of now, and would be staying to see to the remains of dead family members and await news on the missing. Jim's cousin Frank tried to prevail on him to stick around for the funerals, but Jim shook his head.

"I don't do funerals," he said. "Stopped going when I was in the Army. We'll remember them in our own way, Frank." That seemed to end it, and they all embraced, and we got on board. Travis livened it up a little by playing a tune on *Scrooge*'s horn, which, believe it or not, sounded a lot like what I imagined a duck's fart would sound. Everybody laughed through the tears. Mourning would go on, but recovery had begun.

As we waddled slowly down the road nobody was talking very much, and I had a lot of time to think about what we'd just done. One thing came to mind immediately. What good had we done? Did we really have to come here?

The short answer: Yes, we did.

Not for any practical, justifiable reason. It was easy to prove that we hadn't made much of a difference to anybody.

A month ago, I would have asked Dad to explain it to me, why I felt so good having done so little, when you got right down to it. We'd risked our lives, after all, the whole family. Was that *smart*?

Maybe it wasn't smart, but that's what human beings *do*. If there's a chance, ever so small, that you can do some good for your family, you *do* it. If there's even the smallest chance that, by *not* doing something, your family will suffer, then you don't allow that chance to pass.

It may be bad logic; but if you aren't prepared to drop everything and charge into danger when your loved ones are threatened, there's something missing in you. If you don't have anybody you'd do that for, or who would do that for you, I feel sorry for you and advise you to find more friends.

IT WAS ONLY a short trip down the road before we saw the tiger.

He was strapped to the hood of somebody's pickup truck with a lot of bullet holes in him, his rough pink tongue lolling out of his huge mouth. Flies were swarming around his eyes. Half a dozen people were gathered around him, laughing and talking. Two children were rubbing his orange-and-black fur.

"Sucker just came walking by, calm as you please," one of the men was saying to the others. "Hardly even looked at me. Scared the hell out of me, though, I don't mind telling you."

Travis had pulled over, and I jumped down from the hood. I wasn't really aware of what I was doing. My feet seemed to be leading a life of their own.

"No zoos around here I know of," another man said. "Probably somebody's pet. You ask me, people shouldn't be allowed to keep animals like that."

I was at the tiger now. I touched its head. The men fell silent.

I have no idea where it came from, or why there or why then, but I felt it rising up in me and it was unstoppable. Everything, just everything. I began to cry.

No, let's be honest here. This wasn't just a tight throat and a few tears leaking from my eyes. This was just short of bawling out loud like a baby. It was on me in an instant, and before I knew it I was sitting on the ground. It was a sobbing, wrenching, snotty-nosed cry, more appropriate to a two-year-old than a high school senior. And I couldn't seem to stop.

Humiliating? You bet. Soon I felt a pair of arms go around me and I looked up, unable to catch my breath, expecting to see Mom. But it was Evangeline, and soon Elizabeth was on my other side. They held me until I could breathe normally, and Evangeline used her sleeve, all she had available, to wipe my face before helping me to my feet. How wonderful. No better way into a girl's affections than to snivel and whine over a dead tiger, right? I wondered if I'd ever be able to look her in the eye again.

Nobody said anything. The guys around the truck were all doing other things, careful not to look my way. It wasn't the first time they'd witnessed a meltdown like that recently, and it wouldn't be the last. Maybe some of them had even had a moment like that themselves.

I got back on the hood with my back to the rest of my family, my legs hanging over the side.

"Ready to go, Ray?" Travis asked. I nodded without turning around, Travis gave a tiny beep of the horn, and we were on our way again.

WE WERE ABOUT five miles away from Rancho Broussard when we finally ran out of gas. Travis nursed *Scrooge* along another quarter mile, sputtering, then pulled to the side of the road and called ahead.

In a few minutes three heavy vehicles pulled up beside us and six heavily armed men got out and held the doors for us and loaded Grandma's stuff into the cargo spaces, and a few minutes after that we were driving through the gates and into a world of peace and quiet that hadn't been touched by the destroying waters.

A huge meal had been prepared, and we all sat down at the table. Some of my family dug in heartily, but I didn't have much appetite. Evangeline sat beside me, Mom on the other side, and I kept getting appraising glances from Mom when she thought I wasn't looking.

I'm okay, Mom, honest I am.

Then there was a long, hot shower, soaping and shampooing myself three times and still not feeling totally clean.

Then there was a big bed in the guest room, with clean satin sheets.

Home. Or close enough.

THE NEXT DAY we checked into the Swan and Dolphin at Disney Universe. The Redmond family was reunited, and of course the stories of what the brats had been doing had to be gotten out of the way before we could fill Mrs. Redmond in on *our* boring adventures. They had managed to destroy only a few odd corners of the resort, apparently. The fire crews had things in hand, the injured had been taken to hospitals, and early reports said the park might be open again in a few days.

We intended to stay there only a night or two until we could arrange a flight to the Falkland Islands to see Uncle Jubal. Usually, it's just a matter of calling him and telling him we're on the way. But for some reason, Jubal was not answering his phone.

The first day Travis kept getting excuses that had to do with the disaster. Distribution nodes down, lines too busy, not enough bandwidth with all the emergency channels operating. Bullshit like that. It sounded fishy to all of us, but there wasn't much we could do.

The second day I went with Elizabeth and Evangeline and the brats to a big water park and we rode the slides and surfed the waves all day. We'd explained over and over to the brats that you had to wear a bathing suit on Earth, but they kept forgetting. I spent half my time trying to locate their discarded duds.

The other half I spent admiring how good Evangeline looked in a bikini made of three scraps of orange cloth, none of which would have covered my palm. They had a great deal of trouble covering Evangeline, too, especially the top two, which had a lot to cover. The girls had bought them from a dispenser outside the changing rooms. When they came out they were giggling. I asked them what the joke was.

"Lots of flesh," Elizabeth said. "Earth girls are *fat*!"

"And I never saw so much pubic hair," Evangeline said. "Honest, three-quarters of them were bushy as . . ."

"Beavers?" Elizabeth said, and they collapsed laughing.

Martian girls depilate everything below the neck. The legs and underarms because that's just what girls do, and the rest because it provides a tighter seal for the sticky device that is needed for urination in a pressure suit. And it doesn't hurt so much when you rip it free.

Evangeline let me put suntan lotion on her back. I did it for Elizabeth, too, but it somehow wasn't the same. At six-two and six-one respectively, Elizabeth and Evangeline turned a lot of heads at the water park when they walked by. I tried to tell myself that I did, too, but the fact is my strength is a wiry strength, and many of the Earth boys bulged with muscles.

Okay, I'm skinny. The only interested glance I noticed was from a guy.

But it was a great day. All the blue, chlorinated water and blazing sunshine seemed to wash and burn away a lot of the memories of filth and decay and wretchedness of the last days, and the sight of all the people splashing around and having fun reminded me again that life goes on.

At times, it struck me as just plain *wrong*. But why shouldn't these people have fun? There just wasn't room for everybody in the United States to go to the Red Zone and help out. In fact, they were asking people to stay away. These people had probably planned their vacations months ago, put down deposits. The people who worked here, and in the other parks, had to make a living—and attendance was down, way down. The park wasn't crowded at all.

At the park's entrance there were barrels for canned food donations, overflowing, and a big clear plastic cube bulging with money. Nobody had forgotten.

Life has to go on. Doesn't it?

WHEN WE GOT back to the hotel room, still smelling of chlorine, Travis was stalking back and forth, cursing a blue streak. A lot of it was incoherent rage, but every once in a while he said something specific and eventually we figured out that he hadn't been able to get through to Jubal.

"One excuse after another," he shouted. "Overloaded circuits. *Bullshit!* Can't be reached. *Bullshit!* He has 'the flu.' *Bullshit!* Storms. Storms, for chrissake, and the planes can't land or take off. *What kind of fucking idiot do they think I am?*"

I knew the answer, and I think he did, too. They just didn't care. They—whoever "they" are, in this case the IPA—were so used to lying they did it reflexively, and didn't much care any more if anyone believed them. What were they going to do about it, anyway? They were the IPA, the *Power Company*. They ran the world.

Well, I thought they had picked the wrong enemy when they decided to fuck over Travis. Nobody fucked with Travis.

"All right, I'm chartering a plane, right now, and I'll fly the sucker down there myself. They can't do this to me, it's in our contract."

He was actually on his way out the door before Dad and Dak caught up with him and grabbed his arms and pulled him back into the room. They gentled him down some until he was willing to listen.

"They'll shoot you down, Travis," Dad said. "You know that."

Travis shook them off, but then he relaxed. He nodded.

"What kills me is, I can't figure out what they're up to."

"Some kind of security bullshit," Dak said. "That seems to cover everything."

"Yeah, but . . . why Jubal? Why are they doing this to him?"

*   *   *

WE WAITED AROUND for three more days. Travis never did get through to Jubal. On the fourth day he took off for Buenos Aires, and we boarded a spaceship to Mars.

The trip back was just another trip.

The weight gradually fell away. I spent most of the time aboard catching up with schoolwork, and with friends. Every day the time lag was less, until it was instantaneous again.

We talked to Travis every day. He rented a big boat and motored out to the Falklands, where he was met by an overflight of fighter planes firing across his bows, then a destroyer, which turned him back. It's a good thing Travis didn't have his own destroyer, or he might have started the Second Falklands War, and I'm not sure which side I would have bet on. But he did turn back.

Then we were on our way down, and on the train into town, and entering the familiar confines of the hotel.

I got back into my own room, which seemed somehow smaller. I dropped my suitcase on the floor.

Home.

11

★ ★ ★

SUMMERTIME ON MARS.

Yeah, right.

There is no logical explanation for why we have a "summer vacation" from school on Mars. There's an explanation; it's just not logical. The reason is, that's the way it's always been done.

Come to think of it, that's the explanation for a lot of human behavior, isn't it?

The actual Martian summer is determined by our distance from the sun, not by the tilt of the axis, as it is on Earth. The orbit of Mars is a lot more eccentric than Earth's so we go way out there and get cold, then come way in and get . . . well, less cold.

The virtual Martian summer begins when it's the end of May on Earth, when summer begins in the Northern Hemisphere. They tell me the reason schools break for summer on Earth is because that's when children have to be on hand for the planting, and later for the harvest. Which makes about as much sense as calling a holiday in December because that's when the mammoths come through on their annual migration, and we have to kill a few to smoke and store in our cave. Come on, it's the twenty-first century.

So it was August. Yeah, right.

The Martian year is longer than the Earth year. Almost twice as long: 697 Earth days. But we don't use Martian years. Nobody I know states their age in Mars years, we all use Earth years. Birthdays are on the Earth calendar, and so is just about everything else. We can't keep Earth time, but we do the next best thing. We run on a twenty-four-hour clock, and use the same minutes and seconds as you do on Earth.

. . . but wait. How can that be? The Martian day is twenty-four hours thirty-nine minutes, and thirty-five seconds. So how do we deal with the extra minutes?

Simple. We ignore them.

It's a messy solution to a messy situation, but the fact is that Mars is a very tiny cultural tail wagging behind a very big dog, which is Earth. In many ways, what's happening on Earth is more important than what's happening on Mars. So it's advantageous for us to live by Earth years and months. We'd live by Earth days if we could—and I can't tell you how many times I've heard tourists complain that we have a longer day. Some of them seem to expect us to speed up the rotation of the planet so they can have their normal Earth day.

When you think about it, what were our alternatives? Well, there have been a thousand proposals for a Martian clock, most of them metric, and some of them even make a certain amount of sense. Twenty hours in a day, for instance, or only ten. Divide each hour into one hundred minutes. Then divide each minute into . . . what? Problem is, a "second" is a standard of measurement of *everything*. Do we really want a Martian second? I don't think so.

Luckily, nobody uses mechanical clocks anymore, and computer clocks can easily be instructed to pause for 39.583333 . . . minutes before resuming again. At first, when people were getting together to thrash all this out, after we'd been living here a while and it was obvious we needed to tell time in a different way if twelve noon wasn't going to work its way around the day, so we'd all be eating lunch in the middle of the night sometimes, they just called it "the Pause." They set it at midnight. All the clocks would stop for 39.5 minutes when it was celestial noon on the far side of Mars from the big human settlements. That way, the Pause would happen while 99 percent of the people on the planet were sleeping.

Then somebody like Mom, who wanted to celebrate the differences between Mars and Earth instead of slavishly imitating our big sister, started a drive to move the Pause from a place where nobody noticed it to a place where you couldn't miss it. Make it a truly Martian thing, something you could talk about when you got home. Come to think of it, the Pause Debate was one of the first really hot political issues to interest the Martian population.

Nobody can get by without politics, but we have a minimum of it on Mars. Basically the things that aren't handled by the owning companies back on Earth, or that they could care less about, are handled by the City Council. It's elected, and everybody over the age of fifteen can vote, even if you just got off the ship. The Council just sort of grew, and I can't really say it's grown that much. Which is the way a lot of people like it. Many of the people who came to Mars to stay, so far, are a lot like native Alaskans, who are famous for not liking other people telling them what do to.

Anyway, moving the Pause had a lot of support . . . but move it where? That was debated for almost a year. Almost any daylight hour had some supporters, and plenty of the evening hours, too. But at last we voted to stop the clocks at 3 P.M., 1500 hours, and to call it the Siesta.

Close second: Happy Hour. After all, we are a planet of innkeepers.

IT WAS THREE months after our trip to the Red Zone. I had graduated high school with honors in English and history and adequate grades in everything else. I had to decide where I was going for my higher education. What should it be? Harvard or Yale? I'd never been to sunny California, so maybe I'd go to Stanford or UCLA. Cambridge and Oxford didn't interest me, as I'd heard the English climate was just awful, plus I'd have to listen to those British upper-class accents all day.

Just kidding. I could "attend" any of those grand old places, but at the freshman level I might as well select my institution of higher learning by what I thought of their basketball team, or even their school colors. And weather wouldn't be a problem, because I wouldn't be going to Earth. Not yet, anyway.

Blame it on the web, like so much else. These days you could attend classes virtually. The universities resisted it, but eventually they were confronted by a *de facto* situation, and gave in. You no longer have to go to Boston to attend Harvard. If you know enough to log on to online classes you can become a web freshman. No entrance exam necessary. Hooray for equality!

Of course, there's equal, and then there's equal.

And there's practical, and there's impractical. There's nothing to prevent you from attending an advanced seminar at the Sorbonne, everything but some highly select honors courses is webcast these days. That doesn't mean you will understand what they're talking about. So all but a few supergeniuses start out in the traditional way, with Physics 101 or Introduction to African History, and work their way up. When you think about it, it's good for everybody. The geniuses can proceed at their own pace, and they can do it from Manhattan or the rudest sheet-metal hut in Calcutta. People who never had a chance to see so much as a blackboard in the past are now able to get an Ivy League education, if they're up to it. Excellence can now actually select itself in academia, at least until the point where you actually arrive on campus and are faced with prejudice and politics and academic bullshit. Or so I've read, in researching the pluses and minuses of web school. Mostly pluses, to my way of thinking, the big one being I could stay on Mars for a few more years, at least, just like that boy or girl in Calcutta doesn't have to figure out how to pay for transportation to and lodging in Paris.

But eventually, the different levels of equality come into play. You can get a degree from Stanford and never leave your igloo in Nome, but it's not quite the same kind of degree you'd get if you'd lived in the ivy-covered dorms. The sheepskin itself will look identical, but simply by googling the student you can find out if he or she actually attended in the flesh. So, people being what they are, an Attending Degree, or AD, was more prestigious than a Web Degree, or WD.

But there's a remedy for that, and so far as I can tell it adds up to what Mom calls "that rarest of human institutions: a meritocracy."

You can start out as I plan to, attending classes via the web. You get graded like everybody else. Then, if you look like *Hah*-vahd material— that is, if you are smarter than some of the legacy admissions already there—you will be invited to attend *in corpore*. Doesn't matter if you're our boy from Calcutta, or a girl from Chad, or some poor child who actually lives in Boston but never had a chance to attend a good school.

As for picking a school, there's another alternative these days, and it's what I'm leaning toward.

Don't pick.

If I'm going to be on Mars anyway, what do I care about singing "The Whiffenpoof Song" with a lot of drunken Elis? I'd never make the rowing team to bring glory to dear old Cambridge. I don't give a hoot about either American football or real football. Other than reasons like that I don't see the point of identifying myself with any particular school. In this academic strategy, you simply attend the classes that appeal to you. On Monday morning you can be in a class in Johannesburg, follow it up with a seminar in California, and that afternoon attend lectures in Japan and Buenos Aires.

If a certain professor turns out to be boring or incompetent, just stop going. Professors *hate* this, they call it the Neilsen Rating system of education. It's mostly the ones whose web attendance is low who complain, though.

You can cobble together your own educational strategy, chart your own path, design your own specialty, if you wish. You may not even want to pursue a degree, you may just want to learn stuff and go from there.

Tentatively, that's what I planned to do. Do what *I* want to do.

There was just one small problem. What *do* I want to do?

Problem . . . I hadn't yet felt what you'd call a real *passion* for anything other than what all boys my age feel. That is, girls. How do you make a career out of girls?

I didn't have to worry about money. I could pick some area that didn't necessarily pay much. I could be a Martian geologist, sifting through rocks with no intrinsic worth. There's no diamonds or seams of gold or uranium on Mars, it's not tectonically active enough to have formed such things. There's no oil, and no market for it if there was. And there's nothing else here that can't be had more cheaply and easily on Earth. But there's still plenty to learn about the history of Mars through studying its rocks. I've been collecting them since I first got here.

I could be a historian. I'd already decided to take some courses in various areas of world history. Find out which place and period I was most interested in.

I could be an English major. I know two English majors. One of them runs the local Shakespearean Society in his spare time, when he's not mixing drinks. The other can recite page after page of *Beowulf* in Old English as he carries your bags to your room in the Red Thunder.

Hard to see myself as any of those things. I knew what I really wanted. I wanted adventure. I wanted to do something like Mom and Dad did, something that people would remember. My one shot at adventure, so far, had been spent slogging through muck and seeing things I'd just as soon forget. A disaster is *not* an adventure, believe me.

Ah, yes, the lazy, hazy days of summer. I decided to take a break from a day of not doing much in particular and take a ride up to Phobos and try to get out of my funk. Dammit, the days of adventure were over, and I missed them.

And that's how I missed the start when Earth invaded Mars.

ONE MORE THING I like about Mars that you can't get on Earth: We are allowed to use bubble drives on our personal vehicles.

On Earth, you can't power a car or truck or even a train with a Squeezer drive. For one thing, it would be impractical. It makes more sense to use the Squeezer bubbles at big central power stations and transmit the electricity. Plus, everybody's paranoid about bubbles in private hands. Sure, it's happened, no security system is perfect, but it stands to reason that the fewer bubbles people have to experiment on, the less chance anybody else will discover the secret of how to make them and then be able to hold the world hostage. Or blow it up.

So the bubbles mostly go to power plants, where they can be guarded more easily. The only place where they're used the way Jubal first used them, as direct power for a spaceship, is in space itself.

But Mars is a spacegoing society. So are the settlements on the moon. Part of the covenant Travis and his lawyers worked out during the Orange Bowl Accord guaranteed that we could have our own bubble-manufacturing plant. Travis was thinking ahead, he didn't want just one society—the Earth, or America, or whatever world government might be formed in the future—to have complete control of all the power in the world. So Jubal himself made just a few Squeezer machines. There are nine, total. Two on Mars, two on the moon, three immobile ones on the Falklands, and two mobile ones on the Earth for heavy excavation and such. Nine Squeezers for all of humanity.

Some people say that's at least four too many. That's the Earthies.

Some say that's *nine* too many.

Whatever they say, we have our two, and we're not about to give them up. It sure makes life a lot easier. It also makes it more fun. Without personal Squeezer engines we couldn't airboard.

I SUITED UP and let the suit check itself and report to me that all was copacetic except I was about halfway down on air. I aired up without even thinking about it, though I wouldn't be using much suit air. Rule One: You always start out with full tanks. You can never be sure just how long you'll be out.

I park my board out behind the hotel, under a hoist. I lowered it, unhooked from ground power, swung aboard, strapped in, switched from suit air to board air, and gave the handle a tiny twist. A puff of exhaust from the bubble raised a cloud of dust, and the board lifted three feet, then six. I shoved forward and was off into the sky, accelerating all the way. The ground dwindled under me. I felt good, maybe better than I had since returning from Earth.

FLYING TO PHOBOS isn't like driving to the corner grocery store, but it's not all that daunting, really, not if you have the power. With the minibubble drive, I had power to spare. It's not even like flying from, say, Los Angeles to San Francisco in a small plane. On Earth, unless the weather is bad, you can see your route, and your destination doesn't move. Going to Phobos, you don't aim at where it is, you aim at where it will be, and when you start off you can barely see it.

Phobos is the only moon in the solar system that rises in the west and sets in the east. That's because it's in close, and Mars revolves relatively slowly. It takes Phobos just seven and a half hours to complete one orbit, so it rises twice every day. It's only a little more than four thousand miles above the surface, just a little more than one Mars diameter. Orbital speed, just under five thousand miles per hour.

That probably sounds fast, if you're an Earthie. Nobody on Earth ever drives anything that fast except spaceship drivers and military pilots, and not many of those. I've been doing it since I was fifteen.

There's a fast way up and a slow way. Nobody I knows takes the slow way. How you do that, you build up your speed as soon as you're safely out of the atmosphere, then you cut your engine and coast until you reach where Phobos is with just enough energy to tangent the orbit, then you speed up some more or gravity will pull you back down. That's how the old chemical rockets used to do it, because it's the most efficient.

I didn't need to worry about that. The way I did it was to blast to the halfway point, then turn around and blast until I was motionless relative to Phobos. Total travel time was about an hour. To put it another way, less time than it would take you to drive from one side of Los Angeles to the other.

There's a fairly loose launch window to do this, because of the power available to us, but there was no point in starting out when Phobos was on the other side of the planet and trying to catch up with it. So twice a day, a lot of people take off for Phobos within about twenty minutes of each other. I saw half a dozen others rising on their boards, one close enough to wave to, which I did. He or she waved back.

I was quickly out of the atmosphere. I called up a navigation window on my faceplate, saw the big curve of Mars moving slowly away from me, the little dot of Phobos chugging along behind me, and the tiny speck that was me right in the center, with several suggested trajectories and one yellow radar alert that meant one of the boarders would get within a mile of me in about ten minutes. No biggie; I adjusted my course a little and the other boarder went green. I leaned against the backrest under an easy one-sixth gee acceleration, set the navigator to beep me ten seconds from turnaround, and ticked up some music to travel by. Selected a nice oldie, "Daytripper," by the Beatles, a group Grandma favored and had turned me on to.

Life was good again.

* * *

PHOBOS LOOKS LIKE a big baking potato. On one side is a really huge crater, half as big as the rock itself, like somebody had scooped it out to put in the sour cream and chives. That crater is called Stickney. I rendezvoused pretty much in the dead center of Stickney and tied my board down.

I entered the air lock with half a dozen other arrivals and we all watched the air gauge, then popped our helmets and took off more or less as a group, though I didn't know any of them, and we pulled our way down a series of corridors with the hand ropes anchored into the walls, fighting off as usual the occasional baffled Earthie going in the wrong direction despite the huge arrows painted prominently on every wall.

Phobos is an irregular carbonaceous chondrite with a long axis of about seventeen miles. It's not much, but it has to do us for a moon, as our other one, Deimos, is even smaller and farther away.

Building big zero-gee habitats in Earth orbit was a lot cheaper with the Squeezer drive than it ever had been before, but still not cheap. Lift costs were of course way down, but space is a harsh environment, and you can't build your space stations out of tinfoil and bubble gum. Also, it's dangerous, particularly heavy construction. People die regularly building stuff like that in free fall.

But with the Squeezer, mining is easy. They bored into the middle of the big rock and then squeezed out a hollow about a mile in diameter. They sprayed the inside with absorbent foam and put in an air system. Phobos became a necessary side trip on your trip to Mars. Buses left every five minutes at the appropriate launch windows. Inside were big attractions and small businesses, carny-type things but adapted to free fall. (Actually, ELG, Extremely Low Gee, since Phobos does have gravity, just not enough to matter, but we use the terms interchangeably.) You could try low-gee drinks, take classes in gymnastics and dancing, watch low-gee shows, and, of course, the thing *everybody* wants to try: weightless sex. You can rent rooms by the hour, and if you didn't bring a companion, one could be found either at the singles bars or commercially. Nobody ever got around to outlawing prostitution on Mars, and as long as you don't get too aggressive and get yourself arrested for disturbing the peace—the basic no-no in Martian society—you can sell what you please.

Everybody who didn't blow lunch in five minutes loved it.

Martians hated it. It was full of Earthies. No Martian would go there unless he had a job there.

So we made another hole, the same size, and made it off-limits to anyone who wasn't a Martian. Most Earthies didn't even know it was there. We didn't really have a formal name for the place, though some called it the Hideaway. An Earthie would have to get pretty lost to even stumble over the entrance, as it is behind a series of doors marked EM-PLOYEES ONLY. One of the perks of being a native.

Very few adults came to the Hideaway, so most of the people you saw were teenagers. This was the place we used instead of a mall or a strip or drag to cruise around in and show off our cars and girlfriends and have a beer and just generally hang around to bullshit and brag and meet chicks and think of ways to piss off adults and now and then get into a fistfight. It was fairly tame, actually. There was more of the old malt shop to it than the old roadhouse. It was more YM/WCA than street rumble. But it was our 'hood, and we liked it.

I said hi to various friends but didn't linger with anyone. Most of them were out of their suits, and I wanted to be, too.

The thing about pressure suits, especially the ones that you can use both on Mars and in vacuum, is that they have to be ready to keep you warm or cool you off, and that's a lot to ask of a machine you can wear.

When you're out on the surface, cold is the problem, even at midday during the real summer. At night, forget about it. Nobody goes out at night if they can help it. In vacuum it's a different story. They talk about the cold of outer space, but space is really no temperature at all. But if you're in the sunshine—and that's most of the time—even out at Mars' orbit, you tend to overheat. So the suit has to protect you from that heat and at the same time dump the heat your body is producing.

Like I said, it's a lot to ask.

When Mom and Dad flew *Red Thunder* to Mars, the secondhand Russian space suits they bought cost them as much as the ship itself; there was no way they could have built a useful suit themselves. Suits are cheaper these days because they are made by the thousands, but they still set you back more than a small car would on Earth. Lots of Martians couldn't afford one at all on their wages, so it's part of the contract when they come here. Use of a suit is a basic civil right.

The main thing you should know about a suit is this: They are almost always a little too cool or way too hot. Not broiling-in-the-desert hot, but warmer than you'd like. You fiddle with the thermostat all you like, you never get it quite right. And they're better on the surface than in space. An hour in one on the way to Phobos and you'll be sweaty when you arrive.

So I headed for the shower. Luckily, I had my own.

WHEN YOU'RE TUNNELING with a Squeezer, you can hollow out a space in any shape you want . . . so long as it's a perfect sphere.

At each of the cardinal points of the compass, and at the north and south poles of the Big Bubble, tunnels had been made that led to much smaller hollows, a few hundred yards in diameter. I didn't really know how big they were, since by the time I started coming all six of them were already at least half-full, you couldn't see the rock walls anymore.

What they were full of was Martian trailers. That's what we called them, anyway, though they usually only made one journey, from the prefab plant on the surface up to the Big Bubble. They were actually modular housing, made in four different standard sizes. They were shaped like loaves of bread, the most common size being eight-by-eight-by-fifteen. They were made of plastic, with insulation sandwiched between two layers, for noise rather than temperature, as they were meant only for use in an environment like the Bubble, and were not meant to provide shelter but privacy. Each was prewired for electric and web, had plumbing and sewage, air circulation and heating, and its own pumps. After that, you were on your own. You could put the door anywhere you wanted, in any of the six walls. You could get a model with a shower and a toilet, and you could have a low-gee kitchenette.

That's what I had, a deluxe Model-B with all the trimmings. Mine was in the North Quadrant. Elizabeth had one just like it in the East Q.

We northerners like to think we were a bit above those equatorial people . . . but they thought the same of us.

I'm not saying the North or any other Q was where the rich kids went, or anything like that. It was more of a neighborhood thing, almost but not quite like turf. We didn't fight any battles over it.

The trailers came with attachment points that you could hook onto other trailers, make a real multiroom house if you wanted to, but hardly anybody did that. It was seen as ostentatious. The Model-A was smaller, and the bigger units were usually shared, common space for dancing and whatever. No, we used the attachments to hook onto other people's units, and made irregular 3-D honeycomb arrangements that would have given a zero-gee bee a psychosis. There was no rhyme or reason to it, except that you knew the units closest to the walls were the oldest residents.

What you did was, you ordered one, it was delivered on a freighter a few days later, and you and a friend wrestled it through the corridors and into the Q you wanted to live in. Then you bolted it to somebody else's unit, hooked up, powered up, and you had a cozy little nest. No formalities at all, except you couldn't block access.

If you ever wander into one of the Qs, don't look for the color-coded arrows you'll see everywhere else on Phobos. What you'll see instead are graffiti-covered surfaces in every color of the rainbow, complicated enough to dazzle your eye even if you're solidly planted on two feet in one gee. They range from murals showing varying degrees of talent to web marks and web numbers and obscene poetry and icons and here and there a slapped-on notice:

⇧THIS WAY TO THE SWAMP⇔
ABANDON HERE, ALL YE WHO HOPE!
ש!!!!! CINDY'S BAT MITZVAH, 3 PM SAT. !!!!!ש

Most of these things were hand-lettered and held on with adhesive tape. Strictly low-rent, and that's the way we liked it.

To tell you the absolute truth, I'd gotten lost myself more than once in the maze. Never on my way to my own place, but trying to find somebody else's. And that was okay, too. It's not like it was that big a place, just confusing.

I made it to my own cubicle without incident, stripped off my suit, and then my clothes, and shoved off a wall and toward the shower.

It looks just like an ordinary shower from the outside. A frosted plastic door that seals tight around the edges, like a refrigerator, lined with blue tile on the inside. That's where it all changes. You have to get the water heated to the right temperature before you turn on the water dispenser because you don't want a hot globule of water clinging to you. It can burn. You set a temperature on a digital gizmo, and in about a minute water starts to bulge out of openings at the narrow ends of the stall, what you might call the top and the bottom. You put on a pair of clear goggles because you don't want soapy water drifting into your eyes. Then you grab handfuls of water and splash them against your body to get wet, then add soap.

All this time there is a blower in operation to keep things moving, which I why I didn't hear the trailer door open or anything else until the shower stall door opened and I looked over to see a pair of naked feet right in front of my face. The toenails were painted a bright red, and they were attached to slender legs, which were attached to . . . the rest of Evangeline. Down at the bottom was her head, and all she was wearing was her big upside-down smile and a tiny pair of shower goggles.

"Oops!" she said, and twisted in the air, pulling herself inside and into my arms. She was already slick with suit sweat, and soon she was even wetter as we drifted among the water globules.

We didn't get much washing done for quite a while after that.

Ah, yes. Life was good.

12

★ ★ ★

THE THING TO keep in mind about low-gee sex is to go slow. It takes a little practice and self-control, but it pays off in two ways: You don't get bumps and bruises or—it's been known to happen—broken bones or concussions.

And low-gee sex is the best sex there is.

Your biggest problem in doing *anything* in free fall is that your muscles were developed to hold you upright against a one-gee gravity field. Your legs in particular are more of a liability than an asset. They will deliver a hundred times more energy than you really need to get the job done, and do it when you least expect it. The muscles of the ankles are usually all you need to move around.

Don't use those thigh muscles at all!

So the basic, or "missionary" position in free fall is for the girl to wrap her legs around the guy and lock her feet together, and for the guy to hold his legs out straight and try not to let his curling and uncurling toes shove the two of you all over the place. Using a tether or a net is considered to be a sissy move.

That's how we started out, but Evangeline is adventurous, and soon we were deeply into positions emphatically not for the beginner. The shower stall was just high enough for one of my favorites, where I put my feet on the "floor" and she puts her feet on the "ceiling," pretty much the position she was in when she first opened the shower door and . . . well, you get the picture.

We worked our way through the free fall edition of the *Kama Sutra,* reached orgasm without injury, and then started washing each other. That's almost as much fun as sex. You can gather small globes of water into big globes and then mash them into little globes again, against her body. Surface tension helps it stick, and adding soap makes it slick, and it's just *lots* more fun than a regular shower. I washed her hair and she washed mine, then we turned the blowers on high to suck out the floating water. That gets chilly pretty quick, so we floated out and dried each other off with big fluffy warm towels.

By then my rendezvous probe was ready for another docking maneuver, and she guided me into her own fleshy capture latches, which were amazingly strong and versatile, and we did it all over again. Practice makes perfect.

After a long time, we fell asleep in each other's arms.

EVANGELINE AND I had become an item on the ship on the way back from Earth. It took me a while to make my move on her, and when I did she was eager and willing. It was a few weeks later before I realized, with a laughing hint from Elizabeth, that she had been setting me up for it for a long time, since back on Earth. Women, huh?

I wouldn't say we were inseparable. We attended different schools, and she was a year behind me, but pretty soon we were spending a lot of time together. About every other night she spent the night in my room. Mom, the progressive, was fine with it. Dad was uncomfortable, but he liked her, and soon relaxed. Most Martians are fairly easy about things like that, anyway, except the Muslim kids and the hard-core Christians.

Was I in love with her? Honest truth, I wasn't sure. I liked her a lot, I liked being around her, liked making love with her. She was smart, gorgeous, we agreed on most things and could argue reasonably when we didn't agree. But from time to time she would make some innocent little statement that indicated she was thinking long-range. I was nervous about that. I don't apologize for it. I agree with both Mom and Dad that marriage is something you need to think about a long time, and it's best if you're closer to thirty than twenty. They had been younger, but statistics showed they were part of the lucky minority, still being together as long as they had been.

I'm not sure Evangeline agreed about that.

When I woke up that day I looked over at her, floating a few feet away from me. She was wearing her stereo now, no telling what she was reading, but it was probably something medical, connected to a summer course. She wanted to be a doctor, she said, and the best way to do that was to ignore the school year and keep at it year-round, because the competition is intense.

Evangeline is more comfortable in free fall than anyone I know. I'm one of the 90 percent who prefers a local vertical. That is, all my furnishings in the trailer are oriented the same way. There is one wall I think of as the "floor," and there are no posters or cupboards on it. The artwork I do have is all oriented the same way, with a top and a bottom.

She is one of the 10 percent who don't give a shit. If she could afford a trailer of her own—which she can't—it would be totally floor-free. She'd use all six walls as walls, and tape up her posters any old way. She is able to read upside down as well as right-side up, it makes absolutely no difference to her. Pictures, too. You handed her a photograph upside down, it would never occur to her to turn it around.

She's right and me and the 90 percent are wrong, of course, I know that. It's embarrassing, in a way, it sounds like an Earthie thing to do, but I'm more comfortable when there is a visual up and down to refer to. This phenomenon has been known since the earliest days of space, in Skylab and Mir and primitive places like that. Most astronauts preferred a local vertical, but a few didn't care.

It must be a brain thing. Something in the wiring, maybe. I can't interpret a face very well if it's upside down to me. Evangeline is often inverted when a group of people gather in Phobos, and doesn't turn around unless someone asks her to.

It may be a bit physical, too. Evangeline has long toes, and can use them almost like a second pair of hands. She is also incredibly limber. She's always up on the latest twists in free-fall dancing, and has invented more than a few moves herself. If she can't hack it in medicine, she might make a living as a contortionist in a carnival. The *Cirque du Soleil* company in the other Phobos bubble would be happy to have her.

I was lazily admiring the long, bare length of her when the doorbell rang. Evangeline twisted, touched a wall with one toe without even looking—and that's another thing, she always seems to know *exactly* where she is, to the inch, even if she's been drifting for an hour with her eyes closed—and headed straight as an arrow for the door button. One foot on the jamb, one hand on the handle, she pulled it open. There was a guy in an orange-and-purple uniform out there. He took her state of undress in stride, but with no lack of appreciation.

"FedEx," he said. "Somebody sign for a package?"

She signed his register with her left hand—she's ambidextrous, too, maybe that accounts for some of it—upside down, and it printed out a receipt card. He handed it to her and turned to go.

"Wait. That's it?"

"Too big a package, lady," he said. "My assistant is Earthside, in Africa, and I'm not going to wrestle it into this mess alone. You'll have to pick it up yourself in the other bubble."

"Well, you don't get a tip for delivering a receipt," she said.

"I'll live without it. Good day to you."

If anybody could slam a door in free fall it would be Evangeline, but that was beyond even her talents. She eased it closed, looked at me—at about a forty-five-degree angle—and shrugged. I was still appreciating the shrug, which is a very different operation in a naked girl than it is in a boy, when I came completely awake and alert.

"Oh, shit," I said. "Where's my stereo?" She toed off and came up with it in the pile of clothes and suits in one corner. In the microgravity on Phobos, everything will drift into the same corner every time. She tossed the stereo, perfectly, of course, right at my hand. I put it on and checked the time, then ticked up my appointment book—not a thick document, nothing like Mom's—and saw what I'd expected.

"I've got a lunch date with a counselor in two hours," I said.

"Go for it."

"You want a ride?"

Her face lit up, and she started tossing clothes at me. She was pressuring me to teach her to board, and I guess one of these days I would, though I didn't relish riding the sissy bar.

We dressed and suited up and were out the door in five minutes. I followed her through the maze, into the Big Bubble, and out to the board park. We strapped in and I eased up very slowly from the parking area, and when my suit told me I was out of the No Turbulence zone I twisted hard on the handle and turned left. Below me and to the sides, the attitude jets got me aimed in the right direction, and the displays in my helmet showed I was a little late for optimal descent.

"How much can you take?" I asked Evangeline.

"At least as much as you can, big guy. Let 'er rip."

"Okay. Hang on to your helmet."

I eased up to half a gee deceleration, then a gee, then a gee and a half.

"Whee!" Evangeline hollered.

Phobos was dwindling. We were going far too slow to stay in any kind of orbit around Mars, but it would take a while for us to fall all that way, and it would leave us a few hundred miles from home when we got there. So I inverted us until Mars was directly over our heads and accelerated again. Up to two gees for a little while, until the external pressure gauge began to twitch just a little.

"Double whee!" Evangeline squealed as she looked up. I turned us back over and used the helmet display to adjust our angle of attack for optimum heat dispersal. In a minute we were showing a wake.

I swung to the north, at about a thousand miles per hour. We could see Olympus Mons almost directly ahead of us as the orange glow built up around us. Then back south, toward the smaller peak of Pavonis.

I deployed the Kevlar wings on their long, composite rods and extended the glide. From below we'd look something like a bat, something like a kite. We could plainly see the complex of hotels and homes that was Thunder City and I was setting up for my final approach when our radios started shouting at us. Just about blasted our ears off, to tell you the truth, and I hastily ticked the volume down.

"*Attention! Attention!* You have entered restricted airspace. You have entered restricted airspace. All nonmilitary aviation is forbidden in this area until further notice. You are directed to land at once or be fired upon."

It's hard to describe on how many levels this didn't make sense.

Restricted airspace? The only such place on Mars was a zone around the bubble generators, and those were on the other side of the planet. Non-military aviation? *All* air traffic on Mars was nonmilitary. We don't have an army or an air force. I couldn't have been more flummoxed if I'd been sitting in the bathtub and a periscope popped out of the drain and somebody told me to heave to or be torpedoed.

"I don't know who you are," I said, thinking it had to be some joker who had hacked the air traffic radios. "But are you sure you've got the right planet?"

"*Ray!*" Evangeline shouted. "Behind us!"

I glanced at my rearview window. Where my firetail had been a few minutes ago there was now something long and black with a bulge in the middle, and it was growing at incredible speed. My collision alarm began to beep, and the display told me the thing was coming up on me at five hundred miles per hour.

There really wasn't anywhere to go. Left, right, up or down, it was too late to avoid the thing, whatever it was. So I did the only thing I could.

"Hang on tight!" I shouted, and this time I felt her arms squeeze around me right through the suit.

There wasn't a lot of noise as it passed, not a hundred feet over us. The air is too thin to carry sound that well. I got a fleeting glimpse of a black airplane, and then the wake turbulence and jet blast hit us. Hard. The left wing fabric more or less exploded and the right wing flapped like a tent in a hurricane. We bobbed up, and then down, and then were caught in a barrel roll, over and over and over on our longitudinal axis. We were wrenched so hard that my hands were pulled off the handle-bars, and as the right hand came off it twisted the grip, which opened the jet ports below us to about 50 percent thrust.

If we'd been anywhere but over the Valles, we'd have been dead. I banged my head several times against the padding inside my helmet, and was woozy for a second or two. When I saw clearly again, we were headed straight down, still spiraling in a crazy motion from the thrust be-low. I kicked at the attitude jets with both feet and got the nose up, but gee forces were keeping me from reaching the handlebars again. If I couldn't reach them, I'd have to steer with my feet, and that wasn't good.

"Push me forward!" I told Evangeline, and immediately I could feel her hands on my back. She was leaning back against the sissy bar, so she had some leverage, and after a few seconds I was able to wrap both hands around the grips and get to work. I don't recall thinking about it, my training and instincts took over, and I slued left, away from an approaching canyon wall, got us upright again, and applied full thrust. We pulled five or six gees for a few moments, close to blacking out, and then rose above the rim of the canyon to about a hundred feet. I cut the drive and we were weightless, in a slow arc that would take us to the ground in about a minute. Ahead was the town, and way beyond that was the black aircraft, banking hard and looking like it was coming in for another run at us, this time head-on.

"I'll *kill* that fucker!" I shouted, with more bravado than sense. But the fact is, if I'd had guns mounted on the board, I'd have been blazing away.

"We'd better get down on the ground," Evangeline said. "He's bigger than you, and I'll bet he's got guns."

"Who the hell *is* he?" I said.

"I have no idea. But if you fight him, you're going to lose."

She had a point. Still raging inside, but feeling more rational, I brought the board down to the ten-foot level and scuttled—that's what it felt like, anyway—over the loose stones to the back of the Red Thunder.

No more than a hundred yards from the door another craft of the same design came swooping out from behind a building, positioned itself in front of us, and hovered there. There was a dark plastic bubble in the front and two things I was pretty sure were machine guns aimed at us.

They were sending us the warning again, but I could hardly hear it over the various alarms my board was giving me, and I didn't have a lot of choice in the matter, anyway. Hovering like that, his downdraft was terrific, and once more the board twisted out of my control. I was still too high to just cut power, so I wrestled with it and managed to bring us to a sliding halt on the left rim of the heat shield . . . and then the wind caught the remaining wing and blew us over. I yanked my left leg up just in time to keep it from getting pinned, and cut power to all systems except the air.

"You okay?" I asked as I struggled with my safety belts.

"No. I think I . . . may be in trouble here."

I didn't like the note of fear I heard in her voice. I managed to get myself free and off the board and turned around. Her leg was trapped under the edge of the board.

Mass and weight. You don't think about it on Earth, you're used to it being the same thing. So though my board massed about as much as a big Harley motorcycle, it weighed a lot less on Mars, and one guy could set it upright.

But because of its mass, its inertia remained the same as on Earth. That means, if you got in its way while it was moving, it would hit you just as hard as that same mass would on Earth. Not something to trifle with. But we hadn't been moving very fast when we hit, so I hoped none of her bones were broken.

I started to tilt the board off of her and pull her out.

"Don't!"

"What's the problem?"

"I don't think I'm hurt, but it feels real cold there. I think I may have a leak."

That word set off a series of actions that had been drilled into me so well that it almost felt like a reflex. I noticed a faint mist in the air around her calf, and some ice rime forming on her suit fabric. I realized the weight of the board was pressing her leg against the ground, and that was probably closing the puncture, at least a little. Leave it there until I was ready, as she'd already realized. I slapped the pocket on the front of my leg and the suit dispensed a patch about the size of my hand. The protective skin peeled itself away from the sticky side, and I knelt beside her.

"Ready?" She nodded, and I shouldered the board off her and dragged her a few feet away with one hand. There was now a pronounced jet of mist.

"Cold," she said.

"I've got it." There was a rock embedded in the suit fabric, about the size of a grape. I brushed it off, and there was a burst of vapor. Bad puncture. I slapped the patch on, held it tight with one hand while sealing the edges with the fingertips of the other. That should hold it, but better safe than sorry. I opened the tiny cargo space under the board's seat and grabbed a duct tape dispenser.

We call it duct tape, and that's pretty much what it is, but you can't buy it on Earth. It's stickier, and resists cold and vacuum. I made three winds around her calf, then a fourth for good measure. The mist was no longer coming out.

"Okay?" I asked her.

She smiled at me behind the helmet glass. I saw her eyes scanning the data there, invisible to me.

"Yeah, all systems go. But my whole leg feels cold. That's going to leave a chilblain."

"Sissy," I said, and held out my hand. She took it, and I pulled her to her feet, and she promptly winced and raised her foot off the ground.

"Ouch. The ankle. May have sprained it. But I can walk on it."

"What's the point?" I said, and picked her up and hurried to the emergency lock door, thinking about who I was going to kill first, the pilot of the first plane or the second one. Far as I was concerned, they were dead men.

WE DON'T REALLY have hospitals as such on Mars, in the sense of big buildings devoted to nothing but medicine. We have any diagnostic or operative equipment you can find anywhere on Earth, but it's scattered. We're too small to need more than one gene therapy lab or organ-growing facility, so the costs of big-ticket items like that are shared among the various corporations that own the tourist facilities.

What we do have is a first-aid station right next to every air lock. Some of them are not much more than a cupboard of medical supplies and a hot phone to call for help, which will be there in two minutes, maximum. But the big locks, the ones used by large numbers of people every day, have full-scale emergency rooms attached.

I cycled through the lock and turned right and went through the emergency room door. The nurse on duty took in the situation at a glance and we both helped Evangeline out of her suit. She only cried out once, when we eased off the boot. The ankle was starting to swell. The nurse briefly examined the site of the puncture on Evangeline's calf, pronounced it to be no problem, and spread a cream on it. Then she wrapped an electric blanket around Evangeline's leg and switched it on.

"We'll X-ray that ankle," she said, "but it doesn't look too bad."

"What the hell is going on out there?" I asked her. She looked up at me, and for the first time I noticed she looked scared.

"Where have you been?"

"Phobos."

"Okay. I don't know much. Nobody does. About an hour ago those ships landed, and they started ordering people around. They say there's bigger ships in orbit."

"Who are they?"

"Soldiers. They're dressed in black, and they're carrying big weapons. Everybody's been instructed to return to their rooms or their homes. I stayed here, and nobody's bothered me yet."

Homelanders? That didn't make any sense. I knew the situation was chaotic back in America, there was a lot of debate about who was in charge and some of it was being settled with planes and tanks. But what did they care about what happened on Mars? Why not invade Antarctica, if they wanted to waste their time? It was a lot closer to home, and would seem to be about as important, geopolitically.

"We didn't get anything from the web on our way down," Evangeline said.

"They've taken control of all the transmitters. All we're getting is these announcements. 'Stay in your rooms. There is no danger. This is all routine, don't worry.' All the time they're pointing guns at people and herding them around. You can't make a phone call, I tried. Not even over the emergency line."

Neither Evangeline nor I was wearing our stereos, and we had our helmets off. I hunted through my suit pockets for mine while the nurse was applying a quick-drying plaster to Evangeline's ankle. In moments it hardened with just her toes sticking out. The toes were turning purple.

Sure enough, no matter what icons I ticked on, all I got was a window with a continuous scroll of EMERGENCY REGULATIONS. They were extensive, but added up to "Stay at home and do what we tell you."

"There's supposed to be some sort of announcement in three hours," the nurse said.

"You okay, Evangeline?" I asked. She nodded. "Then let's get out of here." We thanked the nurse and headed for the door to the emergency room.

It took us right into the spacious lobby of the Red Thunder. I'd never seen it looking like this. It was almost deserted. A couple who looked like tourists were at the front desk, looking very angry. There was nobody behind the desk. That had never happened, in my experience.

In fact, other than the couple who probably intended to ask for a refund, there was no one in the lobby at all except for armed guards in black uniforms stationed at all the four portals to the concourses and the escalators to the lower levels.

Then four men in black uniforms came up the escalator, in a big hurry. They turned left and came straight at us. Something in their attitude made me think they weren't here to apologize for almost killing us.

I wasn't familiar with the uniforms—no surprise, Earth has so many armies only an expert could keep track of them—but it was clear these were of a different class than the grunts guarding the doors. They were dress uniforms, officers. The largest of them, slightly ahead of the others, had stars and ribbons and medals all over the front of his uniform. Clearly the man in charge. We waited for them. They had sidearms, but they were in holsters on their waists. Evangeline grabbed my arm and held on tight.

They stopped with the "general" about three paces from us, and the other three men moved to form a loose circle around us.

"Ramon Strickland-Garcia?" he asked.

"My friends call me Ray. But I don't think we're gonna be friends."

He ignored that. I felt a hand grip my right arm, and looked down to see the guy over there holding on to me. He reached into a pocket and came out with a set of handcuffs.

"And who are you?" the general asked Evangeline.

"My name is Evangeline Redmond," she said, and took two quick steps toward him, timed so that she was set perfectly to swing her foot with the cast on it right into his crotch. It lifted him six inches in the air before he quite knew what hit him.

"Run, Ray!" she shouted.

Well, it wasn't quite the strategy I'd have taken if I'd had time to think about it, but suddenly it felt right.

Not the running part, though. Where would I run?

I jerked to my left and the guy holding my arm pulled harder. I reached down, grabbed his forearm, and then leaped into the air and did a backflip. I took his arm with me, but not his body. I could hear something cracking in his shoulder, and his grip came loose.

I was hearing a high-pitched shriek from the general and a whimper from my guy when another of the officers started toward me. He was reaching for his weapon. I aimed a punch at his head and he reacted. He *over*reacted, which is what I was counting on in a guy who hadn't gotten his Mars legs yet. His muscles, which should have just tensed, pushed him about six inches in the air and he hung there longer than he wanted to, which gave me time to sweep my leg under him and he found himself lying sideways, overcompensated again, and I kicked him in the face before he hit the ground.

The guards at the portals had noticed something was happening. They started running toward us, and two of them promptly jumped way too high and didn't land well. I was watching their guns, and they weren't pointing them at us. If they had, I'd have given up right there. No point in getting shot. But I was hoping they didn't have orders to shoot, and it looked like they didn't. Any one of them was big enough to tear me limb from limb, but they'd have to catch me first.

Adrenaline can slow time for you. That's what I felt, like I had all the time in the world with these clumsy Earthies. I remember turning and seeing Evangeline as though she was frozen in midair, but the foot with the cast on it moved lightning quick, to the side of the head of another officer. How many was that? I'd lost count, and reinforcements were coming up as fast as they could, not knowing the proper way to run on Mars. I grabbed Evangeline's hand before she even hit the ground and pulled her toward me. She almost slugged me before she realized who I was. Her eyes were wide and she was grinning, out for blood. In fact, there was a little blood on her lips. Not hers; she had bitten one of the officers.

"Let's go!" I said, and got us both headed for the front desk. That was about all the plan I had at the moment. My helmet was back at the lock, and she didn't have any part of her suit, so outside wasn't an option. But I knew places in the hotel even the staff didn't know about. I figured we could hide.

Then Evangeline stumbled and dragged me down, and when I looked at her I saw her eyes were rolled up in her head and she was jerking spastically. I noticed two sets of thin wires with hooks at the end pricking the fabric of my suit and realized we had both been tazed. My suit had protected me.

I scooped her up in my arms again and as I was rising, looked up to see a soldier with a billy club. I saw the club coming down, and that was that.

13

I LATER LEARNED that those were the only casualties inflicted on the occupying force during the invasion of Mars. Some military statistician somewhere at the rear must have cataloged them all:

One (1) shoulder: dislocated

One (1) jaw: broken

One (1) concussion

One (1) laceration (bite: human)

One . . . well, probably two (2) very, very sore jewels: family

So although they won the war, technically, we sure beat the living crap out of them, didn't we?

But that was later.

*   *   *

I WOKE UP in a cell. It wasn't much longer than I was, had a bunk and a steel sink and a steel crapper. The bunk was hard, the room was cold, and I was naked.

I didn't know where I was, I didn't know what had happened to Evangeline, I didn't know where my family was, I didn't know what the soldiers taking over was all about. I didn't know anything at all except that I needed something to hang on to or I was going to start bawling like a baby, so I concentrated on hoping that the guy I had kicked in the head was hurting ten times worse than I was.

When I got tired of that, I thought of ways to kill the pilots of those planes. Slowly. I was very imaginative, it would have made you sick to see into my head during that time.

I don't know how long it was. The light in the ceiling was very bright and it never varied, and there were no windows.

At some point a guy opened the door and frowned at me for a moment. There was an armed guard outside the door. The guy came in and shined a light in my eyes, pinched and prodded me in a few places, touched the top of my head with a rubber-gloved hand. I yelped, and saw that his hand came away slightly bloody, which scared me.

"He's all right," the guy said, and they left. Medical care, I guess, as required by the Geneva Convention, as if anybody even knew where to *find* that anymore, much less abide by it.

Somebody came by a few minutes later, opened the door a crack, and tossed in a plastic bottle. I got up, moving slowly. Picked it up. Snapped off the lid. There were about a dozen aspirin inside. I swallowed them all and lay down.

I must have slept.

I GOOGLED IT later, under "interrogation" and "brainwashing." Fear and isolation and disorientation are all useful in the early stages.

But that was later. Then, I felt exactly what they wanted me to feel. Scared, isolated, disoriented. I probably would have even if I'd known it was part of their technique.

I was left alone for a long time. It might have been only a day, but it felt a lot longer. The light never varied. I could drink out of the sink by cupping my hands. At what seemed like irregular intervals the door would open and someone would set a piece of fruit or a sandwich wrapped in paper on the floor. The sandwiches were tuna fish or bologna or egg salad. The wrapping paper was printed with the words "Red Thunder Hotel" in the tasteful red script we use in the restaurant to wrap the hamburgers. But the food didn't come from the hotel. Mr. Redmond would never have let that shit into his kitchen, much less out of it.

Were they making a point with the paper? I didn't think it was a coincidence. I had a lot of time to think about it, and I'm sure that's what they wanted me to do. They were telling me they were in control of my family's business, and therefore, my family. I began thinking of more interesting things to do to these people if I ever got the drop on them in some dark alley.

Never going to happen, I knew that even then, but it's amazing how much it can buck up your spirits. Their screams for mercy resonated in my head and covered up the throbbing.

I WAS ASLEEP when they came for me. (See Interrogator's Manual Chapter Two: Grogginess is Good.) Two large guys in black uniforms and body armor barged into my cell. They handcuffed me and tied my legs together. I guess I can't blame them, considering what we'd done when they kidnapped us. But instead of taking me out of the room, one of them held a rag to my face and I smelled a chemical. I went out pretty quick.

I woke up in a room right out of a cop movie. It was dark, with a bright light over me. In front of me was a long table with four chairs behind it. There was a large mirror set into the window to my right. I was bound to a chair with tape, arms and legs, and I was wearing just a pair of boxer shorts. There wasn't much else to see, except two wires, a red one and a blue one, coming out the left leg of my shorts and trailing across the floor to a device sitting on the table. I could feel some sort of clips attached to my scrotum. There was a dial on the top of the device, which was plugged into an ordinary wall outlet by a long, orange cord.

They left me that way for maybe an hour, to think it over.

So this is the part where I chew through the tape on my wrists, use my toenails to unscrew the chair bolted to the floor, hurl it through the one-way mirror, and wait for the bad guys to come on, a sharp shard of glass my bleeding hand. I dispatch all five or six of the people who arrive using my superior Martian combat skills, strip the uniform from one of them, which just happens to fit my tall skinny frame, fight my way out of wherever it is I am, get back to civilization and rally all my oppressed Martian comrades and we repulse the evil invaders.

I thought about it, believe me, but I never got past the chewing through the duct tape part. It turns out duct tape is strong enough to loosen teeth, and it tastes awful.

The rest of the time I spent trying not to think about how I really, really had to go to the bathroom. *Now.*

There were three of them when they finally came. All were dressed in black uniforms. The insignia on them didn't quite fit, like old patches had been torn off and new ones sewn on. They were two men and one woman, all wearing opaque-lensed stereos with that clunkiness that spoke of military issue. There wasn't anything remarkable about any of them. The woman had short black hair. All three were white, racially. None of them ever smiled.

Somebody brought in coffee and served it to them, and they didn't say thank you. I hoped their moms would be ashamed of them, but I didn't say anything. Then they just sat there for a while, looking at me— or their faces pointed at me, anyway, though I never saw their eyes.

Finally, the guy in the middle spoke.

"Where is Jubal Broussard?" he asked.

I thought that over, knowing there was a sharp, witty remark I could make that would put this bastard in his place, but I couldn't think of it.

Then I had it.

"Huh?" I said.

"Where is Jubal Broussard?"

"Jubal . . . he lives on the Falkland Islands."

"That's where he lives. Where is he now?"

"How should I know?"

"We think you do."

"Then you got a problem, because I don't know. I didn't even know he had left."

"No, Ray, it's you who have a problem, because we know that you know where he is, and you are going to tell us."

I knew there must be a way to convince him that he was wrong, so I opened my mouth to tell him so.

"Fuck you!" I explained.

His hand moved to the big dial that was connected to the wires that were connected to my balls, and I peed my pants.

HE DIDN'T SHOCK me, it was just nerves and the need to go. And I don't think he ever intended to shock me. It was the humiliation he was after. It worked.

"Where is Jubal Broussard?" he said again.

And that's how it went for a long time.

They seemed endlessly patient, and so totally, impassively sure of themselves that I eventually began to wonder if it was *me* who had gone insane. Did I know where Jubal was? Did somebody tell me and I forgot? Who the hell was Jubal, anyway?

I kept waiting for the shock in my crotch, for them to bring out the hot screwdrivers and the splints to jab under the fingernails. I kept waiting for *anything* to change, and for a long time nothing did.

I want to say that I would have held out. I want to say that if I had known where Jubal was, I wouldn't have told them. But part of me is pretty sure that I probably would have told them. Sitting in your own cold urine, almost naked, strapped to a chair, not knowing where you are or where your family is, facing some implacable *power* that you know can wipe out your life like a mayfly . . . well, trained soldiers have cracked under pressure like that, as I found out later. What do you expect from an eighteen-year-old kid?

What kind of gumption I had expected from myself was a lot more than what I managed to show, and I knew it was something I would carry with shame for the rest of my life. No one else will ever know just how long it took them to make me cry, how long it took before I was begging. I'm not going to set it down here. I'll just say that, in time, I did cry, and I did beg. The best I can say for myself in the self-respect department is that I never got around to bargaining.

I'm not saying I didn't think about it: "Go ask my mother and father. *Please!* They're tougher than me." I never said that.

Maybe I would have, eventually. Sneer at me if you want to, but not until you've been through it yourself.

But finally the woman pressed a button I hadn't seen, and the door opened. In came the "doctor." It was the guy who had shined the light in my eyes, anyway, though I suspect that if he had a medical degree it was from the University of Dachau.

There were no formalities at all. He came around the table, and I saw he was holding an old-fashioned syringe, the kind with a metal frame and a long, wide needle that looked like it would hurt real bad. I struggled, I guess because that's just what you do when you think somebody is about to kill you, no matter how hopeless it is. And it did hurt, like the dickens. I watched as he depressed the plunger and about 10 cc's of some yellowish liquid went into my arm.

After that, I didn't worry anymore.

THERE ISN'T A lot I can say about what came next. My memories are vague. I would be in the chair, no longer strapped in because I didn't need to be. I had no more initiative than a garden slug, and about as much as strength. They'd ask me questions, and I'd answer them. It was sort of free association. I'd start off answering the question they asked, and then I'd wander off into dreamy stuff. I'd laugh. I'd cry. They listened to it all, and then they asked more questions. I don't remember what the questions were. Then I'd be in the cell, thinking about absolutely nothing. I don't recall my mind ever actually being blank before, but it was then. If they put food in front of me and told me to eat it, I'd eat it. If they didn't bring any food, I didn't get hungry. It was all the same to me.

Then I'd be back in the interrogation room again and then back in the cell. This cycle repeated more than once, but that's all I'm sure of.

Looking back, I really don't know why they bothered. It must have been clear to them even before they drugged me that I couldn't tell them what they wanted to know.

All I can figure is that it was part of a routine. The manual says you question him for X days. Then you do one of four things: you torture him physically, you kill him, you put him in jail and forget about him, or you let him go. The possibility of a trial with a judge and lawyers didn't even occur to me. These weren't trial sort of people.

Routine, rote, going through the motions. Brutality is the reflex of fascism. It's not a fallback position, it's where you start.

Then, for a while, nobody bothered me. I woke up two times in a row in the narrow bunk, and in between times of sleep they fed me twice. Call it one day. I didn't do much of anything. My head still felt like glue.

I woke up again, and for the first time in a while I was sure what my name was, how old I was, and that I lived on Mars. I didn't recall much else. I remember that, for a while, I knew I had a mother and a father, but I couldn't recall their names. I thought about it for hours. It made me angry, then sad. I cried about it, alone in that bright cell. I think I may have cried myself to sleep. All I know for sure is I woke up again and was served some slop for breakfast, and I felt a lot better. Not quite ready to appear on *Jeopardy!*, but at least with my important memories intact.

I SPENT ANOTHER day in the lockup and saw no one except the guy who brought lunch and dinner. I slept again. I woke up when someone opened the door and tossed some clothes into the room. They weren't the clothes I'd been wearing under my suit, but they were mine.

I dressed, and was met by two guys in the black uniforms I'd become familiar with. They led me down a curving hall and for the first time I was able to study the insignia on their chests and shoulders. Most of it didn't mean anything to me, things like service ribbons or things indicating their ranks. There was nothing there with any writing on it. No HOMELAND SECURITY, no U.S. ARMY, no UNITED NATIONS or COMEUROPE. The most prominent patch was on the right shoulder and over the heart, and it was a white circle with a black lightning bolt flashing across it.

Who *were* these guys?

They took me back to the torture chamber. My main interrogator and the woman were sitting behind a table. I was taken to the single chair across from them and set down roughly in it. I just sat there, trying not to breathe hard, hanging on to what little dignity I could muster by not letting them know how terrified I was.

The woman shoved a paper toward me.

"Sign that," she said.

You want to know how beaten down I was? You want to know just how quickly and thoroughly they can crush the spirit out of you? I almost did. I had the pen in my hand and was about to scrawl something in the space marked SIGN HERE.

Then I put the pen down and read it. It was short, and said that I agreed never to discuss anything about the events of the last seven (7) days, including but not limited to the conditions of my treatment, the manner of my incarceration, and the subjects of the "voluntary statements" I made.

"Sign it," the man said.

"What if I don't?"

"The question doesn't arise," the woman said.

"There is nothing voluntary about it, and you know it."

"Who cares?" the man said. "I'll spell it out for you. You have no witnesses, and nobody would care if you did. What this is about, is you never mention that we asked you as to the whereabouts of Jubal Broussard. Not to anyone. As long as you live."

"What if I do? You throw me in jail?" I knew that wasn't it as soon as I said it. The cat would already be out of the bag: Somebody has misplaced the most important man on Earth.

"I told you this was stupid," the woman said, not to me.

I stared at them for a little longer. The man sighed.

"What will we do to you? Nothing."

"We'll kill your family," the woman said. "You'll watch. It will take a while. I will probably do it personally." She pulled her stereo down to the end of her nose and looked at me over the top. It was the first time I'd seen her eyes.

I never put a lot of stock in this "eyes" business. But her eyes definitely were different. Call it my continuing state of disorientation if you want, but the only word I can find for her eyes is reptilian. Nothing so obvious as slits for irises, but a blankness there, a predator without emotion. She didn't blink. I wouldn't have been a bit surprised if a forked tongue had slithered out of her mouth.

I never saw the other guy's eyes. He never took off his stereo. Probably would have turned me to ashes with his laser vision.

"You're getting a big break here," the guy said, not unreasonably. "We could charge you with resisting arrest, assault and battery, but none of those guys want to press charges. We can bring them ourselves, though."

We. Who *are* you?

Didn't surprise me that the general didn't want a fuss made about how a Martian girl kicked him in the nuts, though.

"This is ridiculous," the woman said, putting her stereo back in place and looking away, suddenly bored with the whole business. "The only way to deal with this is to kill them all, like I said."

"Your opinion has been noted," the man said. "You were overruled."

I signed the paper.

IT WASN'T JUST fear that made me decide to sign. No, really. I mean, I admit I was scared, I'd have done most things they might have told me to do. But signing a paper? Who the fuck cares about that, at this point? I might as well have recited the Boy Scout oath, spit in my palm, and sworn "Honest Injun!" It would have been equally meaningless. These people were *way* beyond legality. They didn't care about any of that shit. Their authority extended from the barrel of a gun and the point of a needle.

So why bother with the signature? Procedures, I guess. Dad told me once that fascists are sticklers for paperwork.

Anyway, after that final and gratuitous humiliation the two guards frog-marched me out of the room and down the curving corridor. They bounced too high, like Earthies, and I was fairly sure I could put a move on them that would twist me free, disable them, and give them or somebody else a good excuse to blow my head off. At that moment, it didn't seem like that awful an option. I didn't know how I was going to face my family, knowing how poorly I'd stood up. I didn't know how I was going to get to sleep, get up in the morning, eat, look myself in the mirror. There didn't seem to be any point to any of it. They had broken me, no doubt about it. My spirit was a squashed dog on the freeway.

They took me to an air lock whose inner door was standing open. They shoved me through, and I found I could still rustle up an interest in life, because for a moment I thought they were going to cycle me through into the outside. They slammed the inner door closed and the outer one started to open, and I braced myself for the killing cold.

But no, there was a long flextube with lights strung along the top, about eight feet in diameter, sealed to the outer door of the lock. It stretched off fifty feet or more, curving slightly to the right. I followed it to another air lock and got inside it. I looked through the window and breathed a sigh of relief.

It was the Grand Concourse, the "main street" of my hometown. I opened the inner door and stepped through.

It was all crushingly familiar, but just a little off. There were not many people around for midday, and many of those I saw had a hurried, furtive look. That was the Earthies. The Martians I saw looked . . . I wasn't sure, but they seemed angry, determined. Pissed off, in a word. I guess they had reason to be. I had no idea what had gone on during my incarceration, but it must not have been fun.

Most of the Martians were moving in one direction. Some were carrying signs attached to metal poles, but not waving them around, and not saying anything.

I got my bearings. All the hotels had grand entrances branching off the Concourse to the buildings themselves, and I was three hotels from home. About a mile.

I trudged along, feeling lower than a snake's belly, as I once heard Travis say. People kept passing me. I was getting closer to home, and to having to tell my tale of cowardice and surrender.

There's a big computer-controlled fountain in the middle of the Concourse about a hundred yards from the road to the Red Thunder that has been a teen hangout since they built it, when I was a kid. The skateboard pits and roller rinks were not too far away. We used to play games dodging the moving jets, which you could only do for so long before you got soaked. Later, older, we'd just hang and shoot the shit. Mostly guys without steady girlfriends; the girls hung out in the nearby hamburger joint in gaggles. Or is a group of young girls a giggle?

I spotted a group of three slackers who basically seemed to live there, hassling some of the younger kids, including me until I got older and too big. They were in their early twenties now and seemed to have no ambition in life except to keep hanging. Elaborate skateboards they seldom actually used were propped against the fountain. I knew what they were doing. They were running the Strip-her program. A silly little bit of software that turns your stereo into X-ray glasses. Or seems to. It makes a 3-D real-time image of whoever you're looking at, but it strips away the clothes and makes them appear to be naked. Just a guess, of course. It won't show if she's wearing a navel ring or if she has tats. Childish, very childish.

Okay, I did it, too, but that was years ago.

"Space!" one of them shouted. I looked over, saw it was Joe Chan, more or less the leader of the group. Too lazy to be really mean, well on his way to alcoholism.

"Joe," I said back.

"*Space*man, is that really you? Ray?"

"It's me, Joe. I haven't got time for any trouble."

"No trouble, my friend. Look, they're carrying your picture."

That made no sense at all, so I started to go on, but I saw he was twisting his head around till it was sideways, then even farther. What? Was he trying to stand on his head?

"That's you," he said, and pointed.

I turned around and found myself twisting just like him. One of the people going by was holding a sign, the pole pointed to the ground so the thick cardboard was upside down. It was two-foot-by-three-foot posterboard. At the top was a picture of me, what looked like my graduation photo. At the bottom was a message:

FREE THE RED
THUNDER TEN!

I was in no shape to make sense of that. The Red Thunder Ten *what?* Some kind of promotion? A giveaway at the casino?

"It's him, space," Joe was saying to one of his homeys.

"What's going on, Joe?" I asked. "Why is that man carrying a picture of me?"

"You a *hero*, man!" he said. Then he snickered, to show how unimpressed he was. "Yo, can I have your autograph?"

Things were happening too fast and making no sense. I was suffering from humiliation, sensory deprivation, and maybe a panic attack. My head felt like it was filled with sludge. I was vaguely aware of a noise building up from the street leading home, the sound of hundreds, maybe thousands of voices, like in a sports stadium, where it's just a roar, and you can't pick out words. And people began to pour out of the street and around the corner ahead of me. They were all Martians, from the way they moved, and they were moving very fast, and all toward me.

"There he is!" someone shouted.

"It's him!"

With my wits about me I'd have known what had happened. Joe Chan had IMed his friends, such as they were, and they had passed it on, and within ten seconds of him identifying me the whole crowd ahead knew where I was.

Right then all I saw was several hundred emotional people charging in my direction, waving signs and shouting, and all they needed was burning torches and maybe a noose or two to look like the angry villagers in a Frankenstein movie.

I turned and ran.

Didn't do me any good. The people on that side had the news, too, and now they recognized me and closed in from all sides. Next thing I knew I was being lifted onto the shoulders of two strangers and others were reaching out to touch me. I finally perceived they were smiling, laughing, joyful. Quite a few were even crying.

So they carried me around the corner and down the smaller concourse past all the flashing signs advertising the delights to be had at the Red Thunder, and into what was the largest crowd I'd ever seen on Mars outside of the soccer stadium. They carried signs, and I saw my face again, and Mom's and Dad's and Evangeline's and Mr. Redmond's and Grandma's and . . . good god, there were the two Redmond brats, too.

A big stage had been set up in the public space leading to the lobby and it was covered with red flags with a paler pink circle in the middle of them, crisscrossed with lines. I realized it was one of those old drawings by Lowell, or somebody, showing the Martian "canals" and "seas." Over it all was a huge banner that read:

MARS FOR THE MARTIANS!

There were television cameras, and they were all pointed at me, and flashes from still cameras, and I could see myself from different angles up on half a dozen big screens erected all around the crowd. Other screens held familiar talking heads, Martian journalists, mostly, and they all looked excited.

I couldn't help noticing I looked a little goofy, sort of like somebody had just brained me with a sledgehammer, which is pretty much how I felt, so I tried a tentative smile and a wave, and the crowd *roared*.

Jesus Christ, what have I gotten myself into?

Then I was passed from hand to hand over the heads of the crowd and set more or less on my feet on the edge of the stage. There were people up there, and they were all shouting and clapping and slapping me on the back, putting their arms around me and smiling for the cameras, wanting to be on the news, I guess. I recognized some of them, political figures mostly, such as we have on Mars.

There were a few media stars, too. A few live on Mars, and a lot of them visit. They like to be seen on the ski slopes on Olympus Mons . . . I guess they like to be seen just about anywhere. I found myself shaking hands with some pretty famous people.

I was still too stunned to be asking any of the questions I wanted to ask, and it apparently wasn't expected of me. Nobody was trying to quiet the crowd, nobody was stepping up to the podium to speak.

But finally the dynamic of the crowd changed. I can't exactly put my finger on it, but it was another stereo thing, and I didn't have my stereo. (In fact, I never got that one back. Probably still stored in some evidence locker on Earth.) Anyway, everybody started looking in the same direction, back behind the stage toward the hotel. I looked up at the screens and on one of them I saw my mom, running. She was running a little faster than the cameraman was backing up, actually, and I saw her face twist as she stiff-armed the asshole and then I had a great view of the ceiling. Served him right.

I broke free of the crowd on the stage and dashed to the rear and jumped down in time to see her closing the last twenty yards or so. A couple other people got in her way and she handed out a few more body checks. She was implacable, which I'm used to, but she was sobbing, which I'm not. She flew into my arms and just held me for a moment, squeezing hard enough to leave bruises. I was doing the same.

But this wasn't the place. Her mind started working again, and she broke the embrace and tugged on my hand. I didn't need any more urging. I pulled ahead of her and started pushing my way through the crowd. In a minute we were in the middle of four husky guys in the red blazers of the Red Thunder security detail, guys she had outrun on her way to the stage.

We crossed the lobby to more cheers from the staff, and a lot of them were crying, too. But they stayed at their posts and gave us our space as we made it to the corridor leading back to our living quarters.

14

IT WAS THE strangest reunion you could imagine.

All of the "Red Thunder Ten" were there. I was the last of us to be released, probably because of us all I'd spent the most time corresponding with Jubal. The Redmonds had been released first, after only four days. Another instance of crossing all the I's and dotting all the T's? I mean, they'd never talked to Jubal, never met him.

The brats, too. They took the brats into custody. Unbelievable.

They said later that nobody was rough with them. Mostly they sat around with some adults and played with toys. Doctors examined them and found no needle marks and the boys confirmed they hadn't been injected with anything. But there were traces of some drug in their blood. It was an inhibition-reducing substance and they probably put it in their ice cream. The boys said they ate a lot of ice cream, and then people got them to play with cool toys to tell the story of all the time they spent with us, the interplanetary terrorists, the Strickland-Garcia family.

Ice cream. Nothing I saw in Florida compared with that.

I learned all this later, because after the first round of hugs and kisses Dad hugged me again and put his lips to my ear.

"There is a name we will not mention for now. And we won't discuss what happened to us."

I looked around. I was at home. *At home.* I started to mouth something, and Dad shook his head and whispered into my ear again.

"Read my lips," he said. And I suppose somebody could, if we were all on camera. And we had to assume we were.

THEY BROUGHT ME up to date. Back on Earth, they were aware of the invasion of Mars, but it wasn't making a lot of news. Some sort of peacekeeping operation was what they were getting from official sources.

It was a very big deal on Mars. Maybe the biggest deal since the spaceship *Red Thunder* landed. For the first time most of us were thinking of ourselves as Martians. We *did* think of Mars as home, and more important, each of us *had* a home here, even if it was usually only a temporary apartment. But these invaders had come and, without so much as a pretty please, had searched the whole place.

I mean *everything*. Every hotel room, every private apartment, every broom closet.

That takes a lot of soldiers and a lot of determination. You don't kick down a door on Mars. Believe me, you don't; 90 percent of the people opened their doors and stepped aside when the official knock came, but the 10 percent who didn't presented a problem. Doors on Mars are strong. They are pressure-capable, by law. They are built to keep you alive if there is a blowout on the other side. Fire most weapons at these doors and the bullets will just ricochet. Fire something with armor-piercing bullets, and you may kill the people on the other side. The only way to get through a Martian door with somebody on the other side who didn't want to let you in is to use small shaped charges and blow off the hinges.

Here's how it went, and I'm so sorry I missed it all:

At first the diehards, the ones who forced the soldiers to blow their doors, were looked at as nuts. What's the big deal? They come in, they look around, they make a mess, and then they go away. A nuisance, but it's over. Then it became clear they weren't going to stop until they'd patted down the entire planet.

Committees were formed. Delegations were sent to the commanding officers, demanding an explanation. They got diddly. More delegations were formed, demanding civil rights. *What* civil rights? the officers asked them. Mars is under martial law for the duration of the emergency; we control your civil rights.

What emergency?

We're not authorized to reveal the nature of the emergency.

Groups of angry people began to gather and discuss possible courses of action. A general strike was called on the third day but didn't really go anyplace. People were still too confused. But they were starting to re-think their position on those cantankerous misfits who, when Big Brother hammered on their door and demanded *Open up or we'll break it down!* shouted back, *Break the fucker down, then!*

It's a big symbolic thing, breaking into someone's home. Be it ever so humble, it's your castle, and it gets your back up. This whole thing might have eventually blown over, things might have gone back to more or less what they were before, except for that. There would have been out-rage, a lot of muttering, but there's work to be done, no use crying over a little invasion of privacy. It happens every day, right? They know everything worth knowing about you, right? So why get so upset that they came into your home and searched it?

But finally, the general population got angry. Suddenly, 20 percent were refusing to passively open their doors. Then, overnight, it was 50 percent. And not long after that, you were seen as some sort of *coward* if you submitted quietly.

Ironically, there was one more thing that made it a more attractive proposition to sit back in your living room and listen to the frustrated soldiers demanding, then wheedling, and finally almost pleading for you to let them in.

In most cases, *you didn't even own the door.*

It was a symbol, it was the drawbridge over the moat into your castle . . . but technically, it belonged to your landlord. The company that owned your apartment building, the owner of the hotel that em-ployed you and provided your housing as a necessary perk of the job. Somebody batters it down, it's not your problem. The landlord had to fix it, just like if your water heater broke down. So it didn't actually *cost* you anything to take a moral stand. When you realize it's not going to cost you anything, it's a lot easier to stand up for your rights, even if, technically, you don't have any.

And if you don't have any rights, you start to wonder why you don't, maybe for the first time.

SOMEWHERE IN THERE my family and the Redmonds became the Red Thunder Ten. We became the rallying cry for . . . Martian independence!

But independence from who? That's what I most wanted to know.

"Nobody is absolutely sure," Mom said. "Things are pretty unsettled back on Earth. We think it's some sort of coalition, and the United States is a big player. Or what's left of it."

America was shattered. We all knew that. Casualties from the wave were 3 million, officially, even higher from other sources. No one would ever have a total count, only an order of magnitude. It was almost certainly the most disastrous couple of hours the human race had ever experienced.

The rebellion in Idaho had been pretty much suppressed, with heavy loss of civilian life. No sooner was that situation over than rebel groups sprang up all over the South, many using guerrilla tactics. Some Army units stayed loyal, others defected to one competing faction or another. There was a President in the flood-damaged White House, and a competing President in Chicago, and states in the West weren't paying much attention to either one. There were National Guard checkpoints at most state lines. The union was showing signs of fracturing, not North/South or even East/West, but into individual states or coalitions of states. There were various international alliances and feuds going on to complicate the situation. Canada had sealed the border to the north. California was dealing with Japan and China basically as an independent nation. Sacramento's relations with Tokyo were a lot warmer than with either Washington or Chicago.

There was corporate involvement in it all, as these days a lot of multinationals functioned basically like governments and were more powerful than many governments.

Then there were the Rapturists. The majority of the people who had more or less dropped out of life with the arrival of the wave had given up and were trying to put their lives back together. Not easy, since most employers weren't hiring *anybody,* especially those who had walked out on them in a time of crisis. These people were finding their homes and cars repossessed, their bank accounts empty or full of dubious currency because they hadn't paid attention to the financial market catastrophe that arrived on the heels of the physical one.

Served 'em right, as far I was concerned. I find it hard to be sympathetic to people who are *rooting* for Armageddon. In fact, I find it impossible.

But there were still hard-core Rapturists waiting for Jesus (hey, he died in A.D. 33; *get over it!*), and a lot of them had been elected to public office in the past decades. Where that was the case, sometimes nothing was being done at all. Police weren't policing, firefighters weren't fighting fires, taxes weren't being collected because of some crazy business about "the number of the beast." Mayors weren't mayoring. I guess nobody was complaining much about the tax situation except those whose salaries were tied to taxes. But here and there people were angry about no police and no firefighters. Here and there they had held new elections, at the end of a rope.

So that was the national situation, as well as I can sum it up. That was the merely alarming news. On the East Coast, things were *bad.*

Through some slow but inevitable process, the devastated East Coast communities had changed, in the minds of the rest of the country, from people in need to The Enemy. Sure, they had a bad break, but things are tough for us all. We gave and we gave, we sweated our hearts out, and now all our political institutions have betrayed us, we don't know which flag to salute or who to call Mr. President, our money has gone into the toilet and other currencies are shaky, my last paycheck was late or I don't have a job at all, food prices have tripled, meat is hard to come by, and you say *you've* got problems? Live on the goddam beach, build yourself a shack. Only rich assholes could ever afford to live where you lived, anyway, so I should worry about you? Besides, I'm thinking of moving to California and voting with the Secessionists.

* * *

I SPENT THE night in my own bed, happy to be back but wondering who was watching as I tossed and turned. In the end I had to take a pill, something I didn't want to do, until Dad told me that even Mom had taken one, that first night, and she hates mood-altering drugs. This one was pretty good. I dropped off in ten minutes, and if I dreamed, I don't remember it.

The next day we all relaxed together. Dad didn't go in to work. We avoided all press interviews, which made a lot of people pretty pissed off. It also wasn't in Mom's nature just to let this slide, every bone in her body wanted to be out there organizing, protesting, and she had a marvelous platform to speak from, being one of the Ten. But there were all those things she couldn't talk about, all those questions she'd have to answer with "no comment." It would have to wait.

THE NEXT DAY, Dad decided to have the apartment painted.

Dad called in the crash crew, the guys who dealt with a suite after musicians had stayed in it. They whisked all the furniture out of the place in half an hour. All our possessions went with it, neatly boxed and labeled. Then, with all that stuff out of the way, Mom decided the carpets were looking a little faded and worn. I thought they looked fine, but nobody asked me.

The painters ripped out all the light fixtures. Then they applied a coat of new paint to every surface. Then a second coat, then a third. They put down the new carpet, and then Mom decided she didn't like our old furniture and had it all put in storage.

Okay, so I'm a little slow to catch on. I thought it was just a flurry of activity to get our minds off of what we'd just gone through. When the crew started moving new furniture into my room I noticed a little guy doing something with a small electronic instrument, going over the walls inch by inch.

When it was all done Dad and Mom called me and Elizabeth into the guest room, which had been left utterly bare, every surface completely painted, no carpet on the floor, no windows. The little guy was there. He was just an ordinary guy, with an indefinable Earthie look about him. I was a foot and a half taller than he was.

"I'm going to give you my standard disclaimer," he said. "Technology today is such that there can never be a hundred percent guarantee that a place is not bugged. The best I can give you is 99 percent."

"Go on," Dad said.

"I found two cameras in every room. Here's one." He dug in his pocket and took out a metal sphere the size of a BB with one glassy surface. "This is the smallest I've ever seen. They are very good, but they can't see through paint. But remember, these are the big guys, and although I think I'm very good, too, I'm only a private detective."

A private detective! I didn't even know we had any on Mars. But I guess anywhere you go, people want to spy on other people. This guy looked about as far from Philip Marlowe or Spenser as it was possible to be.

"I found plenty of listening devices and took them all out. But be aware that a lot of electronic equipment can conceal a listening device that can record and save, and be tapped later, so there's no radio signal."

"We understand that," Dad said. "Thank you, Basil. You can send your bill to the hotel."

The man ducked his head for a moment.

"Begging your pardon, sir, I think it would be best if you paid me now."

There was an awkward pause, and Dad nodded. He produced a credit card and made a funds transfer on the spot.

"Sorry," Basil said, "but things being the way they are . . ."

"I understand," Dad said. I wasn't sure if he meant the shaky condition of the financial markets—lots of people were asking for cash these days and hoping that the cash would retain its value—or the uncertain status of our own freedom.

"Okay," Dad said, after Basil the Detective left. "New house rules. Only family and close friends in this apartment. I'm not going to install a metal detector or pat anybody down before I let them in here. I'm not going to let them push me that far. But until we figure this all out, we need to keep everything close, okay?"

Elizabeth and I agreed.

"This room"—he pointed to the door to our former guest room—"is secure. And it's going to stay that way. Nobody but family gets in there, for the duration. Okay?"

We all nodded.

"In fact, I don't even want you and Elizabeth in there, Ray. Kelly and I won't be going in, either. It's the only way to keep it clean."

"Clean for what, Dad?" Elizabeth asked.

"We'll talk about that later. Things have changed, people. We have to be on guard, and that means no idle talk about any of this. I don't know what the hell is going on, but we're working on it. We'll tell you when the time comes. Okay?"

So we set about the task of putting things back together. And it was a sobering one. In my room, every box I opened, every object I took out, was no longer the old friend I had left there a week ago. Now it was a suspect, a possible spy. I put each object through a third degree, asked it to account for itself.

You *look* like an old copy of *Winnie-the-Pooh* that used to belong to my father, but are you *really?* Are you harboring a parasite? Or are you really a book at all, but actually a clever replacement? I looked through the pages, bent the spine, and peered down into the space there. I shook things, looked at them with a magnifying glass. I started throwing stuff away. There was no point, I knew that, but suddenly I didn't want to own so much stuff. I had no use for most of it anyway. I kept only senti-mental objects and things I couldn't do without.

In that first category, most of it was from Jubal. I lined up all his lit-tle gizmos on the shelf where they had been, including the last one, the one he had sent me on the day of the tsunami. I hadn't even had a chance to open it until I got back from Earth.

It wasn't as impressive as most of the stuff he'd sent me, in fact, it was quite small, just a flat black plastic rectangle an inch on a side, with a red button on it. They called them holosnaps, you could buy them for five dollars down at the gift shop of the Red Thunder, record a message to use as a keepsake. Usually they had a graphic on the back: Greetings From (fill in tourist destination). This one was blank.

I pressed the little red button and set the unit on the table. A little holograph of Jubal's face grinned at me.

"Just a little lucky charm for my main man, Ray! Keep dis wit' you an' you always have good luck! See you soon, me!"

Weird, huh? It was such a pointless little bagatelle.

THEN ONE DAY Travis walked in the front door, looking grim, sparing only a short hug and kiss for each of us. He looked a lot older than he had when we'd parted in Florida. His hair seemed grayer, he had more worry lines on his face.

He was carrying an ordinary plastic packing box, which he took to the newly fortified guest room and set inside. We all joined him and sat on cushions, the only things in the room. Travis got a small lamp out of his box. It was battery-powered. He set it in the center of the circle, and Dad closed the door. I noticed for the first time that there were no light fixtures left in the room. He started removing small boxes from the big boxes and handed one to each of us. They were small e-mail inputs, just keyboards and screens. We turned them on. Again, battery-powered. He took out a small black metal box and set it beside the lamp in the middle, and handed us each a patch cord. He connected his keyboard to the box and showed us that we should all do the same.

The last thing out of Travis's magic box was a small music player. He turned it on and it began to play something I wasn't familiar with. He turned the sound level up a bit. Then he looked at all of us.

"This stuff was all randomly selected, off the shelf. I'm working on the thesis that they can't bug everything on Mars. No more talking. The planet's smallest chat room is now open for business."

TRAVIS: Maybe this is all a waste of time . . . maybe we could sit around and quietly discuss this like free human beings.

KELLY: I think it pays to be careful.

MANNY: Agree. They told me not to talk about Jubal. I'm not going to, to anyone else. But we have to discuss it as a family. They made threats.

KELLY: They told Manny and me they would kill our children while we watched.

RAY: Ditto.

ELIZABETH: Everybody thinks I was raped. I'd almost have preferred
   rape to the drugs. It was mind rape.

KELLY: Ditto. Ray, did they

RAY: They wired my balls, Mom. But they didn't use it.

ELIZABETH: Ditto. My labia.

KELLY: Same here.

TRAVIS: I think we can assume we were all treated about the same.

MANNY: You, too?

TRAVIS: Oh yeah . . . they appeared to enjoy it . . . my money didn't
   help me . . . nor did my American citizenship . . . I don't even
   know where they took me . . . they kept me for seven days . . .
   I was sure I was a dead man . . .

KELLY: They need us. They expect us to lead them to Jubal.

ELIZABETH: What the fuck is happening, Travis?

TRAVIS: What is happening is . . . Jubal has escaped . . . the powers
   that be thought we knew where the most valuable man in the
   world is . . . maybe we should get some refreshments in
   here . . . this is going to take some time . . .

Escaped. Incredible.

Jubal was the most carefully guarded person on Earth. With modern
surveillance techniques, the sort we were hiding from at that very moment, it was possible to keep an eye on *anybody,* twenty-four/seven, no
matter where they went. How hard could it be to keep one strange little
fat guy secured on an island a thousand miles from anywhere? If Jubal
had pulled it off, and it looked like he had, then the Prisoner of Zenda
and Houdini and Jean Valjean had nothing on him.

TRAVIS: Things on the Falklands are not quite what you may have
   thought they are . . . Jubal has been a virtual prisoner for 22
   years . . . but virtual is the key word . . . they always know where
   he is, but that doesn't mean they are actually looking at him . . .

KELLY: What's the difference?

TRAVIS: He's not under surveillance, physically, all the time . . . he
   was at first, but we protested . . . it pissed me off, I thought he
   deserved privacy . . . so I made a fuss . . .

MANNY: How do you make a fuss with those people? We've just seen how powerful they are. I figured they just do what they want to do.

TRAVIS: Looks like they do now, whoever they are . . . but it was different until recently . . . and you're right, I've got a lot of money, I've got some power, but you don't push these guys around . . . what you do, you play them against each other . . . there's different nations with different interests, and I learned all the conflicts between them . . . when I needed something, I'd set India against China, or Japan against Germany, or almost anybody and everybody against the US . . . and I could usually get my way . . . as long as it wasn't something big . . . I kept saving that one . . . I thought of it as the nuclear option . . .

ELIZABETH: ?

TRAVIS: Old slang for the threat of last resort . . . I could always tell them that if they didn't treat Jubal well, we'd take our Tinkertoys and go home . . .

KELLY: You could do that?

TRAVIS: Legally, yes, anytime he wanted to, Jubal could just leave . . . Jubal was a voluntary exile, he's a free man, theoretically . . . I figured it would be fought out in the courts, unless some big nation decided to kidnap him, which could be done with, say, the American Atlantic Fleet . . . but plenty of people would have gone to war over that . . . oh, hell, it gets confusing, politically . . . just believe me that I had some leverage down there, and the big boys were a lot happier not fighting so long as the things I asked for weren't real important . . .

RAY: So what did you ask for?

TRAVIS: The main thing was privacy, like I said . . . first I got them to stop examining his mail, ingoing and outgoing . . . a small thing, but it was a major concession for them . . . who knows what he might have been sending out?

RAY: He sent me a lot of stuff.

TRAVIS: Like what?

RAY: Just little gadgets. I'll show them to you.

TRAVIS: See? . . . a lot of people were opposed to it because of just that . . . who knows what a "little gadget" Jubal made might do? . . . but I was able to convince them that if Jubal made anything important, I'd be the first one to let everybody know because I'm the one who would get rich on it . . . anything Jubal makes belongs to us . . . to US, goddam it, not to anybody's government, not to the UN, not to the Power Company . . . I told them we're not fucking socialists, and if they didn't like it

KELLY: You'd take your Tinkertoys and go home.

MANNY: You'd take your Tinkertoys and go home.

GRANDMA: You'd take your Tinkertoys and go home.

RAY: What's a Tinkertoy?

ELIZABETH: What's a Tinkertoy?

The next thing Travis asked for was that Jubal's labs should be off-limits to observation, like his bedroom and bathroom.

Then a lot of years went by.

It is the security dilemma, according to Travis. You start out alert, whether it's just a shift guarding something or someone, or a career of guarding. But when you've been guarding something for over twenty years and nothing has happened . . . well, you start to assume that nothing *will* happen.

That helped Jubal's escape. Another thing that helped was even more basic. He had never shown the slightest *interest* in escaping. They figured he bought his "protected guest" status, that if he wanted to leave, he'd *ask*.

But when he decided to split, for reasons Travis either didn't know or hadn't revealed to us yet, he didn't ask anybody. He figured out how to do it himself.

He built himself a spaceship and blasted right out of his laboratory.

TRAVIS: I've made friends over the years . . . people have retired and moved into nice houses on what I paid them . . . Nobody I know on the Falklands knows the whole story, but some of them knew pieces . . . It seems Jubal was real upset when the wave hit . . . kept saying it was his fault . . . he tried to call me, tried to call you, Ray, but the phones were out . . . then he quieted down and seemed to accept his situation . . . what he was really doing was figuring out how to bust out of the joint . . . Jubal being Jubal, he seems to have taken the direct approach . . . he built the spaceship right there in his lab, single-handed . . . he must have built it strong, because he blasted right through the roof when he took off . . .

KELLY: Is he okay? Do they know that?

TRAVIS: They can't know . . . but the spaceship worked . . . it tore out of there at five gees . . . by the time they could mount a pursuit it was almost beyond radar range, heading Solar south . . .

MANNY: South? There's nothing down there!

TRAVIS: Part of the escape plan, apparently . . .

We call ourselves spacefarers, and we've been to all eight or twelve planets (depending on who is defining what a planet is) and all the major asteroids between Mars and Jupiter, and all the moons worth visiting, and have even tracked down and landed on thirty or forty Centaurs, which are large bodies found between the orbits of Jupiter and Neptune . . . but we've only touched down on a few dozen of the comets in the Kuiper Belt, and as for the postulated trillion or so long-period comets in the Oort Cloud, we still don't even know within a hundred billion just how many are out there.

Space is vast. We only travel in a tiny slice of it. Forget about galactic clusters 14 billion light years away, forget about even our near galactic neighbors. Don't even think about stars on the other side of our own galaxy, or even in the next spiral arm over. In fact, aside from the exploratory ships that have gone out toward stars within a thirty-light-year radius of our sun, we don't even know what's to be found within half a light-year of us.

And even there, except for a few scientific expeditions, we know only the plane of space where all the planets lie, what we call the ecliptic. A million miles above the Solar South Pole there is . . . nothing. No rocks, no planets, no human presence at all. Ten million miles, same deal. Keep going, and the next thing you'll hit will be another star system. There's just no reason to go there.

Bring it in even closer. In the space around the Earth, the plane of the ecliptic where both the Earth and the moon spend all their time, space is fairly crowded. Near-Earth space is swarming . . . but only out to about a thousand miles. Ninety-nine percent of all orbital activity is equatorial. GPS, weather, and photographic satellites are in polar orbits, but all those benefit from being close in. Go out twenty thousand miles above either pole, and you'll find practically nothing man-made, and nothing at all that's natural. The geosynchronous circle, twenty-two thousand miles above the equator, is another swarming point, thousands of satellites, but still plenty of room for more. There are multiple habitats at the Lagrange points, before and after the moon in its orbit. And that's about it.

Head to the north or the south, and you're in *very* empty space. No one would expect a spaceship to go there. Why would it? It's like some nasty Earthie once said about Mars: There's no *there* there!

TRAVIS: The only stuff that's prepared to accelerate like that is military, and that's mostly on Earth, in close-Earth orbit, or on the moon . . . A few interceptors gave chase, I think, but it was fifteen, twenty minutes before they scrambled . . . By then Jubal was already out of reach and . . . when they lost him on radar he was still accelerating, still going in a straight line . . . bottom line, there's just too much space out there to search . . . so . . . take your pick.

ELIZABETH: Pick from what?

TRAVIS: Worst case, the ship came apart . . . best case, he shut it down himself and he's coasting, he figures to get well out of range before he decelerates . . . how long he could wait would depend on how much air and water and food he brought along

. . . .

GRANDMA: Okay, I'll break this long silence. You look like you've thought of a third possibility, Travis.

TRAVIS: Yeah . . . maybe he just intends to . . . keep going . . .

15

★ ★ ★

WE HAD SEVERAL other meetings in the safe room, but basically, that was all we learned. Jubal had busted out, and nobody, not even Travis, knew where he was.

There was one huge problem with the idea of Jubal leaving the Falklands in a spaceship, though.

Jubal doesn't fly.

Not on spaceships, not on airplanes. When they took him to the Falklands, he went on a military ship. In fact, Jubal's list of phobias could probably be used as a reference for a diagnostic manual. Of the most common ones about the only ones he misses are arachnophobia and herpetophobia. Jubal likes all animals except people. He doesn't like heights, or small spaces, or crowds, or cities, or strangers. Basically, what he likes are solitude in the outdoors, preferably a swamp or river or lake; boats; inventing things; his family, and my family.

We were all having a hard time imagining him getting into the sort of small spaceship he could build secretly in his lab, much less taking off in it. We tossed around other ideas, but none of them made any sense. Stowing away on a supply boat? Getting on it would have been impossible in the first place, and he would have been missed in twenty-four hours, and how far could a ship go in that time?

Submarine? No way it could sneak into those protected waters. No way he could build one, launch it, and get far enough away to not get recaptured. Besides, a submarine is claustrophobic.

Disguise? Pretend to be someone else? Don't make me laugh.

Travis came up with the only other possible explanation, and it wouldn't have made sense for anyone but Jubal.

TRAVIS: Maybe he invented a teleporter and beamed himself up to
    join Captain Kirk and Mr. Spock.
RAY: Who's Captain Kirk?

Things gradually got back to normal. It's amazing how quickly you sort of adapt to living in a police state.

Not that we didn't resent it. Nobody likes to see troops in black uniforms with giant guns posted at every intersection. Once we knew for sure that they had orders not to shoot unless physically attacked, it became fashionable to spit toward their boots every time you walked past one. At the end of a shift you didn't want to walk too near them. Slippery.

Taunting was popular, too. Wise guys outdid each other coming up with insults, chants, nasty signs. Groups gathered to insult them. Mooning was popular and, since most of them were males and no Martian woman would be caught dead keeping company with them, not even the prostitutes, groups of high school girls liked to get together and pull up their shirts or drop their pants and challenge their manhood.

Funny, we'd never had a demonstration before they came, and now we had three or four of them every day. Most of them didn't amount to much more than "Earthies Go Home!" but there were more thoughtful people who had come to see the invasion as a political opportunity.

The word most people were using was "participation." Martians wanted more say in our destiny. Up to then, most people thought of "Martian destiny" as making as much money as possible. Down deep, most of us still thought of ourselves as Earthies. The invasion started changing that.

*　*　*

ONLY A FEW things happened worth mentioning during the next month. Travis told us the real reason the Power Company was so upset about losing Jubal, and we had our second and third invasions.

It was starting to look like they were lining up out there to invade us. "All nation-states, corporations, power-mad billionaires, and disgruntled liberation groups wishing to invade Mars please take a number and wait your turn," as a popular comedian put it.

The point of the joke was that we didn't know who the second and third waves of invaders were. We still didn't have much of an idea who our *occupiers* were, though theories abounded, and most people agreed it was an extragovernmental coalition of corporations.

If *who* was in dispute, *why* was even more problematic, except to members of my family and the Redmonds, who couldn't talk. There were rumors that Jubal was dead, vigorously denied by all concerned and backed up by some excellent videoshopped news stories that showed a smiling Jubal working happily in his lab and talking to some visitors, casually referring to various current events. Anyone who knew Jubal knew in an instant that it was bullshit—it took an event the size of the tsunami to get Jubal's attention at all—but nobody but my family and the staff in the Falklands really knew Jubal, so they got away with it.

It's on Mars. Who cares? We got problems of our own.

Evangeline and I just happened to have a front-row seat for the second invasion. Well, I guess we did for the first one, too, but it's not the one I would have picked, seeing as how we almost got killed.

We had been coming out onto the roof of the Red Thunder in the evenings. We'd sit together, watch the sunset. Martian sunsets are pretty, if you like pink. No, we didn't get it on, nobody's figured out how to do that in a pressure suit. It was *night*, you understand, and basically, Martians don't go out at night unless it's an emergency. What you do if you *have* to go out after dark is put on an insulated oversuit, stay in groups of three or more, and get back inside as soon as you can. And still you get cold.

What we'd do those summer evenings was sit on electric pads, lean back against our airpacks, hold hands, and watch the stars come out. Watch Phobos move across the sky, see the blazing exhausts of ships blasting for Earth or the outer planets. Watch for meteorites burning up. Sometimes we talked about anything and everything under the sun, sometimes we hardly said anything. We'd stay out there until our feet and hands started getting cold, then we'd hurry inside and down to my room and jump under the covers until we'd generated some heat.

Dad and Mom didn't know where we went those evenings. It wasn't permitted, strictly speaking, and it was just a wee bit dangerous, though we were always within ten seconds of the pressurized and heated freight elevator. Sometimes you just wanted to get away from people, you know?

Then one night, all ten of the black ships that had surrounded the city for just over a month blasted into the air.

"Whoa!" Evangeline breathed, and we both sat up straighter. We were almost blinded by the light of their bubble-drive exhausts, bright enough to partially polarize our faceplates. "What's going on?"

"You got me."

The black saucer-shaped ships were soon invisible against the black sky, but the exhausts were still there, and dwindling fast.

"They must be pulling five gees," she said. "What's the hurry?"

"Beats me. Maybe they just got tired of pushing people around and decided to go home." She was looking at me, trying to decide if I was kidding. She laughed.

"Yeah, right. Well, good riddance." She pointed a middle finger skyward and let out a whoop. "Take that, you fuckers! And never come back!"

That was the moment that one of the black ships exploded. We stared at it, stunned, a huge white flower like a fireworks burst. We could actually see bits of it twisting and turning, trailing fire.

Evangeline was still standing there, finger extended like she didn't quite know what to do with it.

"Don't ever point that thing at me, okay?" I told her.

"That's not funny."

It was miles and miles away by then. We watched until most of the wreckage had fallen beyond the horizon. For the next fifteen minutes we watched the first space battle in history develop over our heads.

Being Martians, and having spent quite a few nights out there on the roof, we thought we knew spaceships. These ships were behaving like ships in a bad sci-fi movie from last century, twisting, deking, slowing, and accelerating. It was an actual dogfight. At the speeds they were moving, it must have been brutal for the crews.

"Those things were purpose-built," I told Evangeline at one point.

"What do you mean?"

"Your normal ship has just the one drive, at the back. It's built to take acceleration stresses from just one direction. There's little attitude jets, but they couldn't put a ship into a turn in vacuum like we're seeing here. For that, they must have side drives, forward-facing drives, all of them highly maneuverable. These things are to normal spaceships like a fighter jet is to the *Sovereign*."

They were armed like fighters, too. We'd see one of them streaking along, a thin line of expanding light, and suddenly there would be a series of flashes and the tinier lines of air-to-air missiles being launched. Actually, space-to-space, I guess, though I'd never heard the term. Aside from a few satellite shoot-downs, the military guys had never been allowed to play their deadly games in space because of international treaties.

Didn't seem to matter to these guys, and I knew they hadn't built these killer ships in the days since Jubal flew the coop. Somebody had been cheating, and hiding it.

We could see the movements of the ships because they seemed always to be under thrust, sometimes sprouting more than one exhaust as they used the only means of turning in space, which was vectoring thrust to one side or another, using secondary engines. Sometimes one bright plume would stop spouting and another would start, in precisely the opposite direction. You get going too fast up there, and next thing you know you're beyond the fight. They didn't take the time to turn ship, they had jets in the nose, and in the sides as well.

We'd see what looked like small explosions . . . and have no way to tell just how big or small they really were, since we didn't know the distance. They could be firecrackers a half mile up, or nuclear bombs a hundred thousand miles away. But some burst in clusters, and I figured they were salvoes of missiles, possibly intending to spread shrapnel in the path of another ship.

Naturally our faceplates were buzzing with small windows off to one side, and normally I'd have been doing a lot of looking and listening to that stuff . . . but how often do you see a thing like we were seeing, live, right in front of your face? The news was a mass of confusion, anyway, the times I glanced at it. One talking-head newscaster was actually in his pajamas, looking like he was at home, just got out of bed, as he relayed the jumbled information he was getting.

Ships taking off. Explosions. Fire in the sky! No reports of injuries . . .

I knew more than he did, so I shut him down.

Then there was a *big* fireball in the sky, and a short time later, another.

"I'm getting real tired of not knowing what the hell's going on," Evangeline said.

"You and me both. Do you think—"

There was a loud emergency signal in my helmet. A face appeared on a larger window, overriding our own stuff. She was wearing the uniform of the Emergency Services, the Martian equivalent of the fire department. They did handle fires, but their main concern was pressure integrity.

"Even when this fighting is over," she said, "we are concerned with debris impacting ships in space and the surface itself. We are advising all airboarders to stay within Phobos, or land as soon as possible. All shuttle flights are canceled until further notice. All deep-space vessels are advised to get as far as possible from the fighting, since our radar is showing literally thousands of high-velocity fragments and we haven't had time to chart the fastest and/or most dangerous ones.

"Everyone downside is advised to remain in their quarters with pressure doors sealed and storm shutters closed, or to seek public shelters on the lowest levels. Follow the flashing green arrows embedded in the floors of all public areas. Remain in the shelters, tuned to this channel, until the all clear has sounded."

I was going to say something, but Evangeline was shouting and pointing behind me. I turned, and saw something big coming down. It burned a bright blue-white, and chunks of stuff were coming off it and bursting. For a moment it seemed to be coming right at us, but that was an optical illusion, I guess, because it passed overhead at least a mile up. I could judge the distance because it still retained some of the saucer shape of the black ships. It looked like a big bite had been taken out of it. It went over the hills to the east of town, there was a moment when we could see nothing . . . then a towering fireball rose into the air just as the sonic boom from its passage overhead hit us.

"I think we'd better get below," I said.

"I'm already on my way."

I got another urgent message as we ran for the elevator. Dad's face popped up in a side window, looking harassed.

"Ray, where are you?"

"On my way, Dad."

"Come to the subbasement shelter if you're close enough," he said. "Have you heard anything from your sister?"

That's the moment it all stopped being a video game for me. Pretty late, I know that, but you had to be there. Until that ship crashed beyond the hills it was very hard to make yourself believe it was all really happening.

The elevator shook as we descended. Evangeline grabbed my arm and held on, and I put my arm around her. Ice was forming on our supercold suits and bits of it flaked off and fell at our feet.

We reached the bottom elevator level and stepped out into a crowd of hurrying people, some of them dressed in suits, most of them in regular clothes. Down a flight of stairs and we were in the pressure shelter, the absolute last line of defense against blowouts, only to be used if you felt the whole structure of the Red Thunder Hotel was in danger of being breached.

Later, Dad had cause to be proud of his workers. We only do shelter drill twice a year, as opposed to pressure drill, where all guests are sealed into their rooms for ten minutes and shown a video of how to don emergency suits, which we do once a week. So you might have expected them to be a little rusty, especially since nobody really took shelter drill all that seriously. After all, what sort of catastrophe was likely to rupture all the multilayered pressure defenses at the same time? No quakes on Mars. No tsunamis. Plenty of tornadoes, but pretty weak in the thin air.

War? Don't make me laugh.

But there they were, hustling the confused and beginning-to-be-frightened hotel guests into the shelter almost as efficiently as the crew of the *Sovereign*, who did this sort of drill once a week. Two big guys in bellhop uniforms were at the entrance, putting a hand on everyone's shoulder to move them along, while the other hand passed out emergency suit kits.

"Move it along, please, take one and move it along, all the way to the end of the corridor. Move it along, break the seal on the suit pack, and you'll be shown how to put it on. Move it along. I'm sorry sir, I don't have time to answer your questions, move it along please . . ."

We hurried down the long, narrow room. TV screens every ten feet or so were showing how to break the seals on the suit packs, how to unfold them, how to step into them, how to zip them up. Very few people had gotten that far. A lot of them were still at step one and not making a lot of progress. Most of them were stuck at step three, trying to stick their legs into the suit arms or putting them on backwards. You can wear them backwards, in a pinch . . . but pinch is the key word. They're just thick man-shaped baggies, designed to be tolerable for about an hour, and survivable for a day. You plug the air hose into the socket in the wall, then you sit there, sweltering or freezing, wondering if the next time the air monitor says you need more oxy, there will be any coming down the line.

How I Spent My Martian Vacation.

Dad was near the end of the shelter with half a dozen employees, working on the more hopeless cases. He was trying to unwrap the air hose from an elderly woman's neck. The old lady was looking a little blue. He looked up.

"Ramon, I need you . . ." A piece of ice flaked off my suit and dropped at his feet. He frowned at it for a second, then at me, then decided to ask me later what I'd been doing out at night. "Get to the pressure control center. They're a man short." He turned back to his charges, and I made myself scarce, with Evangeline following behind me.

The control center was just off the middle of the tube. There were three chairs in there, each facing consoles. From them we could access any of the hundreds of cameras in the Red Thunder complex. I slid into a seat. I recognized Patil Par-something, never could remember his last name, our house detective.

"What the situation?" I asked.

"We've got about a dozen rooms where the guests refused to leave," Patil said, and shrugged. "They're safe enough, probably. We've sealed their doors, lowered the shutters. Still maybe forty or fifty in the halls and on the elevators, on their way here."

"Have you heard from Elizabeth?"

Patil pointed to one of his screens. "Your sister's on her way."

I saw her hurrying through an almost deserted mall. Behind her was a solid wall of transparent Kevlar, which I'd always thought of as plenty safe enough but, considering the impact I'd seen, suddenly looked like delicate crystal with my sister framed against it. Of course, solid steel would have been no better against a missile hit.

I noticed something else behind her. There were four of the soldiers, the black troops, standing together.

"Looks like they took off in such a hurry, they left the grunts behind," Patil said, with a trace of satisfaction.

I heard a disturbance behind me. It got louder, with people shouting. I jumped up and stuck my head through the door.

One of the black troops was in the shelter. He had thrown off his helmet and was shoving his way through the crowd, his huge weapon held out in front of him.

"Lemme through, lemme through!" he was shouting. He was a huge man, red-faced, either bald or with a shaved head. He was shining with sweat as he passed me, and breathing heavily. His eyes were all over the place, like a trapped animal.

I knew what was going on. They call it pnigophobia, which is fear of choking, but it's actually a fear of vacuum. This dude must have been medicated to make it to Mars at all, and he'd certainly been in terror during his whole stay.

He reached my dad and grabbed him by the arm.

"Gimme one of those," he shouted, and took the suit bag Dad was holding and started trying to do two things at once with one hand: tear open the suit bag and unbuckle his big equipment belt, which would make him too bulky to fit in the suit. It wasn't working, so he set his weapon down and concentrated on the equipment belt.

Dad watched until the guy got the belt off and dropped it. Then Dad kicked the weapon along the floor, reached down and pulled the billy club from the belt ring, and hit the guy in the face like Babe Ruth swinging for the bleachers.

Blood sprayed, but the dude didn't go down. He shook his head and looked pretty pissed off. Dad swung a second time, and the guy grabbed the billy and twisted. Dad was no match for the guy's Earthie strength, but he rolled with it and let go and backed away as the guy started into a karate kick.

I don't doubt he was a real terror on Earth, all these guys were obviously elite soldiers, Rangers, SEALs, Delta Force, whatever bullshit name they were using these days. But the gravity fooled him, and he hit his head on the ceiling and landed flat on his face.

The next thing that happened was truly astounding. A little girl who couldn't have been older than twelve stepped forward and kicked him in the ear. Lots of nerves in the ear. Must have hurt like a bastard.

He roared and reached out for her but she skipped out of the way, and two more people kicked him from behind. Two people stepped forward and grabbed the billy club and held on as three people jumped on his back. He got up as far as his knees before more people started piling on. The sound of it was frightening, the pent-up rage. They were shouting, screaming, growling . . . It seemed everybody wanted a piece of him, and if they'd continued, I'm pretty sure they'd have literally torn him to pieces.

"Stop!" Dad shouted. "Stop it right now!"

It took a while, but with the help of a few others Dad dug him out of the pile. He was bloody, his uniform was in tatters, and it looked like a piece of his ear was missing. Dad had the weapon in his hands.

He poked the man with his foot, and the guy didn't move. He was out.

"He's still alive," Dad said. "Take him to the infirmary." When nobody moved, he looked around at the people. "Nobody's going to be killed in my hotel if I can help it."

A couple guys stepped forward and picked up the soldier and carried him, not in a manner I'd call gently, to the infirmary. Dad hurried over to me. So within less than a minute I'd found two more reasons to be proud of the old man.

"Ray, get back to your screens. I need to know where everybody is."

I jumped back into my chair. Me and Patil scrolled quickly through the cameras on all the floors. The halls were all empty. The camera just outside the shelter showed half a dozen people still trying to jam through the door. None of them were black troops. I switched through half a dozen screens and saw no one. The last screen showed the four troops I'd seen earlier, and they seemed to be arguing. Then they seemed to come to a decision, and started to jog.

"They're headed our way," I said.

"Get those stragglers inside," Dad said, "and then seal the doors." He stood up straight and wiped sweat from his brow. I saw his hand was trembling. "I won't have anybody killed in my hotel, but I won't shelter those monsters, either."

THE MONSTERS CAME to the door and banged on it. We could hear them, but only faintly. Like I said, Martian doors are strong and thick, and there were two of them here, an inner and an outer one. There was no glass in either one.

Dad herded the people to the far end of the tunnel and then stood there facing the door with the weapon in his hands. I switched back and forth between the inside and outside cameras, between my dad and the guys outside pleading to get in.

Three reasons to be proud.

We couldn't hear what they were saying, but it was getting rough. One was shoving another, and that one shoved back. One of them leveled his weapon at the outer door, another knocked the barrel away—apparently the smarter of the two, as he realized that it wouldn't do a lot of good to get inside by destroying the air lock. Stupidity won out, though, and the first one got his weapon pointed right again and let off a burst. *That* we heard, very loudly. Dad jumped, but held the weapon steady.

It didn't work like it does in the movies. In real life, you shoot bullets like that into a hard surface and the suckers like to ricochet. When the smoke cleared, two of the troops were down. One was writhing in pain, and the other wasn't moving. The door wasn't hurt.

They didn't fire any more rounds.

IN ALL, WE stayed in the shelter for eight hours. Things got organized fairly soon, and before long we were getting reports about the various explosions, and the debris, and the expected impact points of the larger chunks.

The debris, the remains of spaceships and human beings, could do one of three things. The largest part of it was moving at escape velocity and went into orbit around the sun, never to be seen again. A smaller part impacted on the surface. A little bit went into orbit, to be cleaned up later. After two hours all the most dangerous stuff was accounted for. We stayed an extra six hours in the shelter, just to be on the safe side.

When we came out, there was some blood on the floor, but no troops. We had seen them dragging the dead or wounded off, and we never saw them again.

Ten black ships took off and went to war. Seven came back. Whoever they were fighting, they either went back home or were destroyed.

NOBODY TOLD US anything. The black troops took up their posts again, but there weren't as many of them, and they gave off a real scary vibe. But it didn't seem directed at us Martians so much as at their own commanders. None of them had died during the attack simply because there had been no blowouts. It turned out they were as safe outside the shelters as we had been inside them. But it wasn't lost on them that they had basically been abandoned.

They weren't supposed to talk to us except to give us orders, or as much as was strictly necessary for things like weapons searches. But a few Martians began to talk to them, and a few of them talked back. Bits and pieces gleaned from these contacts began to be heard on underground networks.

Believe it or not, they didn't seem to know a lot more than we did. They were a mercenary force, as we had figured, but they didn't know who was paying the bills. True to the mercenary ethic, they didn't really care so long as the money was good. You got the impression that a lot of them would have been a lot happier in a situation where they actually got to kill folks. Apparently they had considerable experience in that department; there were dozens of places on Earth where people with their skills were in great demand. Same old story.

But none of them were what you'd call space warriors for the simple reason that no war had ever been fought in space, or on another planet. These guys were used to fighting in hostile environments, in deserts and jungles, basically all the shit holes of the world, where so much of the violence was concentrated.

What they weren't used to was fighting in a place where you hardly dared shoot your weapon for fear that you'd cause a blowout that could kill you. They figured they could survive in any place on Earth, but the only place they could survive on Mars was amidst the "hostiles," in a controlled environment. And since they were not trained in low-pressure combat and were not expected to go out on the surface . . . they hadn't been issued pressure suits.

The word went out: *Leave the grunts alone.* Where did "the word" come from? Nobody was sure. But there was a "revolutionary" under-ground, and it was communicating in the good old low-tech way, by whispering into ears in dark corners. You can't bug every place, and what the supercomputers couldn't hear they couldn't analyze. The big advan-tage in staying clandestine was that the invaders had very little "humint," as the folks in the spy game put it: human intelligence. They couldn't put agents among us, they'd stand out like cows in a herd of horses.

Am I saying we had no traitors? No Benedict Arnolds?

No, of course not . . . but we had a lot fewer than you'd think. Not really from any overwhelming sense of "patriotism," that idea hadn't re-ally caught on yet. But we were mightily pissed off, okay? We were an-gry enough over the "Red Thunder Ten" business, and now the invasion . . . enough already, okay? It was us versus them, and I guess that's where patriotism starts out.

Plus, one day the names of six collaborators were put out on the grapevine, and those six somehow got the living crap beat out of them by people who they were all unable to identify. Worse, after that nobody would talk to them. *Nobody.* The thin trickle of human intelligence our occupiers had been paying good money for dried up to no more than a drip after that. It seemed wiser, if you couldn't really see yourself as a Martian, if you couldn't stand with your oppressed brothers and sisters, if you only wanted to get on with your business, to at least *shut the fuck up!*

But that was the real key to our stiffened resistance, when all was said and done. Getting on with our business.

Business was bad.

The only thing that prevented all the hotels on Mars from being empty the day after the invasion was that there just weren't enough ships to carry all the tourists at once.

You want to make a Martian mad? Do something to screw up the hospitality industry. *Now* you've got our attention.

16

★ ★ ★

KELLY: So Travis, do you know anything at all about what's going on?

TRAVIS: Very little . . . I'm not the CIA or a Homelander . . . have a few sources in both places . . . they're not talking . . . bottom line everybody thinks it's some sort of corporate fight . . . maybe with political backing from the Chinese or the Americans . . . though the Americans are pretty busy with other stuff like a few million dead people and 400 million very angry ones . . .

MANNY: What do they want with us? Is it Mars they want, or . . . us?

TRAVIS: It's us . . . because we're the only possible link to Jubal, if he's still alive . . . and Jubal is the key to everything . . . to a lot more than you know . . . and I'm afraid Jubal did a very rash thing before he took off . . .

Travis then told us the first part of why everybody was *really* so anxious to find Jubal. Even then he didn't tell us all of the reason. Maybe he wanted to break it to us gradually, just what a hole we were in.

* * *

TO THE EYES of the world, Travis had handed over the responsibility for the Squeezer drive to the assembled leaders of the world and its citizens that sunny day at the Orange Bowl before I was born. In the *real* world, it wasn't over.

Travis had always known the Squeezer drive was incredibly dangerous, much worse than any atomic bomb that had ever been built. Squeezer bombs could literally blow up the Earth. Could humanity handle all that power? But did Travis have the right to be the anti-Prometheus, denying humanity the free power that could do so much to solve so many problems? Bubble power could lift vast parts of humanity out of poverty, stop its reliance on increasingly scarce and polluting resources like oil, coal, and uranium. It gave us the power to travel the solar system, and even reach the stars.

Travis decided he didn't have the right to hold it back . . . but Travis *always* hedged his bets. He did a lot of hedging, and only some of it was public knowledge.

The system they came up with had worked well for over twenty years, and there were three parts to it:

1. Primary Squeezer units, the ones that made the bubbles and could control their size and hence the degree of compression inside them, were made only on the Falkland Islands, and only by Jubal and/or the small number of scientists Jubal schooled in the techniques of making them. So far, no one else had figured out how to do it for themselves.

2. Once made, there was nothing safer than a bubble. Just what a bubble *was* was still a subject of fierce debate and terrible frustration in physics labs all over the world. Travis and Jubal had never allowed them to be studied, and though a few had fallen into unauthorized hands over the years, nobody was any the wiser yet. Squeezer technology had upset a lot of applecarts in the world of physics, and what fruit they had managed to stack up again was badly bruised. But one thing was known, and that was, once you'd made a bubble, there was nothing you could do with it without the *second* unit, the one that introduced what Jubal

called a "discontinuity" in the perfectly smooth, perfectly round, perfectly impenetrable surface.

3. Jubal's original Squeezer, cobbled together from parts gathered around his lab and a few mysterious items he'd never publicly described, for obvious reasons, could make bubbles *and* produce the discontinuities. But when they began to be produced in bulk, the machine was divided into two components: the primary Squeezers, of which there were only a few, and disrupters, of which there were many. A disrupter could be installed in a spaceship to provide direct thrust, or in a power plant to generate electricity. So they came in all sizes and could be found in many different types of machines, but they all had one thing in common: You fuck with them, they go *boom!*

This had nothing to do with the bubbles themselves. If an airplane powered by a bubble drive crashed into the ground, the bubble was not harmed. You might find it in the wreckage, if it didn't simply float off and waft its way into the upper atmosphere and then deep space. No, disrupters blew up because of booby traps built into the disrupter mechanisms. Jubal had built the booby traps, connected to ordinary explosive charges, just enough to ensure that the disrupter would be destroyed.

Naturally, over the years some nasty people had gotten their hands on disrupters and tried to take them apart. *Boom!* Hell, I had a tiny disrupter unit in my airboard. I had no doubt that if I tried to take it apart, I'd lose a hand, minimum.

So far, Jubal seemed to have thought of everything. If you X-rayed a disrupter with enough power to see anything . . . *boom!*

Magnetic resonance imaging? Sure, it had been tried. Subject a disrupter to a strong enough magnetic field and . . . not *boom*, not yet, but the unit suffered a meltdown internally, and if you tried to take it apart then . . . *boom!*

Nobody talked about it much, but there were well-documented stories from people who had worked on these projects, in China, America, England, France, and other countries. The list of corporations that had tried to take them apart was long, too, as well as a few terrorists. The result was always the same. Jubal had built them well.

Crushing a disrupter unit was simplicity itself, of course. They weren't invulnerable. Just put the unit in a hydraulic press and turn it on. Crunch! *Boom!* And what do you have? A free-floating bubble and a crushed disrupter. Oh, my, the studies that had been done on those crushed disrupters! The smoking remains had been taken apart atom by atom, probed by microscopic nanobots. Thousands of experimental models had been built from the bits and pieces of knowledge painfully put together by destructive testing, then turned on . . . and nothing. They just sat there.

Though there were a few diehards out there still trying, bubble research was so frustrating that not much of it was going on today. From time to time a theoretical physicist or a group of them would issue an impassioned plea to be allowed to communicate with Jubal, citing the enormous leaps in human knowledge that could be gained if only they understood . . . well, what the fuck a bubble *was*. So far, Travis and Jubal and the High Priests of Squeeze had resisted all attempts to let the genie of unlimited power out of the bottle.

That was the *public* bet hedging, the part everybody knew about.

TRAVIS: You know me . . . a belt and suspenders man . . . I learned piloting VStars that there's never too many backups . . . so what if it all went very, very wrong? . . . what if somebody got their hands on a Squeezer machine and started making bubbles and putting them in suitcases with stolen disrupters? . . . the disrupters that are given out . . . there are thousands of them on Mars alone, they won't make a bubble blow up, they won't turn them OFF . . . but they can make them blast at such a rate that it might as well be an explosion . . .

KELLY: What did you do, Travis?

TRAVIS: Hey, don't type in that tone of voice with me . . . anyway, suitcase? Hell, they could be small enough to fit in your pocket and be able to destroy half a city . . . So I asked Jubal to build a booby trap into all the PRIMARY Squeezer units, too . . . he built it into the software, it's buried real deep, I doubt if anybody could find it even if they were able to look, and naturally nobody but the folks at the Falklands have access to ANY of the insides of a primary unit . . .

MANNY: I'm afraid to ask what the booby trap was.

TRAVIS: Nothing fancy . . . nothing that's going to hurt anybody . . . there was a password . . . too long to memorize and you had to enter it three times in a row . . . only Jubal and I have it . . . it makes the important stuff, the guts of the Squeezer unit, melt down into slag . . .

RAY: And Jubal . . .

TRAVIS: This is speculation, people, but it's the only thing that could account for why they want him back so bad . . . sometime just after he left . . . it had to be after, because if it was BEFORE they'd have been on him in a flash . . . Jubal must have sent out the password . . .

ELIZABETH: How many did he shut down?

TRAVIS: There's only one way to do it, hon . . . sending out the signal would shut ALL of them down . . .

So now Earth was virtually without power, right? The vast machine humanity had constructed since the Industrial Revolution was grinding to a halt; they'd have to start dusting off the coal-burners, rebuild the torn-down dams, start drilling for oil again . . .

Well, no.

Not yet, anyway. So far, no one but those at the very top knew anything was wrong. Which was why there was a power struggle—literally—like the world had never seen to get Jubal back and make him start building primary Squeezers again.

Squeezer bubbles came in a variety of sizes. The ones used in the big power-generating plants naturally had a lot more energy inside them than the little one that powered my airboard, which would last for about a year of heavy use. The amount of matter that was squeezed into a particular bubble was precisely measured and appropriate to the task. And just to be on the super, super, *super* safe side, even the power-plant bubbles didn't contain enough energy to run the plant forever. Typically, they needed a new bubble twice a year. And new ones were sent ahead, so most of the plants had a year or two on hand. So it would be a while before the machine began to sputter. Enough time to at least begin to start looking for alternative sources of energy . . . if anyone dared even suggest that. Trouble was, firing up an old nuke or any power plant would raise some pretty awkward questions.

You say you can't make any more bubbles?

You say Jubal Broussard blew up all the Squeezer plants?

You say that the most carefully guarded man on Earth slipped through your fingers? You say you lost him?

I'd call those awkward questions. Not the sort of thing the electorate would want to hear at any time, even less in the wake of the worst catastrophe since the Second World War, at a time of financial panic.

But *wait* a minute . . .

RAY: Something I don't get, Travis.

TRAVIS: I think I know where you're going.

RAY: Why don't the . . . what do they call themselves? Why don't the High Priests of Squeeze just make some more Squeezers?

TRAVIS: . . . yes . . . why don't they . . . .

KELLY: . . . my clock says it's been two minutes, Travis . . .

MANNY: Three minutes. Spit it out, Travis. What haven't you told us?

TRAVIS: . . . brace yourselves . . .

And Travis told us his last secret. It was a doozy.

I NEEDED TIME to think. We all did, I guess.

I think best in my hidey-hole on Phobos. I hadn't been up there since the invasion . . . the *first* invasion, now. Tell you the truth, I'd been a little scared about getting back on my board. They say, on Earth, a shark takes a bite out of your board, you should get right back up on it, like if you're thrown off a horse, or you'll start thinking about it too much. I kept seeing that black ship swooping toward me like some predatory bird . . .

So I let Evangeline drive, even though she didn't have her license.

No problem. Evangeline's instinctive feel for free fall made her the best seat-of-the-pants boarder I'd ever seen. Maybe a little hard on the accelerator, for a rookie, but she never came close to getting into a jackpot I couldn't have gotten her out of.

We did what we usually did when we got to my trailer. It was wonderful. She seemed to think I was the best thing that had ever happened to her. I'm only average-looking, I've got no illusions, girls didn't sigh and stumble when I walked by. She made me feel better-looking than I really am.

And let's get the word right out there. Love. I was pretty sure I was in love with her. I wanted to make her happy more than I wanted to make myself happy. I wanted to take care of her, have fun with her, be around her no matter what we were doing.

I was jealous when other guys looked at her. Is that bad? Given her looks, it was going to happen a lot, but I never had to fight over her. She could shut a guy down with a few words, making him feel like he was something she'd scraped off the bottom of her shoe. It was awesome to see. Where do girls learn that? I guess beautiful girls have to learn it or never have a moment's peace.

Afterward, we relaxed with a pipe of Phobos Red, reputed to be the best marijuana in the solar system. I wouldn't know; I'd never smoked anything else. It's not illegal on Mars. Some people say it will lead to hard, dangerous drugs, like alcohol, but that's not been our experience on Mars.

I had a problem.

I had sworn a solemn oath not to reveal what was discussed at the last meeting in the safe room, which had included only Grandma, Mom, Dad, Travis, Elizabeth, and me. And that didn't seem right to me. It's not like I wanted to tell the Redmond monsters . . . but I thought Mr. and Mrs. Redmond had a right to know just why they'd been put through so much hell, and of course, Evangeline.

But I wanted to talk. Boy, did I ever want to talk.

I took a last hit and was about to try to ease into the subject when the doorbell rang. This time Evangeline pulled on a robe and when she opened the door the FedEx guy looked sad, as if he remembered the last delivery, which he probably did.

"See, here's the deal, spacegirl," he said. "That package you guys never did pick up? Tomorrow's the last day before I have to send it back. Do you want it or not?"

I'd forgotten all about it. I'd been sort of busy for a while after we made our last departure from Phobos.

I didn't get a lot of packages. Most of what I did get was from Jubal. That would be interesting enough in normal circumstances, but considering his status as a . . . what? fleeing felon? I guess destroying the Squeezers was probably against the law, even though he'd built them himself. Anyway, this must have been the last thing he sent me before he became a wanted man. Maybe it had a clue as to where he'd gone.

"We'll be down there in a minute," I told him, and this time I gave him a tip. We made it down to the freight office before he did.

IT WAS A standard shipping box, a four-by-four-by-four plastic cube with rounded corners and ridges on sides to make it slide easier. Stickers had been partially peeled off it or messily covered over with thick felt-tip pens. There was no single sticker still intact to tell us what its contents might be. The only things readable on the outside were the label addressed to me, Phobos, Big Bubble NW, and a red sticker with a white arrow that said THIS SIDE UP. Pointless in Phobos.

We herded the box back to my trailer. You don't carry things in Phobos, you walk behind them and urge them, or go ahead and tug them. We got it inside, pulled the handle, the lid popped up, and it seemed somebody had send me a box full of . . .

. . . dried grass.

"It's from Jubal," I said.

Evangeline laughed. "It's not smokable, is it?"

"I guess you could smoke anything, but this wouldn't do anything for you. This is plain old tussock grass. Now that the sheep are gone from the Falkland Islands, it grows pretty high all over the place. Great habitat for birds."

"So . . . what? You think he was planning to send you some penguins? This was to feed them?"

"It's packing material. Like excelsior." I sighed. "Jubal does things different than other people do. He doesn't like foam peanuts."

We pulled out handfuls of the stuff, and pretty soon we came to a black hole.

I don't know how else to describe it. It was like nothing else I'd ever seen. Nothing anyone had ever seen. It was like an antibubble.

Like a Squeezer bubble, you couldn't really touch it. I mean, you could put your fingers on it, but you couldn't grip. Your fingers just slid right off. Nothing clung to it. The dried grass was full of dust, dirt, seeds, but none of it clung to the bubble.

But where a normal bubble is totally reflective, this thing was the absence of reflection. Imagine an eight-ball on a pool table . . . and now forget it. An eight-ball is shiny. Imagine a ball made of charcoal . . . and forget that, too. Charcoal is dull and black, but you can see it. It reflects enough light to see features on it.

It had no temperature. It had no features. It looked like a hole in space.

We pushed it out of the box and it hung there.

"I don't *like* that thing," Evangeline said, softly.

Here's the best thing I can think of to describe how it looked. It made the real world look like a photograph with a perfectly round hole cut in it and nothing behind it but outer space.

"I *really* don't like this thing," Evangeline said. I agreed. Black is okay, I like black as a color. This was so far beyond black . . . did you ever see that movie *2001: A Space Odyssey*? Those black slabs in that movie? Compared to this thing, those slabs were bright as an emergency magnesium locator flare.

"What the hell are you supposed to do with it?" she asked. "It's from your uncle Jubal, right?"

"Couldn't be anybody else."

Then I remembered Jubal's "lucky piece," the little holosnap he'd told me to carry around with me as a "lucky piece." Luckily, I had it in my pocket.

"What's that? Holosnap?"

"Jubal sent it to me."

I thumbed the red button, expecting to see the little image of Jubal.

"—ull of Grace, The Lord is with thee. Blessed art thou among . . ."

The black hole was gone, and hovering there in the air, curled up in the fetal position, was Jubal.

Who promptly began to scream, then to vomit.

THINGS GOT PRETTY confused for a while. Evangeline didn't scream, but she let out a little squeak. Hell, I probably squeaked myself.

"I'm fallin', I'm fallin'!" Jubal was shouting. "Make it stop!"

There was nothing I could do about that, but I tried to put my arms around him, to at least give him some comfort.

Bad idea. First I got smacked in the face by one of his flailing hands. I was sent swirling head over heels to the far wall. Jubal is strong, and he was in total panic, like a drowning man. I waded back in. Evangeline had hold of one of his feet and was hanging on for dear life. I grabbed an arm, and we all three did a violent dance around the small space, banging into walls.

Finally, I worked myself into position in front of him and grabbed his face.

"Jubal! Jubal! Ease up, you're hurting me!"

He stared at me and started to cry.

"Oh, Ray, oh, Ray, I'm so sorry, me! I can't . . . *I'm falling!*"

"Just hold on to me, Uncle Jubal, just hold on, everything will be okay."

I DIDN'T BELIEVE it, and neither did he, but he did calm down a little. He puked again, all over my shoulder, and then he buried his face in my chest and shook with great racking sobs. He was vibrating like a tuning fork.

Evangeline wasn't doing a lot better. I saw building panic in her face, and I couldn't have that. One panicky person was more than enough.

"Ray, what are we going to *do*?"

"First we've got to get him calmed down. We could use some falling sickness pills. You know anybody who's got any?" Evangeline, who'd never had a second of falling sickness in her life. But I had to ask.

Having something to do seemed to focus her mind and calm her down.

"I'll be right back," she said, and was gone out the door.

I spent a long ten minutes. At some point one of the little gizmos he'd made and sent me floated by in the chaos of stuff we'd stirred up and, without thinking about it, I grabbed it. It was the little box with the hand that came out and turned the machine off.

"Jubal, Jubal, look at this!" I said. "Look, Jubal! It's that great thing you sent me. Remember, Jubal? Remember? Look, I'm going to turn it on." I flipped the switch, and the little box rumbled and groaned and the lid flipped up and the little plastic hand came out and grabbed the switch, pulled it, and popped back into the box. "See, Jubal? What a neat thing this is. Thank you for sending it to me."

His eyes were fixed on the box like he was seeing Jesus.

"Do it again," he whispered.

I punched the button again, and the little hand came out. It turned off the machine. I did it again, and again, and again. We were still doing that when Evangeline returned. She held up a small hypodermic and showed it to me.

"They told me this will tranquilize an elephant," she said.

Mistake.

Jubal's eyes rolled toward her, saw the needle, and rolled back to me.

"No shots!" he wailed, and began to struggle again. Evangeline quickly hid the syringe behind her back, but the damage had been done. It took another couple minutes to get him back to the cowering, passive state of panic he'd been in before.

"I've got some motion sickness pills, too," Evangeline said in a small voice.

"Give them to me. Here you go, Jubal. Take a couple of these. They'll make you feel better."

"No shots?"

"No shots, I promise."

Jubal put the pills in his mouth and chewed on them. I looked over my shoulder and nodded to Evangeline. She jammed the needle into his butt.

So I lied.

*   *   *

IN A FEW minutes Jubal was a lot calmer. In fact, he was too damn calm. He was so loopy from the drug that he was unable to answer any of the thousand questions I had for him. About all he could do was giggle and float around the trailer like a short, chubby balloon. He seemed to enjoy bouncing off the walls.

"What was that stuff you gave him?" I asked her.

"I don't know. The guy said it would calm anybody down."

"What guy? How did you find him?"

"I know people," she said, unhelpfully, and I left it alone.

"I'm going next door to borrow a puke-sucker," she said, and was out the door again. Naturally, we'd never needed one of those handy little airvacs, but we had a neighbor who was subject to sudden eruptions if he moved around too quickly. Embarrassing, but some people never entirely adjust.

We got the place more or less back in order. I was terrified for several hours that there might be a concealed camera or mike that my spy sweeper had missed. I didn't bother Evangeline with that thought. What was the point? If one was there, somebody would be along to collect us all in a very short time.

When enough time had passed, and Jubal was snoring gently, loosely tied into a corner so he wouldn't hurt himself, we devoted ourselves to two questions. How had Jubal gotten here, and what the hell were we going to do about it?

Evangeline didn't know the whole story, so I filled her in on what Travis had told us. I know, I'd been sworn to secrecy, but Evangeline was a part of it now.

She was quick on the uptake.

"That rocket that blasted off from the Falklands," Evangeline said. "That must have been a diversion."

"I think so, too. Who would have suspected that Jubal would *mail* himself out?"

Because that's what must have happened.

But how had he gotten himself into that . . . black bubble, and how had he gotten the bubble inside the box, sealed it up, and dropped it off into whatever mailbox they used at the Power Company?

Jubal was first and foremost a tinkerer. With the facilities he had, it would be child's play for him to build a machine that would load up the box and ship it.

Now, if I was running the place, the moment that phony rocket ship blasted through the ceiling of Jubal's lab, I'd have sealed off the whole island tighter than a gnat's ass. Nothing would come in or go out until I'd figured out where Jubal was. So Jubal must have sent the package out *before* the ship took off.

It could be done. It was an insane idea, but it was the only way out of his prison for a guy who couldn't fly. Leave it to Jubal to come up with such a solution, thinking outside the box, as it were.

But what was the black bubble? Jubal wasn't in any shape to answer that, so we tried to find out what we could from the clues we had.

He was dressed in his usual Hawaiian shirt and khaki shorts. We went through his pockets. There was no money, no wallet, no keys. What use did Jubal have for any of those things? There was a little notebook with pages covered in Jubal's childish scrawl, most of it seeming to be about penguins.

There was another little black box.

Jubal must have been holding it when the black bubble opened, then lost it in his panic. But when I was gathering up the garbage I saw it, grabbed it, and gave it a look.

"Is this yours?" I asked Evangeline. She frowned, and shook her head.

It had all the earmarks of one of Jubal's gizmos. I say "box," but it was irregularly shaped, and I saw it would nestle neatly into my left hand. Jubal is a lefty. It was maybe eight inches long, three wide, an inch thick. There were maybe a dozen buttons on the front of it, and several dials on the side, and a blank screen. None of them were labeled.

"You couldn't pay me enough to punch one of those buttons," Evangeline said.

Me, either. It seemed likely that this was the thing he'd used to make the black bubble around himself. I had no desire to see the inside of one, even though I knew Jubal had survived it. I carefully wrapped it in a cloth and put it in one of my drawers with some other junk.

*　*　*

"SO WHAT ARE we going to do with him?" Evangeline asked.

"I don't know."

We stared at him for a while longer. Then Evangeline cleared her throat in that way people do when they have something to say and are having a hard time getting it out.

"What?"

"Ray, don't hate me, but I sort of have to suggest this."

"Spit it out."

"What if we . . . turned him in?"

I had known that was coming. How did I know? I'm not proud of it, but the same thing had occurred to me.

"We can't keep him here," she pointed out. "He's just barely manageable when he's doped up, and we can't keep him doped up forever. Tell you the truth, I'm not happy about doping him up at all."

"To get control of him, for the time being . . . you do what you have to. I understand that. And it was my idea, and I got the stuff . . . but what now? Where can we take him? Where will he be okay?"

"Only place I know of is Earth," I said. Which was true. He wouldn't like the low gravity of Mars any better than he liked the almost zero gee of Phobos.

"I mean, I can't understand why he left in the first place," she went on. "You say he destroyed all the Squeezers on Earth, and that's another thing I don't understand. Why did he do that?"

"I have no idea. Lately he seemed to have sort of adopted me as his conscience. He never really got over his shock at how the Squeezer could be used as a weapon."

"Jiminy Garcia-Strickland."

"Yeah. We had long talks about things."

"So did he ever hint that he was going to escape?"

"I've been thinking about it, and scanning through our correspondence, and all I can see is that he sent me that key *before* all of this came down. So he had been *thinking* about escaping. But he never talked about it. I know he'd gotten paranoid. He thought people were listening in."

"They probably were."

"Most likely. So he couldn't just call me up and say 'set and extra plate for supper, bubba, I'm on my way.' "

She sighed. Then she looked at me out of the corner of her eye.

"Ray . . . it just doesn't add up. All this fuss over him. There's something you aren't telling me."

She was right.

So there it was. I'd sworn a solemn oath not to tell anyone. Evangeline was mentioned specifically.

But screw that. Evangeline was as deep in hot water as I was now, and she deserved to know everything I did. The problem was how to tell her. It was just so goddam *crazy* . . .

I sighed. "There's no way to ease into this, I just have to come out and say it. It's simple, really. Jubal is the only one who can make Squeezers."

She kept looking at me, waiting for the punch line. Then she shook her head.

"That's crazy."

"That's exactly what *I* said."

IT WAS ACTUALLY what I *typed*, and so did Dad, at about the same time. Mom, too.

I decided to tell it the way Travis had. It was the only way that made any sense. If it made sense at all.

"Quantum leaps," I said.

"Don't get all mathematical on me, Ray. You know I'm not good at it."

"Neither am I, at least not on that level. But you understand the concept, right?"

"Uh . . . something about jumping from one state to another, without exactly occupying any of the spaces between?"

"Works for me. You go along for a long time and things stay pretty much the same, maybe you make a little progress here and there. Then, out of the blue, you're kicked up to the next level."

"What next level?"

"The next level of anything, but we're talking about knowledge here, or technology. The Squeezer was a quantum leap in both senses . . . but it seems like it was only a quantum leap in *knowledge* for

Jubal. For the rest of us, it was a leap in technology, we suddenly had a new thingamajig that did neat stuff . . ."

GO BACK TO the Stone Age, Travis had suggested. Or farther, back to the missing link between apes and men. Monkeys that walked upright on the African plains.

Enter language, tool use, and fire. I don't know if anyone knows what order those came in, and it doesn't really matter. They were all quantum leaps, and nothing was ever the same after any of them were first used.

Sure, language must have evolved gradually, it wasn't a case of one ape man suddenly coming out with "to be, or not to be, that is the question." Tools, too, to a lesser extent. One ape starts to use a rock to pound on stuff, and the other apes notice, and it's monkey see, monkey do. Then an ape finds out you can do better with a stone with a sharp edge, then another figures out how to chip an edge . . . and on and on. Took a long, long time before prehumans were making spears and bows and arrows, but not that long in evolutionary terms. Not as long as it took them to learn to stand upright.

Fire must have been different. Maybe that's why it's still almost a mystical power to us. Think of how many religions use fire for sacrifices. Picture it: A guy walks into the cave, and he's got some fire on a stick. He pokes the stick into a pile of wood he's gathered up. You'd be impressed, wouldn't you? Probably you'd run away from it at first, but after you'd had some cooked meat and saw how you could handle the stuff, and how you could poke it into the face of a saber-toothed tiger and watch the sucker run away . . . well, you just couldn't help loving the stuff, right? My guess is that, once some genius figured out how to handle fire, *all* the tribes of cavemen, *everywhere*, were using fire by the end of the week. It was just too damn good to ignore and so easy to use.

But did they know how to *make* fire? Maybe not. Maybe they had to wait for lightning to strike and start one, then try to keep it going. It goes out, and they're screwed.

The fire had gone out on Earth, and everybody was hard at work trying to track down the modern Prometheus.

In case you didn't know, the whole title of Mary Shelley's book was *Frankenstein: Or the Modern Prometheus*. Just thought I'd toss that in.

"WE'VE HAD OTHER quantum leaps," I told Evangeline. "But probably nothing like the discovery of fire. The Industrial Revolution was just a series of more efficient ways to use fire."

"Power," she said.

"Exactly. The steam engine, electricity . . . none of it was for free. You could trace all energy back to the sun, which is big-time fire. Even hydro power is the sun evaporating water that falls on the land. Oil, gas, all stored solar energy. The sun is what makes the wind blow."

"Nuclear power," she suggested.

"Another quantum leap. A different kind of fire, and at first it looked like something for nothing. You know, they were talking about free power, just giving it away, when they made the first nuclear reactor. Turned out that building them was a lot harder than they thought. Fusion . . . still working on it, that turned out to be even harder, but nobody's working on it too hard now that we have the Squeezer.

"There was no worldwide research leading up to the Squeezer. Jubal was more like Alexander Graham Bell, working in his lab, suddenly he's got a telephone."

"But Bell built on other people's work," Evangeline said. "Electrical experimenters, chemists . . . I don't know. Didn't Jubal?"

"I don't *know*," I had to admit. "When you can get him to talk about it, he talks about superstrings and branes and esoteric stuff like that. I don't understand it at all. I'd always assumed that other scientists did . . . I mean, the ones they picked to go to the Falklands and study at his feet. I guess *everybody* assumed that."

"And you're saying they were wrong."

She thought about it. I could practically see her mind going down the same paths my own had taken when Travis revealed this to us. She shook her head.

"It doesn't make sense. Look at your caveman. He starts a fire, and everybody sees how he does it. How hard can it be?"

"Pretty tough for somebody with an IQ of maybe five, and an instinctive fear of fire. All animals fear fire except us . . . and we treat it with healthy respect."

"Still . . ."

"You're looking at it wrong. Say the caveman genius comes into the cave with a shotgun. He's figured out how to make one. And think about what all that would take. One, he has to invent gunpowder. Two, he has to figure out how to make iron, cast it, bore it out, make some sort of spark mechanism. And I wasn't kidding, much, about the IQ. Say he tries to explain how to *make* one to these other people, folks who have a vocabulary of nine or ten words and still haven't quite figured out all the uses of the opposable thumb. You figure they'd be able to mix gunpowder? Could a chimpanzee?"

"You're saying the best minds on the planet are so far behind Jubal that they're like apes?"

I shrugged. "No, it doesn't really work that way. Analogies only go so far. Jubal's the smartest man I've ever met, but there are people who are just as smart as him."

"So what's the story?"

"I wish I knew. Jubal's head's been examined just about every way a head can be examined, trying to find out what's different about it. Your first thought has got to be that when his dad nearly killed him, beating him with that nail-studded two-by-four, something happened to his brain. One theory is that some part of his brain adjusted, some cross connection to the higher math functions or something like that—and he was already very good at higher math before he was hurt—but it's all guesswork. There's been fights about who gets Jubal's brain when he's dead, and plenty of people who'd like to take it apart while he's still alive. Some of them even claim he'd survive the experience."

"Which brings us to the golden goose."

"The goose that laid the golden eggs."

"Whatever."

"Yeah, but in Jubal's case it's more like that old joke about my brother is crazy, he thinks he's a chicken. We'd get him some help, but we need the eggs."

She looked over at Jubal again, snoring quietly in his safety web.

"Poor guy. All he's ever wanted is to be left alone."

"That's why he's tried so hard for twenty years to teach gunpowder making and iron smelting to the other monkeys. But there's something about the Squeezer that no other human mind has succeeding in grasping. Not yet anyway. There's a thousand theories about what that might be . . . but they're monkey theories, they're bound to be wrong. Jubal's *brain* is the quantum leap this time. He seems to have the first human brain that is able to deal with quantum mechanics on a practical level. And there's only one of them."

"And we have him," she said, quietly.

We both looked at him for a while.

"We are so fucked," she said.

"You said it."

"What are we going to do?"

"HELLO . . . MOM?"

"Ray, where are you? And why aren't I getting a picture?"

"I'm at my trailer." No need for specifics. And there was no picture because I'd turned it off. "I guess the camera's broken. Listen, Mom—"

"Have you finished those applications, Ray? The school year is beginning soon, and I've told you and told you."

"Mom . . . I need to see you."

Long pause.

Do all moms have extrasensory perception, or is it just mine? I can pull off anything with Dad, just distract him a little and there you go. But something in the very little I said, or in the way I said it, had tickled her trouble radar.

"Sure," she said, cautiously. "Come right over. I'm home."

"I sort of need to see you here. And sort of . . . soon."

Longer pause.

"Are you in trouble, honey?" Not *What have you done?* I really appreciated that.

"There is some trouble, yeah."

Very short pause.

"I'll be on the next bus."

I'D MADE THE call from the other bubble, the one that used to be packed with tourists but was pretty deserted now, what with the recent violence.

I'd moved out here so in case I was traced and someone came to do something about it, Evangeline would see me being rousted and try to think of something to do with Jubal before the troops descended on my trailer again.

As to what exactly that would be . . . we hadn't gotten that far.

But if they were watching, they were subtle. Mom showed up along with a few other passengers and I jetted over to her. She looked a question at me, and I just shook my head and took her hand and led her along toward the trailer.

Let me tell you, I was never so happy to have someone to dump a problem on.

17

★ ★ ★

ABOUT EIGHT HOURS later a guy and a girl guided another guy down the wide tunnel leading to the Phobos air locks. They each had hold of an arm. All three of them were in space suits, as you'd expect of people heading toward a lock. All three of them had their helmets on and locked down.

How do you tell a drunk in a space suit? By the barf on his faceplate. This chubby little fellow's was coated with the stuff, and there were big splashes of it on the outside, too, and from time to time a bit of it flew off. Everybody gave the trio a wide berth, given the behavior of vomit in free fall.

Not an uncommon sight in Phobos, at least the tourist part. The three people were the very picture of two disgusted employees and one fat Earthie with a load on.

At least that's what we hoped. If only we could get Jubal to curse and wave his arms around and protest that he'd get us fired, the picture would be perfect. But Jubal was sound asleep.

DID I MENTION that sometimes my mom can be a little scary?

She pushed into my trailer, glanced at Evangeline, who pointed forlornly at the far corner of the room. Mom looked over there, at Jubal snoring peacefully. I think her eyes widened a little bit. I can't be sure. Then she faced me.

She sighed.

"Tell me about it," she said.

We filled her in on the story, such as it was. I'm sure glad we had Jubal there with us, or I wouldn't have believed it myself. Mom heard us out and then was silent for a few minutes.

"Okay," she said, finally. "We've got to get him someplace secure."

"Preferably with some gravity," I pointed out.

"Evangeline, do you have any more of that dope?"

"Mrs. Garcia, I—"

"Hon, it's Mrs. Strickland-Garcia, but if you're going to be seeing my son, I'd prefer it if you'd call me Kelly."

Evangeline had a hard time, but eventually choked it out.

"K-k-kelly, I don't use that stuff, I don't do any drugs, I just know—"

"Evangeline, I don't care about that right now. In fact, right now I'm glad you had the contacts. So do you have more?"

"I can get it."

She handed Evangeline a wad of money. "If possible, get something that will sedate him without totally knocking him out. We need him able to answer questions, at least as much as he's ever able to. Lord help me, I'm brokering a drug deal with a teenager. Never mind. While you're out, rent a suit. Short, portly, would be my guess. And pick up a can of soup. Vegetable would be good. Unless you have some, Ray."

"Soup . . ."

"Close your mouth, son, some of the garbage in this dump might drift in. Never mind. Soup, Evangeline. And scissors and a razor—"

"That I've got, Mom."

She favored me with half a smile and touched my cheek. Well, I did need to shave. Sometimes every other day.

Evangeline left and Mom and I extracted Jubal from the safety web. She set me to work shaving off his beard and cutting his hair short. I ended up with a completely different Jubal, one I'd never seen before. Nobody else had, either, which couldn't hurt.

"It will fool people, but it won't fool scanners," Mom said. "But I have an idea about that," Lord, she hated those things. You never knew when one might be probing your eyes, scanning your irises like the UPC code on a packaged steak and comparing it to the universal identity database.

Evangeline came back from her shopping trip, and we all worked together to stuff Jubal into the suit and get it fitted as best we could. His eyes were wandering around. As a precaution we tethered him in place with a few tie-downs hooked to rings on the suit.

"What have you got, Evangeline?" Mom asked.

"Pills. Still in the bottles."

Mom read a few labels, googled the names, and settled on a little pink one. Evangeline got a water bottle, and Mom gave Jubal the pill.

"Stop her," he said.

"Stop who, Jubal?" I asked.

He shook his head, looking groggy. He worked his mouth a few times, his eyes rolled around. He tried again.

"Stop her."

We all looked at each other.

"Not stop. *Her*," he said, desperately. "*Stop*-per. Where my stopper?"

"Does he mean a stopper, like a cork?" Evangeline asked us.

"Don't feel too *good*, me. My . . . stopper. Little box I brung with me. Maybe it's under these silver pants . . ." He started groping futilely at the outside of the suit.

I went to my shelf and got the little box he'd had with him inside the black bubble. I showed it to him. He reached for it. Mom put out her hand and stopped him.

"Is this the thing that makes the bubbles Ray told me about?" she asked.

"This is that thing," he agreed.

"I don't think you should have it right now, Jubal, I think—"

I thought he was going to cry.

"Please, Kelly, I have to have that thing. I have to."

"Jubal, I don't think it's safe."

"It safe, I promise, me. Oh, it real safe." Then he mumbled something.

"What was that?" I asked.

"My fault," he said "All my fault. But this, it safe. Can't hurt nothing, this." He let out a weak laugh. "Harmless, this. Safe, this."

Mom looked dubious, but she handed it to him. He flipped a switch on the side, and Mom winced. Nothing happened.

"Safety," he explained. "It turned off, now, this thing." Then he wrapped his hand around it and curled up and seemed to go to sleep.

That's when somebody started pounding on the door.

"You expecting anybody?" Mom asked.

"Nobody who pounds." I admit it, my heart was in my throat.

"Back door," Evangeline said, and headed toward it. She was still in motion when somebody started pounding on that one, too. For the first time I saw Evangeline disconcerted in free fall, flailing wildly and smacking one hand painfully against a shelf as she tried to twist and somehow claw her way through the air back toward us. In a cartoon it would have worked, but in real life she had to wait until her feet hit the back door, and she pushed off from it like it was on fire, coming back toward us too fast. I caught her in my arms and hugged her. She was shivering, and didn't seem to notice that she was bleeding from a small cut on her pinkie.

"Open this door at once. I repeat, open this door at once."

Mom started toward the door. I reached for her, not wanting her to be behind it if shooting started, but she was just out of my reach. She opened the little peephole and took a quick look, then slammed it closed.

"A soldier," she said, quietly.

"Just one?" I asked.

"How many do you need, if he's armed and we're not?" Mom asked.

"At least one at the back door, too," Evangeline pointed out.

I was in no mood to give in without a fight. I had to have a plan. The pounding started again, making it hard to think.

"Open this door at once," the voice said.

"If they blow that door, somebody's going to get hurt," Mom said. And I knew the fight was over. And really, what sort of fight could I have put up? The closest thing I had to a weapon in that trailer was a kitchen knife.

"I'm going to count to three," the voice said.

"Don't bother," Mom shouted. She looked at me. "Unless you have a better idea?"

"No, Mom," I said, quietly. I put my arms around her, gave her a hug.

"You get the back door, I'll get the front." She started to turn, then looked back at Evangeline. "Honey, that was brave, what you did when the invasion started. But no ball-kicking this time, okay?"

"No, ma'am. I promise."

Mom nodded sadly, and we went to open the doors. I'd just opened the back one when the guy at the front shoved his way in past Mom, cracking her on the side of the head in his haste to get in. I thought I might explode, watching it. But Mom shot me a look that clearly said to leave it alone. I swallowed bile, and did.

The second guy came in more cautiously. I wondered who was the leader, the backdoor guy or the cowboy? Both were large, male, and decked out in the full black fascist regalia of our conquerors, helmeted, visored, in full body armor, following their weapons into my home and pointing them at everything in sight.

"You, asshole, get over there with the women," the cowboy said. I realized he was talking to me. "Cover them," he said to the other guy. He shoved his way past me and poked at Jubal with his weapon.

"What hav—"

And he was instantly replaced by a five-foot black hole.

I saw the corporal start to turn around, looking over his shoulder.

He said "What the fu—"

"—ust do it, Jubal, goddam it!" Mom was screaming.

Or at least that's how I saw it.

Evangeline and Mom swarmed over me from only a few feet away, and Jubal was out of his nest of cargo webbing. My stomach lurched. The sense of dislocation was enormous, unprecedented, completely outside of my experience.

I'd had a few minutes snipped out of the filmstrip of my life.

WHAT HAD HAPPENED was, Jubal missed with his second shot. Seldom had anything looked less like a weapon. But most things can be used as a weapon, and this was a singularly nonviolent one. What it did was to *postpone* the violence.

At the end of the trailer where Jubal had been there were now two black bubbles, held down with the cargo netting. Inside them were one fascist who had been about to roust Jubal, and one fascist who had just seen his buddy get swallowed up by a black hole. At some point in the "future"—if that word meant anything in the face of Jubal's newest invention—they would feel exactly the way they had been feeling when they were encapsulated. That could be minutes from now, like what had happened to me, or months from now, as Jubal had experienced.

Or millions of years from now.

Or never.

During the confusion as Mom and Evangeline made their way toward Jubal, things got sort of confused. By the time they realized what had happened, there was no way to be *sure* which bubble had me inside.

Turning off a bubble was simplicity itself, as I'd shown by accidentally setting Jubal free. But once one had formed, there was no way to tell what was inside, or to tell one from another unless they varied greatly in size.

Jubal and Mom thought I was in one of them. Evangeline was adamant I was in another one.

The problem, of course, was that if they picked the wrong one what was going to come out of it was a very confused and soon-to-be-angry man with a weapon powerful enough to destroy the whole trailer.

For once in her life, Mom lost the argument. Evangeline was so sure which one I was in that she actually shouted at my mom. That probably wouldn't have done any good, but then Evangeline reminded her of the stories I'd told of her uncanny sense of orientation in free fall and, reluctantly, Mom gave in.

So they armed themselves with the only useful weapons they could find, which were thick plastic shelves ripped from the walls, and stationed themselves on opposite sides of the bubble . . . because there was also no way to tell the position of the person inside the bubble. Would the soldier emerge facing them, or facing away? Upside down? Sideways? They decided if they saw a lot of black, they'd start swinging, and

Jubal was standing by to make a new bubble if the wrong guy came out.

It wasn't much of a plan, but it was all they had. Luckily, Evangeline was right.

"They won't be the last ones," Mom said. "When these guys don't report back, somebody will come check on them. We've got to get moving."

We did. Mom answered the riddle of the vegetable soup by ripping open the pouch and squirting the chunky yellow-brown stuff onto the inside of Jubal's faceplate and smearing it around. It made very convincing vomit. We spattered the outside of his suit with it, too. When we clapped it over Jubal's head and sealed it he was too far withdrawn to protest. In fact, he seemed to feel a little more secure in a space suit, something he had never worn, and didn't mind at all that he couldn't see out.

WE TRIED TO think of a way to get one of the soldiers' weapons, but didn't waste a lot of time on it. Even in hindsight, I don't know how we could have, with the resources at hand, nor what real good it would have done us. They'd come out of their bubbles armed, dangerous, and raging mad. We decided that Evangeline and I would escort Jubal to the air lock, where Mom had a rented shuttle waiting.

When we left the trailer a few faces popped back into their trailers . . . then slowly emerged again, like prairie dogs. There were some other people hanging around at the first corner we came to.

"No problem," I told them. "Just a drunk."

"No business of mine, space," my next-door neighbor said. Obviously most of these people had heard the pounding on my door, and some of them had seen the soldier. So some of them knew a black trooper had entered and not come out. There were probably people around my back door, wondering when that guy would come out. Nobody seemed upset at the idea that something bad might have happened to the dude, but you never know what's in someone's heart.

"You think there's any squealers in that bunch?" I whispered to Evangeline.

"Nobody who plans to ever call himself a Martian again," she said.

"Still."

"You're right. Let's hurry."

We made good time to the air lock, Mom following a little bit behind, not obviously associated with us. She would be able to keep watch on our backs to see if anyone was after us.

We got into the air lock. I held the door for Mom, and we all cycled through. The outer door opened, and we piled out, Evangeline and I tugging Jubal between us.

"Over this way," Mom said on the private channel we'd chosen. We shoved off through the parking lot, past hundreds of airboards, to the part where private vehicles were tied down. Mom had arrived in a red-and-white Avis Sport Utility, about the size of a small city bus on Earth, the kind of thing the more adventurous tourists rent to explore the outback for a few days, comfortable and idiot-proof when the autopilot is engaged.

We wrestled Jubal inside the lock, which was just big enough for two people. Mom was the smallest, so she squeezed in beside him and cycled the lock. When it opened again Evangeline and I went through.

Mom had taken Jubal's helmet off and was cleaning it out, and he was waving feebly.

"No, don' do dat thing," he said. "Leave it on. I like it better, me."

I looked at Mom, who shrugged, and clamped it back down, not what you'd call clean inside but not opaque, either. All I could figure was, claustrophobia or not, the suit and helmet might be a comfort. It's a womblike feeling, being in a suit, and most people take well to it.

"You drive, Ray," Mom said. I went to the front and settled into the pilot seat, strapped in, with Mom and Evangeline close behind me. There was plenty of room up there, and a wide wraparound windshield.

"Where are we going?" I asked Mom.

"Just . . . out, for now. I've got a call in to Travis, but until we can rendezvous with him in something bigger than this little jitney I think it's best if we put a few million miles between us and—"

She looked past me and frowned. I followed her eyes and saw a bright light down near the surface of Mars. It expanded rapidly.

"Oh, no," Evangeline whispered.

And that was the first shot of the third invasion of Mars from those goddam idiots from Earth.

* * *

EVANGELINE AND I had now seen space combat from the middle, from the bottom, and from the top. These were the best seats, in a horrifying way. But if we'd had a chance, we would have missed it entirely.

I had the ship in manual mode and tried to give it the little jog that would start me moving away from Phobos.

"I'm sorry," came an automatic voice. "All traffic is currently grounded. Please be patient until the current alert is ended."

We watched the battle unfolding. It had a certain lethal beauty. Ships' exhausts drew bright white lines across the night surface of Mars, which was three-quarters of the globe from where we were, which was almost over the city.

On the other hand, after a few hours you began to think, when you've seen one space battle, you've seen them all.

Trying to make sense of it, stuck and unable to get out of there, we speculated about what we were seeing. We analyzed some of the trajectories and decided that a lot of those ships were robot-controlled. Humans couldn't stay conscious during some of the maneuvers they were making, and probably couldn't even survive the most extreme ones. Some of those ships were accelerating at fifty gees.

So maybe nobody was dying. At first.

Most of it was happening well away from the city. All three of us were following everything we could on our suit faceplate stereos, naturally, and I have to say the Martian news media had gotten a lot better at this, whether or not the invaders had. They had reporters all over the place, in the deserted malls, down in the shelters, up on the surface getting some spectacular night shots of the battle when a ship or a missile streaked overhead. It looked pretty risky to me, but I guess newspeople always think they're invulnerable, and always have their eyes on the prize. Pulitzer Prize.

There were long periods when nothing seemed to be happening, and we wondered if it was all over. Maybe they were regrouping for the next attack. Nobody had any idea who was winning and who was losing. There were six hours of that. We had to give Jubal another pill when we heard him whimpering back there.

Bottom line, after eight hours of sitting in the same place and watching a lot of strangers trying to kill each other, we really could have cared less who won. The ideal outcome would have been if they *all* killed each other off. Then something hit Phobos, about a mile away from us.

Later it was determined to be a stray missile. It made quite a flash, and sent up a plume of rocky debris. Not like an explosion on Earth, where the dirt goes up for a bit and then splashes back down. Everything just kept moving. A few seconds later we felt a small tremor jolt the ship.

There had been a few dozen people visible on the surface around us. Now they all headed back toward the air lock, as fast as they could go.

None of us said anything. Something *pinged* off the windshield. Evangeline pointed, and I saw a tiny star-shaped pit in the supertough Lexan. It couldn't have come from the explosion. Anything traveling fast enough to chip our windshield would be halfway to Deimos by now.

"Lots of debris flying around out there," I said. You'd better believe it. Even when there was no actual shooting going on, the most spectacular display was of millions and millions of tiny particles from the explosions and the impact on Phobos entering the atmosphere and burning up.

"Ray, go check Jubal's suit again," Mom said. "I don't trust a suit I haven't checked out myself."

Another hour passed.

Wars have an ebb and flow, even if they're over in less than a day, as all our invasions were. We couldn't see it at first, and never got it all straight, but at some point it became clear that the operations were moving close to the city. We had made a little more than one complete orbit of Mars, and the city had crawled back around until it was almost under us again.

We could see it down there, getting close to morning now, but still lit up like Miami Beach or the Las Vegas Strip.

Then there was a huge explosion, and all the lights went out.

18

★ ★ ★

WHAT CAN I say? My heart stopped. I stopped breathing. I cried out.

I may have done all or any of those things, but I don't remember. I remember bumping my head hard off the slanted windshield in front of us. Somehow I had unstrapped myself and just lurched up, I guess. All I remember was the extreme urge to *do something*. And the slowly dawning realization that there was nothing I could do.

All the camera feeds from below had cut out when the lights went off.

Mom had been talking to Dad on the phone. That conversation was cut short.

Evangeline had had Elizabeth on the line. Gone.

I had been trying to raise Travis on a frequency Mom had given me. No answer.

Then, a flicker here and another flicker there, some of the lights below came back on. Not the big gaudy neon and laser and xenon meant to be visible from space, but just some faint glows.

"Power station," Mom whispered. "Maybe they just hit the power station. Please let it be the power station."

All the hotels and malls had emergency power, big banks of the same sort of batteries used to power cars on Earth. Those small, faint lights should be from hotel room windows and emergency lights under the Lexan-covered malls . . . which would mean that the hotels and malls were still there, not smoldering ruins . . .

Things began to come back together in about five minutes. Alternate transmitters were dialed up, connections reestablished, reporters began breathless stories. We watched a stand-up from a newsman in a suit standing in the middle of a mall in front of a shattered fifty-foot pane of Lexan, hip deep in debris generated by the blowout. "No casualties to report here, Marilyn, at least not yet, though as you can see people might be down at the bottom of this mess, or possibly lying out on the surface. Everything just picked up and *zoomed* out of here, I had to hang on to a railing and I was lifted off my feet! We are sealed off at the moment, naturally, but we've got plenty of air. It's getting cold . . . I hope rescue crews are on the way . . . though I don't suppose it'll help anyone who might be under all this." He paused, with what sounded like a genuine catch in his throat. "We'll do what we can. Back to you in the studio, Marilyn."

Marilyn came on to assure viewers that rescue parties were on the way, but they were spread pretty thin, what with all the other blowouts . . . Marilyn looked harried and more than a little frightened. I wondered where her studio was.

Somebody began a delayed feed of the events of a few minutes before. At first the camera was rock-steady, aiming at the sky, then everything shook, the cameraman seemed to drop the camera. It lay there on its side for a moment, and we could see a fireball moving sideways across our screens. The reporter was just short of babbling. Her voice shook with adrenaline.

"Holy shit! . . . uh, there's been a major explosion . . . Jim, did you see . . . um, looks like something hit the ground, I repeat, something hit the ground, something big hit the ground about five hundred meters from . . . Jim, I don't know the town from . . . is that Burroughs High? Ah . . . Marilyn, it looks like one of the invader ships came down not far from Burroughs . . . that's right, it's Burroughs High . . . it just fucking *crashed*, came right over our heads . . . I don't know where that fireball came from, nothing will burn out here, in fact I'm fucking freezing . . ."

The cameraman and the reporter were hurrying toward the low domes of my recent alma mater. They cut to a live feed. The reporter was still breathing hard, but had established herself with a smashed dome in the background.

"It appears that a large piece of debris scored a direct hit on the Burroughs High School gymnasium. We can only pray . . ."

I had a lump in my throat. I had no real affection for the place, I was glad to see the last of it. All I cared about was deaths and/or injuries. We watched and listened and surfed all possible news sources, and so far there were no confirmed reports of casualties. But we all knew it would take a while.

Then there was an image of home.

"I'm standing outside the historic Red Thunder Hotel, the sun is coming up, and the full extent of this disaster is becoming more apparent. As I speak, rescue crews are making their way through the Red Thunder and all other hotels, going room to room. As you can see, this building took a heavy hit. I've counted six major breaches, and some other windows appear to be blown out . . ."

In the pale pink dawn of early morning, I could see what he was talking about. Something had hit the north side of the tower at the third, fifth, and tenth floors. There was a piece of twisted, smoking metal sticking out of the side like a broken harpoon. Smoke was coming out of the top of the building. Nothing will burn in the thin carbon dioxide air of Mars, so I couldn't figure it out at first. Then I had it.

"That stuff must have been very hot. If it punches through someplace, and then the emergency systems seal it off, it could start fires on the carpets or beds."

"It can't burn long," Mom said. I couldn't see her face very well through the helmet, but I thought her eyes looked red. Evangeline squeezed my hand tight.

"They're all in the shelter," she said. "Isn't that what your Dad said?"

"That's right. The shelter should be okay. They'll be okay in the shelter."

I felt a hand on my shoulder and almost jumped out of my skin and suit at the same time. I twisted, and saw Jubal floating back there, staring fixedly at the windscreen. How long had he been watching?

"All my fault," he said. There was no particular emotion in his voice. It was just . . . dead. Hopeless. "All my fault."

I was about to reassure him that it wasn't, but then thought better of it. I saw Mom turn and stare at Jubal.

"What do you mean, Jubal? Because you ran away?"

He looked puzzled. The amount of drugs he had in him, I was surprised he could talk at all.

"No," he said, at last. "I had to do that, me. I had to take the stuff away from them before things got worse."

"So what do you mean?"

Jubal just shook his head. Then he sighed and gestured to the window.

"All this, it gotta stop. It gotta stop."

Mom studied him a moment. Then she asked a question that would have been nonsense, asked of anyone but Jubal.

"Can you stop it?"

He frowned. He started to shake his head, then frowned again. He opened his mouth to say something, stopped himself, and let his breath out, slowly. I had the creepy feeling that Jubal was thinking, in his own special way. I say creepy, but of course it was also wonderful. It's just that you never know what's going to come out of that box once you open it. You know there will be good stuff, but there's likely to be bad, too. But if anyone could deliver a miracle here, Jubal was the one.

"The killing, it has to stop," he said, finally. "No more killing."

AN HOUR LATER the space-traffic control center judged the area within fifty thousand miles of Mars was reasonable clear. The advisory said that combat operations seemed to have ended, and most battle debris had either impacted or left the area.

I started easing the ship slowly away. Traffic was tight, as everybody else who'd been grounded for all that time hurried to shove off and get back down to find out what had happened.

There were still no phones. We called Dad and Elizabeth and Evangeline's family every five minutes: "We are hard at work to restore your phone service to the high standards you are accustomed to, so please bear with us!"

"So what do we do now?" I asked.

Mom looked troubled. There were several things that needed to be done, and it wasn't possible to do them all. We needed to get away from there, *far* away, with Jubal. We also needed to get to the surface to find out what had become of our families.

"I guess we still need to get out of here," she said. "Evangeline, what do you want to do? This isn't your fight."

I could see she was torn. She wanted to know about her family, but she also wanted it to be her fight. She wasn't part of our weird family, which included Jubal and Travis . . . but I was pretty sure she wanted to be. Before she could answer we got a phone call, just sound, no picture, that changed everything.

"Kelly? Can you hear me, Kelly? Ray, Evangeline, anybody who can hear me, please pick up."

"I'm here, Manny," Mom shouted.

"Oh, great. Ah . . . I'm okay, I've accounted for all the Redmonds. Are you guys doing okay? We haven't been able to get any news from Phobos."

"We're fine, Manny. I don't think anybody got hurt. Where is Elizabeth?"

"I don't know, hon. I've got calls out, but things are very patchy. I don't know how long this connection will last. I'll let you know as soon as I know anything, of course, but I'm pretty busy here with damage control. There are five dead so far—"

"Oh, my god!"

"—don't know if they were guests or staff, it's sort of . . . well, they were in a room that got hit. I'm getting reports of dozens of deaths and some injuries . . . just a minute, something coming in on the other . . . on the other channel here . . ." There was a long silence. "Okay. Okay, ah, Kelly, Elizabeth's been hurt. I don't know—"

Buzz. Pop. Hiss. And then silence.

The silence didn't last long. Mom went into Emergency Mother mode in a heartbeat. Maybe two heartbeats.

"Ramon, give me the code for your airboard."

I gave it to her. "But Mom, you've never flown a board."

"How hard will it be to find a boardhead willing to fly yours?" She was already out of her seat and headed for the air lock.

"Hang on, Mom," I said. "We're about a quarter mile away. I'll bring—"

"No time for that. I'll jump. Evangeline, do you want to come with me?"

"No, ma'am. My family is okay. Ray will need some help."

"Good girl."

"*Mom!*"

She stopped, half into the air lock.

"What do you want me to *do*?"

"Go north. You should hear from Travis soon. He said he'd be able to find us. Don't boost too hard or too long. If you haven't heard from Travis in . . . twenty-four hours, turn around and head back. I'll have something organized by then.

"Remember, Travis doesn't know we have Jubal. He doesn't know *anything* except that I sent out an urgent message. Use high encryption when you talk to him, until you're together."

And with that, she closed the door behind her. I know I should have been flattered, and I was, believe me. I was also scared half out of my wits. Suddenly I wasn't just the driver of a silly little shuttle. By the laws of space travel, I was the captain of a deep-space-bound ship, crew of two, one a girl even younger and more scared than me, one a helpless child-man genius that the most powerful people on Earth had proven themselves willing to kill innocent people to get back.

I could feel it when Mom shoved off, since the shuttle started a slow yaw away from Phobos. I canceled that vector and added a little more, and we rotated until I could see her, boots toward us, moving away at a clip that was maybe a tad too fast for my liking, but not alarming. I saw her rotate to bring her heels toward the surface, saw her knees bend to soak up the landing without pushing herself back into space, saw her use tiny spurts of her suit jets to move her along the surface, not touching, until she reached a group of people hanging out around their boards. She turned and waved at us. She was very small at that distance.

Everything suddenly looked very small, most especially my little ship. Soon, even Mars would look small.

"Well, I guess we'd better get going," Evangeline said.

"Yeah." Still I did nothing.

"Off we go."

"Into the wild black yonder."

We looked at each other.

"Okay." I eased the control stick forward and felt the acceleration build up.

BY ANY RATIONAL standard, one random bucket of space should be pretty much like every other bucket: empty. Say your bucket is a cubic AU—Astronomical Unit—about 90 million miles on a side. Same difference as if it was a bedpan. Just space, nothing there, no matter what size your sample is.

What is so hard to communicate to people who haven't actually been out in it, is how *big* "outer space" is. Say we had enough energy and potato chips and Dr Pepper and oxygen to last us for a few centuries, and accelerated in the direction Evangeline and I were going—or any direction at all, picked at random—until we were almost at the speed of light. Say we were passing through cubic AUs at the rate of about one every eight minutes—which would seem like fractions of a second to us, because of the relativistic time dilation. AU after AU after AU we intrepid explorers would have this to report:

Nothing there. (Actually, a few molecules of hydrogen in a cubic yard, a speck of dust too small to see, maybe ten molecules in size, in every cubic mile. And that's in the *dense* parts of interstellar space.) We could continue on and on and on until all the food was gone and the ship was filled to the ceiling with poop, and be far, far around the curve of the universe before we had a reasonable chance of hitting anything.

I mean *anything*: a piece of gravel, an asteroid, a planet, a star.

We could fly out of our galaxy and take a long time before we hit another . . . and fly right through that as though it was almost all empty space, which it is.

So logically, going north or south of the plane of the ecliptic of the solar system, where all the matter is, shouldn't be any different than following the well-traveled space-lanes between the big globs of matter where we make our tenuous homes. Just a little emptier. Just a little farther from everything that is familiar.

Bullshit. It was spooky. Every second took us farther away from all that was safe and familiar. It was, I'm a little ashamed to admit it, a deeply superstitious feeling. With every second that we accelerated, that distance increased.

That's right. Accelerated. If it had been up to me, I'd have got up to a certain speed and then shut down the drive. Coasted until Travis contacted us. But as soon as we started boosting, at what a Martian would call "one gravity," a strange thing happened. Jubal got better.

He came walking up behind us, bouncing a little too high like an Earthie, but he had a tentative smile on his face. He removed his helmet.

"Hey, this ain't so bad," he said. "I feel kinda light. Kinda funny."

"It's one Martian gravity, Jubal," Evangeline said. "A little less than .4 gee."

"Yessum. I figgered. I kinda like it."

"What about your . . . ah, claustrophobia," I said.

He looked around.

" 'Bout the size of a school bus," he said. "I been on a school bus, me."

Evangeline and I looked at each other. Shrugged.

"We *are* on a spaceship," Evangeline said. "I thought you didn't fly."

"Never have," he said. "Mebbe it be gettin' *on* that thing scare me so."

I'd never thought of that. Maybe it was just weightlessness he couldn't tolerate. Maybe he'd even get used to that. People do.

So that's why we were boosting constantly. It was no problem with a bubble drive. We'd run out of food and water long before we ran out of fuel. There *was* a problem, though, if we were to rendezvous somehow with Travis. Boosting for a while and then shutting down would have put us on a straight line at a constant velocity. Travis could get to us a lot sooner. Constantly accelerating, our speed was constantly increasing, and we'd be much, much farther from Mars when Travis started his search, which would make it much harder.

In fact, it would have been impossible, except for one thing I had thought of and called in to Mom just before we were getting out of the radio range of the shuttle and the GPS satellite web around Mars. I told her I'd be riding the axis. I mean, *really* riding it. I got the ship aligned so that if you drew a line through the Martian north and south poles and then extended that line north, you'd find me within a hundred yards of that line even if we were 100 million miles out. It took me a while, but the computers were easily able to cope with that degree of accuracy. Even at a billion miles, we shouldn't stray more than a mile from that line.

"Good thinking, Ray," she had said. "You're really using your head."

That made me feel good.

What was less comforting was the thought that, at the rate we were accelerating, we'd be a billion miles away a lot sooner than I'd like.

THE HOURS STRETCHED out. We realized that the critical parameter was food and water and oxygen.

We took inventory. The oxygen would last us about two weeks. There was a good amount of water and a tiny toilet, a dry one, so we wouldn't be wasting water with that. Food was going to be a problem. Remember, if we didn't hear from Travis there was only one thing we could do. We'd have to turn ship, blast until we were motionless relative to the solar system, then start accelerating again. Halfway there we'd have to turn again and decelerate. We had to get back with enough oxygen.

We did the math, and found that we could blast for only three days, to leave a safety margin. Twelve days, out and back. We'd be mighty hungry when we got back.

Food was just not something they stored much of on these tourist buses. People brought their own picnic lunches and warmed them in the microwave. There was a little pantry and a little fridge.

"Let's see. We got plenty of olives." Evangeline held up a gallon jar.

"Have they got dem red things in 'em?" Jubal asked.

"Pimentos. Also almonds. Also unpitted."

"I like the pimentos," Jubal said. "I suck 'em out."

There were lots of nuts, cashews, trail mix, dried fruit mix. Nachos, Cheetos, bags of candy, and bars of chocolate.

"God, by tomorrow I'll be one big zit, I eat stuff like this," Evangeline said.

There were also big cans of caviar, a dozen kinds of dip, and lots of boxes of crackers of various kinds. Potted cheese. Marmalade. I hate marmalade. There were a dozen kinds of mineral water, soft drinks, tonic water, ginger ale.

What we were best supplied with was liquor, all of it in those tiny little bottles. Evangeline studied the list, a small bottle of Jack Daniel's in her hand.

"Jeez! Look what they charge for this! Highway robbery."

"Outrageous," I agreed, and didn't tell her that the Red Thunder charged twice as much. Hotels make a fortune selling stuff like that.

"Gimme that lil bottle, *cher*," Jubal said. "We got ice?"

"Ice we got," she said, opening the ice maker. "We got enough ice to get to Alpha Centauri and back."

"So what's your drink . . . ah . . ."

"Evangeline," she said, gently.

Jubal smacked himself in the forehead.

"Oh, I am a polecat idiot! You too young, right, *cher*?"

"You going to card me, Jubal?"

He thought about that for a moment, then laughed, that big hearty roar I hadn't heard in a long, long time, and had wondered if I'd ever hear again.

"None of my business, Evangeline. That's a nice name, Evangeline. *Acadien!*"

"*Mais oui!* And my drink is vodka, rocks, a twist of lemon peel rubbed around the edge. Toss me that Absolut."

We all fixed drinks and sat around the little fold-down table and wrote out an inventory. We argued rationing, tried to figure out menus of the rich but scarce stuff we had. After a while I wasn't focusing too well, and we were laughing a lot more than the situation warranted. It was better than the alternative, which was worrying about what might have happened to Elizabeth. No word on that yet, and most of the news channels didn't reach us out where we were. Correction. They *could* have reached us, would have done so if we'd been in any kind of decent ship, but the piddling little shuttle was only equipped for reception in near-Arean space, and we were getting next to nothing.

TWO DAYS PASSED.

There was one deck of cards in a drawer and a Monopoly set. We used Monopoly money when we played poker, and it's a damn good thing, as I would have lost most of my inheritance in the first twenty-four hours. My own damn fault for playing cards with the smartest man in the world, right?

Wrong! Evangeline cleaned both of us out. I wondered if Jubal was being gallant, letting her win, but I don't think so. Jubal just isn't that subtle, and the look on his face as he tossed in three eights he was so confident in, only to have it stomped on by Evangeline's full house . . . well, Jubal just wasn't that good an actor.

We got our revenge, though. She had no luck at all at Monopoly. You should have heard Jubal cackling when she landed on his Board-walk hotel.

We lost our taste for olives pretty quickly. Jubal still enjoyed sucking on them, and we dutifully ate them as part of the skimpy meals we had planned out. After nursing moderate hangovers following our first sleep period, we rationed the booze, too. None of us were heavy drinkers.

We tried not to look at the radio too often.

I had established the channel to monitor from Mom, and if she had contacted Travis as she felt sure she could, he would know where to transmit and on what freq. We got nothing. The silence of the radio could make me sweat, if I thought about it much. I just underlined how very, very far away we were from anything human. When I thought about that, I tossed the dice and brought myself back to cutthroat capitalism. What were the chances of Jubal tossing a nine next turn, ending up right on Illinois? Is it worth my while to put up another house before he gets there? Did I have enough cash? These questions came to seem very important.

JUBAL HAD BEEN sleeping well. His adjustment to being in a tin can a billion miles from nowhere was just short of miraculous, if you'd known him before. Gravity seemed to make all the difference, even if it was acceleration gravity. And, as Einstein observed, there is absolutely no way to tell one from the other unless you look out the window. We had pulled the shutters on all the windows long ago.

Then the third night I heard him sobbing.

"All my fault," he was moaning. "All my fault."

I sat up and switched on a reading light. We'd folded up most of the chairs, made the rest into bunks. Evangeline and I had, of course, remained chaste, sleeping apart, because we were unmarried, and Jubal had old-fashioned ideas about that.

The bunks were lumpy, but in .4 gee just about anything is comfortable enough.

"All my fault."

I got up and gently shook Jubal by the shoulder. His eyes snapped open, and he gasped, but quickly got himself under control.

"You were having a bad dream, Jubal."

He rubbed his eyes and looked up at me with a wan smile.

"No dream, Ray. No dream."

"You want to talk about it?"

He glanced over at Evangeline, who was sitting up. She swung her legs over the side of the seats and walked over to the fridge and got three glasses filled with ice. She set them on the table and Jubal and I joined her.

"Last bottle of Jack," she said, pouring it over the ice for Jubal, then a vodka for herself and another for me. I didn't really want it, but what the heck? We were only a few hours from the time we'd have to stop accelerating and start slowing down. I no longer looked at the ship's computer very often. I just didn't much like the speed figure, and I liked the distance from home even less.

"Thanks you, *cher*, I need it." Jubal took a big drink and made a face.

"So what did you mean, Jubal, my friend? The invasion?"

He shrugged. "I guess that my fault, too. I thought I run away, I might stop the killin'. But I'm not good at that kind of thinkin', me. Should listen to Travis, he always tells me right."

"Jubal, that escape was pretty good thinking. I mean, it was a good plan."

"It was?"

"Sure. I'd have thought it was impossible to get away from that place. They were watching you all the time . . ."

"Not all the time." He looked a little smug. "I figgered I could use those little bitty times Travis worked it out so I'd have some, what he called, dignity. Privacy. But I couldn'ta done it without I invented that stopper."

"Stopper?" Evangeline asked.

"That what I call the other bubbles. The reg'lar kinda bubble, it squeezes. Them black bubbles, they stop."

"Stop time?"

"Weeell . . . it ain't exactly time. I mean, there's different kindsa time, see? The kind we use, you can't stop it and you can't turn it around. But there's two other kinds of time, and . . . oh, man, Ray, I can't 'splain it real good."

"That's okay, Jubal. No matter how you went at it, I wouldn't understand it, anyway."

"Well, what it *look* like, and what it *feel* like, is that time stops inside that stopper bubble, so that's what I called 'em."

"So, for all practical purposes . . ."

Jubal thought about it. "Yeah, I squinched up real tight, me, and I turn on de stopper bubble, and soon as I touch that button . . . dere I am wit' you guys, and I'm fallin', and pukin' . . . sorry about that."

I thought about it.

"What if I hadn't thought to use that little gizmo you sent me?"

Jubal smiled.

"Well, then, if de guys say the universe will stop blowin' itself up, if the whole shebang come to a stop and then start to fall back in on itself, in 50 billion years or so, and it all fall back into a new cosmic egg all ready to be born again . . . why, there'd I'd be, sittin' right on top of that cosmic egg, me, halfway tru a Hail Mary."

That brought a moment of silence. Evangeline broke it.

"And that . . . that didn't worry you?"

"Why worry?" Jubal wanted to know. "Time, it ain't flowin', ain't no way to worry, nor nothin' to worry 'bout. Course, I did wonder what would happen to my soul. Do souls care about time? I ain't figgered that one out yet, me. And anyhow . . . not ever comin' out that bubble be better than sittin' aroun' the way I was. I had to stop all the killin'. Like I said, it's all my fault."

"The invasion . . ."

"No, Evangeline, *cher.* Oh, that probably my fault, too, they was tryin' to ketch me." I remembered that Jubal didn't know we'd been invaded not once, but three times, and decided that wasn't something he needed to know. Not just yet, anyway. That we had all been picked up and tortured was something he didn't need to know, *ever*.

"And anyway, I never went to Mars. It's the other thing that's all my fault."

"What would that be, Jubal?"

"Why, the big wave. The sumammy."

I looked at Evangeline and saw she was looking at me.

"Jubal . . ." I began.

"It was a ship, Ray. One of them starships went out a long time ago."

"You're sure of that?"

"Nothin' else it could be. Somebody went out there, long, long way, and stopped hisself, turned hisself around, and headed back home. Then something go bad. Maybe all the people on that ship, they get sick and die. I dunno. Whatever, the ship just keep on going. Brain in that ship, it probly navigate its way home, but don't nobody tell it to stop. Ain't no way it hit the Earth on a accident. Take good aimin', hit a planet at that speed. Real good aimin'. I shoulda thought of that, me, before we give it to the world. All we thought about was, don't let no crazy people get hold of no bubbles so's they can 'splode 'em. Shoulda thought of that thing. Those bubbles, they aren't a good thing. Wish I'd of never thought of 'em. All my fault."

So we were back to the old argument. Were Einstein and friends responsible for Hiroshima and Islamabad, et cetera? Up to you, judge it for yourself. Personally, I couldn't hold Jubal responsible for the "sumammy." Of course, some would.

"Do you have any idea of who it was, Jubal?" Evangeline asked.

"No idea, me. Maybe Travis will know. Last time we talked, just before they cut us off and I started plannin' to bust out, he said he'd look into it, him."

That would have been a good time for Travis to call, but in fact it wasn't for another two hours, as I was just getting back to sleep, that the phone rang.

19

★ ★ ★

I'D SET THE ship's com unit to an old-fashioned ring, since none of us saw the point in wearing our stereos when we had no net connection. It rang once, and I sat up with a jerk, and then it began its message.

"Travis Broussard, calling for Ray Garcia-Strickland and Evangeline Redmond. Come in Ray and Evie. Travis Broussard, calling for . . ." and repeat. I hurried to the front of the shuttle and grabbed the mike.

"Ray calling Travis, Ray calling Travis. Come in, Travis. We're reading you loud and clear." I said that several times, then shook the sleep out of my brain and set the transmitter to repeat the short message. No telling how far away he was, but it could be very far, indeed, if he was using a directional antenna pointed at our extrapolated position. There could be quite a time lag. There was also no telling when he'd be close enough to pick up our weak signal, but Travis always had the best equipment available, and if any ship could pick us up from out here, he'd be the one.

He was also the best space pilot I'd ever known, something I'd held close to me in the darkest hours of doubt, early in the morning, for the last few days. He'd get to us.

It was ten minutes before the reply came.

"I'm reading you, Ray. Good job of flying, my man! You're within about a half mile of the line I projected, and only about ten thousand miles farther away than I expected you to be." I had nothing to say to that. With a computer and an autopilot anybody can be a great pilot, as long as you're traveling in a straight line. Travis's job, it turned out, had been a lot harder.

"I was on my way back to Earth, see about finding out some things, when your mom's message came in. Sorry I couldn't be faster. I had to cut a chord across a lot of empty space. Lonely out here, huh? Over."

"Elizabeth," Evangeline hissed in my ear, her fingers digging into my arm. I nodded. I'd been there already.

"Roger that, Travis. How is Elizabeth? Over."

Long silence. I forgot to turn on the timer, but it turned out to be around thirty seconds before we heard from him again. So he was closer than I had thought.

"Elizabeth will be all right, you guys. Ah . . . hell, she was working with a volunteer rescue crew and she . . . she was working her way through some debris to get to a guy who . . . ah, turned out to be dead. She had to have known he probably was, but she kept at it, and she picked up . . . a tear in her glove. Got a pressure sleeve on it, got hung up trying to get out . . . hell, there's no easy way to say this. She may lose the hand."

Long silence. Then . . .

"Over," he said.

I gulped and looked at Evangeline, who was crying.

"Copy that, Travis. Is everyone else okay? Over."

Thirty seconds.

"All your family members are okay. They were all pretty busy last time I talked to them. There was a lot of damage, lots of stuff to clean up. I don't know if you've heard a casualty report. Last I heard, it was over a hundred, with a few dozen still missing and presumed dead. Most of them are natives. Sorry, I mean Martians. Over."

"My god," Evangeline said. I couldn't think of anything to say for a moment. That was okay, because Travis resumed in a few seconds, in spite of the 'over' business.

"Ah, might as well give you some more information. Your countrymen are not taking it lightly. Some of the black ships have landed again, and they're not being welcomed with open arms. There have been riots. A few of the troops were killed in the blowouts, and Martians got their guns, so the locals are not entirely unarmed now. They've killed a few of the soldiers, and the soldiers have killed a few Martians. I wouldn't call it an all-out fight, there's too much damage to clean up, and too much worry about causing more blowouts. But tempers are, as they say, running high. I wouldn't wear any black clothes if I was out there in public pressure. In fact, most people are wearing red. Over."

I glanced at Jubal, who had popped another pill after his disturbing dreams. Just as well. I'd be able to tell him that Travis was coming to the rescue without upsetting him with more stories about death and . . . injuries. Oh, my poor sister.

"Roger. Ah, Travis, I don't know what Mom told you, other than to come get us. Over."

Twenty-nine seconds silence.

"She didn't say much, except that y'all had to run. I assumed it had something to do with the invasion. Over."

"It does, in a way. You know the thing we don't ever talk about? I probably shouldn't say any more over an open channel. Over."

Twenty-nine seconds. Then thirty-five. Then forty. I was about to call again.

"No fucking way," he finally said. There was a small note of hope in his voice.

"Way," Evangeline said.

He'd hear that in fourteen seconds, but he went on—or had gone on, considering that we were hearing his words fourteen seconds after he spoke them.

"Okay," he said, taking a deep breath. "Okay, this is great news, if you're saying what I think you're saying. But I'm afraid I have . . . oh, hi, Evangeline, nice to hear your voice. Like I was saying, I've got some bad news. I have company.

"Ah, I don't know where they picked me up, but I've got three black warships only a few miles behind me. I've been pulling two gees for two days, I should catch up to you in a few hours."

"Should I . . ." I shut up because he was still going on.

"They'll be catching up at pretty much the same time. Obviously they've been following me to find you, and, hell, they're listening, so we might as well say it. Is what we don't talk about aboard? Over."

"Roger that, Travis. Should I keep boosting? Should I cut the drive? You should know that he will get very sick and very scared if I cut the boost. Over."

Pause.

"Fuck me if I know how he's surviving the trip at all. You must be a miracle worker. No, you might as well keep boosting. You don't have to worry about consumables anymore, I've got plenty on board for all of y'all. Not that it'll matter much, because as soon as I get there I expect we'll all be captured. Right, Captain whoever-the-fuck-you-are on that command ship?" Short pause, but no one on the black ships answered him. "Over," he said, sounding infinitely sad and tired.

"But Travis . . . can't we do something? I mean . . . we've come so far . . . over."

Evangeline covered the mike with her hand and whispered in my ear.

"Hello, anybody home? He just told you the assholes are listening in. Do you think he should be discussing tactics with us?"

Oh.

"Maybe he's got a few tricks up his sleeve," she said.

"Travis usually does," I whispered back.

"I'm open to suggestions," Travis said. "But if you have any, it might be best if you wrote them on a piece of paper, tucked it in a bottle, and chucked it over the side, if you get my drift. Here's the situation as I see it. Correct me if I'm wrong, Captain Shitbag on the SS *Snotbucket*, and all y'all on the other two ships, too . . ."

WE HAD TWO big advantages. The three black ships could have blasted us to hell and gone, but they wanted Jubal alive. And they were warships, not cargo carriers. They had no means of grappling us, no way at all to capture us without risking violence that would kill us. They could chase us forever, but they couldn't stop us.

We had two big disadvantages. First, we were unarmed.

"What can I say?" Travis asked, defensively. "When I had this ship

built I never thought about having to fight pirates. I got no laser cannons, no blasters, no space torpedoes. I got a good shotgun, a rifle, and
three handguns. That's it."

The second drawback to our situation was that we had nowhere to
go. They might not be able to stop us or capture us, but they sure as hell
could follow us. Forever. Where we were heading there was nothing at
all. Behind us were all the possible ports of call, and every one of them
would be infested with more black ships, alerted by these fellows, waiting for us to land. We might fly around for months, but eventually the
food and oxygen would run out.

"Stalemate," I said.

"Well, no," Travis said. "Not even a Mexican standoff. It's a traveling
siege. Sooner or later they'll wear us out. All we can do is decide when."

"Situation like that," Evangeline said, "best thing to do is put it off as
long as possible. Something might change."

"I agree," Travis said. "You hear that, Captain Scrotum? We're not
turning ourselves in just yet. What I'm going to do is rendezvous with
my friends, take them off that flying breadbox, and then turn around
and head for home. Maybe somebody else will be in control when we
get back, we can work a deal with them and watch them shove it up
your asses. Maybe the mass-murdering pimps who are paying your
wages will be too busy fucking your mother to pay attention to you. Of
course, they'd have to tie a dirty towsack over your mother's face to fuck
her . . ."

Neither Captain Scrotum nor Captain Shitbag nor any of the other
colorful captains Travis addressed over the next hour had anything to
say. Maybe their feelings were hurt.

Probably not.

Over the next half hour the time lag gradually lessened. We didn't
use the radio much, as we didn't have anything to say that we wanted
Captains S & S to hear, just a time check now and then so the ships'
computers could calculate the rendezvous.

Finally Travis's ship hove into view beside us and we got our first
look at it. I'd heard about it but never seen it. It was pure Travis.

He'd based the design on an old movie, *Destination Moon*. It was sleek
and silver, and had four landing fins because it was designed to enter the

atmosphere of Earth—or Mars or even Titan—and come down on its landing jets. It was quite large, maybe bigger than the black ships. It wasn't the largest private space yacht, but it was up there in the top twenty.

Written on the side in old cursive, like the U.S. Constitution, was the name: *Second Amendment*.

Evangeline had gotten Jubal prepared while our ships matched speeds. He was in his suit but not his helmet. He was shivering and holding a sturdy barf bag up to his face.

We cut thrust at the same time, and drifted side by side. I turned on the headlights and rotated the ship to the sounds of Jubal's volcanic heaving. A cargo bay was opening on the side of the *Second Amendment*. Inside was a land/space vehicle in the same family as my nameless little shuttle, a boxy thing like mine, but slightly larger. As I watched it crawled forward, extended its front wheels over the lip, and then with a little spurt of its jets, moved past us and into the darkness, presumably into interstellar space, as we would have no place to put it and no way to find it later. Expensive, throwing something like that away, but Travis had said not to worry about it.

I jetted forward and into the bay. It wasn't meant to be entered while in space, normally a crane would lower it to a planetary surface or it would be used as a lifeboat. But there was enough room for me to ease in and position the shuttle in the center of the cargo bay.

"You clear of the door?" Travis asked.

"All clear," Evangeline said from the back.

"Closing doors." I couldn't see anything, but Evangeline told me when the doors were shut.

"Resuming acceleration." Slowly the thrust built up and the shuttle settled down to the floor. Then it came on stronger, until it was half a gee.

"Don't get out yet, guys," Travis said. "I'm watching . . . damn. Oh well, it was a long shot."

"What's that?"

"I was hoping one of those guys back there might hit my shuttle. I tried to get it in the right position, maybe they wouldn't notice it, they were five miles back . . . like I said a long shot. Okay, I'm pressurizing the bay."

We could see the air rushing in, as water condensed and froze into hard little ice crystals, then we could hear it. A green light came on and Evangeline and Jubal went into the bay, Jubal holding a second barf bag like a holy rosary. It cycled, and I went through, helmet in hand. They were already hustling toward the air lock/elevator at the front of the shuttle. It was cold in there! Frost had formed all over the shuttle but heated air was flowing all around us and melting it, where it dripped onto the rubber nonskid floor. We all three squeezed into the air lock, which sealed, and immediately rose five decks to the bridge, just under the pointed nose of the *Second Amendment*.

Travis was there when the door cycled open. Jubal practically leaped into his arms, sobbing and shouting with happiness. Travis was grinning like a fool, slamming his hands against Jubal's broad back. Evangeline and I hung back. I looked at her, and she wiped away a tear. Then Jubal and Travis were beckoning to us, and it was a very small but very happy little party there for a while.

Jubal didn't want it to stop, he was babbling happily, trying to tell all of his story at once, in no particular order, much of it in Cajun French. But Travis brought us all down to Earth . . . so to speak.

The bridge was a wide, comfortable cylinder, like a wheel of cheese. There were sofas and tables around most of it, with about a quarter devoted to the captain's chair and a control console array. There were windows all around, but they were closed. He had drinks laid out on a table, and some snacks. Mostly crackers and cheese . . .

When we'd stopped laughing and explained about our diet for the last three days, Travis produced sliced ham, bread, mustard, and apples from a fridge concealed in one wall, and we all made sandwiches while Evangeline and I brought him up to speed.

"Okay," he said at last. He produced a video screen on another wall, and we looked at three black disks, about evenly spaced, outlined in bright, flickering light like a solar corona during an eclipse. I knew they were the saucer-shaped black ships, seen from the top, accelerating along with us. Actually, getting closer, it looked like, as the distance between them was gradually increasing.

"They're moving up," Travis confirmed. "They'll have us surrounded in about thirty minutes. They're taking their time. No hurry.

They'll get us boxed in, and then I guess they'll make their move, if they've got one."

"Do you think they can do anything?" I asked.

"I haven't been able to think of anything. Not and be sure of getting Jubal alive. Even if they had some sort of grappling equipment, and I'd bet a billion dollars they don't, it would be easy for us to keep jigging and jagging away from it. To risky, too many things to go wrong and destroy both of us."

"So we're fu—*ouch!*" Evangeline glared at me and rubbed her arm where I'd pinched her. I'd never impressed on her strongly enough that Jubal was depressed by blasphemy and obscenity and she'd forgotten.

"I don't know," Travis said. "I figure if they're ever going to talk, it'll be when they're alongside. Then they'll make whatever offer they're going to make. Jubal, tell me about the black bubbles. The . . . what did you call them?"

"Stoppers," he said. "See, there ain't really no bubbles at all, no. I mean, they look like bubbles, so that's what I call 'em, but they really . . . the word the other folks use for 'em is superstrings, but that's stupid. They ain't strings, and they ain't super."

"I thought superstrings were incredibly tiny," I said.

"Tiny don't signify," Jubal said, shaking his head. "Somethin' got sixteen dimensions, all twisted up in a way . . . well, it make my head hurt when I think about 'em, so I don't think about 'em much. But you can unscrew 'em some. They can unfold, if you know how to give 'em the right *twist*." He opened an imaginary mason jar in the air.

"But why are these different from the first kind?"

"Sixteen dimensions," Jubal said. "Four squared. Four of 'em is . . . time dimensions. Different kinds of time. So if you unwind a string a different way, the stuff inside it . . ." He frowned. "Inside ain't the right word. The bubbles don't have no insides, see. They's not even really all here, the silvery part you see is just the part that sticks out from where they really are into where we really are." He looked at us hopefully.

"So where are they really?" Travis asked.

"I ain't figgered that part yet. Some other infinite universe. Or someplace, make us look like little bitsy meebas in a microscope." Meebas? Oh, amoebas. "Anyway, I ain't thought about it much, because it hurts my head, but I figgered how to unstring one a them strings so that it can be any size. Didn't know what it'd do to something inside it. Killed rats, it did." I remembered that the rat they'd placed inside a Squeezer bubble had turned into a fine gray powder. "And if you can make 'em any size, what's inside can be squished real right. That's the Squeezer bubbles."

"And the stoppers?"

"Well, time is different in 'em. Maybe time is zeroed out, I still haven't figgered all the equations for that one."

"Why'd you make it?" Evangeline asked. "Oh, dumb question. You made it so you could escape."

"No, ma'am. I made it because I don't like frozen fish, me."

There was a suitable silence. Travis sighed and made a go-ahead motion toward Jubal. He was used to this.

"Lotsa fish in them Falkland Islands. I like to catch 'em, me. But some days I don't catch any, and then if I want fish, I got to take some out of the freezer."

"Jubal, they'd have flown any kind of fresh fish you want in if you'd asked for it."

Jubal stared at the floor.

"I don't like to ask for stuff. And I like to catch my own. Tastes better. But you know fish, it ain't as good the second day, and the third day . . . whew! Forget about that thing! So I wondered how I could keep fish fresh longer."

It made perfect sense, didn't it? When you thought about it? But Jubal was just . . . ah, *warming* to his subject.

"Keep stuff hot, too. Cook up a étouffée, put it in a stopper, and a year later you open 'er up and she still be steamin'! Never have to freeze nothin', nothin' ever have to spoil, no! Keep your drinks hot or cold, dependin' what you want."

Travis looked at us, and he looked as astonished as I'd ever seen him. It actually was a pretty damn good idea. Of course, there were about a thousand other ways to use a stopper bubble that the three of us could think of without breaking a sweat, some of them with scary implications . . . but that was Jubal. He was the theory man and the engineer. Travis was the practical one.

We were interrupted by a beeping sound. Travis sighed.

"Jubal, you okay with me opening the windows?"

"Think I wear my helmet, me," he said, and put it over his head. When he was safe with whatever comfort the suit gave him, Travis opened the windows all around the bridge and we saw the three black ships surrounding us. Their exhausts were so bright the windows darkened until we could barely see the ships themselves. They were equally spaced, and seemed to be around the same size, which was the same size as the ones that had first landed and taken me and my family prisoner. Say a bit bigger than the *Second Amendment*. Travis picked up the old-fashioned mike from his console and spoke.

"Captain Broussard of the SS *Second Amendment*, calling Captain Jerkoff of the good ship Pus-bucket. Come in, Pus-bucket. Don't you think it's about time we talked? You're bound to have a proposal for me. A threat? An offer? A heartfelt plea?"

"You are instructed to cut your drive immediately and prepare to be boarded," somebody said, in a voice that sent chills up my spine. It was a woman's voice. It was hard to be absolutely sure, but it sounded a lot like the voice that had interrogated me for endless hours and then threatened my family.

"Oh, an instruction, is it? Am I addressing Captain Jerkoff herself, or are you merely a lackey? By the way, did you know it's customary, by the ancient and honorable laws of the high seas and high space, to identify yourself when communicating from one craft to another?"

"Who I am is none of your concern. Cut your drive and wait to be boarded." She was trying for the calm, even voice she had used during interrogation, but there was anger there in the rising tone at the end.

"*Hoo!* Getting a little cranky, are we? Boosting at two gees for three days didn't agree with you? Hard to sleep, isn't it? Man, I've got a crick in my neck, hurts something awful." Travis put the mike down and cracked his knuckles in front of it, grinning at us. He was enjoying this. I tried to smile myself, but that voice took most of the fun out of it.

"You are ordered to cut your drive at once, and—"

"Or what?"

There was a silence. When Travis spoke again, there was steel in his voice.

"Or what, Captain Douchebag? Cut the baloney and lay your cards on the table. Tell me why I should cut my drive, or I'm going to keep blasting until somebody's food runs out. I got a *lot* of food aboard. Enough to feed the four of us for about a year. How much do *you* have?"

Silence again. Travis winked at us.

"Not that much, huh? Course, at the speeds we'll be reaching, it might be enough to last a hundred years, back home. That would be awkward, getting back home and finding out the people who were paying you for your atrocities have forgotten who you are."

"Who's bullshitting now?" she said. I saw Jubal wince. "You people have families. You wouldn't want them to all be dead when you got back."

"Touché," Travis said. "So we both have to turn around at some point. But I don't see why I should do it in your custody."

"Keep thinking about family, Broussard," she said, and the menace and confidence was back. "And you, too, Ramon, and you, Evangeline. I'm sure you remember the things that were told to you when you were in custody. Are you really willing to sacrifice everyone who is dear to you to protect that . . . that freak?"

I'd have been shocked, but I'd already been there. Once someone threatens your family like that, you know where your real vulnerability is.

Would I? Would I beg Travis to stop the boost, get down on my knees, and plead with him to surrender Jubal to these people if I thought they would hurt my family, or Evangeline's?

You betcha.

If you wouldn't have done the same thing, there's something wrong with you. Don't forget, the worst that would happen to Jubal would be getting locked up again in a prison like the Falklands. They didn't want to kill him; they wanted what was in his head.

I'd already worked it through in mine. These were people who didn't mind using any amount of force, who would drug children and actually seemed to like psychological torture. I knew without question that they'd enjoy physical torture as well, or if they didn't, they'd hire somebody who did, who was good at it, who was a Michelangelo of torture. Maybe they figured they could force the secrets of the Squeezers out of Jubal. Maybe they actually *could*. I didn't know. Would I give him up, with the certainty that they'd use any means necessary?

Sorry, Jubal. I love you, I really do. But I'll turn you in if it comes to it.

But first, before I start pleading, let's hear what Travis has in mind.

He seemed to have been reading my thoughts. He looked at me and Evangeline and shook his head. He covered the mike with his hand.

"Not gonna happen," he said, quietly. "We will all do whatever it takes to protect your families."

"Ray, Evangeline," Jubal said, quietly, "came to it, I'd give myself up. I done caused too much trouble already. Don't y'all worry none about your families."

Evangeline looked away from him. There were tears in her eyes.

"Not gonna happen," Travis said again. Then he spoke into the mike.

"That sounded like a threat to me, Captain D. Would you mind repeating it for the recording, so we can play it at your trial?"

"Just turn off your drive, you motherfucker, or I will personally supervise the slow deaths of everyone you ever held dear."

"Got it," Travis said. "Give us one hour to talk it over, okay?"

"Are you out of your fucking—"

"Come on, Captain. We've come this far, and we've got a big decision ahead of us. What's one more hour?"

"There is one more thing you should know," she said. "You understand we want Jubal Broussard alive. But even more important than that, we want to make sure that no one else gets their hands on him. Do you understand what I'm saying?"

"I'd understand it a lot better if I knew who you are, and who the 'no one else' is."

"That's not something you need to know. All you need to know is that, if you don't stop accelerating and allow yourself to be boarded in one hour, your fucking ship will be destroyed, and your fucking families will *still* die."

"Got it. Talk to you in an hour."

There was a short silence after Travis turned off the radio, then he turned to me and Evangeline.

"First, what happens out here will have *no bearing* on what happens to your families, I can promise you that. I don't know if they've been rounded up, there's no way to know what's happening. But those folks on those ships out there aren't going to be sending any orders back. They're fixing to disappear."

"You mean . . ."

"I mean, I'm going to take them *out*!" We both jumped at the savagery in his voice. The amiable, easygoing Travis was gone for a moment. He looked away and got himself under control. Then he looked at Jubal.

"What do you think, Jubal?"

He was looking at his hands twisting in his lap.

"That lady got a nasty mouth on her, sure enough." He looked up. "She really kill their families?"

"I think you can count on it."

He shook his head. "I didn't want no more killin'. There already been enough killin', and it all my fault."

"It's not your fault, Jubal," Travis said.

"He's right," Evangeline said. I nodded when Jubal looked at me.

He was still shaking his head.

Travis sighed, then looked at me and Evangeline.

"Give me and Jubal a minute, you guys."

He put his arm around Jubal and took him to the far end of the bridge. Evangeline went to the other side, keeping our backs to them, and looked out at one of the black ships. We could see a bubble on top, with windows, and somebody was standing there, looking out at us. They were too far away to make out, but I thought it was a woman in a black uniform.

"Want to give her the finger?" Evangeline said. I shivered.

"No, I think Travis should handle poking at snakes with a sharp stick. All I want to do is run."

"Me, too."

We thought about that for a while. Well, I actually thought about kicking myself repeatedly in the ass if I could bend my leg enough. *Idiot!* You're supposed to brag and swagger about what big balls you have to your girlfriend, aren't you? This is the girl who kicked an armed soldier in the nuts while you stood there with nothing but a dumb, stupefied grin on your face. What would have it have cost you, popping the rod to that murdering bitch across the way? But it was too late to do it now, it would look stupid. And too late to reassure her with brave words after what you'd just said.

All I want to do is run. *Idiot!*

"I'm glad you're here, Ray," she said, and put her arm around me. I did the same.

"I'll do what I can," I said. Idiot!

"I know you will, Ray. I know you will."

Well, maybe all was not lost.

We heard only a few phrases from across the room, mostly when Travis raised his voice in frustration, but several times we heard Jubal, sounding determined.

"I don't want no more killin'," he said. "Been too much killin'."

Then, just a little later, Travis said, "I don't see the difference. Six of one, half a dozen of the other."

Jubal said something, and I watched the reflection in the glass as Travis shrugged, but he looked a lot happier than he had.

"How long do you think it'll take? We only got fifty minutes."

"Ten minutes. Maybe fifteen."

"Go to it, then." He took Jubal to a section of the control panel that had only a few basic dials and a joystick on it. He turned some catches under the console and lifted it from the front. Jubal bent over and stuck his head inside. Travis came over toward us, and I laughed aloud.

"What's funny?"

I spoke quietly, because I knew Jubal could take offense, being laughed at.

"He just looks like a mechanic working under the hood."

Travis looked over his shoulder; I heard Evangeline giggle.

"When he's done, the rascal will probably pad the bill."

"Travis, don't you think it's about time you told us what's going on?"

"Yeah. I was trying to convince—"

"It done, Travis." Jubal had straightened up and collapsed into one of the control chairs. He didn't look happy.

"Already?" Jubal didn't answer. Travis sighed, put a hand on each of our shoulders. "Might as well just do it and explain it later. This is my decision, okay?"

I didn't know what else to do but nod. Travis took his seat, looked out the window at what we figured was the command ship, and picked up the mike.

"Calling the unidentified ship," he said. "Answer at once."

"Did you make up your mind?" came the awful voice.

"No more games, no more insults," Travis said. "I'd sort of like to know your name. Is that you at the window?" He waved at the dark, distant figure.

"My name is no concern of yours. Have you made up your mind already?"

"Yes, we have. We've decided to take you out. That's why I asked your name. It doesn't seem right to kill someone I'm looking at without knowing her name."

She could actually laugh. I hope she enjoyed it, because it was her last one.

"You are incredible. If you'd had weapons that can take me out, you'd have used them already."

"No, *you'd* have used them. That's the difference between us, and I know it's a weakness, but I like to give somebody a chance to do the right thing. It's still not too late. Turn yourself in, do a little time, start a new life. There's always work for sadists."

"You have thirty-nine minutes."

"No, you have five seconds. And the last lesson you're going to learn in your miserable life is this: Never assume a ship called the *Second Amendment* is unarmed." Travis clicked something on the control panel, and we saw her react. She didn't like what she saw. Evangeline and I turned around, and the other two ships were gone.

Just . . . gone.

Travis waved to her, and we saw her turn to shout orders to somebody, and Travis clicked the thing again, and her ship was gone.

20

JUBAL RETIRED TO a stateroom, refusing to talk to anyone. Travis was skulking around with such a sour expression that neither Evangeline nor I thought it was the right time to talk. There was a lot of time before decisions had to be made, anyway. I didn't have the foggiest idea of what those decisions would be, or much of a notion of our alternatives, though I was chewing that over in my mind a lot.

Meantime, the only thing we could do was slow down. The first thing Travis did, after Jubal left us, was to turn ship and start decelerating. It would take about four days, at one-half gee. We told Travis we'd be okay with a full gee, but he said he thought he'd need us rested and alert, and he couldn't see any reason to hurry. At the end of the four days we'd be motionless relative to the solar system, and then we'd have to decide where we were going.

Evangeline poked around the fully equipped galley and told me Travis had been telling the truth. There was enough stuff in there for a trip to the stars. Knowing Travis, I wouldn't have been at all surprised if he'd had that in mind when he had the ship built. He planned for any contingency, including warfare in space, as Captain Whoever-she-was had learned in her last moments of life.

I asked myself how I felt about that. We'd just killed an unknown number of people. Almost certainly in the hundreds. Most of them were probably just folks doing their jobs. I sure wasn't going to be hypocritical enough to say I wept for the captain . . . and probably a good part of the people under her command. I was glad she was dead, only regretted she hadn't seemed to suffer. But many of those people aboard were probably only doing their jobs. Maybe some of them didn't even know what the others were doing.

Well, I figure you've got to choose your job carefully. Read the fine print. If it has anything to do with invading people and torturing them, find another job or suffer the consequences when those folks fight back.

Evangeline was a wonderful cook. I'd had no idea, but her father was the chef at the Red Thunder, so . . . duh. She whipped up a jambalaya to die for and set four places at the table. Travis started wolfing his down, not looking at either of us. She spooned a big portion onto the fourth plate and went to Jubal's room. She came back without the plate.

"He wouldn't let me in," she said, "but he took the food."

I let a little time go by, let Travis get almost finished.

"So . . . Travis . . . what's he mad about?"

Travis tossed his fork onto the plate and leaned back.

"My fault," he said, and swallowed the last mouthful. "Jubal's too gentle to hang around with me. You heard what he said, he didn't want to kill anybody."

"We didn't have any choice," Evangeline said.

"He knows that. Jubal's not stupid, he's just not real logical when it comes to emotional things. He was always a sweet soul, even before his injuries. Now he just can't handle ugliness like that."

"So that's what you were arguing about?"

"Not exactly. He knew we had to do something. He was arguing we should use his new thing. His stopper bubble."

Evangeline brightened.

"So that's what you did? You put them in those bubbles? That means they're still alive then, right?" She caught herself, as if ashamed she was relieved to find they were alive. "I mean, that means somebody can let them out when this is all over. Put them on trial for what they did. I mean, that's better than killing them, isn't it?"

I hugged her with one arm. I was half through the jambalaya, and I wasn't hungry anymore.

"That's what I did, all right," Travis said. "Jubal put his new machine in the weapons system, and we froze them in those bubbles. So they're all in there, just like they were a few hours ago. That bitch, the captain is still turning around, still about to give the orders to blow up this ship. If somebody ever finds them, they'd better be ready when the bubble turns off, because she's going to be shooting at anything that moves."

"Well, you look like you're not happy about it," she said. "Maybe I'm too soft, but I think it's better not to kill, when you can."

"I'm with you, hon. But it's really academic."

"'Six of one . . .'" I said.

"Half a dozen of the other. Evangeline, how do you figure we're going to *find* them?"

"Well, we know where they were when you . . . when you stopped them."

"That's right. We were about a billion miles north of the sun, traveling . . . I don't even remember, but it was millions of miles an hour. Now, I don't know if they kept traveling. Jubal wouldn't tell me. Maybe he doesn't know. From what you guys described, I think they might have just . . . stopped. Dead in their tracks. Remember, I've never seen one, and you say they're so black the only way we'd see them was if they blocked out some stars. Whether they stopped or kept going at their original velocity, they are a long, long way from anything. If they're still moving, they could be halfway to Polaris by the time anyone gets around to organizing a search."

"But you said they probably just stopped. No mass, right?"

"Like I said, it's way too much of a physics problem for me. But take the best case. Best case for them. They're motionless, a billion miles above the solar system. How is anybody going to find them?"

She started to answer, then closed her mouth. Physics isn't her thing, but she had an instinctive feel for space and spatial orientation. Maybe that would take her to the answer I'd already arrived at.

"They're going to be hard to find," she said, quietly.

"Next to impossible, I'd say," Travis said. "They don't reflect light or radar. We know their position—*if* they aren't still moving—within about five hundred miles. Now, I guess you could come out here with a really big net and start casting around."

"But why would they?" she said.

"Exactly. I have a strong feeling they would be an embarrassment to whoever hired them, if this all comes out the way I'm hoping it will. Best just to forget about them. I doubt anyone even knows they were out here except for the people who ordered them to follow me . . . and the four of us."

We were quiet for a while.

"It's really sort of a theoretical question, I guess," Travis said, at last. "That's why I gave in. I told Jubal if he could modify my Squeezer to make a stopper, then we'd use that. If he could do it in less than an hour. He must have known he could. Anyway, in a philosophical sense, he's right. He's been in one, and he came out fine. Time stopped for him. If I'd used the Squeezer, we'd know that everything inside just came apart. This way, they're at least potentially alive in there. Probably for a very, very long time."

I remembered Jubal's image of what would have happened to him if I hadn't thought of opening the black bubble with the thing he'd sent me. Jubal, inside a black bubble, sitting on the cosmic egg after the biggest squeeze of all, as every atom of matter in the universe collapsed into one unimaginable thing where mass, matter, energy, time, inertia, gravity . . . none of it existed . . . and the bubble floating on top.

"I'm not going to swear anybody to secrecy," Travis said. "Y'all can do what you want to do. But Jubal and I decided there was no reason to ever tell anybody what happened out here. I'd like to just leave it that three ships came chasing out after me, and I never even knew they were there. I found you guys, took you aboard . . . and they vanished."

"Well, that's what happened, isn't it?" I said. "The last part, anyway. I don't see any reason we have to tell anyone the story. I'll probably tell Mom and Dad, though."

"You go ahead and do that. I'd trust Manny and Kelly with anything."

Evangeline looked at us. She shrugged.

"I won't miss the bastards. I may tell my dad, but I might wait a while to do it."

"Like I said, do what you think best. Now. Anybody got any ideas where we should go?"

THAT WAS THE question, of course. Soon we'd know if our families had been picked up, but for now we were in the dark about that. Even decelerating, every second took us farther away from the solar system. Then it would take a while to build up some speed on our way back home. It would be a week before we even made it back to the region of space that might or might not contain the three black bubbles with people frozen in time inside them.

It was then we would have to decide where to go and what to do when we got there.

Mars was out. We had to assume that somebody was still in charge there, and it wouldn't be anyone friendly to us. Earth and Luna were out, too, for even more obvious reasons. Where else was there?

There were small settlements on and inside a few asteroids, on some of the moons of Jupiter and Saturn, some free-floating space habitats near the rings of Saturn. Most of them were tourist destinations or scientific research stations. Pretty tough to hide in any of them. The rest were "communities of affinity," as the sociologists called them. There was a large group of Mormons on Ceres, all-Muslim colonies on Enceladus and Tethys, various New Age philosophical retreats here and there. There was New Africa on Ganymede. Even harder to hide in any of those.

Jubal came out of his room on the second day and acted as if nothing had happened. That was his way. He'd . . . brood, or sulk, or pout, depending on how you wanted to look at it, then it would be forgotten. He didn't bear grudges, and he didn't dwell on slights or disagreements. A day alone and he was back.

Still, we all sort of tiptoed around each other for the next day, as people who had shared in something we knew had to be done, but couldn't find it in ourselves to be proud about. Nobody talked about what we had done, and we all seemed content to leave it that way.

I pretended to sleep in my stateroom, but every night when Jubal was safely tucked away I made my way down the dim corridor to

Evangeline's. It was annoying, but worth it to keep Jubal in a good mood. She did most of our cooking, helped by Jubal, who knew a thing or two. Jubal was lavish in his praise of her cuisine, which leaned heavily toward Cajun and soul food. It was a great deal for me and Travis, since both of us were helpless in the kitchen.

WE'D NEVER HAVE known it if Travis hadn't told us, but we eventually reached what we'd been calling the zero point. That meant we were no longer moving away from the sun. Without a pause we began to move in-system again.

"Lady and gents," he said, "this is as far from the sun as I've ever been. If we were in the ecliptic, we'd be out beyond Neptune."

I guess that impressed him more than it did me and Evangeline. He'd grown up in an era when it would take a long time to get out here. We had always thought of Neptune as a place we'd probably visit someday. But I'd never expected to be out in this direction.

For the first time since the black ships, Travis called us all together after the evening meal that night. And he got right to it.

"Ray, Evangeline, I know Jubal told you his take on what is probably the worst-kept secret of this century. Just what it was that hit us and caused the Atlantic tsunami."

"He told us it was a starship," Evangeline said.

"Had to be," Jubal said. "Nothin' else that big could go that fast."

I didn't say anything. The "official" explanation was that it was some previously unknown natural phenomenon. That was their story, and they were sticking to it. Currently they were trying to make the math work such that it might have been some sort of ejecta from a supernova. Which just proves you could always find *somebody* to whore for the government in any field, including astronomy.

"That's what I've been working on since you guys went back to Mars," Travis said. "Obviously it was something propelled by some sort of stardrive, either the bubble or something invented by some other civilization. My money was always on it being one of ours, and now I know it was."

I'd always expected it, too, and that was certainly the dominant theory buzzing around the web. But it was sobering to see that Travis believed it.

"Jubal told you he thought it might have been an epidemic. Maybe they got to another star system, landed, picked up some sort of virus, headed home, all died, and the autopilot just kept them blasting for home.

"I never liked that. If I was making an autopilot, I'd set it up to turn ship automatically when the time came, and decelerate until it parked itself in Earth orbit, even if it was full of dead people. But I know some people can do some damn-fool things, and a lot of damn fools were building and launching starships back when this one must have taken off."

He was right about that. I'd read about it in history class. A lot of nations, not all of them with much of a history of engineering excellence, had built starships and launched them soon after it became possible to do so without busting the national budget. Some nations who *couldn't* afford it, piss-poor countries headed by strongmen, military dictators, or just flat-out psychotics like the people who ruled North Korea at the turn of the century, went ahead and did it anyway, as a matter of "national pride." They'd hire an astronomer to pick out a star known to have planets that nobody else was heading for already, hire engineers who hadn't made the grade in other jobs, slap something together fast and cheap, and set out for the glory of the Great State of Fuckupistan.

Energy was unlimited, so size was not a problem. The fastest and cheapest way was to find a smallish asteroid, hollow it out with Squeezer bubbles, and use the squeezed matter to boost the ship. Build your crew quarters and hydroponic farms inside the hollow.

A few of those ships were overdue. Nobody knew how many, because beyond a few light-years communication was impossible, and because nobody knew how long an exploratory crew would choose to stay. Maybe some of them had landed on Earth-like paradises and had no intention of returning to Fuckupistan and its glorious leader.

But most starships hadn't returned yet because they were probably still on their way out. Even at the speed of light, star travel takes time, and we knew from the ships that *had* returned that there were no habitable planets within ten light-years.

"There were plenty of groups with a grievance who made hollowed-out asteroid starships, too. You could buy one for only about 100 million dollars, unfurnished. I've been looking at those to see who could have done it, too. It had to be a big one, not one of those economy jobs the real nutcases took off in. Even at the speed of light, the *Second Amendment* wouldn't have nearly enough mass to do the damage that was done. Neither would a ship the size of the *Sovereign*. It had to be a fairly big rock."

"But it *could* have been an accident, right?" I asked.

Travis shook his head.

"I wanted to believe that. And the one thing that bothered me about the suicide-flier scenario was that there was no *message* attached. Something that big, you want people to know it was you who did it. But nobody stepped forward to claim responsibility." He waved his hand. "Check that. A hundred groups of nuts have claimed responsibility, just like they always do, but not a one of them has any credibility. Nothing but wannabes. If there was somebody on the ground who knew this was going to happen, it would have made sense to brag about it a day or two before it happened. It's not like flying an airplane into a building, you can't shoot it down. You can't even see it coming, it's moving so fast. So why not taunt the people you are planning to hit? Why not get your message out, hit us, and then say 'I told you so, and here's what we want you to do or we'll bring down the wrath of fill-in-the-blank *again*.' "

"Nobody ever said terrorists are smart," I said.

"Amen to that. But still . . . anyway, I moved on to—"

"Wait a minute," Evangeline blurted. Everybody turned to look at her. A few hints of body language told me she was wishing she'd kept her mouth shut. She needed to work on her self-confidence, at least when it came to subjects like this. But she plowed on. "Maybe . . . well, I just thought, maybe these guys . . . say they're a small group, and they can't afford to buy their own ship. So they get a group of them aboard as passengers, and sometime later they take it over. Kill everybody aboard."

"Gas would do it," Travis said.

"You've already thought of this," she said.

"Go on. I want your thinking."

"Well, they take over the ship. Turn it around and . . . do what they did."

"Why no announcement?" he asked.

"That's what just occurred to me. Say they're a small group, a few dozen, a few hundred, I don't know. The hijackers have to go a long way out, then they have to slow down, like we did. Then they have to build up speed again. They probably took off a long time ago."

"Maybe as long as twenty years ago. Go on."

"Okay, while they're doing all that . . ."

"The group goes belly-up!" I said.

"That's what I was going to say."

"Let her tell it, Ray."

"Sorry."

"It's okay. Anyway, like you said, they don't have to be very smart, and the trip doesn't seem very long to them, because during a lot of it time is hardly passing at all because of the . . . what's the word?"

"Lorentz-FitzGerald contraction?" I said.

"No, that obsolete," Jubal said. "You talkin' about time squeezin'."

"Yeah. They're gone twenty years, but it only feels like a year to them. They get back to the solar system and their group is dead . . . and they don't even know it."

"And there's no way for them to find out," Travis said, smiling. "No way for them to communicate, call Uncle so-and-so and even see if what they're hoping to accomplish might even have already *happened*."

"Idiots," Jubal muttered.

"Exactly. It works out as a classic 9/11 situation. One relatively good planner who got away with it because nobody was expecting it. Maybe a dozen others who are mainly idiots, plus some aggrieved idiots on the ground who may have blown themselves up in a bomb factory, or all got caught at something, or just got old and tired of the whole terrorist lifestyle. It's a young idiot's game, not an old idiot's. Anyway, like you say, Evangeline, that answered my question of why there was no warning on the ground."

He let us think that one over for a while.

"On the ground," I said, finally.

Travis pointed his finger at me. "Bingo. I thought about myself sitting in the control room of a starship that's moving so fast you can't see anything out the front window. Only way you know you're approaching

Earth is the ship's computer says you are. It's tough to put yourself into the head of—"

"Wait a minute," Evangeline said. "Why can't they see anything out the front window?" She looked around at us. "Maybe I'm dumb . . ."

"No, *cher*, not dumb," Jubal said, with a chuckle. "Everythin' up front been blue-shifted. No more visible light."

"Okay, I *am* dumb. What's blue-shifted mean?"

"Have you heard of the red shift?" Travis asked.

"I think somebody mentioned that in science class. Something about all the galaxies moving away from us?"

"That's right. All the galaxies we can see are moving away from us, and the way we can tell is that the light coming from them is shifted into the red end of the spectrum. It's like when a train goes by—"

"It sounds higher when it's coming toward you, and lower when it's going away. I remember that."

"Works the same way with light. The light gets stretched out, it becomes redder. The farther away it is, the faster it's moving away from us. Out at the edge of the universe, some of them are moving away at close to the speed of light, and the light is shifted way down into the infrared. If it's coming toward us—"

"Wait a minute. I've never understood why they're all moving away. Why aren't some of them coming toward us? Those galaxies, way out there, they've been moving away from us for a long time, right? So what happened. Did some really, really big dinosaur fart?"

There were a few seconds of silence, then Jubal whooped. Did I mention that Jubal has what you might call a low sense of humor? He's not much for jokes or puns, but he loves a whoopee cushion. And once you get him started . . .

He roared, he giggled, he literally fell on the floor and rolled. After a weird moment, Travis began to laugh, too, then me and Evangeline, though her face was pretty red, wondering if we thought she was stupid. I kept trying to tell her it was okay, but I was laughing too hard, and she eventually realized nobody was laughing at her. It was one of those situations where you feel you've almost got it under control, then somebody will laugh again, and you start all over. Laughter is a real contagious thing, sometimes, and after a while it becomes painful, but still you laugh. Until finally you are all sitting there, worn-out, still being hit by little waves of giggles.

I know. It wasn't that funny. But you had to be there. You had to have been through what we'd been through, and probably you had to be facing the bleak choices we were facing. Anyway, it helped. Lord, how it helped. I felt more emotionally cleaned out than anytime since . . . well, since I cried after seeing that dead tiger.

Travis finished his lesson, Red Shift 101, and then moved on.

"Blue shift is exactly the opposite," he said. "Something is coming toward you real fast, the light waves get compressed, they get bluer. They go into the ultraviolet, then into X-rays, and finally gamma rays when you're moving *really* fast."

"Same thing with radio waves," I said.

"Bingo again. So I started . . . well, let's go back to the bridge of that starship, the SS *Tsunami*. A human can't fly it. Forward, you can't see anything, the light has been shifted up out of the visible spectrum. You've got a computer that's making some really, *really* tough calculations. It's putting together some sort of image from the hard radiation coming from in front, it knows where the sun is, and has an idea where the Earth should be. But it's not getting as much information as it's used to. Probably not anything usable from the solar navigation arrays."

"Those are the satellites in solar orbit," I said, "like the global positioning—"

"Got it," Evangeline said.

"He's flying by dead reckoning and inertial records and probably a lot of prayers to whatever god he worships.

"But how accurate can he be? Jubal worked on that problem, and I got some other friends to work on it, too, and the answer we came up with independently was . . . he was lucky to have hit the Earth at all. If lucky is the word.

"One, he's been traveling for a long time, a long distance. Determining your current position is *everything*. And if you're off by a few feet a light-year away, it's going to add up to thousands of miles at your destination.

"Two, things are happening *fast*. He'd be crossing the distance from the Earth to the moon in less than a second, every second. He will, or the computer, actually, will try to make course corrections as far out as possible, because it will have more effect out there. You try to deflect something the size of an asteroid from a point close to your target, you'll need a lot of thrust.

"Three, not only is it moving fast, but he's *slowed down*. Time has contracted for him. Every second for him—and for the computer—is a week for us on Earth. The computer is compensating for that, but it's one more thing to complicate the equation."

"Jee . . . oh, man," I said. "I don't see how he managed to hit his target *at all*."

"I don't think he did," Travis said. "Or not the one he was aiming for, anyway. Take a look at this."

He turned and called up an image of the Earth on a big screen. A line appeared, and I was taken back to that awful moment in the gym when it all began. It was the image left by the remains of the starship and some cubic miles of seawater that had instantly smashed into hot plasma with the impact. Travis worked a cursor and the line extended itself down to the southwest.

"Here's the incoming path. Here's the point of impact. Now draw a diameter around the Earth, at right angles to the path." That all happened, and then the picture zoomed in and the globe turned a bit. "Now I'm going to move the point of impact over Washington, D.C." That happened, and the line that traced the path of the ship moved with it. "What do you think?"

Evangeline and I stared at it. The line began in D.C., and passed over Philadelphia, New York City, and Boston.

"You're kidding," Evangeline breathed.

"I wish I was. I can't be sure, of course. But it looks to me like this guy, these guys, wanted to impact Washington. I'm no physicist, but I figure the whole city would be vaporized. How far that damage would reach, I don't know. It might depend on how shallow the impact was. It might skim right along the surface, plasma hot as the middle of the sun, all the way to Boston. Instead of 3 million dead, we might have had . . . I don't know, 50 million? 100 million? Plus, you might *still* get a tidal wave that would hit Europe. I just don't know, I can't make my mind wrap around that much evil . . . but I think he missed."

We pondered that for a while. He was right. It was hard to even imagine.

"So we got lucky?"

"Almost. Just a little bit more inaccurate, and he'd have missed us entirely. My gut feeling, he got lucky to hit us at all. But he wanted to do more."

I remembered something else.

"Wait a minute. You said you knew this was intentional. So far all I've heard is speculation. He probably did this, he might have done that, he got lucky."

Travis nodded.

"The message," Evangeline said.

"Bingo three times. I imagined him in there, he's busy as a one-legged man in an ass-kicking contest, trying to keep it all straight in his tiny little head, monitoring the computer, probably worrying every time the computer set off a correcting boost, saying his prayers. The seconds are ticking down, a week at a time. *Then . . . oh my god! I forgot to send out the message. They have to know who did this. I, whatever my name is, the greatest terrorist mastermind and hero of my people or my cause, dealing out death to those who deserve it. How else will they sing my praises?* So he sends the message out at the last minute."

"And we got it?"

"Some people did. It took them a while to figure out where to look, and when they had it, they kept it to themselves. They don't know how to deal with it. If they'd asked me, I could have told them. You *can't* deal with it. There's no way. We don't even know if this guy was the first. Anybody less accurate than this guy was, we'd probably never have even seen him pass through the solar system, not even if he only missed by a thousand miles. If one was on its way right now, this instant, we could do nothing. We'd have a fraction of a second response time. The people in control, the handful who know the full story, they just *hate* that. Hate it worse than normal people do, because control is *everything* to them. I think that's another reason they want Jubal back so badly. They think he's the only one who can find an answer."

Jubal shook his head, sadly. "Ain't found one so far, me."

"But how did *you* find out?" I asked.

"Same way things usually get done. Connections. I know a lot of people at the Jet Propulsion Laboratory. I realized that if a message was sent out, it would arrive as X-ray or gamma ray bursts. So I found an old friend, and he didn't want to tell me, but I can be persuasive. Turns out they went back and checked some astronomical instruments that look for those things. There was a burst just before the impact. It was in Morse Code. They had to process it a lot before the message came out."

He stopped and looked down at his hands.

"Okay, I'll ask," Evangeline said. "What was the message? Who did it?"

"The message was 'Death to.' "

We waited. Slowly, realization dawned on me.

"That's it? *Death to?*"

"You probably ought to put three dots after it, or maybe a dash, whatever you do when somebody is cut off. He got out two words, and then he crashed."

I DON'T KNOW how the others spent that night, but I kept turning it over and over in my mind. A cosmic joke. Proof that God has a sense of humor, though a pretty rough one.

Well, we always knew that. Read the Old Testament.

Travis told us he had made a stab at figuring out what group might have been behind it all. It was almost impossible. Something like eight hundred large starships had gone out over the years, only a few dozen had yet returned. He started by eliminating the seven octants of space where the ship did *not* come from. It had arrived from south of the sun, from the solar southwest, but that had been a popular area for adventurers, it had a lot of stars with known planets.

He had it down to about ninety possibles. That is, ships that had gone out in that direction. Among there were three groups Travis thought might have decided on a destructive suicide pact.

One was a Brazilian millennialist cult supported by a billionaire who had left their town deep in the Amazon, whose theology included the idea that the Earth would soon be destroyed by "The Hammer of God," and who thought that would be a good thing. Had they decided to be the

Hammer? It didn't seem to jibe with the words "Death to . . ." which sounded more angry than jubilant, but who knows?

There was a group of Muslim extremists from Indonesia. Muslims were always going to be suspect in a thing like that since 9/11/2001, and they had a long history of suicide attacks.

Then there were the anti-Federal extremists from the American Northwest who had often said things like the only thing wrong with that guy who blew up the Federal Building in Oklahoma City last century was that he hadn't used a nuke, and he hadn't set it off at the U.S. Supreme Court. They had taken off in that direction with the announced intention of forming their own perfect, all-white, all-Christian utopia and returning someday to restore America to its original glory, which I presume would have included black slavery.

Take your pick.

And there was always the "small cabal" theory, of a group taking over a spaceship and turning it into an instrument of mass murder. Maybe even one person could have done it, your classic "lone gunman."

That's the theory I was leaning toward. The only good thing I could see in the whole awful mess was that no one would ever know his name.

21

★ ★ ★

THE NEXT DAY we all met again to try to hash out our two big problems:

1. Where to go, and

2. What to do when we got there.

So far, the only sensible answers we'd been able to come up with were:

1. The nearest neutral country, and

2. Surrender.

It wasn't a conclusion we came to lightly. We wanted to protect Jubal. We didn't want him to fall into the hands of the Power Company, any of the unknown contending factions, the Americans, the Chinese, the King of England, the Catholic Church, an eccentric billionaire, or even the International Red Cross. We wanted to fight. Hell, we wanted to get even.

We'd been able to follow the news from Mars, which was not good.

Occupiers were still there, though they were no longer patrolling public places, they were staying in their ships on the ground and in orbit. Now that they knew Jubal wasn't there, there wasn't really much point in keeping Mars, but I guess if you've worked real hard to steal something, it's tough just to give it back. Plus, they may have been pissed, too; they'd lost some people, which was one reason they weren't showing their faces in the malls anymore.

It was nothing to how pissed the Martians were. The deaths seemed to have united my countrymen . . . and words like that were being used now. Countrymen! And countrywomen! Resisters, comrades in arms, patriots! Martians! Down with the Earth invaders! What had been a mutter of discontent had become a roar of revolution.

All the deaths had in been what the military calls "collateral damage." Meaning that nobody was actually shooting at us, we had been killed by stray missiles and crashing spaceships. Try telling that to the loved ones of the "collateral casualties." One firebrand had this to say about it: "Tell 'em to cram their collateral up their asses. It was murder, plain and fucking simple!" Roar of applause.

I was sad to be missing it all.

We saw Mom on a podium, one of a group of people gathered at a mass rally, and I thought I spotted Mr. Redmond. If any of us had been taken prisoner again I'm sure somebody would have mentioned it. They knew now where Jubal was . . . to within about a hundred million miles. They knew that he had fled with me and Evangeline because they had chased us.

Then we all vanished, dropped off the screen. And we had to *stay* vanished, at least until we decided what to do. We longed to call in to our families and tell them we were okay, but we had to maintain radio silence. Radar was unlikely to find us, but there was no better way to give away our location than to send out a message.

So . . . surrender, or . . . what?

Travis was beside himself with frustration.

"God . . . sorry, Jubal. People, we have one of the most powerful, effective weapons ever invented. And I don't know how—"

"I didn't want to make no weapon, me," Jubal said, morosely.

"I know you didn't, *cher*, but ever since humans picked up a tree branch to whack a saber-toothed tiger on the snout, just about anything anybody's ever invented can be used as a weapon. And sometimes you have to fight, Jubal! I know you don't like it. But believe me, if they get their hands on you again, the power that you've unleashed will be in the hands of people who will set up a dictatorship more powerful than anything the world has ever seen."

"So what would *we* do if *we* kept Jubal and his secrets?" Evangeline asked.

"Set up the most powerful dictatorship the world has ever seen," Travis said. "But run by people who don't want to hurt anybody."

"You?" she asked.

He gave her a sour look.

"Evangeline, if I wanted the job I could have had it before you were ever born. We worked long and hard to come up with an institution where no one nation or company could control all that power. It worked for twenty years."

"Stopped workin' when I busted out," Jubal said.

"Would have one day, anyway," Travis assured him. Jubal didn't look convinced. I wasn't, either, frankly, but I was withholding judgment on that. What Jubal had attempted, in his fumbling way, was to take the power away from *everybody*. That would have thrown the economy of Earth into a tailspin, no question, but it wouldn't have been as bad as the tsunami, and his *intent* was to prevent more of those. Jubal can only think of one thing at a time, and when it's not physics, he doesn't always hit the ball out of the park.

Should he have left? Probably not. But he did, and we had to deal with it. There had to be a way to do it that didn't involve handing him to these powerful interests who were willing to invade and kill to get him. But how?

"If not you . . . who?" Evangeline pressed on.

"I don't know. But this is our only opportunity."

"Pretty slim one," I said.

"Yeah, but it's all we have. Let's go through it again.

Evangeline groaned, and Jubal just sat there, staring at his hands.

Here was the problem:

We had the most powerful spaceship that had ever been built, because it was the only one ever built with a primary Squeezer machine in it. Jubal had installed it on the sly when Travis landed it in the Falklands shortly after it was commissioned. The thing people kept forgetting was that a Squeezer wasn't a big device. The first one fit in your fist. The one Jubal installed on the *Second Amendment* was even smaller.

Travis said it was like a World War II battleship going up against the Spanish Armada, but that didn't work for me. If we engaged the enemy, if we went into battle around the Earth or around Mars or anywhere else, we could slaughter them if they came at us one at a time, like the endless chumps in a Kung Fu movie who patiently wait their turn to take on the hero. But they wouldn't come that way. They'd come in masses, and even though we could program the computer to take them out at a pretty good rate, they could stand off millions of miles and fire a virtually unlimited number of missiles at us. We'd be bound to miss one of them. And when they saw how the fight was going, they could fire nuclear missiles. Oh, yes, there were still plenty of those around. With a nuke, you didn't even have to come very close. Anything within a few miles, the shock wave would kill us.

So hiding was out. Combat was out. What was left?

We didn't think of a thing. We decided to sleep on it again.

I SNEAKED INTO Evangeline's room again that night and we got naked, as usual, and into bed, as usual, and petted, as usual. But eventually we both admitted we didn't really want to make love, for once. There was just too much to think about. Instead we cuddled, and I learned that, sometimes, that can be more comforting and intimate than actual lovemaking. We couldn't seem to get close enough, we wanted to get inside each other's skin. I think it was that night, not all the previous nights of hot and heavy sex, that made me sure at last that I was in love with her. Lying there on my back with her face nestled against my neck, her breasts squeezed against my body, one smooth and soft-skinned and muscular leg thrown across me, feeling her sweet little toes stroking my calf . . . it was the only place in the universe I wanted to be.

I think we may have stayed that way for as much as an hour, shifting position once in a while, not saying a word, exploring each other with our hands. And suddenly we did want to make love, and it was long and slow and gentle. When we were done Evangeline got up and lit a candle and set it on the head of the bed, and I watched her in the golden glow as she rummaged in the pocket of her space suit on the floor and came up with a pipe and a bag of Phobos Red. She sat beside me, legs folded in lotus position, and lit up, then passed it to me. She held it in a long time while I smoked, then released a slow breath.

"It always helps me think," she said. "We're gonna need to think real good if we're gonna figure out how to save civilization as we know it."

We looked at each other for a moment, then burst out in a fit of giggles.

"Right," she said, when it subsided. "Like *that's* gonna happen."

"So we have three choices," I said. "We make a stand of some sort, we run away and hide, or we surrender."

"Fight, flee, or fuggedaboutit," she summed up.

"Is that really all we can do?"

"Well . . . one of my teachers was always saying 'Think outside the box, class. Think outside the box. The best solutions are the ones that sound crazy when you first think of them.' I always thought she was full of shit. But we've pretty much decided that fighting is just suicide, hiding is impossible . . ."

"And surrender is unacceptable."

"I'm with you there."

"So what *other* alternatives are there? Come on, let's think outside the box."

We did, for five minutes or so, punctuated by regular fits of giggles. It was very good stuff.

"Okay, okay, get serious here," she said, patting the air with her hands. "This is the most serious decision we're ever likely to make. There has to be something else."

More silence.

"Well . . . we could demand that they surrender."

She giggled, then stopped herself and took another toke.

"Okay. I said outside the box. That's sure outside. How do we do that?"

"Ah . . . we make a broadcast from Earth orbit. 'Lay down your arms, ground your ships, or . . . or you'll be really, really, *really* sorry!' "

She collapsed on her back and kicked her legs in the air, howling with laughter.

"God, I love you, Ray. Okay, okay, okay . . . how about . . . we write a really nasty letter to all the zines on Earth. Tell the Earthies they should be ashamed of themselves for invading Mars, and they should be even more ashamed for making it so tough on poor old Jubal, who didn't never want to hurt nobody, him."

"Appeal to their better nature."

"Exactly."

"Let's leave that one on the table a while." I was still thinking about *I love you*.

"How about political asylum?"

"Didn't we agree that one was pretty much the same as surrendering? Who is there on Earth who could protect us?"

We went through the possibilities once more. The husk of the United Nations? Nah. The International World Bank? The gnomes of Zurich? Trouble was, neither of us knew enough of the political situation to know what was realistic. Travis, who did, thought Switzerland was our best bet, and it was still pretty much surrendering.

"How about some legal process?" I suggested.

"You mean some international court?"

"Yeah. There's a ton of 'em. Some of them are set up to handle international disputes."

"You mean between Earth and Mars?" She looked dubious.

"Except, technically, Mars isn't an independent state. But I guess they negotiate with rebel groups, too."

"We have to declare our independence."

"That's up to the folks back on Mars," I said. "Sounds like they're close to it. But we can't do anything about it out here."

"No, I mean us. The . . . the Independent Republic of the *Second Amendment*, population: four."

We thought about it.

"I get to design the flag!" she said. Once more, the giggles.

"Tell me about it."

"Okay. Ah . . . a field of red, with a big, *big* silver ball in the middle."

"The Bubble Republic," I said. "That's sure a symbol of power for the modern age. Nobody'd dare stand up to it."

"So we win!"

And I'm sorry to say that's about as far we got that night. So much for thinking outside the box, huh?

After a few more hits we finally managed to get to sleep. That night remains in my memory as one of the best nights I ever had. We were far from home, and our home was in danger. Maybe all of human civilization was in danger. We didn't know where we were going or what we were going to do when we got there. All in all, there wasn't much to be happy about. But I had my love nestled in my arms, naked and soft and warm, and I was positively goofy with happiness.

I recall having the glimmering of an idea as I drifted. I made a mental note not to forget it while I slept. It was important, I knew, it was a possible way out. I *had* to remember it.

When I woke up all I remembered was that I'd had an idea.

BREAKFAST THE NEXT day was a bleak affair, despite Evangeline's delicious *huevos rancheros*. Jubal, usually an eater of vast enthusiasm, pushed his food around on the plate while praising it, as he'd been taught to do. Not even a loss of appetite would interfere with Jubal's manners. Travis ate in silence, and Evangeline and I didn't have a lot to say, either.

There was one bright moment. A few days before we'd released the high-tech equivalent of a message in a bottle. It was a little rocket that held a high-power radio transmitter. Evangeline and I had recorded messages to our families—nothing anyone could use, just "Hi, Mom and Dad, we're alive and well as of" and the date. We had launched it behind us, in the general direction of Mars. It accelerated for twenty-four hours, to the point where it would be impossible for anyone to trace it back to us, and then switched to transmit. With any luck, some of the ships occupying Mars might take off after it.

So as we were putting the dishes into the washer, the phone dinged and Mom's and Dad's faces appeared on the screen. Behind them were

Mr. and Mrs. Redmond. Their faces were a mix of happiness and worry. Mom spoke for them all.

"We're keeping this short, Ray and Evangeline, Travis. I don't know what all it might be safe to say. But we are so, so happy to hear you're alive. I . . . oh, this is so frustrating, there are so many questions I want to ask, and I know you can't answer. So I'll try to tell you the important news here.

"Elizabeth is doing well. She's walking around . . . they had to take off her left hand, Ray, I'm sorry, they . . ." She broke up, and I felt I would, too. Evangeline was crying. Dad took over.

"She's in good spirits, kids. She wanted to be here, but they want to keep her another day. She's very angry, as we all are, but she doesn't seem to worry much about her injury. We've seen the new prosthetic, and it's . . . very good. They say it'll be just about as good as the old hand." Mom stepped forward again, having pulled herself together again.

"We'll try to broadcast with Elizabeth tomorrow at this same time, kids. Meantime, I suppose you've seen some of the news from here. Everybody is very angry, but so far no one has come up with any idea, just a lot of talk, talk, talk. You know, the sort of stuff I'm good at. But I'm losing patience with talking.

"We don't know what you're up to out there, Travis, kids. If I know you, Travis, you've got some sort of scheme. All I ask you is this. Don't put the kids in danger. I've spent all the time since you all left angry at myself for sending you out there in the first place. It's not worth it. I know how you feel about Jubal, but I don't see any alternative but to take him home and let things go back to the way they were. We can work on a political solution here on Mars, and lobby for a voice back on Earth. We've picked up some support, gotten the word out about what's been happening here. There are investigations going on, and maybe something can be done. But we just don't see a solution that will allow Jubal to be free. I'm so sorry, but that's just the way it is. Travis, bring my son home to me and bring him home safe. We love you."

"Love you, son," Dad said, his voice breaking. They signed off.

Jubal was crying quietly.

"That's it," he said. "Take me home, Travis."

"You got it, *cher*. Absolutely." Travis's face might have been set in stone. He got up, walked across the bridge, and pounded his fist furiously against a bulkhead until I was worried he was going to break the bones in his hand.

"Jubal, pardon me, but God *damn* it! Here we sit, with the most powerful weapon ever made, and we can't do anything but crawl home with our tails between our legs and give it *back* to them."

"Nothing else to do, my frien'. Nothing else to do. I never should of left, me. I was just feelin' so bad. I done read me on them boys, made the atomic bomb back in that big war. They thought they was doin' the right thing, yes sir. Some of 'em, they never regretted it. But since the wave hit . . . I ain't had nothin' but regret."

Something was tickling at the back of my mind.

"Oppenheimer regretted it," Travis said.

"That Oppenheimer, he was plenty smarter than me."

"Atomic bomb," I said. Everybody looked at me.

"Outside the box," I said.

"Which box would that be?" Travis asked.

"Surrender," I said.

"That's what I plan to do. It twists my gut into a knot, but that's all that's left. I'm so sorry we got you kids into this, but—"

"We're not kids, Travis, and I mean we can make *them* surrender."

If I expected everybody to stand up and cheer, I'd have been severely disappointed by their actual reaction. Which was pretty much no reaction at all except for Evangeline frowning as if to say this was no time for silly jokes. I kept waiting for somebody to say "How?" I mean, the idea was so crazy, I wanted a *little* bit of encouragement to even get it out. Nobody did.

"I was thinking about it last night as I was falling asleep," I said, jumping in with both feet. "When Jubal talked about the atomic bombs I thought about where they were first used, in Japan."

"Ain't gonna hurt nobody," Jubal said.

"I don't think we have to. Not even any 'collateral damage.' What we need to do is give them a warning. Fire a shot across their bows that is so convincing, so scary, that they'll let us alone. We can figure out what to do later, after they're off our backs."

"What kind of warning would that be?" Travis asked.

"Listen, in history class we were talking about Hiroshima. Somebody advised the President of the U.S. . . . ah . . ."

"Truman."

"Right, Henry Truman. Some of his generals wanted to drop the bomb on Kyoto, the old Imperial City. Somebody else talked them out of it because of its historical value. Somebody else said drop it on the Emperor's Palace in Tokyo. Somebody—MacArthur?—said that would make the Japanese hate Americans forever. Then another idea was floated. Explode the bomb high over Tokyo harbor. A warning shot. Tokyo harbor is big, and there were a lot of people who lived there, they'd—"

"Would have killed a lot of people," Travis said.

"Sure, but not nearly as many as died in Hiroshima. Conventional bombing had already killed over a hundred thousand people in Tokyo earlier that year, 1945, right?" Travis nodded. "So, eighty thousand were killed in Hiroshima, not quite that many in Nagasaki. Wouldn't killing five or ten thousand around Tokyo have been better than that? And a lot of Japanese would have seen it, heard it, felt it, and survived to talk about it, including the Emperor. It always struck me as a better solution, or at least a better first try. If it didn't work, *then* you decide what to do next."

"Don't want to kill *nobody*," Jubal said, forcefully.

"Neither do I, and if we can't figure out how to make this work, then I vote for going home."

"You don't get a vote," Travis said, not unkindly. "Neither do you, Jubal and Evangeline. This is not a democratic ship. So, until you convince me you know how to scare the bejesus—sorry, Jubal—out of the most powerful people on Earth, without hurting anybody . . . well, then we're on our way to Mars to get y'all back to your folks."

I turned to Jubal.

"You said you could make a Squeezer bubble just about any size, didn't you, Jubal?"

He shrugged, clearly not interested in this discussion. Mentally, he was already pacing the limits of his exquisite prison again.

"Any size, *cher*. Big, little, turn a big one into a little one, a little one into a big one . . . it don't matter, since it ain't really in this universe anyway, and it don't use what we think of as energy, and the mass inside ain't really inside, not the way we think of inside . . . it's complicated . . ."

"So here's what I know about bubbles," I said, and began to tick points off on my fingers. "They can be any size. Whatever's inside comes apart. Whatever's inside can be squeezed, and the energy let out gradually." I paused. "And they are perfectly reflective."

And I laid it out for them. After about an hour that started out with shouting and ended with dawning realization, we shaped course for Earth.

WE WERE ABLE to go slow getting there. The trick I had in mind could be done at any time, but would be most effective within a week of the vernal or autumnal equinox, and the latter was not far away, September 22. Jubal spent some of that time working on his gizmos, but it wasn't all that complicated. Meantime we all discussed the plan, every possible detail of it, trying to think outside of the box, trying to come up with flaws, trying to think of every *possible* thing we might have forgotten. You never can, of course, so it was an edgy time.

Early on we sent out another bottle rocket with another message, this one frankly designed to mislead. We told the folks on Mars—and anybody else who might be listening in—that we were on our way home. We expected to arrive back at the dear old Red Planet in two weeks. With any luck, a great part of the fleets of the various invaders would be waiting for us there, to take Jubal back into custody, or at least fight for the right to do so.

That was fine with us, because it was a fight we intended to miss. With the right luck, it would be a fight that would never happen.

The messages from the families came back pretty quickly, reassuring us we were doing the right thing, the better part of valor, sometimes you just can't win, etc. Elizabeth was the only dissenter.

"You must be crazy," she said. "If I was out there with you, I'd fight! . . . but you go ahead and do what you think is best." She showed us her new hand, and it was a marvel. She was already picking up things with the thumb and forefinger. Honest, you could hardly tell it wasn't flesh.

WE EASED BACK into the normal traffic patterns of the ecliptic so as not to attract a lot of notice from the wrong people, sort of lost ourselves in the stream of spaceships that now plied the spaces between planets.

Then . . . there we were, hovering about four thousand miles above the North Pole, where there was very little but GPS and spy satellites in close orbits and no inhabited structures at all, and feeling very alone and conspicuous.

Travis suggested that I should make the broadcast, since I was the one who had come up with the idea. The very idea completely terrified me. Luckily, I never had to admit to that. Evangeline scoffed right away.

"Yeah, right. You keep calling us kids, so you think an ultimatum from either one of us would carry a lot of weight? It's your ship, and your cousin, and you are the guys who started all this. Plus, whoever does this is going to piss off a lot of people. Ray doesn't deserve that. And anyway, everybody on Earth pretty much hates you already, so what's the difference if they hate you a little more?"

Travis thought this over, then grinned, and it was clear that the idea that everybody on Earth hated him had a certain appeal.

So we all sat down at the control seats on the bridge, and he aimed the camera at himself and started to speak.

"Hello, y'all, it's me again, Travis Broussard. How are y'all doing? I'm here with my cousin, Jubal, and first I want to tell you that our hearts go out to all of you who have lost loved ones and property in the tsunami. Your leaders haven't told you what caused it, so I guess I'd better."

He summed up the one certainty we had, and mentioned a few ways it might have happened. I was watching the radar screens.

"Five ships have started to move from low-equatorial orbit and look like they're headed our way," I said, quietly.

"Your leaders have just sent ships out to take us prisoner," Travis said. "But we still have a little time to tell you the truth."

"Some of you will blame us for the tsunami. That's okay. That's fair. We tried our best to give you this crazy source of power without making it possible for some pissant maniac to blow all of y'all to Hell, and it worked for a while, but we just plain never imagined the depth of human cussedness. The only thing I can say in our defense is that nobody else thought of it either.

I was still watching the screens. "Projected arrival of the first ship in . . . twenty minutes," I told Travis.

"Something else they haven't told you is how Jubal escaped from the Falkland Islands prison . . . and yeah, they'd turned it into a prison, believe me . . . and why he did, and what they've been doing since then. They haven't told you the truth about the recent events on Mars, and what they're all about. In fact, even *we* don't know the whole story. All I can tell you is, there are economic and political forces jockeying for the most valuable thing in the solar system: my cousin Jubal's brain.

"You're going to have to ask them about that. All I have time to tell you right now is, Jubal is a human being, not a commodity, and he wants his life back. In a few minutes your leaders, or the people who have bought and paid for your leaders, are going to try to take us captive or, if they can't do that, kill us. They'd rather nobody have the secrets of the Squeezer than let their rivals have it."

"Five more ships headed our way," Evangeline said. "No missiles so far." Travis nodded, and went on.

"So far I've been talking to all the people of the Earth. Now I'm going to talk just to the people who own the warships that are heading our way, but I want all the people of the Earth to listen in, so if the worst happens, you'll know whose fault it all was.

"None of y'all have ever really grasped just how powerful the Squeezer is. I can forgive you for that, a little bit, because until recently I didn't understand it all, either. If I had, we might never have used it to go to Mars, and we'd all still be stumbling around trying to make our oil supplies last another decade or so. We might just have buried the damn thing, never told anyone, and a lot of lives would have been saved. I still think I did the right thing, but I'm a lot less sure than I used to be, and I know I'll go to my grave with that question hanging over my head. Even now, I'm tempted to just head out for the stars with my cousin and let y'all hash it out for yourselves without Squeezer power. I expect you'd muddle through . . . but I believe human beings should go to the stars, no matter what the risk, and I don't know of any other way to do it but with the Squeezer.

"So what we're going to do is show y'all something. You'll all be able to see it, it's something your leaders won't be able to hide from you. It's going to be frightening, but no one is going to be hurt. We just thought we should show you what we *could* do, if we chose to. And what your *leaders* could do, if they ever got ahold of the Squeezer technology.

"And a special message to the leaders. Both those obviously in power, and those behind them, pulling the strings. Like I said, we expected you to attack us, and that's what you're doing. We're going to take out your ships if they come too close. We don't want to, but we will. So here's your ultimatum. Call off the dogs, or lose them. *All* of them. And believe me, we don't know who all of y'all are, but we know some of you, and if you don't surrender, *immediately*, we are coming to get you. We know where you live, whether it's in presidential palaces or regular old mansions. We will squeeze you, you motherfuckers . . . sorry, Jubal . . . we will squeeze you and anybody who's around you, and we'll keep coming, and keep coming, until you all are dead. And then we'll piss on your graves and sow them with salt.

"So call your ships back, *now*, and pull all your troops off Mars. When I know Mars is free of invaders . . . then we can sit down and talk."

He paused and looked around at all of us. He had been sounding glib and even carefree, as he usually did, but his face was covered with sweat.

" 'Squeezer technology,' " he muttered. "That's gotta be the biggest lie I ever told. Far as I can tell, it's magic, if only Jubal can do it."

I'd had the same thought myself.

"Okay, friends. Now let's see if we can pull off the biggest bluff in human history. Jubal?"

We'd had to increase the dose of Jubal's medicine. This had all taken a lot out of him. He looked up, vaguely, then seemed to realize where he was.

"Oh, right," he mumbled. He turned to his own console as I watched the ships getting closer. The first few were about ready to turn and decelerate. That was important as a signal of their intentions. If they didn't turn, if they kept accelerating at us, that meant they didn't intend to capture us, they were going to come in shooting, with their missiles moving very fast. We would be very busy for a while, trying to fight them off with our Squeezer.

Jubal's console had been jury-rigged, as most of his things were, and not cleaned up nice and neat. He'd engineered the most important part into a single button, which would start a series of events that would be handled by a computer. His thumb hovered over the button. He looked up.

"Y'all sure this is the right thing to do?"

"Best we could come up it, *cher*," Travis said. "Nobody will get hurt."

Jubal sighed and pressed the button.

We had been hovering directly above the North Pole, which took only a little thrust. That meant the Earth was behind us, invisible. Ahead was nothing but black, empty space.

And then it wasn't empty. Right in front of us, seeming only a few thousand miles away, was another Earth. Half of it was almost blindingly bright, and even the dark side gleamed with lights. I could pick out Oslo, Stockholm, London, Paris . . . hell, the whole night side below the Arctic Circle seemed lit up. Lots of people down there. Billions and billions of people.

Travis let a few seconds pass, let people down there have a chance to take it in, then waited a few more seconds after that. Then he leaned into the mike.

"Any questions?" he asked.

22

AND THAT'S HOW I saved Mars and maybe the whole human race, and in the process kicked some of the most powerful people on Earth in the butt.

Well, I had some help. And of course, it wasn't as quick or as easy as that. It never is. But it *was* my idea.

What we did, Jubal built two of his famous little gizmos into two of Travis's bottle rockets, and we programmed them to fly to positions over the Earth's poles. The north one was right outside our window, the other four thousand miles over the South Pole. When the button was pushed, the Squeezer generators did that crazy thing they do: unraveled something that might or might not have been a superstring, something so tiny that we hardly have words or even numbers to describe how small it is, caused it to unfold itself a bit here, a bit there, through the seventh dimension, the eighth dimension, maybe the nine hundredth dimension (I'm as much in the dark here as anybody else), until a part of it that looked like a silvery sphere extruded itself into our universe . . . and kept unfolding it, and unfolding it, all in a time that Jubal said couldn't even be measured in the dimension *we* used for time in *this* universe . . .

. . . and they got bigger and bigger . . .

. . . and *bigger*, and *bigger* . . .

. . . *AND BIGGER* . . .

. . . and bigger . . .

. . . and bigger . . .

. . . and bigger . . .

. . . and bigger . . .

. . . and bigger . . .

. . . and bigger . . .

. . . until it was . . . well, *really* big. One million miles in diameter, both of them. Large enough that, if the Earth were inside it, it would rattle around like a BB in a battleship, according to Jubal.

Large enough to contain the sun.

Food for thought, we figured.

And then we skedaddled. Couldn't go north; there was the little matter of a million-mile bubble up there. So we aimed ourselves away from the closest group of ships headed our way and blasted at two gees.

I'd never done two gees before, for any period of time. After ten minutes or so, it begins to, well, *weigh* on you. Naturally Travis had provided his ship with the best acceleration couches money could buy. We nestled into them without our stereos—you don't want anything on your face that might suddenly weigh five times what it used to—and watched the ship's screen from our supine positions.

For a while, nothing happened. The ships hadn't started to decelerate, but they hadn't fired any missiles, either. That was not good news. We *wanted* them to fire a few.

"Missile away," Evangeline said. Travis swung his head in her direction.

"I got it. Locking on."

"Estimated time to impact, three minutes."

"Let's fire back at them, Ray."

"Okay." We had drilled extensively on this. Travis's missiles weren't armed with anything, but the black ships back there wouldn't know that. They did have seeking radar on them, though, and I locked a missile on each of the pursuers and fired them in sequence, five seconds apart. We watched them leave, pulling fifty gees.

"More launches," Evangeline said. "Four, five . . . six. Fifty gees."

"Okay, that's a few more than I wanted," Travis said. "So let's show 'em how far we can reach." He worked on his Squeezer control board. There was a joystick there, just like an old video game. He centered the cursor on each of them in turn and blip, blip, blip, they went away, wrapped in stopper bubbles that you wouldn't ever want to open.

No reaction at first, then the ships began sideways maneuvers, trying to evade our missiles. Their options were limited, with Earth on one side and the bubble on the other. I felt claustrophobic, with the real Earth visible out one window and the reflected Earth out the other. I thought it would be even worse for them, and wondered if they'd figured out yet what it was they were seeing . . .

A BUBBLE A million miles in diameter presents a flat, mirrored face, for all practical purposes, the curvature being so slight you'd need a fine instrument to measure the degree of distortion of the image. With the Earth currently sandwiched between two bubbles that size it meant that everyone standing outdoors with no cloud cover was able to see the reflection of one of them. Folks close to the equator could see parts of both.

How big did they look? Well, they were four thousand miles away, which made the virtual image appear to be eight thousand miles away. At eight thousand miles the Earth covers forty degrees of arc. Compare that to Luna, which covers one-half degree. The image the people of Earth were seeing was eighty times the width of the full moon, and it was visible whether it was night or day where you were standing.

I'd call that a pretty impressive demonstration. It scared the hell out of *me,* and I'm the one who thought of it.

Getting there at the equinox was a bit of luck, but it would have worked pretty well even if we hadn't. At any other time, the sheer size of the bubbles would have blocked the sun entirely and Earth would have gone totally dark. Maybe that would have been even scarier.

Suddenly Evangeline shouted, "One of the ships is decelerating!"

We all had our eyes glued to the screens, where one of our pursuers was now showing a reverse vector. Our missiles were closing in . . . and in another few seconds they flew harmlessly by, as they'd been programmed to do.

"Another one is slowing," she said, tensely

"Come on, guys, you don't want to die, do you?" Travis whispered.

And then, within a few seconds, all the others began showing negative acceleration. The distance between us began to increase. No more missiles were fired.

Travis waited a decent interval, and we all watched the curve of the Earth in case something nasty might be hiding back there waiting to jump us. But there was little chance of that. Finally, Travis sighed.

"My friends," he said, "I think that was the shooting match. I think the most powerful people on Earth just blinked."

We all cheered, and Travis cut the acceleration to half a gee so we could get out of our couches without the risk of breaking bones. Travis gave us all high fives, we shouted, we danced, Evangeline kissed Travis, then Jubal, then me.

Then Jubal threw up.

WE KEPT ON going in the direction we had been going, still on alert. Within fifteen minutes the invitations started to come in. People wanted to talk to us. Like reasonable people, most of them said. Never mind that we just tried to kill you . . . and anyway, it wasn't really us, it was those sharks over at . . . any number of accusations were made against countries, corporations, individuals. It was impossible to keep all the name-calling and finger-pointing straight, and we didn't even try. Travis had made a checklist of people he *knew* were involved, along with a longer list of possibles. Within an hour we'd heard from all of them. Same message:

Let's talk.

Only please, please, *please turn those things off!*

We didn't do it. We couldn't, and wouldn't have if we could. The original plan was to leave them in place for twenty-four hours, so everyone could get a nice, *long* look at a possible doom hovering over them.

Technical detail, revealed here for the first time:

There were a *lot* of those million-mile bubbles. As soon as one formed, the solar wind and sunlight pressure started pushing it away, just like a vagrant breeze stirred the first one that Dad found in Florida. A sphere with that much surface area and no mass is going to start moving. In fact, it's going to have a high velocity instantaneously. Before long, you'd notice the movement, even in something that large. So Jubal set the Squeezers to generate a bubble about once a minute. Then it would turn that one off and replace it with another, in a nanosecond, in the place where the first one had been. From the ground, or even up close where we were, you couldn't even tell it was happening.

There was some negotiating between Travis and people on the ground. Actually, not much negotiating; it was a matter of Travis telling them what they were going to do and them doing it, chop-chop, ASAP, right *now!*

They were instructed to remove all troops and ships from the surface of Mars, and to do it within two hours.

"Figure that gives 'em enough time to get off those Martian whores, pull up their socks, and get back to their ships," Travis said.

"Martian whores have better taste than that," Evangeline sniffed.

They were to take the ships to Phobos, land, tether down, and await further orders. When we got word from people on the ground that that had been done, Travis ordered everyone off the ships and inside Phobos, where they would peacefully submit to being disarmed. And they would surrender all space suits. No need to put them in prison if they didn't have suits; the whole big tourist bubble in Phobos became their prison. Another four hours and it was confirmed that had been done.

"Okay," Travis told his conference call audience. "Whoever those ships belonged to, company, nation, or individual, kiss 'em good-bye. They invaded Mars flying no flag, never revealing their identity, and under international law that makes them pirates. Well . . . if international law doesn't say that, it *should.* Anyway, the ships are forfeit. They are now part of the Martian Navy. The crews will be held for war crimes trial by the Martian authorities." He covered the mike with his hand and made a face at us. "Whoever *that* may be." Then back to the phone:

"Here's how it's going to go. You guys rely on bubble power for *everything*. I reckon you could go back to oil and gas and solar and nuclear and woodstoves, for a while, but that will take a lot of time, and it'll all run out soon. You don't even want to *think* about what will happen to your economies and your big companies without bubble power. Anybody out there who doesn't understand that perfectly well? Or should I explain it more?"

He waited for ten seconds, and no one on the other end had any questions.

"Right now, all the working Squeezers in existence are on Mars, and the only guy who can make more is with me, and we're going to Mars. As I've just demonstrated, you don't want to mess with us. Understood?"

Again, no objections, though I fancied I could almost hear the gears grinding in those powerful heads coming right over the radio, all of them trying to find an angle, an advantage . . . and a way to trip us up.

"And that's the way it's going to be, for a while. I don't know how long. You'll be all right, we'll ship you bubbles, your machines and cars and microwave ovens and computers will keep working. It won't be for free, the Martians are going to charge you for it, but it wasn't free before, either, it was just cheap. How cheap it stays will be up to the Martians.

"Because that's what I'm going to do. I'm going to hand this all over to the Martians, who will be declaring their political independence real soon now, as soon as they can get organized from all the disasters you caused them. I don't know what they'll do with your Martian investments; that's up to them. Maybe they'll nationalize them, maybe they'll decide to work with Earth investors and owners like they have before. I suspect that most of them will just want to get back to work, to earning a living, like they did before you attacked them. They may want to extradite some of y'all and put you on trial. They'll have to work that out.

"I got shoved into this situation once before, and did the best I could, which wasn't enough. Y'all are too fractured down there, you got too much bad history, you got too many rivalries, too much bad blood. Too damn many people, too, and as far as I can see, not a damn 'democratic' country that still retains much democracy. I don't know what Mars will do, but I think they'll have sense enough to set up some sort of democracy, because lousy as it is, it's still the best system we've come up with. But maybe it'll need a dictatorship, maybe there needs to be a stronger hand at the controls of something this powerful. I don't know who I'd trust to do that, other than my cousin Jubal, and he's not . . . inclined to do it. Jubal's too nice. I don't even trust myself to handle it, not by myself. In fact, thinking it over, I realized that the only people I would trust to do the right thing—and there's only a handful of them—are all on Mars. My friends and my family. I'm hoping that most Martians are like that, enough divorced from the old political and social lines on Earth to be able to think like a human being, like a citizen of the solar system.

"That's why I'm renouncing my American citizenship, and all allegiance to the planet Earth, and intend to become a Martian just as soon as I set foot on Martian soil again . . . and as soon as those newly free people figure out just what it means to be a Martian. We're throwing our lot in with them, and I've just shown you we have the power to handle anything you throw at us and, as a last resort, take you all down with us. And don't think I wouldn't do it. Now, get your butts in gear."

PREVIOUSLY, TRAVIS HAD told them about his "Sword of Damocles." He said there was a Squeezer generator somewhere out there, waiting for a signal. If it got that signal . . . Earth would be enclosed in a bubble for all eternity. This was told only to the top dogs, not to the world in general. Travis didn't mind that most people on Earth might hate him, but there were limits. And it might cause a panic even worse than the one we'd already caused by our demonstration of power.

Another bluff. There was no such device. But they could never know that.

"One of those times when it would be better to just die, rather than 'win,'" Travis said. "All we've got going for us, right now, is that they don't know our limitations. An all-out assault would kill us, and they'd at least know that no one *else* had Squeezer power. But that's how their minds work. You have to have them by the balls before their hearts and minds will follow. And you have to understand that these guys, if *they* had something like this and knew they were going down . . . they *would* destroy the Earth. *They* would kill billions of people, so they can believe I would. It just makes sense to them."

This was all said with Jubal out of the room, not doing too well with more stomach upset. And to tell you the truth, I had a hard time believing what he said. Would people really do that? *We* had the power to do it, and we had never even considered it, not for a nanosecond. It was altogether more insight into the dark side of humanity than I wanted to think about . . . but Travis had seen a lot more than I had, and I had to consider that he might be right. History tells me that, for many decades, the whole benighted green globe of Earth was gripped by a horror called "Mutual Assured Destruction," the idea that if one country launched a massive nuclear attack, enough missiles would survive the first strike to guarantee the destruction of the aggressor nation. It worked, I guess . . . but what if it hadn't? If America had sustained an attack that killed 300 million people, would the gnomes down in the silos and deep underwater and in the bombers follow orders and kill 300 million Russians, just out of hatred?

"Bet on it," Travis said, and I knew he was right.

SO WE WENT home and were welcomed as conquering heroes. They staged parades for us, carried us around on their shoulders . . .

Dream on.

We stole in like thieves in the night, managing to miss the swarms of media and sneak into my home in the Red Thunder. We glimpsed the damage on our way in, and it was painful to look at, but nothing like the pain I felt when I saw how much it had all aged my dad. He'd never lost a paying customer before, except to suicide, and dealing with it all had taken a lot out of him. But his welcoming hug was strong. There were tears and laughter, and a big feast that no one ate much of.

Then it was back to reality.

For a while I thought it might come to blows between Dad and Travis. There was bad feeling between Mom and Dad, too, and between Mom and the Redmond family. I'd never seen her so subdued. Even though it had all worked out well—so far, anyway, though none of us thought it was all over yet—the burden for placing us two "youngsters" in danger was falling on her shoulders.

I tried to protest that it had been my own decision, and so did Evangeline, but we quickly saw that was just making the situation worse, so we retreated from the battlefield with Elizabeth.

"I'm with you guys," she whispered. "I just wish I'd *really* been with you."

"You had your own little adventure," Evangeline said. "Let me see that hand."

I was horrified. I figured Elizabeth would be devastated by the whole thing, and I hadn't planned to talk about it at all unless she brought it up.

But Elizabeth rolled up her shirtsleeve and undid a strap, and handed her new hand and forearm to Evangeline. The stump was wrapped in a soft bandage.

"Almost healed up," she said. "The implants inside are still programming themselves to my nervous system. They say it takes a few months to get really fine control. Watch."

The prosthetic Evangeline was holding made a fist, then, slowly, the middle finger extended at us. Evangeline laughed, then began to cry. Elizabeth put her good arm around her and hugged her.

"Don't worry about me, sister," she said, calmly. "The way things are going, I expect I'll have a cloned hand one of these days soon. And this one isn't all that bad. Hell, it's a concealed weapon. It's an iron fist in a plastic glove."

She had a point there. I touched it, and it was warm and soft like human flesh. Still, I wouldn't have traded, and I don't think she would have, either, if she'd had a choice. But that was Elizabeth, making the best of a bad situation.

The family squabbling settled down fairly quickly. None of us were the type who tended to stay mad just because they wanted to be mad. And there was too much good history between them all. Mr. Redmond's heart never had seemed to really be in the argument, considering what our family had done for him, and I think he was actually proud of how well his daughter had done in a crisis. Mrs. Redmond was a little more steamed and never completely cooled off, but she was mad at Mom and Travis, not me, so I wasn't too worried. Mom would eventually bring her around.

By the end of our first day back home, everyone seemed ready to put past mistakes behind them and move on to the considerable problems ahead with a minimum of recriminations. After all, it had all worked out well, hadn't it?

Well . . . not exactly.

SO THE FAMILY reception was a little rough. But the part about the parades and stuff, my fellow Martians *would* have done all that, if we hadn't been staying out of the public eye to retain a little privacy, right?

Well, yes and no.

The fact was, this was a lot to drop into the laps of Martians, who hadn't asked for it. Suddenly we were a world power. Sure, everybody and his idiot cousin on Earth had an atomic bomb, and it would only take one of them to wipe us out—and believe me, a lot of people brought that up in the discussions that followed. And we couldn't tell anybody about Travis's Damoclean bluff, which probably wouldn't have helped, anyway. Half of the people would probably believe there *was* such a thing and that Travis would use it to protect his cousin.

In the end, it was the invasions that finally made the birth of the Martian Republic a necessity, and a sure thing. Nothing could have united us more than the contempt those acts had implied, both for human life and for us as a people. Martians were mightily pissed, our honored dead were hardly cold in their graves, and a good half of them probably *would* have used the Sword of Damocles if it had existed and we were attacked. I mean, not only had they killed Martians, they had killed *tourists*. They had interfered with our *business*. Our hotels were empty, the casinos were quiet. It was going to take a while to get our economy going again.

The Squeezer was suddenly the only thing we had to sell. And most people were in favor of making "those damn Earthies" pay through the nose.

So in the end, everybody rolled up their sleeves and got to work. It's what Martians do, and I say that with considerable pride.

The usual civic leaders stepped forward and tried to take the reins of power . . . and we turned them down. There were endless meetings, rallies, passionate speeches, protests from every imaginable interest group. But in the end it was all decided on the web. We threw it open for discussion, and boy, did we ever discuss.

Anybody could participate. No age limit, all you had to do was be able to read and write. Any language, as computers could instantly translate into the Martian *de facto* language of English.

We went through the age-old possibilities. Direct democracy has a strong, gut attraction to individualists like us, and it works fine . . . until "The People" vote for some damn-fool thing that just can't work. Representative democracy has its attractions . . . until you look at any number of horror stories from Earth and see how easily money can buy the whole shooting match. Even the royal system can work pretty well . . . until the wise king dies and power moves to his idiot son.

In the end, after six months of shouting, we ended up with the first open-source constitutional government. Anybody could write the laws and constitution, but nobody could be sure his bright ideas would stay there. We started out with some of the noblest documents of civilization: The Declaration of the Rights of Man, the U. S. Constitution and Bill of Rights, the United Nations Charter, the Geneva Conventions. Every sentence was passionately argued, with a deadline, and revotes happening all the time. After a while they were debating the fines for not picking up doggie poop.

At the end of six months the constitution was frozen, and we had to live with it for a year. One *Martian* year, if you please. Then we could start rewriting it again, to fix the things we screwed up. I figure we'll be doing a *lot* of rewriting, but what's so bad about that?

We ended up with a Prime Minister and a small parliament. There was provision for a cabinet, and last time I looked Mom was ahead in the polls for Finance Minister.

And we actually had a Navy! In fact, with most of the powerful nations on Earth stripped of their secret fleets, which had violated dozens of international treaties, we had the most powerful space force of any nation.

Manning it wasn't a problem. The day it was announced, most of the male population of Mars between eighteen and twenty-five and more than half of the women that age went and volunteered. We didn't need nearly that many, and those who got in were instant heroes in their snappy new uniforms.

I didn't volunteer. I'd had enough of space combat.

And then there was the problem of Jubal.

TO PUT IT bluntly: Mars didn't really want him. And at the same time, we couldn't get along without him. He was our biggest danger and our cornucopia. As long as he was alive and on Mars, there would be the constant threat of attack from Earth. But if he left, we would be just another pissant little settlement.

Luckily for Jubal, his fate was not up for a vote.

Jubal talked to nobody, was hardly even aware of all the controversy swirling around him. People tried to influence Travis, instead, but he wouldn't get into any arguments about government.

"I'm a cranky old bastard when it comes to government," was all he'd say. "When y'all come up with a system, let me know. I'll take a look at it, and if it looks like it will protect Jubal, then we'll stay. Otherwise, we're off for Pluto and points outward."

Travis did agree to stay until the government was established. The Martian Navy was on patrol by then, and nobody on Earth was showing any signs of wanting to upset the new status quo. Most of them had a lot on their plates already. The United States was still seriously crippled, nobody knowing from one day to another just who was in charge. There had been several military coups. Many other countries weren't much better off than that. Several world leaders had been impeached, or overthrown. Civil wars raged everywhere. The Earth economy was barely staggering along. Nobody wanted to think about how much worse things would get without cheap Squeezer power. Even billionaires can be made to see sense now and then: If society collapses, your money ain't worth squat. So, by and large, people Earthside were happy with the new situation.

Martians settled down and accepted it, too.

In the end, the only one who wasn't happy was . . . you guessed it. Jubal was miserable.

The only time he was reasonably happy was when he was in his lab, making primary Squeezer units. I don't know much about that, it was shrouded in secrecy by Travis and the guards he hired. That was fine with me, I didn't want to know anything about how many they were making, where they were going, what security would surround them, what sort of nasty stuff Jubal was building into them to prevent them being of any use if somebody managed to steal them. The lab was located all the way on the other side of the planet, down by the South Pole.

They built a habitat for him. Some people called it the Jubal Zoo, but of course people couldn't go look at him. It was a circular mile of a damn good imitation of Louisiana swampland. There was a lake, and bayous, and little creeks. Whole huge cypress trees were imported and planted, and the waters were stocked with alligators and birds and fish. The alligators had to be taken out; they were a bit too frisky in Martian gravity. But the rest of it worked well enough. Jubal lived there in a two-room shack with a woodstove and no television.

Nobody visited him but family. Evangeline and I dropped by at least once a week, and Travis practically lived there. We'd row out in the lake and fish, and talk about things. He never complained, never talked about his feelings, but some days he didn't say much of anything at all. All he ever asked about the outside world was when Travis was with us, and then he wanted to know how the Squeezer project was going. If it was "finished."

Finished? I hadn't known there was an endpoint. I figured Jubal would just keep working, and we'd all just stay on our toes. It had worked for twenty years on Earth. All that was different now was Jubal was in a new place, right?

Actually, there was a lot that was different. The despair that had driven Jubal to escape in the first place was still there, and stronger than ever. There was only one thing in the world Jubal really wanted, though he seldom talked about it.

He wanted to go home.

The Jubal-Dome was a nice try, but no cigar. The fact was, he hated Mars. He hated pretty much every place except Louisiana. He'd not even been that wild about living in Florida, but it was acceptable. Mars was definitely not.

* * *

ONE DAY ABOUT a year after our adventures Travis summoned Evangeline and me to the dome, and the four of us went out fishing. We both noticed the change in Jubal. He was laughing and talking. We relived old times, and he told a lot of his childish jokes. If you squinted, you could believe you were actually far up a bayou. The bass were practically leaping into the boat.

When the artificial sun set—just a light on a track, but amazingly bright—crickets and frogs chirped as we rowed back to Jubal's dock. Travis filleted and skinned the fish, which we fried up in hot oil and corn bread batter, and stuffed ourselves with fish, okra, hush puppies, and a fiery Cajun sauce.

After the meal, Jubal grew increasingly nervous. Evangeline and I kept exchanging glances. We knew something was up, but we had no idea what. At last Jubal cleared his throat and spoke.

"I wanted y'all here so's I could say good-bye," he said, looking at his shoes.

"Where are you going, Jubal?"

He smiled at us.

"On a big adventure, me. I'm goin' to the future."

We both waited for the punch line.

"Course, we all goin' to the future, one second at a time. I'm just gonna skip a lot of 'em."

"You're going to skip . . ." I got my first inkling of what he had in mind.

"I done all I need to do here," he went on. "Travis can keep things going, and you young folks got lots to do. Me, I'm not happy here, no."

"We knew that, Jubal," Evangeline said. "I wish there was—"

"There ain't nothing, *cher.* 'Less you can lift this burden off my back." He pointed to his head, to the knowledge he held in there that was so unimportant to him and so vitally important to so many powerful people.

"Ain't no big deal," he said, with a shrug. "Nobody don't get exactly what they want in this life, no. I thought . . . I thought for a while of committin' a real big sin."

"He wanted to kill himself," Travis said, quietly. "Jubal wanted you two to know about what we decided to do instead. In fact, you're part of it."

SO THAT'S HOW we ended up in the living room of Jubal's cabin that night. It was homey, with a comfortable couch, lace curtains in the windows. The room was lit with kerosene lamps. There were old rugs on the floor.

In the center a space had been cleared for a single chair that was hung in the middle of a ball made of thick metal struts. There were springs on the wires, as if whoever was sitting in the chair in the middle expected there might be some violent motion in his future.

His future. Never had anyone's future been more up for grabs. Jubal was truly going on an adventure.

"'Member, Travis," he said, dithering around, trying to put it off. "None of y'all are s'posed to open me up, 'less I can go home."

Open me up. Those words brought home the enormity of what Jubal was proposing to do.

"That's not what I agreed to," Travis said. "And it's not what you asked them to agree to. I told you, I'd turn off the bubble under only two conditions. One, we all agree that it's safe for you to go back home, without anyone bothering you."

Yeah, right, I thought. Like that's going to happen.

"The other condition is . . . we need you, *cher.* You agreed, if something real bad comes up, we can open the bubble."

Jubal wouldn't look at Travis, but at last he sighed and nodded.

"'Kay. But make sure it's *big* important."

We all embraced Jubal, one at a time. I didn't know how to feel. Jubal wanted this. He hated his life so much that he intended to skip as many years as necessary to reach a better one. He was going to get into that contraption in the middle of the room, and he was going to switch on the stopper bubble . . . and there would be nothing left of him but a black hole in space.

How long? Many years, surely. As for an emergency . . . I could think of plenty of things that might come up that would lead Travis to "open him up." So maybe it wouldn't be a long time before we saw him again.

On the other hand, we might never see him again.

He climbed into the metal sphere, and Travis helped him strap in. Good thinking. Who could tell what might be waiting for him in a time that, to him, would be no time at all. If it was me, I'd have wanted to be sitting there with a gun in my hand, but that wasn't Jubal's way. I know he expected to be uncorked, if he ever was, and meet a smiling circle of his friends, a bit older but still his friends, welcoming him back.

If he was ever opened at all, and he was prepared to take that risk.

He was sweating. He held a rosary in one hand and the little device that would generate the bubble in the other and he made eye contact with us, one at a time. Then he started mumbling.

"*Hail Mary, Full of Grace, The Lord is with thee. Blessed art thou among women, and blessed is the fruit of thy womb, Jesus. Holy Mary, Mother of God, pray for us sinners now, and at the hour of death.*"

He squeezed his eyes shut tight.

"*Hail Mary, Full of Grace, The Lor*

Author's Note

Some events in this book were obviously inspired by the atrocities of September 11, 2001. Over a couple of years I speculated what would happen if a large object, traveling at a very high velocity, crashed into the Earth. Not an asteroid or a comet; that's been done many times, in movies and books. A deliberate hit.

By December of 2004 I was a good ways into writing about it. I had the object striking in the Indian Ocean and creating a huge tsunami. I was hampered in my writing by the lack of images of what such a wave would look like. The historical accounts of tsunami I found included few photographs. I imagined it arriving as a breaking wave, of the sort so memorably depicted in the movie *Deep Impact*. Not quite that big, but big enough to do a lot of damage. By Christmas I was well into the description. I had the tsunami devastating Indonesia, Thailand, Sri Lanka, India, and Bangladesh.

Then the day after Christmas I woke to see the images I had been looking for all over the television news. To say I was disturbed is putting it mildly. I got out the maps, and discovered that the earthquake epicenter was less than five hundred miles from the point I had selected for the impact of my fictional large, light-speed object.

I was so spooked I considered abandoning the whole idea. I was afraid people might accuse me of cashing in on the human misery I was seeing day after day, as the magnitude of the disaster became clear. I have never been one to claim that science fiction writers predict anything. We're not even all *that* good at predicting technological advances, a few notable exceptions aside. No writer I know claims any special insight into the future. To have been so amazingly, horribly right about something like this was not what I had in mind when I started writing.

But it was still a good idea. I thought it over, and decided that I couldn't subject the good people of Indonesia, etc., to another tsunami, not even in fiction. So I moved the point of impact, which changed the shape of the story considerably. I believe it made it a better story because it brought it closer to home. To *my* home, the USA.

I know how unlikely this all sounds, but there it is. You can believe it or not, it's up to you. I can only say that it happened.

As I write this note, in September of 2005, Hurricane Katrina has just swept through the Gulf Coast, and once again I am stunned. I had postulated a breakdown in civil order, but the event I imagined *dwarfs* Katrina. I had no idea that the scenes I described some months before would occur in such a (comparatively) small disaster, and as quickly as it did. I guess I should have known better. It is always perilous to underestimate the inefficiency of government, particularly one that is in the process of being made small enough to be "strangled in a bathtub."

Today, September 11, 2005, I began writing the last chapter of this book.

So you are holding a book that was inspired by one horror, and the writing of it was bookended by two others. I don't believe in omens, and if I did I wouldn't know how to interpret this one. I just thought you might like to know.

John Varley
Oceano, Cahleefornia
September 11, 2005